Belinda Alexandra has been published to wide acclaim in Australia, New Zealand, France, Germany, Holland, Poland, Norway and Greece. She is the daughter of a Russian mother and an Australian father and has been an intrepid traveller since her youth. She lives in Sydney with her husband, Mauro, and a menagerie of adored pets. Visit her website at www.belinda-alexandra.com

Sapphire
Skies

BELINDA ALEXANDRA

**SIMON &
SCHUSTER**

London · New York · Sydney · Toronto · New Delhi

A CBS COMPANY

First published in Australia by HarperCollins*Publishers* Pty Limited, 2014
This paperback edition published in Great Britain by
Simon and Schuster UK Ltd, 2015
A CBS COMPANY

The right of Belinda Alexandra to be identified as author of
this work has been asserted in accordance with sections 77 and 78

Simon & Schuster India, New Delhi

A CIP catalogue record for this book is available from the British Library

Paperback ISBN: 978-1-47113-872-0
eBook ISBN: 978-1-47113-873-7

Printed and bound in Great Britain by
CPI Group (UK) Ltd, Croydon, CR0 4YY

To Halina and the lightworkers of the World League
for Protection of Animals,
may you be blessed and supported in the angelic
work you do.

ONE

He had never stopped searching for her and now the moment of truth had come.

Dawn was breaking over the Trofimovsky Forest when the military car that had carried General Valentin Orlov and his son, Leonid, from Moscow came to a stop at the beginning of a fire trail. A dozen people with shovels and buckets were standing around a mechanical digger and drinking tea from thermos flasks. The summer jackets and pants they wore were crumpled and the men were unshaven. They must have been here all night, Orlov thought, running his hand through his own neatly parted hair. He recognised his friend Ilya Kondakov, the aircraft archaeologist, among them.

Orlov respected Ilya. Although their annual searches of the old battlefields of Orël Oblast were motivated by different reasons, at least Ilya had regard for history and the twenty-seven million Russians who had lost their lives during the Great Patriotic War. Orlov had discovered too many graves and crash sites where relic hunters had been before him. He shuddered at the memory of the skeletons left open to the elements. The

I

stolen identification capsules and personal items meant that those soldiers would forever be missing: both in official military records and in their loved ones' lives.

The driver stepped out and offered his hand to Orlov to help him out of the car. The gesture was a courtesy but it irritated Orlov. He might be retired but he did not like to be reminded of it. In his mind he was still the youth with the smooth forehead and chestnut hair who had first put on a military uniform nearly seventy years ago.

'Good morning, General Orlov,' said a young man in an air-force uniform, saluting him. 'I am Colonel Lagunov. I hope that the overnight drive was not too arduous for you? Marshal Sergeyev was certain that you would want to be present today.'

The representative from the Russian Ministry of Defence made Orlov realise how seriously this new find was being taken. What had they discovered that caused them to be so sure this was Natasha's crash site? As a result of his and Ilya's searches, many Russian pilots had been recovered but Natasha had always eluded them.

Ilya strode down the slope and shook hands with Orlov and Leonid. It seemed that he and Lagunov had already met.

'I'm glad you could come. I wasn't sure if it was too soon after your operation,' Ilya said to Orlov. 'I'm sure this is it.'

'Why?' asked Orlov, ignoring Ilya's reference to his health.

Ilya indicated the fire trail and Orlov walked beside him towards it. Lagunov and Leonid followed a few steps behind.

'The area is being surveyed for a new road,' Ilya explained. 'This is virgin forest and the trees are so close together and the undergrowth so thick that if it wasn't for the piece of wing the surveyors stumbled across, I doubt the site would have been found.'

'Yes, but what makes you so sure it is ... Senior Lieutenant Azarova's?'

Ilya stopped and looked directly at Orlov before reaching into his jacket and taking out a piece of bent metal. 'We did a topsoil search around the site. Among the bits of metal and Perspex we found the data plate with the numbers 1445 on it.'

Orlov drew back at the sight of the plate. He had an urge to fall to his knees but resisted. Instead he jutted out his chin. He was used to mastering his emotions. The serial number of the Yak that Natasha was piloting when she went missing had been 1445. It was as good as confirmation.

'How deep is the plane?' Orlov asked. There was a quiver in his voice. Ilya would have noticed it but he was sensitive enough to pretend he hadn't.

'I'm guessing from the readings from the metal detectors it's somewhere between four and five metres under the surface,' he said. 'We didn't want to use the mechanical digger until you arrived.'

'Thank you,' muttered Orlov.

The forest closed around them and the men trudged along the trail in silence. The balsamic aroma of the birch trees stimulated Orlov's nostrils. The grassy undergrowth was damp and springy against his legs. There was something comforting about the white trunks of the trees, resplendent in their summer foliage. 'Birch' was an ancient word that meant 'to keep'. The forest had held Natasha all these years. It would have hurt her to know that all this beauty was doomed. She had once told Orlov that the world was being destroyed by mankind's incessant need to be somewhere else. Natasha had been referring to the Germans who had invaded their country in 1941, but over the years Orlov had often wondered what she would have said about his career. He had spent his post-war life training men and women to go beyond the spheres of human existence.

A twig cracked on the trail ahead of them. Orlov glanced up and for a moment the mists of his inner turmoil parted and there stood Natasha, beautiful with her white-blonde hair and grey eyes. He had loved her with his heart and soul.

'I knew you'd come ... eventually,' he heard her say, as her mouth curved into a smile.

A weight pressed on his chest. 'I've missed you,' he said. 'How I've missed you!'

Natasha's image faded and Orlov found himself staring at a deer. The animal lingered for a moment, her red-gold hide twitching before bounding away. He took the map of Orël Oblast from his pocket, although he'd carried every field and stream of it in his memory for years. In the summer of 1943, the Trofimovsky Forest had been deep in enemy-occupied territory. What had made Natasha disobey rules and fly so far into it? Was it because of what he had told her that afternoon?

The sounds of birdsong and summer insects gave way to human voices as they approached a clearing marked out with stakes and ropes. A female journalist with the *Moscow Times* printed on her notepad was speaking with one of Ilya's volunteers, while a photographer took pictures of the surrounding area.

'When a fighter plane like the Yak Senior Lieutenant Azarova was flying hits the ground nose first at full speed, it torpedoes into the earth to a certain depth,' the volunteer explained to the journalist. 'If the ground is soft, it forms a crater which quickly fills. Unless there is noticeable debris around the area, the crash site and the pilot may never be found. There are secret tombs like this all over Europe.'

The journalist was only half-listening. She was distracted by Orlov's appearance. 'Is that who I think it is?' she asked.

Orlov lifted his gaze to the tree line. His eyes discerned where the plane had sheared through the trees and younger saplings had taken root around the site. He saw for himself the truth of Ilya's description: you could walk within a metre of this place and never realise that a plane was buried there.

His thoughts were interrupted by the rumble of the mechanical digger approaching along the fire trail. What he would give for a moment of quiet so that he could stand alone with Natasha in the majesty of the forest and remember her as she had been, before this whole grisly business got underway. The other volunteers walked in behind the digger. Orlov grimaced when he saw Klavdiya Shevereva with them. The retired school mistress had managed to find out about every recovery operation for Natasha's plane. Klavdiya was responsible for establishing a collection of newspaper clippings on Natasha, and had even persuaded Natasha's mother to donate her daughter's dancing shoes and scrapbooks to the small museum she ran in the Arbat. While Orlov appreciated Klavdiya keeping Natasha's memory alive — 'Natalya Stepanovna Azarova is a national heroine who deserves to be honoured as such' — he sometimes found her interest in his beloved distasteful, like that of an obsessed fan stalking a film star.

Behind Klavdiya marched a group of school students. They were accompanied by a priest clothed in the gold finery of the ancient church. The priest was a thoughtful gesture, organised by Klavdiya no doubt. It was something Natasha would have appreciated. Orlov regretted his unkind thoughts about the school mistress. Natasha, who had been obsessed with film stars herself, probably would have liked her. But Natasha had possessed the gift of getting along with people. Orlov leaned against a tree and acknowledged that he was irritated because he had always wanted her to himself. Now he had to share this intimate moment with the whole world.

The priest sprinkled holy water over the site and blessed the operation. Klavdiya gave her usual speech: 'Young women like Natalya Stepanovna Azarova fought alongside men in the Great Patriotic War to save the Motherland. We must never forget her ultimate sacrifice.' Then the digger moved in and began its work.

As the grey earth yielded to the machine's power, Orlov saw the eighty-three years of his life pass before him. It seemed to him that he had barely been alive before he met Natasha; and after her disappearance his life became an exercise in endurance despite all his achievements. The whole reason for his existence had been squeezed into the months he had known her.

At around two metres into the ground the digger bucket struck metal. Orlov recoiled at the sound. Ilya moved in and brushed aside the mud to reveal tailplane wreckage. The stench of airplane fuel was overpowering. Volunteers stepped forward to sift through the soil for anything that would confirm the identity of the pilot and plane. It seemed to Orlov that after all these years of waiting, things were moving too quickly. He wiped his face and realised he was sweating.

More pieces of the airplane's frame were discovered. Then the twisted fuselage was lifted from the ground. Leonid stepped forward and took Orlov's arm to support him. 'Are you all right, Father?' he asked. Orlov didn't answer him. He couldn't take his eyes off the mud that was being washed from the cockpit. She'll be in there, he thought.

He had a sudden urge to flee the scene but he remained where he was, his eyes fixed on the volunteers who were sifting through the soil looking for human remains. Orlov knew the skeleton would be fragmented. The plane had gone in nose down. No pilot would have stayed in one piece at that level of impact. His hope was that Natasha had been killed in combat and was already dead when the plane hit the ground. At least there was no evidence of a fire.

When the cockpit was clean, Orlov shuddered to see how well preserved it looked despite the bent foot pedal and smashed instruments. Ilya waved to Orlov and pointed to the control column. 'The gun button is still set to FIRE,' he called out.

All Orlov could hear after that was the blood pounding in his ears. His chest felt tight. Leonid insisted that he take a seat on a nearby rock. He accepted a sip from Leonid's water bottle but it tasted salty and did nothing to ease his parched throat. Dear Leonid. His son was a grey-haired fifty-seven-year-old and a father himself, but Orlov still thought of him as the sweet boy with the brown eyes who always looked up to him. Did Leonid ever suspect that his mother had not been the love of Orlov's life?

One of the female volunteers gave a cry. She had been washing something in a bucket and now ran towards Ilya holding whatever it was she had discovered in a towel. What had she found, Orlov wondered, dread pressing in on him. Teeth? Toes? A piece of shattered skull with strands of hair still stuck to it? He winced at the memory of a previous summer's dig when he and Ilya had discovered the deceased aviator's boots with the remains of his feet still in them. Orlov did not want to think of Natasha's creamy white body appearing like that.

He shut his eyes again and remembered her as she had been: leaning against her plane and surveying the sky in that intense way she'd had. She was only five feet tall but she'd had a way of walking and standing that made her seem like a person of much grander stature. Even as an old man he still swooned at the memory of the silkiness of her skin the first time she had lain beneath him.

'The important thing is to stay calm,' he could hear her telling him. It was her way of making fun of Orlov, for that was his famous saying. It came as the result of an attack on their airfield a few weeks after Natasha had joined the regiment. A hangar was damaged and two planes on the runway were destroyed. Orlov and Natasha had thrown themselves into a ditch seconds before the ground they had just been walking on was strafed. 'The important thing is to stay calm,' he'd said and she had never let him forget it.

'Can you identify these? They were in the cockpit.'

Ilya's voice startled Orlov. He looked up to see his friend holding out the towel. His breath caught in his throat when he realised what Ilya was showing him. They were not human remains, but the sight of them still made him weak: a gold filigree compact and a matching lipstick holder. They identified Natasha as the plane's pilot more unequivocally than even the data plate. An image of Natasha powdering her face and applying lipstick before going into battle flashed before Orlov. Make-up was strictly against air-force dress code and, as her squadron leader, he had sent her to the guardhouse many times for ignoring the rules. Eventually, after realising the foolishness of locking up his best wingman when good pilots were scarce, Orlov had turned a blind eye to her disobedience.

He nodded at Ilya. Over the years, he and Ilya had dug up nearly eighty sites together. Every pilot had mattered to them, but this site was the most important of all. Yet even with the proof of the data plate and cosmetic cases, Orlov still had trouble believing that they had finally found Natasha.

'This is it!' Ilya told the volunteers, who had stopped working to watch Orlov's reaction. 'This is Natalya Azarova's crash site.'

The dig continued. The volunteers, driven by the fact they were now excavating the grave of a famous heroine, worked with double the energy. Klavdiya, despite her bent back and varicose veins, worked the hardest. She cried with triumph when she discovered ammunition boxes and guns that were also marked with the serial number of Natasha's plane. Orlov could no longer stand passively by. His doctor had warned him against too much physical exertion, but he no longer cared. If this is my last day then so be it, he told himself as he got down on his hands and knees to sift through the dirt piles. He was momentarily distracted by the shrill cry of an eagle. It soared above the clearing, wings outstretched. It was massive; most likely a female.

Something sharp pricked Orlov's skin. Glancing down he saw that he was holding a round object and that his palm was bleeding. He took whatever it was to the rinse bucket. When he had washed away the dirt and recognised what he had found, a wave of grief overwhelmed him. He sat down in the dirt and tugged at his collar. Leonid, frightened that his father was having another heart attack, rushed towards him. But he stopped short when he saw the delicate object Orlov was holding in his trembling fingers: a sapphire and diamond brooch.

'It was her call sign, wasn't it?' asked Leonid. 'Sapphire Skies.'

'It was her lucky charm,' Orlov replied softly. 'But it didn't help her that day.'

By late in the afternoon, the mechanical digger had removed all the wreckage of the plane and the volunteers had searched the topsoil of an area wider than had originally been marked out. They had located most of the interior of the plane — the seat, controls, Natasha's personal belongings — but nothing of Natasha herself nor her parachute. Ilya walked around the site deep in thought then gave the volunteers the instruction to secure it and gather the search equipment. Klavdiya placed the cosmetic cases and brooch into a protective metal box and pressed it to her chest.

Leonid indicated to his father that the military car had returned to take them to their hotel.

Ilya approached Orlov and the two men held each other's gaze. There was no need for them to state the obvious. The day's dig had finally solved the mystery of where Natasha's plane had crashed, but without Natasha's remains, Orlov was in turmoil. He did not want to look at Lagunov, the air-force man. Instead, he glanced at the setting sun, as if the answers he sought might somehow appear there. For years now, he had been convinced that his beloved had been killed in an air fight. There could be no other explanation for why she had not returned to him. But today's discoveries had made it very clear: Natasha had not gone down with her plane.

TWO

Moscow, 2000

Lily was having that dream again. She was hanging from the side of a ship with only a piece of rotting rope to cling on to. The sea churned beneath her dangling feet. If the thirty-metre fall didn't kill her, then the propellers would, or the sharks that lurked beneath the surface. Her heart pumped like a piston. The rope creaked and began to fray …

'No!'

Lily gave a start and opened her eyes. Pushkin, who had been asleep on her legs, blinked at her. She glanced at her alarm clock: 6.30 am; then looked up at the ceiling and the brass pendant light fitting that hung above her head like a guillotine blade.

'Come on,' she said, reaching down and rubbing Pushkin's chin.

The geriatric cat stretched his rickety legs and jumped onto the floor to join the two kittens, Max and Georgy, who were staring at Lily with their guileless eyes. One of the good things about street cats, thought Lily, swinging her feet to the floor and feeling around for her slippers, is that they're patient.

She remembered her family's cat, Honey, who wouldn't have tolerated waiting for her breakfast.

The cats followed Lily to the kitchen, their untrimmed claws clicking on the parquet floor. Lily filled the kettle with bottled water and plugged it into the wall socket before opening a can of cat food and spooning the contents onto a plate. She placed the plate on the floor and leaned against the refrigerator, watching her feline guests lap the food.

'Before you go to sleep,' the counsellor back in Sydney had advised her, 'think of something you like and examine it from every angle. A cat, for instance: imagine the rumble of a cat purring; the caramel smell of its fur; the warmth that transfers to your hand when you scratch its belly. Cats are therapeutic.'

Lily shut off the memory of those sessions with the counsellor. If she started thinking about them again she'd have trouble getting through the day and she had an important meeting with the advertising agency. 'Moscow in winter isn't a place you go to cure depression,' Lily's mother had told her before she departed from Sydney airport seven months earlier. But Lily had found Moscow cocooned in snow strangely comforting. It was summer now and the trees on Tatarskaya Street, where she lived, were in full leaf. Yet Lily felt the same sense of despair she'd had when she'd arrived. She was thirty-two years of age and she had lost all direction.

She made herself a cup of smoky-tasting Russian tea with lemon and carried it to the living room. She sank down onto the floral sofa, and stared at the imposing mahogany wall unit where she'd placed her television and CD collection. How had they got that thing up to the fourth floor, she wondered each time she sat in this spot. She'd decided that it must have been carted up piece by piece. All the furniture in the apartment was too big for the space and added to the cramped feeling inside. It was the antithesis of the breezy beachside cottage she'd shared with Adam in Sydney's north.

She sipped her tea and, despite her intentions, began thinking about the day she and her fiancé had thrown a barbecue for their friends to mark the completion of the renovations to their cottage and the bombshell that had fallen on them.

'Hey mate, you better get that spot checked out,' Adam's best friend, a nurse at Royal North Shore Hospital, had told him that afternoon. Bradley had pointed to a pink bubble on Adam's shoulder, so tiny that Lily, who thought she knew every inch of Adam's skin, hadn't noticed it before.

'I'll make an appointment for you,' she told Adam. 'I'm sure it's nothing, but best to get it looked at.'

Lily had been felled when the specialist's face turned grave as he examined the spot under a magnifying lens. 'We'll have to do a biopsy and then a test to see where the cells might have spread to,' he told them.

They had walked back to their car in a daze. Weren't melanomas meant to be big black ugly things that let you know they were dangerous, like funnel-web spiders?

They postponed their wedding to focus on Adam's treatment. While the surgeons cut a chunk out of his shoulder, Lily researched alternative therapies. She read books on juicing, and about how cancer survivors had defied stage-four diagnoses by drinking bicarbonate of soda mixed with molasses. She took Adam to his reiki and reflexology appointments. Together they posted positive affirmations on their fridge and on their bathroom mirror: *I am healthy, healed and whole*; *I now claim perfect health*.

At first, the surgeon was confident everything had been taken out. But a few months later lumps appeared on Adam's neck, which were lymph nodes that needed to be removed.

Adam fought his worsening prognosis with everything he had, and Lily fought alongside him. To the amazement of the medical profession, Adam's scans and blood tests started to come back normal. At his follow-up appointments over the next year, he passed every one with flying colours.

After all they'd been through, Lily would have been happy with a simple service on the beach. But Adam insisted that she have her dream wedding, with a string quartet, lavender and vintage pink rose bouquets, a pale lavender cake, flower girls, and a dress that swished around her ankles when she walked.

They'd booked the reception venue in Bowral for the second time when Lily woke up one night to hear Adam retching in the bathroom.

'Was it the green curry?' she'd asked him. 'Do you have food poisoning?'

One look from Adam and Lily had understood that this wasn't the first time the vomiting had occurred.

'I'm sorry,' Adam's doctor told them. 'It appears you have tumours in your stomach and bowel.'

That night, Lily's dream of falling into an abyss began. Eight months later, Adam was gone.

Max jumped onto the wall unit, sending CDs clattering to the floor and jolting Lily from her painful memories. She picked the kitten up and placed him on the windowsill, then glanced at the clock. She'd have to get a move on if she didn't want to be late for work.

The bathroom was squeezed between her bedroom and the narrow entrance hall. She picked up a towel from the cupboard, heard a snarl and jumped back just in time to avoid the paw that swiped at her from under the telephone table. She'd forgotten about Mamochka, Max and Georgy's mother. The tortoiseshell was the latest addition to Lily's cat sanctuary, courtesy of

Oksana, her landlady, who charged her a reduced rent for taking in the overflow of stray felines that she herself rescued. Lily had four in her apartment. Oksana, whose apartment was only bigger by two rooms, had thirty.

'Sorry,' said Lily, making as much space as she could between the cat and herself. Unlike the other strays, Mamochka was wild. She only came out to eat after Lily had gone to bed, and anyone who approached was repelled with a growl and a stomp of her paw.

'Don't worry, my darling,' Oksana had assured Lily. 'With love and affection Mamochka will come around. They all do.'

Lily turned on the shower and stood under the spray. For two weeks of the year during summer, Moscow's city council turned the hot water off so the pipes could be maintained. Lily had grown accustomed to the ice-cold water on her skin; it was bracing and numbed her thoughts like an icepack numbed a bruise. After her shower, she dressed instinctively in what her friends called 'Lily's Park Avenue Princess look': a Ralph Lauren shirt dress, tan court shoes, pink-brown lipstick and a touch of mascara around her amber eyes.

'Lily, you dress up for everything,' Adam used to say with a fond smile. 'Even the beach!'

Adam, who'd been a freelance web-page designer and a volunteer surf lifesaver, thought 'dressing up' meant discarding thongs for a closed shoe. Lily's mother had been a fashion and beauty writer for a newspaper and Lily had picked up the habit of dressing well from her. Now her smart clothes and fashionably blow-dried long brown hair had become a way of coping: making the outer shell presentable while inside she was in pieces.

Before leaving the apartment, she put out fresh water for the cats. Pushkin rubbed against her legs and she bent down to pat him. 'Okay, sweetie,' she said. 'I'm off to work.'

It was only when she'd closed the door and turned the three deadlocks that she realised she'd spoken to Pushkin the way she used to speak to Adam. Her heart sank and she sensed another difficult day ahead.

With many Muscovites away at their dachas for the summer, the city had taken on a more relaxed atmosphere. The traffic had eased and Lily felt for the first time that she was breathing oxygen instead of the acrid fumes of diesel.

A trail of commuters were making their way to the Paveletskaya metro station and Lily joined them. She descended the long wooden escalator to the platform and managed to squeeze herself onto the next train. The first stop was Novokuznetskaya. A group of tourists stared in confusion at the Cyrillic signs; there wasn't a single notice in English. 'Why do the Russians give things such bloody long names!' she heard one of the tourists lament.

The collapse of the Soviet Union had seen an influx of foreign investment and international companies, as well as tourists pouring into Russia. It was the reason why Lily, with her marketing experience and bilingual skills, had found a job in the city so quickly. She glanced at the metro station guide: Bagrationovskaya; Shchyolkovskaya; Krasnogvardeyskaya. Even if you could read Cyrillic, you needed to be able to read it quickly or you'd miss your stop.

She alighted at Tverskaya Station and took the underpass to reach Pushkin Square. The underpass was like a mini shopping mall, with kiosks built into the walls selling everything from potato *piroshki* and icons painted on wooden eggs to pirated CDs and counterfeit watches. The air smelt of *kvass*, the fermented beverage made of rye bread that was popular among the Russians in summer. Lily dreaded this part of her trip to work. Her parents had told her that when they'd come to the Soviet Union in 1969, the government had made sure the drunks and the homeless were hidden from foreign tourists. Now they were out in full view. It turned Lily's stomach to see men lying comatose with people stepping over them, or kneeling before paper cups and begging for coins. The sight that affected her most was the old women standing near the exit. Some of them sold potatoes and beets to supplement their meagre pensions, but the very elderly or crippled simply held out their withered hands. Lily knew these were the ones who had survived the bitter winter; there were many more who hadn't.

The face of the grandmother Lily had loved and had lost when she was nineteen years old flashed before her. That trip Lily's parents had made in 1969 was to smuggle her grandmother out of the country. If her parents hadn't taken that risky venture, Alina might have ended up like these old women in the underpass.

When Lily had first walked through here, she'd been tempted to find some other way to cross six-lane Tverskaya Street so she didn't have to witness the old women's suffering. But then she'd found something inside her that hadn't been depleted during the ordeal of the past four years and had reasoned that even doing something small was better than doing nothing at all. She'd stopped buying takeaway cappuccinos, CDs and lipsticks she didn't really need and now kept the saved roubles to give to the impoverished women. It was a ritual for each Friday, yet on the other days she still couldn't bring herself to look the women in the eyes.

'You know that Moscow's beggars are the highest paid in the world,' the concierge from the Mayfair Hotel, where Lily worked, had told her one day when he saw her dispensing the money. She was shocked that he could be so heartless. It might have been true of some of the young people kneeling before cups in the underpass, but how could it be true of these frail old women?

'Please! Take it!' Lily said today, handing her roubles to the oldest of the women. When she had nothing left to give, she ran up the stairs and emerged into Pushkin Square. She closed her eyes and took in gulps of air. When she opened them again she found herself face to face with an old woman clutching a dog.

The woman pushed a sign in English towards her. It read: *Please buy my dog and take good care of her. We have nothing to eat.* The woman was aged, but beneath her mottled skin she had high cheekbones and a well-defined chin. The yellow blouse she wore was faded but clean and her white hair was neatly coiled into a French roll. The dog resembled a fox terrier and had a smooth coat and bright eyes. Compared to those in the underpass, this woman didn't appear destitute, yet her demeanour exuded such hopelessness that Lily felt crushed by it.

Although she'd distributed her charity budget for the week, she reached into her handbag and took out her purse. She handed over a fifty-rouble note and the woman's eyes filled with tears. She kissed the dog and whispered something in its ear.

'No! No!' Lily protested in Russian when she realised the woman intended to give her the dog. 'I don't want the dog. Just take the money.'

The woman looked surprised that Lily spoke Russian. 'But you must take my dog,' she said, holding out the little creature.

Lily stepped back, overwhelmed by the situation. She turned away from the woman and rushed across the square. She was close to tears. The world was a mess and she felt powerless to fix it.

'You stupid foreigner!' a drunk man sitting at the base of Pushkin's statue shouted out after her as Lily passed him. 'It was a trick! She was never going to give you the dog!'

*

The Mayfair Hotel was a boutique establishment that occupied a restored eighteenth-century palace and catered to executive business people and affluent travellers. Lily rushed past the floral centrepiece in the marble reception area and waved to the desk manager before making her way to the sales office. She stopped at the staff bathroom along the way to check she hadn't smeared her mascara.

'Come on, pull yourself together,' she said to her reflection.

There was a brass plaque above the sink, placed there by Lily's boss, the director of sales and marketing: *You never get a second chance to make a first impression.* Scott, an American, never seemed to have a black day, or even a blue one. His Monday morning motivational meetings were renowned. Not only did his staff have to share their work goals for the week, but he assigned them each a personal affirmation which they were to repeat to him the first time they saw him each day of that week. The affirmation Scott had selected for Lily for the current week was *My life is a super success story!*

'The irony!' she muttered.

She noticed cat fur on her dress and quickly brushed it off then rolled her shoulders to loosen their tension. She breathed deeply as she stepped out of the bathroom. Making the transition from her sorrowful personal life to her professional one had become second nature to her, but her veneer of composure nearly crumbled when the first person she laid eyes on in the office was Kate, the perky sales coordinator.

Kate beamed when she saw her. 'Good morning, Lily!'

Lily felt her face sag but tried to smile back. Twenty-five years old, blonde and beautiful, Kate had fallen in love with a fellow Englishman who worked in the hotel's guest relations department, and was returning with him to Cornwall in September to get married. Everything was being organised by Kate's mother, aunt and three sisters, who were determined to make Kate's wedding 'the most beautiful ever'. Lily could tell by the look on Kate's face that she had another 'delicious' detail to share with her.

'They've ordered the cake!' Kate squealed, rising from her chair and waving a picture in front of Lily's face.

The cake was spectacular. The icing was shades of ivory and mocha and decorated with sugar flowers of tea rose and lily of the valley.

'Look!' said Kate, pointing to the top and bottom tiers. 'The piped lace design is taken from my wedding dress.'

Lily felt light-headed. It wasn't Kate's fault. Lily hadn't told her colleagues what had happened back in Sydney, why she'd fled to Russia.

Fortunately, at that moment Scott got up from his desk and came towards them, giving Lily a chance to escape.

'My life is a super success story!' she called out as he passed her.

Kate followed with her own affirmation for the week: 'My life is an exciting adventure!'

'Good morning, ladies,' replied Scott, grinning. 'The demands of life awaken the giant within me!'

Lily used the interruption to flee to the kitchen and make herself a cup of coffee.

When she returned to the office, Kate was sharing her wedding cake picture with the sales manager. Mary was in her early fifties and divorced, but was making the same ooh-ing and aah-ing sounds that Lily had a few minutes before.

Lily sat down at her desk and switched on her computer. 'Come on!' she muttered to the screen when she opened her email program. Internet connections in Russia were frustratingly slow. She tried to shut out the voices of the two women. *Does Kate's bliss hurt Mary the same way it does me,* she wondered. Maybe not. Mary had been through the experience of a marriage and her wedding was probably only a distant memory. Lily's dream, on the other hand, had been stolen from her.

The sound of an incoming email brought her back to the present. She pressed her palm against her forehead and willed herself to get on with the day. The message was from her best friend, Betty. *Are you crazy?* was her opening line. *What are you doing with all those stray cats in your apartment? Don't you know that Russia has rabies?* Lily felt a rush of warmth for her friend; Betty's outspoken personality was legendary. The email was long and Lily saved it to enjoy later.

Betty was the daughter of Lily's mother's best friend, and she and her siblings had become the brothers and sisters that Lily, an only child, never had. Lily shivered. She had no immediate siblings, but before she had come to Russia she'd discovered that in fact she had dead half-sisters — the children of her father and his first wife. They'd been burned alive, along with their mother, by the Japanese during the war in an act of random revenge against the Russian population of Tsingtao. All her life, Lily had believed that the scar on her father's face had been caused by a work accident. It was only when she'd decided to come to Moscow that her mother had revealed the truth: Ivan had been burned while trying to save his family.

Lily glanced back at Kate, who had now settled down to work. How different their families were, she thought. Kate's family had lived in the same village for generations. They even had a family tree in the vicarage that went back three hundred years, so Kate had told her. How unlike Lily's parents, who had endured revolutions, wars and exile. They were grateful to have ended up in Australia but were haunted still by ghosts, secrets and missing persons. At school, surrounded by friends with aunts, uncles and cousins coming out of their ears, Lily had felt like a freak. All she had wanted with Adam was a settled family life. Now she wondered if she had tragedy in her genes.

'Hey, Lily! Daydreaming again?' It was Richard, the marketing assistant. He handed her a copy of the *Moscow Times*. 'The ad for the special rates is on page three.'

'Thanks,' said Lily, taking the newspaper from him. Had she been cocky like that with her first boss? She doubted it. As far as she remembered, she'd never even referred to her supervisor at McClements Advertising by his first name.

She opened the newspaper to look at the ad they'd taken out for the hotel. Her gaze drifted to the article next to it: *Pilot's Plane Found after 57 Years but the Mystery Remains.* Accompanying the article was a black-and-white photograph of a pretty fair-haired woman in a military uniform. Lily was pleased. Attractive people drew the readers' attention to a page.

'Bloody traffic! I thought everyone was supposed to be on holidays!'

Lily looked up to see Colin, the publicity manager, hanging his jacket on the back of his chair at the desk opposite her.

'Hey, Colin!' called Scott from his office. 'The demands of life awaken the giant within me!'

'Yeah, yeah,' said Colin, sending Scott a wave but not replying with his own affirmation. He sat down at his desk and muttered to Lily, 'The demands of life bloody piss me off!'

Colin's dry humour was a lifesaver to Lily. Despite her aching heart, she smiled into the newspaper.

THREE

Moscow Times, 4 August 2000

PILOT'S PLANE FOUND AFTER 57 YEARS
BUT THE MYSTERY REMAINS

*The Defence Ministry confirmed today that a Yak fighter
plane recovered in a forest in Orël Oblast last week is
that of missing air ace Natalya Stepanovna Azarova.*

*The find comes after years of controversy over the
Great Patriotic War heroine's disappearance while
on a mission in July 1943. Supporters of Azarova
argue that because of her ace status she deserves to be
posthumously awarded the distinction of Hero of the
Russian Federation. However, while Friday's find has
shed some light on the mystery of Azarova's fate, many
more questions remain unanswered. No body and no
parachute were found in the wreckage, lending fuel to the
claim that Azarova was a German spy whose cover had
been blown and who faked her death in order to avoid
arrest. Many sightings of Azarova in Paris and Berlin
have been reported over the years, although none has
been confirmed.*

*General Valentin Orlov, one of the founders of
the Soviet Union Cosmonaut Program and Azarova's
squadron leader when she fought in his fighter aviation
regiment, has long refuted the claim that Azarova was a
spy. Since the war he has searched tirelessly for Azarova's
crash site, and in 1962 was joined in his quest by
airplane archaeologist Ilya Kondakov.*

*General Orlov, who has suffered ill health in recent
years, declined to make a statement after last week's
discovery. He said he would only do so after the
wreckage had been properly examined by the Ministry
of Defence and the forest thoroughly searched.*

*Klavdiya Shevereva, who runs a small museum of
Azarova memorabilia in Moscow, vows that the fight
to prove Azarova's innocence will continue.*

Orlov sank down on the velour couch of his Presnensky district apartment and lined up his medications on the coffee table. His doctor had told him to take the tablets after meals and with plenty of water. Orlov hadn't thought to ask if the procedure could be followed by a shot of vodka, but he poured himself one anyway. Finding Natasha's plane after all these years had brought on a tightness in his chest that had nothing to do with his age or his state of health.

Taking a nip of the burning liquid, Orlov cast his eye about the apartment. He stared at the red wallpaper, the teak side tables and the amber-tinted glass that separated the living room from the kitchen. He had not changed anything since his wife, Yelena, had passed away from a stroke ten years earlier. It was Yelena who had decorated the apartment; Orlov had been too busy with his work at the space centre to pay attention to domestic life. Homes were the creations of women; even though the women in his life had a habit of not staying around as long as he would have liked. He had been only five years old when his mother died.

The sky outside the window darkened and Orlov watched it for a while, wondering if another thunderstorm was on the way. His mind drifted to Leonid. His son's wife, Irina, had asked Orlov to come and live with them. She was concerned about him being alone when his health was failing. Orlov had refused. What good would an old man be to Leonid and his family? If he was a woman, that would be different. He could mend clothes, prepare meals, help with the shopping. But an old man with nothing but memories would be a burden.

Orlov had often wished that he could be one of those people who gave themselves freely to their loved ones, whose presence lit up a room. But a lifetime of secrets and guarding his thoughts had made him too introspective. Yelena had understood and accepted that about him. Even Leonid didn't seem to bear any grudge about having an emotionally distant father. Only Natasha had been able to open up that side of him. Natasha …

Orlov stood and walked to the sideboard. He took out the copy of *Doctor Zhivago* from the drawer and opened it to the page where he kept the photograph hidden. It had been taken in 1943 and showed him and Natasha standing by his fighter plane. They were looking at the camera but in front of them was a map spread out on the plane's wing. They were both smiling. For a moment, Orlov was startled to think that the handsome young man with dark hair and chiselled features was once him. It was during the battle for Kursk and the tension of flying several sorties a day had made them war weary. Yet in the photograph he and Natasha looked radiantly happy.

'The absurdity of youth and being in love,' he mumbled.

Ilya Kondakov had told him that now they had recovered the plane, the next step was to search the forest for Natasha's body. He was drawing plans for how far she might have drifted with her parachute. It wasn't considered chivalrous to shoot a pilot in their parachute; their downed plane was enough of a victory. But the Great Patriotic War had been a bloody battle with atrocities committed by both sides. The other possibility was that Natasha's parachute had been damaged when she exited the plane and hadn't opened for her. Orlov didn't like to think about that too much.

He returned to the couch and poured himself another glass of vodka. When Natasha went missing, he'd fantasised that she had bumped her head and suffered amnesia. In his daydreams she was safe and well, living among some peasants. All he had to do was find her. He did not accept that she could have survived the crash and not come back to him. Every morning he had woken up wondering if this would be the day that she returned. After years of waiting with no sign of her, Orlov had gradually accepted that he had to make peace with the unresolved and get on with his life. But it hadn't stopped him searching.

As the vodka put fire in his veins, he thought about the events of that last day he had seen her. Their regiment had been deployed to Orël Oblast, where German forces were concentrating for a planned offensive. The weather was unbearably hot, so instead of sitting in their cockpits, the pilots had been waiting in a hut. They had expected the Germans to start their attack in the morning but there was no sign of the enemy so far. Alisa, another female fighter pilot in the regiment, was sleeping. Filipp was reading a book but didn't appear to be turning the pages. These two, along with Natasha and Orlov, were the pilots who had survived since the battle of Stalingrad. The other pilots were new. Some people said that the longer you flew the more likely you were to survive, but others said the opposite.

While waiting for the call to scramble, Orlov and Natasha would usually remain silent, each focusing on the task ahead of them. Occasionally, when it seemed unlikely they would be called on to fly they would dare to look to the future. How many children they would have, what they would do for work, how they would spend their summers. Natasha told him that the war had destroyed her love of flying, and after it was over she wanted nothing more than to be a good wife and give piano lessons to children. Orlov remembered studying his lover's face that afternoon and the frown lines between her eyes. She had balled her hands into fists as if trying to restrain herself. She normally had a way of putting death out of her mind. 'It's no use mourning the fallen,' she used to say. 'I have to keep my head so I can fight for the living.'

The knowledge that the Luftwaffe was preparing for a massive air attack to halt the Soviet advance was sobering enough, but Orlov sensed that the peculiar tension in Natasha's manner had another source. Perhaps it was because their beloved regimental commander had been killed a few days before. Natasha often said her worst nightmare was to go down in flames. Was it the death of Colonel Smirnov that was bothering her?

Her edginess worried Orlov, but when he suggested substituting another pilot for her she wouldn't hear of it. She had forced a smile and attempted to lighten the mood by telling him about the time she had met Stalin. 'I thought it was the most exciting day of my life. I was fourteen years old.'

From the moment Natasha had come into his life, she had been a dazzling light to Orlov, all paradox and enticing mystery, a tough fighter pilot one moment and at other times as innocent as a child. Although he had never liked her veneration of Stalin, he had learned to tolerate it. But he had to tell her the truth and this might be his last opportunity.

'Listen, Natasha, there is something you should know,' he said.

When the ingenuous expression on Natasha's face had crumpled, it was as if he had taken a favourite doll from a child and trampled it into the dirt. But before he had any chance to explain himself further the alarm had sounded. German bombers had been spotted and they had to scramble for their planes. That was the last time he had spoken to her.

Sometimes Orlov wondered if what he had said that afternoon had caused her to go over to the other side, to assist the Germans. But he found that impossible to believe. Natasha was intensely loyal. She would not have betrayed her friends. Perhaps instead what he had revealed had destroyed the things that made her a great fighter pilot — her determination, her passion and her concentration. Maybe she had panicked and made a fatal error.

Orlov had never lost a wingman in battle until then; when he did it was his precious Natasha.

He covered his face with his hands and he wept. His shoulders shook and his chest heaved as tears poured from his eyes. Those events had taken place over half a century ago, but it was as if she'd vanished only yesterday.

FOUR

Moscow, 1937

I met Stalin once. I thought it was the most exciting day of my life. I was fourteen years old.

'Natasha, we are here!' cried my father, when the official car we were travelling in passed St Basil's Cathedral and approached the Spassky Gate.

I stared out the window at the red walls and towers of the Kremlin. I had seen the outer fortress of the ancient city many times but this was the first time I had ever been inside. I squeezed Papa's hand as the car passed under the archway and I caught a glimpse of the secret gardens. The golden domes of the cathedrals sparkled in the fading autumn light. The Ivan the Great Bell Tower dominated all the other buildings. It was said to mark the centre of Moscow. People no longer worshipped at Assumption Cathedral and the Cathedral of the Archangel, but something of the grandeur of imperial coronations and funerals of the past remained in the atmosphere. A thrill ran through me when I imagined ladies dressed in velvet and bedecked in jewels watching soldiers on parade. But I caught myself. Of course life was much better for us now that Comrade Stalin was in charge.

The Tsar Nicholas and his predecessors had done nothing for the Russian people except exploit them.

The car stopped outside the Grand Kremlin Palace and the driver opened the door for us.

'Come on, don't dawdle,' teased Papa, reaching out his hand to help me from the car.

'So this is where Comrade Stalin lives?' I whispered.

'Not quite, Natasha,' my father replied, grinning. 'I believe his rooms are in the Amusement Palace.'

My grandfather had been the official confectioner to the Imperial House and Papa had been to the Grand Kremlin Palace many times with him. After the Revolution, when Lenin was in power, my family became 'class enemies', and none of us had been inside the Kremlin since. Now Stalin was in charge, things had changed again. Papa and I were there as guests to a gala dinner in honour of the aviator Valery Chkalov and his crew for having performed the first non-stop transpolar flight to America.

I smoothed down my silk dress, made by my mother especially for the occasion, and followed my father to join other guests waiting at the entrance. I recognised some of their faces from the pages of *Pravda*: there were famous chess players, footballers, dancers from the Bolshoi Ballet, as well as celebrated workers and peasants. I spied Olga Penkina, a milkmaid who had received the Order of Lenin for overfulfilling her farm's production norm.

'Do you think Marina Raskova will be here as well?' I asked my father.

The wall above my bed was covered with pictures of famous aviators, and Raskova had pride of place next to my portrait of Stalin. Whenever a pilot broke a record, I'd go with my family to join the crowds cheering them as they were paraded down

Tverskaya Street. That was why my mother had forgone her place at the dinner so that I could accompany my father.

'I wouldn't let you miss out on this, Natasha. Not for anything,' she'd said.

My father nudged me. '*There's* someone you'll be interested to see.'

I turned to where he was looking and spotted Anatoly Serov alighting from a car. The dashing fighter pilot was a hero of the Spanish Civil War. I was even more excited when I saw he had brought his actress wife, Valentina, with him. She was so beautiful. I had tried to copy her look by pouring lemon juice through my blonde hair and sitting in the sunshine, but I had never been able to achieve Valentina's shade of platinum. A guard appeared and invited us into the palace. We ascended the staircase to St George Hall in an unruly group. The peasants stepped timidly on the red carpet, getting in the way of ballerinas who pranced behind them. The footballers spoke loudly, while the factory workers ogled the bronze wall lamps. My father and I followed behind Serov and his wife. How elegantly Valentina moved! There was something feline about her. I watched her every step of the way and tried to imitate her stalking gait.

At the end of the staircase, we were ushered into the reception hall, where we uttered a collective sigh. The snow-white walls, lit by chandeliers, were dazzling, and the pattern on the parquet floor was of such an intricate design that for a moment I thought it was a magnificent carpet. At the far end of the hall, under a vaulted ceiling, tables were arranged in banquet style, with a head table and several oval-shaped ones placed around a dance floor. A chamber orchestra played Tchaikovksy's 'Nocturne in D Minor'. I was surprised when the head waiter led my father and me to one of the front tables.

When we were all seated, one of the guards marched to the double doors and announced that Comrade Stalin had arrived. We rose to our feet. I noticed the worker opposite my father and me wiping his trembling hands on his thighs.

'Don't get excited,' my mother had cautioned me about meeting Stalin. 'Let him do the talking, and don't express your opinions ... on anything.'

Stalin entered the hall accompanied by three uniformed guards. He wore a grey marshal's uniform and his hair was brushed back from his forehead. He moved slowly and deliberately, meeting the eye of anyone who was bold enough to look into his face. I lowered my gaze when he looked in our direction. Stalin emanated authority, although he was shorter and older looking than he appeared in his portraits. He was followed in by the heroes Valery Chkalov, his co-pilot Georgy Baidukov and navigator Alexander Belyakov, and several commissars. They took their places and Vyacheslav Molotov, the chairman of the Council of People's Commissars, welcomed us and proposed a toast to 'our great leader and teacher of all peoples'. Then he toasted Chkalov and his crew as 'knights of culture and progress'.

The meal began. The feast set out before us included Olivier and beetroot salads, caviar and pickled vegetables for starters, followed by mushroom soup and fish. What impressed me most wasn't the variety and abundance of the food, or the champagne and fine wines served in crystal glasses, but the quality of the bread. The rolls were so soft and sweet that they dissolved in my mouth; they didn't need butter or oil to make them palatable. I had never tasted bread like it. Our family was spared the queues for bread rations because my father's position meant that we received special parcels of items that weren't always available in the stores. Even then the bread was often hard and bitter. The shortage of bread, I had discerned from whispered conversations around me, had something to do with the peasants in the countryside — with their farms being turned into collectives. When I'd asked my mother about it, I'd received the mysterious reply: 'You can't make an omelette without breaking eggs.'

After the main course of chicken cutlets and vegetable pie, our leader rose to give a speech about aviation and its importance to the Soviet Union.

'Vast expanses of our great country are still not linked by roads and railways,' he thundered. 'Air travel is the most promising solution to this problem. The Motherland needs courageous and determined pilots with this vision.'

He spoke like he moved: unhurriedly and with intention. Each word penetrated my consciousness. But he didn't need to convince me. I already had ambitions of learning to fly like my brother, Alexander, who was a cadet in the air force. I'd learned from my instruction that women in the Soviet Union were the equals of men, unlike women in the West. Even those from poor families could go to university to study science or engineering, or rise to become factory managers.

Valery Chkalov stood up to speak next. Although I had read every thrilling detail about his transpolar flight in *Pravda*, it was exciting to hear the story from the man who had lived it. I hung on each word while Chkalov described how the plane's compass had become inoperable as the crew neared the polar region, and how from then on Belyakov had to rely on dead reckoning and a solar heading indicator as his guides. I gasped along with everyone else when Chkalov explained how headwinds and storms caused the fuel to be consumed faster than anticipated and depleted the crew's limited oxygen supplies. Then he related how General George C Marshall was there to greet them on their arrival in America and went on to describe the cheering crowds who turned out as they were paraded through New York City. I imagined each scene as if it was I who had experienced it. I saw myself waving to the adoring crowds from the open-topped car, attired like Valentina Serova in a dress with shoulder pads and high-heeled pumps. My platinum-blonde hair glistening in the sun as President Roosevelt shook my hand and the press cameramen rushed forward to take my picture. I was lost in the glory of my celebrity when Papa nudged me. Chkalov had proposed a toast.

'To Comrade Stalin, who teaches us and rears us like his own children. Even in the most dangerous situations, we feel his fatherly eyes upon us.'

I leaped to my feet with everyone else and raised my glass. 'To Comrade Stalin!'

The waiters brought us dessert of peach compote and raspberry ice-cream. The fruity flavours reminded me of summer days at our dacha.

Anastas Mikoyan, the commissar for the food industry, who was seated at our table, leaned towards my father. 'Ice-cream — like chocolate — used to be available to the working man and his family only on special holidays,' he said. 'Now they can be mass-produced by machines. Why would anyone want to eat handmade ice-cream or chocolates when they can have them produced by shiny modern equipment?'

'Indeed,' replied my father.

I wasn't sure that Papa agreed with Mikoyan's sentiments. His family was once famous for their fine handmade chocolates and pastries. But my father wasn't a political man. He had not been able to find employment for several years after his family's disfavour, and now he enjoyed his job at the Red October chocolate factory, where he had been given a free hand in inventing new chocolate recipes. As long as he was allowed to make things that delighted people, he was happy.

I noticed Stalin was watching us. He stood up slowly and held his glass up to my father.

'I now propose a special toast to Comrade Azarov, chief chocolatier of the Red October chocolate factory,' he said. 'The factory has not only overfulfilled its annual plan for the past two years but has, thanks to Comrade Azarov, also improved the variety and quality of chocolates available to the Soviet people. He has invented two hundred new types of chocolate.'

Papa was caught off guard; he had not expected to be toasted. He blushed and moved his hand to his throat, flustered, and in his usual self-effacing way attempted to deflect the praise onto others.

'Thank you, Comrade Stalin,' he said, rising to his feet and holding up a champagne glass. 'And I would like to propose a toast to Comrade Mikoyan, who has not only been responsible for our success by ensuring the supply of the raw materials needed, but also has made champagne available to every man and woman.'

Stalin's eyes narrowed for a moment as if he were trying to discern some hidden meaning behind what my father had said. But then he smiled and lifted his glass again. 'Indeed, comrades, life has become more joyous! Life has become more fun!'

He turned to the orchestra, which had been joined by a saxophonist and jazz bass player, and nodded. They started up a foxtrot.

Papa shook off his embarrassment and led me to the dance floor. We weaved and turned to the jazz music playing, which was now officially approved. We were good dancers. We had to be — my mother was a ballroom dance teacher. She had trained to be an opera singer, but after the Revolution things changed. During the hard years, when my brother and I were born and my father and other artisans had no work, she supported the family by giving lessons in piano, dance and art to a small number of students. Now, as my father's fortunes had changed, my mother's had too. As I had read in *Pravda*: *Once, the good life was the realm of the tsars and nobles. Under Comrade Stalin, it is for every man, woman and child to live well.* My mother not only gave lessons in ballroom dancing to former working-class couples but also taught them deportment, elocution and music appreciation. Stalin encouraged his people to try new things and to show what bright lives the Soviet people lived, unexploited, outside the capitalist system.

As Papa and I danced, I noticed Stalin moving between the guests with a glass of cognac in his hand, but his eyes were constantly on me. Or, to be more precise, on my feet. My shoes seemed to bother him. Indeed, they did not go with my lovely dress. They were a pair of black court shoes that I had inherited from my mother and kept for special occasions. We had polished them as best we could but there was no hiding that they were old. Shoes were the most difficult item of all to obtain, even for a family like mine who had access to special stores. Occasionally we would hear a rumour that shoes were available at a certain store, but after lining up for hours we would discover that they were only of a single size or of such poor quality that they would fall apart after one wearing. My brother explained that it had to do with supply and demand and a shortage of raw materials. But when I asked him more about it, my mother had quickly cut us short. 'Never, never say anything that could be interpreted as a criticism of our state!' she'd warned.

Papa and I returned to our table and I was surprised to see Stalin approach us.

'Comrade Azarov,' he said, 'I must compliment you on your beautiful young wife.'

'Oh no!' said my father, becoming flustered again and not realising that Stalin was joking. 'This is my daughter, Natalya.'

'My mother was ill so I came in her place,' I told Stalin, repeating the white lie she had instructed me to tell if anyone asked why she hadn't attended.

'You see, Natalya is a budding pilot,' added my father. 'I had to bring her tonight.'

'Is that so?' Stalin asked, taking the seat Mikoyan had vacated to dance. He stroked his thick moustache and studied my face.

I remembered my mother's warning not to say too much, but Stalin's interest in my ambition got the better of me.

'Yes, Comrade Stalin,' I said, tucking my feet under my chair so that my shoes wouldn't distract him again. 'I hope one day to be one of your eagles and bring great glory to the Soviet Union.'

Stalin grinned and nodded approvingly to my father.

'She wants to do the parachute jump in Gorky Park every time we go there,' my father told Stalin. 'We hope that she can commence glider school next year.'

'Next year?' Stalin took out some Herzegovina cigarettes, broke off the ends and used the tobacco to fill his pipe.

'She will turn fifteen in December, Comrade Stalin,' my father explained. 'But she has to wait until she is sixteen to enrol.'

'She's only fourteen?' Stalin raised his eyebrows as he lit his pipe, then inhaled deeply. The air became saturated with the aroma of tobacco. 'Your daughter seems more mature than that.'

'Indeed, you would think so,' agreed my father. 'She has studied every book from the library on aviation.'

Stalin stared at his pipe as if he were thinking something over. 'I tell my sons that to improve themselves they must study, study, study,' he said. 'I myself am an old man and yet I still try to learn something new every day.'

I was thrilled to be having a personal conversation with Stalin. I was about to ask him what he liked to study when one of the guards stepped forward and whispered something in his ear.

Stalin nodded and turned towards us. 'I must go, but it has been a pleasure to meet you, Natalya. You must make your father proud of you.'

On the way home in the car, I replayed every word Stalin had spoken. He wasn't the enigmatic figure of my first impression. He was kind and fatherly, just the way Chkalov had described him, although he was more serious and considered than my own good-humoured father. I was more determined than ever to become one of his esteemed pilots.

FIVE

Moscow, 2000

After the meeting with the advertising agency, Lily worked on a promotional brochure for the hotel's restaurant. She read the brief from the French chef, in which he waxed lyrical about 'the scientific study of deliciousness', and wondered if she should use his term *molecular gastronomy* to describe his dishes.

'What do you think?' she asked Colin.

He swivelled on his chair and looked thoughtful for a moment. 'Leave it in,' he said. 'The Yanks will love it. And if you can get the word *gastrophysics* in there as well, you'll get the Germans on side too.'

Lily wasn't sure if he was serious, or whether he was still in a bad mood from the morning's traffic. She'd ask him again later to see if his answer was the same.

When five o'clock came around, Lily printed off Betty's email, picked up her bag and headed towards the door. Kate and Richard were discussing a new rooftop sushi bar they wanted to go to that evening with Kate's fiancé, Rodney, and some other staff friends.

'Would you like to come?' Richard asked Lily.

She shook her head. 'Thanks, but I've promised to do something else tonight.'

Kate grinned. 'A date? You're so secretive, Lily!'

'I know,' agreed Richard, winking at Kate. 'She's a woman of mystery!'

Lily wished them a good time and headed towards the reception area, dodging an American tour group with their trolley loads of Italian-designed suitcases and tote bags. As she stepped out into the street she pondered her colleagues' perception of her. A woman of mystery! What would they say if they knew what she was really going to do later on?

When she reached Pushkin Square, Lily looked around for the woman with the dog but couldn't see her. It was possible what the drunk had said was true and the dog was a ploy to elicit money from people. But Lily thought the woman had sounded desperate.

She made her way to Tverskoy Boulevard, a park set between two lanes of traffic and bordered by the former mansions of the aristocratic class. The ladies walking their Pomeranians and dachshunds in the dappled shade of the lime trees, and the Versace-clad patrons eating French confectioneries in the newly opened Café Pushkin, added to the fashionable atmosphere. She passed a busker playing a *bayan*, a Russian piano accordion, and stopped in front of an Empire-style mansion with buttercup-yellow walls and a white colonnade. It wasn't the grandest building on the boulevard but the arched windows and the pair of heraldic angels on the pediment made it elegant. It was the house where her maternal grandfather, Victor Grigoryevich Kozlov, a colonel in the White Russian Army, had lived before he'd fled to China after the Civil War. Lily sat on one of the park's wrought-iron benches to admire the home. She pictured her grandfather as a young man coming out of the door with his two sisters to promenade along the boulevard with the other noble families.

After the Civil War, her grandfather's family were arrested and never heard from again. The year before Lily arrived in Moscow, the house had been converted into luxury apartments. A real estate agent had shown her around and explained that after the building was requisitioned by the Soviets 'for the people', it had been turned into a communal living space. The stained-glass windows were vandalised and the carved oak windowsills ripped out and used for firewood. The property developer had restored the exterior but Lily was disappointed to discover that the apartments inside were ultra-modern with open-plan living spaces, chrome finishes and recessed halogen lights. She had no desire to go inside the building again; she preferred to sit opposite it, close her eyes and imagine herself inhabiting her grandfather's body. She would stroll into the ballroom with its gilded cornices and life-sized statues before wandering into the library, where she would sit down on a chair with swan-head armrests and gaze in appreciation of the shelves of beautifully bound books and the rare engravings on the walls.

Lily had never met Victor Grigoryevich or even seen a picture of him — all the family photographs had been destroyed in Harbin after the Second World War, along with the house her grandfather had built there. Her grandmother was not allowed to take anything with her when she was deported back to the Soviet Union, nor her mother, Anya, when she'd fled to Shanghai. Still Lily felt a connection with her grandfather. The first time she had come to see the house, a ripple of joy had run through her. She liked to think that in coming here she was somehow bringing Victor Grigoryevich back home.

*

When Lily returned to her apartment, she fed the cats and changed into jeans and sneakers before slumping on the sofa with a cup of tea. Acting upbeat at the office all day drained her. Marketing managers were expected to be ebullient not melancholy. It would be easier to be an accountant, she thought, and hide herself behind budgets and figures rather than talk excitedly about new target markets and consumer perceptions. She finished the tea then picked up a canvas bag that she kept near her front door and went out again.

While Tverskoy Boulevard had retained much of its historic beauty, the rest of Moscow was transforming into a modern metropolis and not all of it was attractive. In the Zamoskvorechye district, not far from where Lily lived, picturesque pastel houses were being knocked down and replaced by gargantuan blocks of apartments and glass-and-steel office towers. Lily's mother had a saying: 'Beauty isn't everything. It's much more important than that.' She wasn't referring to physical beauty or fashion, but the beauty of nature or of something superbly crafted — the kind of loveliness that had the ability to touch the human soul. The destruction Lily saw around her in Moscow made her wince in the same way she did whenever she visited her parents' bushland home in Narrabeen and discovered that more ancient gum trees had been chopped down to make way for block-like cement houses and gardens of gravel with spiky plants in ceramic pots.

She approached a construction site with a billboard at the front advertising a 'New Moscow Signature Style' apartment block: a hideous mix of neo-classical and neo-Stalinist styles, complete with neo-medieval — if such a term existed — domes and turrets. She looked at the mint-green house with pale pink trimmings beyond it. The workers had left for the day but the damage from the latest onslaught by their jackhammers made

Lily's heart grieve. Only the outer walls remained now, and with the last swing of the wrecking ball the ancestral home of her maternal grandmother would be gone. Alina had been born in China, where her father was an engineer on the Trans-Siberian railway, so she had never seen the house herself. Lily had discovered it through research of the city records: the house from where Alina's forebears had transformed themselves from enterprising peasants into successful cotton merchants and later engineers. She gazed over the remains of the wrought-iron fence and the broken fountain and decided this would be the last time she came this way. She said goodbye to the house that had seen so much history but was destined to become another victim of progress.

It hadn't been Lily's intention to visit what was left of the house that evening. Her destination was a few streets away: another construction site where a pre-revolutionary house had been reduced to rubble a few months ago. A planning dispute was delaying the construction of a high-rise apartment building on the site and that had bought its remaining residents some time. Lily glanced over her shoulder to make sure no one from the apartment building opposite was watching, then she quickly scaled the safety fence and scurried across the site to an unoccupied caretaker's van. She opened her bag and pulled out a can and spoon. Gently tapping on the can, she made soft 'Tchi! Tchi! Tchi!' sounds. As if she were a sorcerer summoning the spirits, cats appeared from everywhere — out of drains, from between crevices, from behind piles of rubbish. There were ginger cats, tortoiseshell cats, black cats, striped cats and even some Siamese and Russian Blue cats. They headed towards Lily, who scooped food from the cans she had brought onto paper plates. She took out a bottle of water and refreshed the tray that was hidden under the van.

When the cat colony had finished eating, Lily picked up the plates and crushed them into a plastic bag she had brought. Oksana had instilled in her the importance of feeding the cats inconspicuously, so as not to attract the attention of any cat haters who might be tempted to poison them. When the building work commenced, the cats would have nowhere to go. Lily was helping Oksana and some other volunteers from Moscow Animals trap the creatures and have them desexed, then tame them and find them homes. But it was only Lily and Oksana who could take the felines into their already crowded apartments, so progress was slow: just a few cats at a time. Meanwhile, four volunteers, including Lily, were on a roster for feeding the wild ones.

'Now, go! Shoo! Hide!' Lily told the cats as she hoisted her canvas bag over her shoulder.

She scaled the fence back onto the street and as she dropped to the ground she heard a voice behind her say, 'You like animals ... and you have a kind heart.'

Lily spun around to find the old woman with the dog standing behind her. 'And you are a foreigner?' the woman continued. 'But you speak Russian with such an elegant accent.'

'My parents are Russian,' Lily replied. She was about to add that she was from Australia, then questioned the wisdom of revealing anything about herself to a stranger. Her mother had once told her the story of how she had been drugged and robbed by a fortune teller when she'd lived in Shanghai.

'You will take my dog?' the woman asked. 'You will take care of her? I knew the moment I saw you that I could trust you.'

'You've been watching me?' Lily asked.

The woman nodded. 'Every morning. I didn't know you spoke Russian till this morning. I had to find someone who could make a sign for me.'

'Didn't you offer your dog to other people?'

The woman cradled the dog's head as lovingly as a mother would protect her child. 'No, of course not. I am not going to give her to just anybody.'

Her reply moved something in Lily. She looked at the dog; it stared back at her with a hopeful expression.

Lily shook her head. 'I haven't got anywhere to keep a dog,' she replied truthfully. 'But here, I'll give you these.' She took out the cans of pet food that she hadn't used. She could always buy more on the way home.

The old lady stared into Lily's eyes as if willing her to cooperate. Lily was overcome by the sadness she saw there. The streets were full of the unemployed and homeless. Only two years ago the banks had failed and the middle class had taken a dive too as their life savings were lost. Lily had heard stories of women who had been teachers and doctors resorting to prostitution to feed their families. The old system of 'from each according to his ability, to each according to his need' had crumbled. It was now every man for himself.

She looked at the woman again and an image of her grandmother flashed into her mind once more. Alina had lived a hard life in the Soviet Union, but after Lily's parents had rescued her, she'd spent the rest of her days in the bosom of an adoring family. Why was this woman all alone, asking kindnesses of strangers? Where was her family?

'Please meet me at the Tverskaya underpass on Monday morning,' Lily told the woman. 'I can bring you something more for your dog and something for you. I can help you that way.'

The woman's eyes filled with tears.

'What's your dog's name?' Lily asked, trying to ease the tension.

'Laika.'

Lily felt a jab to her heart. What a name! Now she was in danger of tears herself. 'Monday? Yes?' she repeated to the woman, knowing that she had to hurry away before she dissolved into a blubbering mess and against her better judgement agreed to take a dog into an apartment already full of cats.

'Thank you,' the woman replied softly.

On the way home, Lily thought about the dog's name. Laika was the stray dog that the Soviets had sent into space in 1957 with no hope of return. The dog's face appeared on the logo of Moscow Animals. Lily couldn't forget the photograph she'd seen of Laika sitting in the space capsule and holding out a paw to one of the scientists. The dog's innocent trust in the men who would betray her made Lily rage against the human race.

She breathed out and realised that she was caught hook, line and sinker now. No matter how much pain she was in herself, she had to find a way to help that woman and her little dog.

SIX

Moscow, 2000

When Adam was alive Lily had looked forward to weekends. Now she dreaded them. On Saturday, she distracted herself by visiting stations in the Moscow Metro. Lily had read that the metro carried over seven million people a day, making it one of the most utilised city transport systems in the world. It was also one of the most beautiful. Stalin had ordered that it should reflect the glory of the Soviet Union, and Lily marvelled at how many of the stations resembled grand ballrooms with their marble walls, high arched ceilings and ostentatious chandeliers. Her favourites so far were Novoslobodskaya, with its floral-themed stained-glass panels, backlit and etched in brass, and Ploschard Revolyutsii, where statues of soldiers, workers and collective farmers flanked the archways. She took a photograph of a statue of a partisan with his dog to send to her parents. Everyone must like that one, she thought — the dog's nose had been rubbed to a high shine.

The statue made her think about the old woman and Laika again. Where did she live? Lily realised that she'd asked the name of the dog but not its owner. That wasn't unusual for

Russia: people didn't like to be asked questions. Russians could appear reserved on the surface but that was the result of years of hiding their true feelings. If you could break through that outer layer, Lily had found, they were usually genuine and warm.

When she returned to her apartment, the light on the answering machine was flashing. The message was from her father: 'Nothing urgent,' he said. 'Mum and I are just calling to see how you are.' Lily glanced at her watch. It was too late to call Sydney now. She stretched out on the sofa and felt a twinge of guilt. Her parents had asked her for pictures of her apartment and Lily had sent them exterior shots of the attractive pink stucco building and the park opposite. The interior was too gloomy and too at odds with Lily's minimalist taste for them not to worry. Even though Oksana had offered to pay for any changes she wanted to make, Lily couldn't muster the energy to redecorate.

She remembered Betty's email and went to her handbag to retrieve it. After the rant about cats and rabies, Betty gave her news about what everybody was up to in Australia. *We all miss you like crazy, of course*, she wrote. *I told Mum that I'm going to visit you next year and she freaked. I'm trying to understand the relationship our parents have with Russia — they seem to revere it as a magical land but they fear it too.*

Lily knew exactly what Betty meant. When she'd told her parents that she was going to work in Russia for two years, her father had been supportive but her mother had worried herself sick. She was terrified that Lily would be arrested by the secret police. 'What your father and I did was highly dangerous and illegal. We smuggled a Soviet citizen out of the country! Don't forget *your* name was in my passport too and we never took the return flight to Sydney.'

Lily loved her mother and would never deliberately hurt her, but she'd stood firm on coming to Russia. It was a new era in the country's history and she was certain that she wouldn't be arrested. After Adam's death she didn't know who she was any more. She needed to flee somewhere — she couldn't stay in Sydney and watch her friends get married. She was pulled towards Russia in a way that she couldn't explain. Perhaps the country was in her genes. After all, she'd grown up speaking Russian at home and among the Russian community in Sydney.

Betty ended her email with questions about Moscow. How was Lily settling in? Were the people at work nice? Was she making new friends? *Please write us more than one line, okay? I want to know how you're really doing.*

A knock at the door jolted Lily from her reading. 'It's me, Oksana,' her landlady called.

Lily opened the door and invited Oksana inside. Before Lily had met Oksana she'd imagined that somebody who lived with thirty cats would be like the crazy cat lady from *The Simpsons* — a spinster whose disappointments in life had led her to shun people and hoard cats. That description couldn't be more wrong of Oksana. Statuesque, with auburn hair and long red finger nails, Oksana was university-educated and cultured. She was in her late fifties but her pale skin was unlined and her style in clothes was tastefully funky. That afternoon, Lily noticed, she was wearing a crinkly floral blouse, black leggings and red ballet flats. She smelled of Allure by Chanel.

'Darling, I hope you have been outside today,' she said to Lily. 'The weather is gorgeous. You know it won't be long before winter returns and we'll be cooped up in our apartments again.'

Lily put the kettle on to make tea. Oksana followed her to the kitchen.

'I have a favour to ask you,' she said. 'Aphrodite and Artemis have to go to the vet to be desexed this Wednesday morning.

But I have a committee meeting for Moscow Animals in the evening and can't pick them up. Could you possibly do it after work? You can use my jeep — I'll go to the meeting by metro. Wednesday is the only day Doctor Yelchin can fit them in.'

'Sure,' said Lily.

Doctor Yelchin had a practice near Filevsky Park and she knew that he desexed Oksana's rescued cats for a nominal fee.

'Thank you,' said Oksana. 'I also came by to see if you want to come to the Bolshoi Theatre tonight. The ballet is *Swan Lake*.'

Lily had no other plans, and staying home and brooding wasn't going to do her any good. 'I'd love to,' she said. 'But how did you get tickets this late?'

Oksana winked. 'I have my connections.'

Lily didn't doubt that. Her landlady had the knack of living well. She kept thirty cats in an apartment that was always scrupulously clean. While she didn't appear to be rich she seemed comfortably off: she wore fashionable clothes, drove a nice car and took an overseas holiday once a year. From what Lily had been able to gather about Oksana's arrangements, when private property had become legal in Russia, her brother, who was a government minister, had acquired her four of the apartments in the building, which must have brought her a reasonable income.

Oksana finished her tea and glanced at her watch. 'Better get going,' she said, heading towards the door. 'I'll come and get you at six. The performance is in the main hall. Let's get dressed up and make a night of it.'

That evening wasn't the first time Lily had been to the Bolshoi Theatre. When her parents had come to Moscow, they had brought Lily with them. The trip to the ballet had been a diversion to avoid raising the suspicions of the KGB, and Anya and Ivan had been accompanied by an Intourist guide, Vera, who was also a friend of Lily's grandmother. Vera had bribed an usher to let them sneak Lily, only a baby, into the theatre with her parents, as Vera's plan involved them all, including Alina, leaving the country that night. Tonight, as the orchestra began to play and the curtain rose, Lily thought of her mother again. Eventually, after seeing Lily's determination and sensing her need to heal the rift inside her, Anya had accepted her decision to come to Russia. 'But please don't try to find Vera or the General,' she'd begged. 'They helped us at great risk to themselves and I don't want to put them in danger.' The General had been Alina's companion. He'd saved her from being sent to a labour camp, and had contacted Lily's parents in Australia to let them know how to rescue her.

Lily tried to imagine all the things her mother and grandmother must have been feeling that last night in Moscow. As she watched Prince Siegfried arrive at his birthday party surrounded by courtiers and princesses, she wondered how much of the ballet her mother had taken in. I've got the bravest mother in the world, she thought. She's sensitive but she always manages to find courage inside herself somewhere. Will I ever manage to do the same?

Lily leaned back in her seat and let the beauty of the spectacle on stage sweep over her.

She left early for work on Monday morning so she had time to meet with the woman and her dog. She waited until quarter past nine at the underpass exit but they didn't show up. I should have expected it, Lily thought, making her way to the hotel. Maybe the woman wasn't impoverished after all and was running some sort of scam that Lily hadn't quite fallen for. Or maybe something had happened to her over the weekend. Lily hoped not.

'Rodney's parents have booked us a honeymoon in the Seychelles,' announced Kate as she spotted Lily arrive. 'It was supposed to be a surprise, but then they thought they'd better tell us so we packed the right things,' she giggled.

Lily made all the enthusiastic comments she could to Kate before excusing herself to go to the restroom. She was glad nobody else was in there. She leaned her head against the cool wall. She and Adam had planned to honeymoon in France. It was going to be four romantic days in Paris then off to a villa in Saint-Rémy-de-Provence.

The rest of her day was spent proofreading elevator posters and the web-page copy for the frequent traveller program. She willed herself not to think too much about the past and not to worry about the old woman and Laika.

Tuesday morning was different. Lily was running late and rushing to get to work when she spotted the woman holding Laika near the Pushkin Square exit of the underpass. The woman's face was grey and she swayed on her feet. Her skin felt clammy when Lily grasped her elbow to support her.

'What's wrong?' she asked. 'Are you sick? Shall I take you to the hospital?'

The woman shook her head. 'No, please, take Laika today. I beg you. Take her.'

There was a flower vendor's stall nearby with a chair for waiting customers. When the vendor saw Lily trying to hold the old lady up, she indicated the chair and Lily eased the woman onto it. Perhaps she'd had nothing to eat all weekend; and the weather had turned oppressively hot again — she could be dehydrated.

'Wait here,' Lily told the woman, before rushing back along

the underpass to a kiosk that sold drinks and light meals. She bought a couple of bottles of water and an egg sandwich.

When she returned, the woman took some sips of water and then poured some into her palm for Laika to lap. Lily waited until she had eaten the sandwich and was pleased to see colour return to the woman's face.

'I have to go to work now,' she explained. 'I've got meetings scheduled all day. But I finish around five-thirty. It's too hot to sit in the square. If you wait down here for me, I promise I'll take Laika for you this evening for as long as you need me to care for her.'

'Thank you,' the woman said.

Lily turned to the exit stairs then stopped. 'I don't know your name,' she said. 'I'm Lily.'

The woman stared at her hands and Lily thought she hadn't heard her. Then she said very softly, 'There is no need to know my name. I am nobody.'

Lily found it difficult to concentrate in the sales and marketing meeting that morning. Her mind kept drifting to the old woman. She wished she could speak to Oksana, but when she tried to call her during the break for morning tea, she could only reach her message service.

She returned to the meeting room, where Kate was pouring glasses of mineral water for everyone. Kate was wearing a silver pencil dress that complemented her blue eyes and tan perfectly. She was a kind person but Lily doubted she would have disrupted her beautiful life to help an old woman and a dog. What was it about Lily that attracted animals — and now people — in need? Why did she feel compelled to help, even when she herself was grieving, while her workmates seemed more interested in which new restaurant they wanted to try next?

During her lunch break, Lily ran back to the underpass but the woman and Laika were gone. The flower vendor spotted Lily and told her, 'That woman you were with this morning said to tell you that she had something she needed to attend to, but she will be waiting here for you at five-thirty.'

Lily thanked the vendor and bought a bunch of irises to lift her spirits. When she returned to the office, she filled a vase with water and noticed the vendor had made a mistake and given her six flowers instead of seven. Even numbers were for funerals, and Russians were superstitious about the bad luck the giver and receiver would attract with an even number on any other occasion. She considered taking the irises back to the vendor, but everyone was heading towards the meeting room for the afternoon session. She placed the vase near her computer before going to the room herself. She wasn't superstitious and what the vendor didn't know wouldn't hurt her.

Scott gave a PowerPoint presentation to the accompaniment of music by Kool & the Gang and success affirmations that flashed at random intervals across the screen, but the rest of the meeting dragged on. Lily kept thinking about what the old woman had said: 'I am nobody.'

When the last meeting ended at five o'clock, she returned to her desk and tidied up, then prepared her to-do list for the following day. She was about to leave when Scott called her and Colin into his office. She remained standing in front of Scott's desk in the hope of keeping the meeting brief, but when Colin sat down she had no choice but to do the same.

Scott beamed at them. 'I've got some great news. The Mayfair Hotel will be opening a sister operation in St Petersburg. I've been given permission to extend your work contract, Lily. We'd love to have you onboard for that.'

Lily didn't know how to respond. It was a compliment that the hotel wanted to extend her contract, but she'd only planned to stay for the two years she'd been hired for. It was impossible to know how she would feel when her original contract expired — would she want to stay or would she want to go home? At the moment, she changed her mind about Russia from one day to the next.

Scott was looking expectantly at her, but before she could answer Kate knocked on the glass panel next to the non-existent door.

'Sorry to interrupt. I've got those figures for you, Scott. We can go through them first thing in the morning.'

'Thanks, Kate,' Scott replied. 'Are you up to anything interesting tonight?'

Kate grinned. 'I'm lining up for theatre tickets. It's Rodney's birthday next month and I want to take him to see *The Seagull.*'

Lily thought of the old woman waiting for her at the underpass exit and glanced at her watch. It was already five-thirty. She hoped the woman would wait. She didn't want to lose her again and spend all night worrying about what might have happened to her and Laika.

Kate left and Scott turned his attention back to Lily and Colin. He didn't say anything further about Lily's contract but instead described the building the hotel had purchased in St Petersburg. 'It's a former Baroque mansion on Nevsky Prospekt and the plan is to incorporate the original interior features into the new design.'

Lily was wondering how to excuse herself from the discussion when Scott himself noticed the time.

'Gosh! Is it already five-forty? Melanie has a function today and I have to pick up the kids from their music lesson.'

'You'd better get going then,' said Colin. 'The traffic will be heavy this time of evening.'

After saying goodbye, Lily rushed out of the hotel and towards Pushkin Square. Surely the woman would wait for her? A noise like two cars colliding took her by surprise. She stopped and looked around. There wasn't an accident in sight, and besides she hadn't heard any screeching of brakes. What had made that noise then?

When she reached Pushkin Square, Lily stopped in her tracks. It took her a moment to comprehend the scene before her. Figures were staggering around covered in soot. Black smoke was pouring from the underpass exit and out of it clambered people with bleeding and burned faces, their clothing torn.

'Get them water!' a woman shouted to the occupants of a nearby building who were watching from their windows.

The smoke began to billow from the exit in greater volumes. What was happening? A fire?

Lily thought of the woman and Laika. 'Oh my God!' she cried and ran towards the exit, but everything had slid into slow motion. Her legs felt like lead. The woman's face and Laika's trusting expression flashed before her. She had told the woman to wait for her inside the underpass instead of up in the square.

A man with a bleeding cut on his forehead grabbed Lily before she reached the stairs. 'Are you crazy?' he screamed. 'A bomb has just exploded! There's a fire! You'll find nothing but dead bodies down there!'

From several blocks away came the sound of sirens as rescue vehicles tried to get through the traffic. Lily couldn't think clearly. Her body had gone numb. She leaned against a lamppost to support herself.

The police arrived and cordoned off the area. Groups of onlookers gathered on the opposite side of Tverskaya Street, trying to see what had happened. More bleeding and burned people stumbled out of the underpass or were carried by others. Ambulance medics lifted the worst cases onto stretchers while other victims collapsed on the ground. An office boy arrived with a mail cart filled with bottles of water. Lily joined in handing out the water to the victims to pour on their burns. The number of injured people was too large to grasp.

'Did you see an old lady with a dog?' Lily asked each emerging one as she handed out the water. They either shook their heads or stared at her blankly, too shocked to understand what she was asking.

The fire-fighters arrived, along with security agents, and rushed into the underpass. Lily looked at each stretcher as it was brought up the stairs. She couldn't tell who was alive or who was dead. Some of the victims had been so badly burned it was hard to believe they were human.

'Did you see an old woman with a dog?' she continued to ask. Then she realised that her question was being echoed around the square. 'Did you see my sister? She sells cosmetics in the underpass.' 'Did you see a man with a child in a stroller?'

She sat down on the pavement and began to cry. Who could have done this? The police diverted the traffic and ordered everyone who wasn't involved in the rescue operation to move away. Lily didn't want to leave. She stared into the smouldering tunnel, hoping she'd see the old woman and Laika delivered safely from the site. A policeman pushed her away and in a daze she walked along Tverskaya Street. Then, in front of McDonald's she saw her. She was sitting down, while a man in a pharmacist's uniform applied a plaster to a cut on her neck; the flower vendor stood nearby and Laika waited beside her, regarding her mistress with concern in her eyes.

'Oh, thank God!' cried Lily, rushing towards them. 'Is she all right?' she asked the flower vendor.

'She's not badly hurt,' the vendor assured her. 'Just a nasty cut to her neck. After the explosion the lights in the underpass went out. All I could hear was smashing glass and screams. I managed to grab hold of her and the dog and drag them up the stairs with me.'

'Thank you!' Lily said. 'I thought they'd been killed!'

The pharmacist closed his first aid kit and stood up. 'The cut's deep but I've cleaned it,' he explained to the two women. 'If it becomes sore or red though, take her to a doctor.' He moved on to attend to other victims.

'I'd better go and ring my husband,' the vendor told Lily. 'He'll be out of his mind.'

'Is there anything I can do for you?' Lily asked her. 'You must be upset.'

The vendor shook her head. 'I'm rattled but it's worse for elderly people like her who lived through the war,' she said indicating the old woman. 'This sort of thing brings it back to them. The sound of a car backfiring used to send my grandmother scrambling under the bed.'

The vendor left and Lily sat down next to the old woman and put her arm around her. With the mayhem all around, she was grateful that the woman and her dog were still alive. What now, she wondered. She'd promised to take Laika but she couldn't possibly leave the old woman alone.

SEVEN

Moscow, 1937

'Come, let's run!' I shouted to my friend, Svetlana, when we alighted from the trolley bus on Arbat Street. 'Mama is sure to have baked us something delicious!'

Svetlana and I hitched our school books under our arms and darted between the pedestrians and through the maze of crooked streets. The Arbat district used to be where Moscow's artists and intellectuals lived side by side with its gentry. Now it seemed everyone was living here as ancient churches were torn down to build residences for Party officials and the mansions of the aristocrats were divided into communal apartments. The elegant Filatov building used to house two hundred people. Now three thousand lived there. This was necessary, of course, I knew.

When Svetlana and I reached Number 11 Skatertny Pereulok, where I lived with my family, we stopped to catch our breath then raced up the five flights of stairs to Apartment 23. Our Armenian neighbour, Amalya, came out of her apartment on the first floor holding her new baby boy. She and her husband had been given permission to move to Moscow after excelling in their roles as Party officials in Yerevan. Now her husband was an engineer with the Ministry of Defence.

'Ah! Here are the twins!' Amalya said when she saw us.

Svetlana and I weren't sisters, of course, but we had similar physiques and round doll-like faces. We were the smallest girls in our class at school but we were the champions at ice-skating and gymnastics. Our compact frames were explosive with strength and speed. But while I was fair with long straight hair, Svetlana struggled to keep her golden brown curls restrained in her braids. At fourteen, my breasts were beginning to swell under the black serge of my school uniform with great promise, and boys were noticing, while Svetlana remained as flat as an ironing board.

'Wait a moment,' said Amalya, her eyes sparkling. 'I have a gift for your mother, Natasha.'

She disappeared into her apartment and returned with something wrapped in a cloth. 'The dried peaches she likes so much,' she explained. 'In return for the jam she gave me the other day.'

I thanked Amalya, and Svetlana and I continued on our way. When we reached the door to our apartment, I was surprised to hear my mother playing the piano. She usually put the gramophone on when she was giving dancing lessons. I opened the door and motioned for Svetlana to follow me. The aroma of ginger, cinnamon and nutmeg wafted around us. Svetlana and I grinned at each other. Mama had baked her delicious cookies.

We took off our shoes and put on the slippers that Mama kept on a shelf by the door. I placed the peaches next to the cookies in the kitchen, then Svetlana and I padded down the corridor towards the living room where my mother gave lessons during the day. At night it became the main bedroom. Our apartment was small but at least we had it to ourselves, a privilege given to my father because of his position at the chocolate factory.

Mama was playing Chopin when we entered the living room. My brother, Alexander, who was on leave from the air force, was leading Svetlana's mother, Lydia Dmitrievna, around the living room in a waltz. Svetlana's father was the manager of a factory and a Party official. Lydia was taking dance and deportment lessons from my mother. Everyone came to a stop when they saw us.

'The gramophone is broken and we couldn't fix it,' my mother explained.

Like me, Mama was blonde with a round face and grey eyes. She was wearing a royal blue dress with a gored skirt and tailored bodice. My mother was always well dressed and made up even when she was doing housework.

Svetlana's gaze drifted in the direction of the gramophone.

'Let Sveta try to fix it,' I told my mother. 'She can fix anything.'

Svetlana planned to go to the Moscow Aviation Institute when she finished school. She was fascinated by the way things worked.

'I've unscrewed the top,' said Alexander, whom my father described as a taller, slimmer and more elegant version of himself. 'But I can't see what the problem is.'

Svetlana picked up the screwdriver next to the gramophone and examined the parts. She asked Alexander to bring her a rag. He returned from the kitchen with one and handed it to her.

Mama started playing the piano again and Alexander and Lydia resumed dancing.

'I've fixed it!' cried Svetlana, winding up the gramophone and watching the record spin. 'There was too much grease around the spring.'

'Marvellous!' said Alexander. 'Can you fix fighter planes as well? Maybe I should take you back to the base with me.'

Svetlana grinned. 'Maybe one day I will design airplanes. And Natasha will fly them.'

'Even as a child my daughter preferred building sets to dolls,' Lydia said proudly. Lydia's eyes were green like Svetlana's but lacked their gentle expression. My mother had taught her how to powder her face and create a beauty mark on her temple to draw attention to her eyes, but Lydia's impoverished upbringing was evident in the smallpox scars on her cheeks and the stains on her teeth. Even though she always smiled at me, I sensed that she disliked me. I didn't know why. Perhaps she resented sharing Svetlana. Like my mother and me, Svetlana and Lydia were close.

'I've made cookies for you girls,' Mama told us. 'Go and eat them and then do your homework while we finish here.'

On our way to the kitchen, I let our dog, Ponchik, out of the bathroom. He was a stray, with fluffy black-and-white fur, that my father had found wandering about on the metro line. Mama put Ponchik away when she gave lessons so he wouldn't get underfoot. I took him to the kitchen with us and shut the door. We ate the cookies and drank a cup of tea with a spoonful of jam in it. Then we settled down to do our algebra homework at the kitchen table. I noticed the fine line that appeared between Svetlana's brows as she concentrated and I watched her write down her calculations in her notebook. Her handwriting was so small, so neat, so scientific-looking that I grabbed the book from her to admire it.

'Ah, Sveta, what a perfectionist you are!'

'What about you?' she replied, picking Ponchik up and cuddling him on her lap. 'You practise the piano for hours! When you are playing, the building could catch fire and you wouldn't notice!'

What Svetlana had said was true. Since I was a young child, music had been my passion and I had planned to study at the

Conservatory. But these days I was more interested in flying. Svetlana and I had finished our homework when our maid, Zoya, came in carrying the special food parcel that we received twice a month. She smiled at us, patted Ponchik and hummed softly as she filled the shelves with cheese, caviar, sugar, flour, tea, canned vegetables and eggs. She pulled out a bottle of red sauce.

'What's that?' asked Svetlana.

'Something called ke-tch-up,' replied Zoya, squinting at the label.

'Oh, I've seen that advertised in the newspaper,' I said. 'It's a condiment that every American family keeps on their table.'

Zoya was still unpacking when Mama and Lydia appeared at the door.

'Come on, Svetochka,' Lydia said, using the familiar form of Svetlana's name. 'We must go home now so you can study for the history examination tomorrow.'

Lydia's gaze fell on the cakes of finely milled soap Zoya was stacking on the kitchen bench. As far as I knew, while Svetlana's family could shop in closed distribution stores, they never received special parcels like us. Although they also had an apartment of their own, it was smaller than ours. It was darker too because all the windows faced the wall of an adjacent building. They had to share the bathroom with a man from Georgia whom Lydia complained was vile and dirty and who spat on the floor.

When Mama noticed what Lydia was looking at, she picked up a cake of the soap and handed it to her.

'No! No!' Lydia protested.

'I insist,' said my mother, pressing the soap into Lydia's hand. 'It smells beautiful and is soft on your skin.'

I picked up another cake of the soap from the bench and inhaled a breath before handing it to Svetlana to smell. Indeed, the fragrance was heavenly: honey and almonds.

'I have something for Svetlana too,' Mama said, disappearing into the corridor and returning with a length of woollen cloth. 'I bought this the other day from my neighbour. I've made a skirt for Natasha. There's enough left over for you to make one for Svetlana too.'

Mama had obtained the material from a woman in our street, Galina, whose husband had been killed in the Civil War. Galina would hear a rumour that material was available and buy it, then sell it for a small profit. Speculation, as it was known, was a crime but there was often no other way for us to obtain certain goods. Sometimes the State produced rolls of material but no buttons, zippers or needles and thread. At other times, the opposite was true. Of course, none of this was Comrade Stalin's fault. It was the result of spies and saboteurs who didn't want the Soviet Union to succeed. 'Really, Sofia, you know I can't accept this,' Lydia said. 'I could get Pyotr into trouble.'

'Yes, you can,' said my mother. 'Think of keeping Svetlana warm.'

Lydia acquiesced and she and my mother kissed each other's cheeks. Svetlana and I did the same.

'I'll see you tomorrow,' I told Svetlana.

Once they were gone, Alexander — Sasha we called him — came into the kitchen and helped himself to some of Mama's ginger cookies.

'Listen, you two,' said Mama, 'I have a message from your father. He received a package today at the factory. He wants you to go and collect it. Why don't you go now while Zoya and I make dinner.'

'Really?' I replied, perking up. 'Who is the package from?'

Mama smiled at me. 'From Comrade Stalin. Natasha, I think you made a good impression on our leader when you met him last week.'

*

The Red October chocolate factory was situated on Bolotny Island, opposite the Kremlin. Mama gave Alexander and I string shopping bags to take with us. Everyone carried string bags now and called them 'just-in-case bags'. Although there were certain staples in the packages we received, some items — kerosene and matches; spoons and forks; paint; nails — were always difficult to obtain. If a person saw a queue outside a store, they joined it. Only after they had secured their place did they ask what was being sold.

On Vozdvizhenka Street, a group of people were huddled around a store window admiring the goods displayed in red and gold boxes. They were the kinds of things we received in our special packages — cups and saucers, eggs, cheese, pens and hair rollers. A sign on the door of the shop read: *Sold Out*.

'Don't you think it's unfair that we receive things that the rest of our comrades go without?' I asked Alexander.

He frowned and stopped on the street corner. 'Sacrifice is necessary to the building of the Socialist State, Natasha,' he said. 'It's not someone privileged by birth who is receiving those special packages. It is our father, an ordinary citizen who has achieved outstanding success for the Motherland through dedicated work. What he and other innovators, leaders and pioneers receive today, every citizen can expect tomorrow.'

My brother spoke articulately but the way his gaze shifted downwards made me wonder if he believed what he said. I believed it. It was a lovely dream and I put my faith in it. After a Socialist State had been constructed in Russia, life would be exactly as Comrade Stalin had described it: more fun and more joyous for everyone.

I could tell when we were nearing the chocolate factory because of the smell of cocoa and roasting nuts that wafted in the air. As well as chocolates, the factory produced caramels, nougat and pralines. But it was the chocolate department that worked three shifts instead of two. My father and the factory's managers toiled from the late afternoon to early in the morning. Those were the hours that Stalin kept and nobody wanted to risk being absent in case he telephoned to inquire about a new delicacy that was being developed or to ask how the imported machines were performing. Although my father was the chief chocolatier and not responsible for production, Stalin often asked for him. He would speak with Papa about everyday things: family life and the challenges of growing older. Papa told us that he thought Stalin sounded lonely and that he had the impression our leader could not trust the Politburo members around him. My father would tell him jokes to cheer him up and Stalin would laugh and say it was good to speak to him. Although Papa never asked for privileges, it was because Stalin liked him that we had a comfortable apartment and use in the summer of a dacha in the pine forest of Nikolina Gora.

The workings of the chocolate factory were secret, but as children of the chief chocolatier we had special access. The guard who stood at the kiosk at the front of the factory waved us through, and Maria, who sat in a booth near the office, opened the door to the factory for us. She led us past the clocking-in machines and the cloakroom and out onto the factory floor.

No matter how many times I visited, I never got tired of the magic of the place. The delicious smell of burnt sugar tickled my nostrils. My eyes opened with wonder at the conveyor belts that whisked chocolate cigars and fruit-filled pillows from one end of the site to the other. The workroom was like a kitchen for giants, with cauldrons that needed ladders and gangways to reach them and enormous vats that bubbled with cherry- and vanilla-scented syrups. Maria led us past the packing department, where women wearing red kerchiefs arranged chocolates into boxes, then the art department, where artists sketched designs for the packaging; sleigh scenes and kittens in baskets being the most popular themes for the New Year. Pavel Maximovich, the factory's chief manager, rushed past us. Normally he would stop to greet us, but Papa had warned us that he was preoccupied these days. After overfulfilling their target for the past five years, the factory was now faced with a shortage of raw materials, especially cocoa beans and coconut oil. Maria left us at the door of Papa's kitchen-laboratory. If the factory was a fairytale land, my father in his white coat and thick-rimmed glasses was its wizard. Papa was developing a new truffle with a caramel cream centre. When in the process of inventing something, he became obsessed by it; even at home his mind was on his creation. He never smoked or ate spicy foods lest they interfere with his sense of taste. Each innovation was a result of weeks, sometimes months, of measuring, titrating and boiling to not only find the right combinations of flavours but to perfect the variables of temperature, pressure and cooling.

When Papa saw us, he put down his notebook and took off his glasses. 'Well, here are the two children that Comrade Stalin has ordered me to be proud of.'

I ran to my father and hugged him, then he and Alexander embraced. Papa went to the cupboard and pulled out a package wrapped in brown paper.

'Here you are,' he said, handing it to me. 'There is something there for both of you.'

The package felt lumpy. I untied the string and handed it to Alexander to roll up — nothing could be wasted. I gasped in delight when I unwrapped the package and saw a pair of dancing shoes. They were silver satin with d'Orsay-style T-straps and pink roses on the toes. Next to the shoes was a box with a fountain pen in it. I handed it to Alexander, then picked up the shoes and held them to the light. Foreign goods were frowned upon, but how could such beautiful shoes come from anywhere but some exotic faraway place? I pulled off my school shoes and tried on the dancing slippers. They fitted perfectly.

'This is a fine pen,' said Alexander, admiring the gold nib. 'I wonder why Comrade Stalin chose this for me.'

'So that you will write to your mother more often,' said Papa, slapping Alexander's back jovially before looking at me. 'The shoes are not all Comrade Stalin sent you, Natasha.' He reached into his desk drawer and handed me an envelope.

'What's this?' I asked, too mesmerised by my beautiful shoes to imagine what else could be in store for me.

'Open it!'

I slit the envelope open with my finger and saw that it contained a letter signed in red by Comrade Stalin himself. My gaze flew to the sender's address — the Moscow Osoaviakhim — before scanning the contents. When I understood the letter's meaning, I jumped so high that I nearly knocked over one of Papa's flasks and had to quickly steady it.

'What does it say?' asked Alexander.

I passed the letter to him and cried, 'It says I am to be admitted to the local glider school — immediately!'

On the walk home, I danced around the lampposts and stretched my arms out, pretending I was a glider plane. Stalin had remembered me!

'You really did impress Comrade Stalin,' said Alexander, his voice bright with pride. 'Only exceptional children are admitted to glider school at your age. I hope you don't join the air force and try to outrank me. I've worked hard for everything I've achieved. You received all the musical talent. Leave protecting the Motherland to me.'

I linked arms with him and inhaled a breath of the fresh evening air. Suddenly the happiness I had felt drained from me. The government's encouragement of young people to learn flying and parachuting skills was not purely for fun but to qualify citizens to form a rearguard army.

'Sasha, do you really think there will be a war with the Fascists?' I asked.

Alexander looked away. It was obvious that he knew something he didn't want to tell me. 'I think Comrade Stalin will do all that he can to avoid it,' he said finally. 'But Hitler … well, he is an unknown quantity. The Soviet Union is rich in resources and we have many enemies: Nazi Germany, the Capitalist countries and Japan.'

'If we do go to war,' I said soberly, 'I will serve the country much better by knowing how to fly planes than by playing the piano.'

Alexander stopped and rested his hands on my shoulders. 'Natasha, war is an ugly thing. The world will desperately need beauty if it does break out. Pretty things like the shoes Comrade Stalin gave you might seem trivial, but look how happy they have made you. Soldiers who are fighting need people who can give them hope.'

We walked the rest of the way home in silence, lost in our own thoughts. While I understood Alexander's point about people needing beauty, I thought that if war broke out, the most important thing would be to protect the Soviet way of life. Afterwards we could worry about music and art again.

When we approached our apartment building I noticed a black van and a dark car parked out the front. There was a commotion taking place on the first floor. I recognised the sound of furniture being dragged around and the contents of drawers being thrown on the floor. I counted the windows to determine whose apartment was being searched. It was Amalya and her husband's. No, surely not!

I was about to count the windows again when Alexander grabbed my arm. 'Quick!' he said, pushing me into a doorway.

I didn't see why we had to hide. We had done nothing wrong. The government was exposing enemies of the people, anyone whose activities were sabotaging the Soviet Union to weaken it in case of war. There had been several arrests in our street. Suddenly the door to the building burst open and Amalya and her husband were marched out by NKVD agents. Amalya's husband walked with his shoulders slumped and his head down. Amalya was crying. Another woman, a neighbour I had only seen a few times, stood in the doorway holding Amalya's baby. The agents pushed the couple into the van as Amalya struggled for one last look at her son, but the men shoved her back and slammed the door.

'Mind the child tonight,' one of the agents ordered the woman. 'The orphanage representative will be here tomorrow to pick him up.'

The car engines started and the vehicles took off down the street. Alexander waited until they had disappeared from sight before he would let me leave our hiding place. Inside the building everything was quiet. As we passed Amalya's apartment I saw that a seal had been placed on the door. Who would have thought that lovely Amalya and her husband were enemies of the people? They had seemed so nice.

Inside our apartment we found Mama and Zoya kneeling in front of the icon of St Sofia that was usually kept hidden in a cupboard. Alexander rushed about shutting all the curtains.

'Mama! Zoya!' he said under his breath. 'You must be more careful. Now more than ever.'

'Only God can help us!' cried Mama. 'Don't you know, Sasha, they are arresting people for nothing now! Amalya and her husband were perfect citizens while we were once "former people"!'

Alexander pushed me into our small bedroom and told me to read a book before closing the door behind him. I wanted to hear what he, my mother and Zoya were speaking about, but they whispered and I couldn't make out what they were saying. I assumed Alexander was upset about the icon. Religion was frowned upon but I sometimes took the icon out myself and prayed to it. I saw nothing contradictory in my behaviour. It was religion and the church that were corrupt and oppressed the poor, not God or the saints. I was faithful to the State but I thought my belief in something higher than myself made me a better citizen.

Since Alexander had returned home on leave, he'd been doing all sorts of strange things. He threw away a pair of binoculars my father used for bird-watching and made my mother get rid of her typewriter. He said anything like that could be used as evidence of spying. Us spies? What NKVD agent would believe that? A chocolatier, his artistic wife and two model children?

I opened the package Stalin had sent us and lay on the bed with the dancing shoes in my hand. Alexander and I shared the room. A curtain on a rope divided it. His side was orderly with a neatly made bed and a desk with only a notepad and pen on it. My side of the room was another matter. I loved pretty things and I put them on display. Apart from the pictures of Stalin and the aviator heroes and heroines on my wall, my writing table was cluttered with ornaments of birds, frogs and bears. Whenever Mama made me a new dress, I hung it on the outside of my wardrobe so I could admire it. It would stay there until Zoya complained of the dust collecting on it and told me to put it away.

I ran my fingers over the satin material of the shoes, then hung them on my bedpost by their straps so that I would be able to see them first thing in the morning and last thing at night.

Out in the living room I heard Alexander say 'Papa' but then he lowered his voice again.

Mama had said that the NKVD was arresting people for nothing now, but that couldn't be true. Stalin would not let that happen.

I thought of Amalya and wondered what sinister secret had lurked behind those shining eyes. Did she and her husband spread subversive material or make contact with foreign agents? I folded my arms under my head and admired my shoes again before turning to stare at the ceiling. The memory of Amalya's stricken face intruded. But I squeezed my eyes shut to make the image go away.

No, Amalya and her husband were guilty for sure. After all, bad things only happened to bad people.

EIGHT

Moscow, 2000

Lily watched the television with the sound turned low. Images of the atrocity of the previous evening flashed across the screen: bleeding people covered in soot; paramedics working flat out. Seven people had been killed. Sixty people were in hospital, many of them seriously injured. 'I saw a young woman die before my eyes,' one eyewitness told a journalist. 'She was horrifically burned and crying. The medics didn't reach her in time.'

Nobody had claimed responsibility for the explosion but everyone blamed the Chechens. The bombings of the apartment buildings in Moscow and other cities the previous September were fresh in everyone's memories. Although there were conspiracy theories about the attacks, most people believed that the Chechens had been involved and so had supported the Russian Federation's second war on Chechnya. Lily rubbed her eyes. She hadn't slept and was still wearing her clothes from the day before. She'd returned home to five increasingly desperate messages from her mother on her answering machine. She had called her parents and spoken with them for over an hour in order to reassure them that the city officials were responding quickly to the crisis, and that the bomb hadn't been directed at foreigners.

There was also a message from Betty. Lily called the bank where her friend worked in human resources and Betty stepped out of an interview to speak to her. They could only talk briefly but Lily was grateful to have people who cared about her.

Her eyes drifted to the bedroom where the old lady was asleep with Laika by her side. Why wasn't there anyone to care about her? She still refused to give Lily her name so Lily had started referring to her as Babushka, grandmother.

She hadn't told her parents or Betty about Babushka. If Betty thought Lily was crazy for rescuing stray cats, what would she have said about her taking in a stranger and her dog? But after witnessing the horror that human beings could inflict on one another, Lily had been overcome by a desire to reach out to someone. Babushka was shocked and confused and needed care. Giving her shelter made Lily feel as if she was doing something to counteract a situation that made no sense.

There was a knock on the door. It was Oksana. Lily had gone to see her the previous night, after putting Babushka to bed, to tell her what had happened.

'Is she still asleep?' Oksana asked, carrying a bag of groceries into the kitchen.

'She hasn't stirred at all,' Lily told her.

'Poor thing,' said Oksana, pulling out a packet of roasted buckwheat and rummaging around in Lily's cupboards for a saucepan. 'And poor you.'

Lily shrugged. Compared to what other people were suffering today, she didn't feel she had a right to complain.

'The cats are calm, I see,' said Oksana, indicating Pushkin, Max and Georgy, who were asleep on the windowsill.

Mamochka was in her usual place under the telephone table. 'They haven't reacted to having a dog in the house?'

'Not so far,' Lily said.

'Strays are like that,' said Oksana, pouring the buckwheat into a saucepan of boiling water. 'They are accommodating. When we had those floods last year, I drove around Moscow and picked up anything that was still alive. Although my jeep was soon full of dogs and cats, there wasn't one hiss, snarl or spit.'

'They were probably grateful,' said Lily.

Oksana touched Lily's cheek in a motherly way. 'Antonia is coming over to look after Babushka this morning, and then I will keep an eye on her until you get back. Are you still okay to pick up Aphrodite and Artemis this evening? If you don't feel like it, say so.'

Lily did feel like it. She had an urge to do things, including going to work today. Anything to get those awful images out of her head. She dreaded taking the metro but she knew that if she didn't get back into normal routine as soon as possible, fear would take hold of her. 'Lightning doesn't strike the same place twice,' she'd told her parents the night before, and the Moscow Metro and streets would be full of police, federal agents and soldiers now.

While Oksana made the buckwheat *kasha*, Lily showered and dressed. She reached up to apply her mascara and realised her hand was trembling.

Oksana had left some *kasha* for Babushka when she woke up. She and Lily sat on the sofa to eat theirs and watched the news. Lily had a hollow feeling in her stomach and what she was seeing on the screen ruined her appetite. She thought that perhaps she should change the channel, but she couldn't make herself do so. Somehow she needed to watch the story again and again, to analyse every nuance with the rest of the anxious population. According to eyewitnesses, two men had left a briefcase, which was believed to have contained the bomb, outside the kiosk that sold theatre tickets. 'We are a country at war and we must act like a country at war,' one city official stated. 'Muscovites must be vigilant now. They must watch their neighbours and report anything suspicious.'

Lily shivered. The menace of the Cold War had dissipated with the collapse of the Berlin Wall. Was this a new type of war?

The television announcer said that the city blood centres needed more donors to help the victims. Lily saw another opportunity to take action.

'Do you mind waiting here until Antonia arrives?' she asked Oksana. 'I want to go and give blood.'

She rang Scott to tell him that she would be late. His voicemail activated and she left a message. On her way down the stairs, she saw her Chechen neighbour, Dagmara, disappear into her apartment and close the door behind her. Dagmara had been evicted from her previous apartment by her landlord after the apartment bombings. Oksana had been one of the few Russians prepared to rent her accommodation.

'The problem with terrorists is they act as if they represent the entire nation when they don't,' Oksana had said. 'They don't care about the consequences for all the innocent citizens when they provoke another nation to war with them.'

Dagmara must be terrified of the reprisals that would result from this latest atrocity, Lily thought.

The line of people waiting to give blood extended out of the hospital and down the street. Lily was glad to stand with Muscovites in solidarity against violence but it was going to be a long wait. After she'd queued for an hour, a nurse came out and told everyone that the hospital had as many donors as it could handle and if more blood was needed they would put out another call on the news broadcast. Lily had no choice then but to leave.

When she came out of the metro and headed towards the Tverskaya underpass the first thing she saw was a city worker washing blood off the tiles. The air was still acrid with the smell of smoke and electrical wires dangled from the tunnel's blackened ceiling. She braced herself to pass the places where people had died or been so badly injured that their lives were now irrevocably changed. As she had suspected, there were police with dogs everywhere. She kept her passport ready in case anyone demanded it.

The kiosks were cordoned off, but the vendors had been allowed to return to see what they could salvage in the piles of crooked metal, shattered glass, pieces of CDs and bits of clothing.

The bomb crater had been turned into a makeshift shrine with bouquets of flowers, icons and candles. Lily stood with the others who had gathered there to say a silent prayer. She now saw how lucky Babushka, Laika and the flower vendor had been. It was only because they were near the stairs that they had escaped serious injury.

The atmosphere at the hotel was subdued. The bellhops spoke in hushed tones to each other and it seemed to Lily that the front desk staff looked at her in a peculiar way. Lack of sleep had left her feeling fragile and she was aware of her rushed blow-dry and hurried make-up, but that didn't seem enough to warrant furtive glances.

Although it was already eleven o'clock she was surprised to find the sales-and-marketing department empty except for

Scott, who was in his office, and Mary, who was staring at her computer screen. Scott stood up when he saw Lily. She thought he was about to announce his affirmation of the week — 'The positive advantage is always mine' — and desperately tried to recall her own.

'Did you get my message?' she asked, hoping to divert the conversation to something else. 'I went to give blood this morning.'

He didn't seem to register that she'd spoken. 'I've told the others to go home,' he said. 'Mary's cancelling some meetings and then she's going home too. Colin has gone to guest relations to see if there's anything we can do to help Rodney.'

'Help Rodney?' Lily asked.

Something wasn't right. Hotel departments didn't send people home because of city disasters unless ... her mind started to churn in an odd slow-motion way ... unless they were somehow affected. She looked at her colleagues' desks. She knew that Colin and Mary were in the office. A full cup of takeaway coffee sat next to Richard's computer; he must have come in during the morning at some time even if he wasn't here now. Her gaze moved to Kate's desk with its display of family photographs and the swatches of bridal lace pinned to her memo board. She suddenly saw a vision of Kate in her silver dress and remembered her words the afternoon before: 'I'm lining up for theatre tickets. It's Rodney's birthday next month and I want to take him to see *The Seagull*.'

Lily froze. The bomb was set off outside the theatre kiosk at a few minutes to six. Kate would have been standing right there when it exploded. White spots began to dance before her eyes. Scott helped her into a chair.

'Kate?' she asked, unable to believe that this was real. Surely what she was thinking couldn't have happened.

Scott grimaced. 'The consul-general said that she was severely burned. She died at the scene. As you can imagine, Rodney and her family are devastated.'

The hotel's director arrived and Scott went to speak to him. Lily sat at her desk in a daze. Her picture of the world had turned upside down. Not Kate. Surely not! Awful events didn't happen to perfect people. Perfect people lived perfect lives. They married perfect partners, had perfect children and grandchildren and maybe even great-grandchildren. They died in their beds at home surrounded by their loved ones. They didn't die at twenty-five years of age, a few weeks before their wedding, killed by a terrorist bomb in a Moscow Metro underpass.

Lily switched on her computer but couldn't read a thing on the screen. If Scott hadn't called her into his office the evening before to tell her about the hotel in St Petersburg, she too would have been in the underpass at the time the bomb went off.

'It's awful, isn't it?'

Lily looked up to see Mary staring at her. Her make-up was smudged and her eyes were bloodshot.

'I can't believe it,' Lily replied. 'It hasn't sunk in yet.'

'Her poor mother,' continued Mary, taking a tissue from a box on her desk and dabbing at her nose. 'She has cancer, you know. Terminal. That's why Kate and Rodney brought the wedding forward.'

Lily felt herself blanch. 'Kate's mother has cancer?'

Mary nodded. 'She took so much joy in planning her daughter's wedding and now she'll be arranging her funeral.'

Lily felt like she'd been kicked in the ribs. She switched off her computer. People were coming in from other departments and putting flowers on Kate's desk. Lily rushed around to find vases for the bouquets but she couldn't think clearly. She'd reach a cupboard and then forget what it was that she was looking for. Kate's mother had cancer?

Finally, she had to stop. She went to the kitchen and drank a glass of water. She had assumed Kate's exuberance over her wedding was a bride-to-be's insensitivity to the mundane lives of others. Now she understood that Kate's excitement was a veneer for her own breaking heart: she had been about to lose her mother. She and Kate had more in common than she had realised. Lily knew Kate's sort of deception first hand. When Adam was ill people used to tell her how well she was handling things, but she was shattered inside. Once he had gone, she'd crumbled.

Lily packed up her desk and said goodbye to Scott. She and Mary hugged. 'We'll get through this,' Mary said, rubbing Lily's back. In Pushkin Square Lily bought a bunch of roses and laid them at the makeshift shrine along with the other bouquets. Despite her anguish, she managed to find the right platform and get onto the right train. Then she remembered the eyewitness account on the news that morning: 'I saw a young woman die before my eyes. She was horrifically burned and crying. The medics didn't reach her in time.' Was that Kate? Everyone else in the carriage was wearing their blank commuter faces but Lily couldn't keep her composure. Tears rolled down her cheeks and she began to sob. What was Kate thinking about as she lay dying? The loss of her dreams? Never seeing her family again?

'I'm sorry, Kate. I didn't know,' Lily wept. 'I'm truly sorry.'

Lily sat in the park opposite her apartment for a while to calm her thoughts after the morning's shock. Oksana had formulated a plan the night before: Babushka and Laika would stay with Lily while she found out where the old woman had been living and if there were any relatives to help her.

When Lily entered her apartment, Oksana's friend Antonia was watching a historical drama on the television. Babushka and Laika dozed next to her on the sofa. Antonia was surprised to see Lily but didn't ask why she was home early.

'She ate some *kasha*,' she whispered to Lily. 'But she hasn't said a word. We changed the dressing on that nasty cut. Oksana thinks she might be anaemic. She's organised for a doctor friend to come and examine her this evening.'

Lily sat with Antonia and watched the television. She tried to lose herself in the story of duels and romances played out against the backdrop of the Tsars' palaces, but she couldn't stop thinking about Kate and Rodney. How awful all those wedding plans would seem to their families now. Lily was relieved when it was time for her to pick up the cats from the veterinary hospital. At least that would occupy her for a while.

'Will you be all right here until Oksana gets back?' she asked Antonia.

'We're fine,' Antonia assured her. She patted Laika's head. 'This little dog is lovely. She hasn't left her mistress's side for a moment.'

Lily had been in the waiting room of Yelchin Veterinary Hospital for only five minutes when she realised that it was the wrong place for her to be. It was six o'clock and the hospital was busy with people turning up to collect their animals after surgery. Veterinary nurses moved back and forth through a swing door, bringing out carry cages containing wide-eyed cats, or walking dogs out on leads. The sight of a poodle with bandaged legs and a cat with stitches down the side of its neck, along with the relieved expressions on their owners' faces, made Lily's eyes well with tears. The last time she'd been in a vet's surgery was the day that Honey, her beloved cat, had been put to sleep. She'd lived a good life to nineteen years of age, but suddenly her kidneys began to fail and she stopped eating. She died six months after Lily's grandmother did; Lily lost her two dearest childhood companions in one year.

The memory made her heart even heavier and she looked around for something to distract herself. There was a pile of magazines on a side table and she rifled through them. They were mostly issues of *Moscow Life* or Russian *Vogue* that she'd read at work. But then a journal caught her eye: *The Relic Hunter*. The subtitle read: *Until all the fallen are brought home*. Lily flicked through advertisements for metal detectors and pictures of German tanks being hauled from bogs and came to a feature on the lost pilots of the Battle of Britain. She was surprised to read that a number of pilots had remained buried with their aircraft until the 1980s, when they were recovered by civilian researchers, because military authorities were against excavating their crash sites. It seemed wrong to Lily that someone should make the ultimate sacrifice for their country and then be denied a proper burial because of red tape.

She looked at the photographs of the pilots that accompanied the article. They were so young, with smooth skin and eyes full of the future. Most of them weren't more than nineteen or twenty years of age, much younger than Lily. If I'm so traumatised after witnessing a bomb attack and losing a colleague, she thought, how did they cope with battles and death every day?

'Aphrodite and Artemis?'

Lily glanced up. A man in a blue uniform was standing near the front desk and holding a large crate. He looked expectantly at Lily, who was now the only person left in the waiting room. He had dark-blond shoulder-length hair and an athletic build. The colour of his uniform complemented his olive skin.

'Yes,' she said, standing up.

The man smiled. Although it was the end of the day, he was still clean-shaven and he sported fashionable sideburns. Lily had pictured Doctor Yelchin as an elderly man with a wise face and stooped back. She hadn't anticipated someone in his mid-thirties who looked like a movie star. 'You must be Oksana's friend Lily?' the vet said, placing the crate on the floor and taking a discharge form from the nurse. He had one of those deep Slavic voices that Lily found hypnotic.

'And you must be Doctor Yelchin,' she ventured.

The man laughed and shook his head. 'Doctor Yelchin is my uncle. He is in the process of retiring and I'm taking over the running of the surgery for him. I'm Doctor Demidov, but please call me Luka.'

Lily blushed. Wasn't using his first name when she'd only just met him too informal for a Russian? If Luka noticed Lily's discomfort, he didn't show it. 'Aphrodite and Artemis are still sleepy,' he said, pointing to the crate. 'I've given them long-acting pain medication and antibiotics but if you notice any swelling or bleeding please call me immediately.'

He wrote his home and mobile numbers on the discharge sheet before handing it to her. Sure that she must be glowing from head to foot, Lily fumbled in her handbag for her purse.

'There's no charge,' said Luka. 'Oksana is a good woman. This practice tries to help her as much as possible. Everything was quite straightforward.'

'Thank you,' Lily said. 'Oksana will appreciate that.' She fumbled again to put her purse back in her handbag and reached down for the crate.

Luka put his hand on her arm. 'I'll carry it to your car. Oksana wanted the cats put in together so I used a dog crate. It's a bit heavy.'

'Thank you,' stammered Lily again.

With his free hand, Luka pushed open the surgery door and let Lily go through first to the car park. She opened the rear door to Oksana's Niva jeep and spread out a blanket on the seat. Luka placed the crate on top of it.

'So you're interested in relic hunting?' he asked Lily, moving out of the way so she could place a towel over the crate. She realised that she was still holding the copy of the journal.

'Oh, I'm sorry,' she said, handing the magazine back to him and securing the crate with the seatbelt. 'I picked it up to read.'

She was blushing so much she was beginning to feel light-headed. Why was she making a fool of herself? Was it because Luka was so good looking? She had loved Adam for so long that she'd never thought of another man as attractive. It was an unsettling feeling and she wasn't sure what to make of it.

'Well, I hope to see you again, Lily,' said Luka, flashing his charming smile again before turning to go back inside the hospital. 'Call me if you have any problems.'

Lily couldn't bring herself to answer. She got into the jeep and started the engine. 'I must be losing my mind,' she muttered, before turning out of the driveway and heading back to her apartment.

Lily found a parking space outside her apartment building. Yulian, a neighbour, spotted her and offered to carry the crate with Aphrodite and Artemis inside. Russian men, Lily had discovered, were chivalrous that way. They caught the elevator to Lily's floor and Yulian placed the crate on her doormat while she searched in her handbag for her key, but Oksana heard them and opened the door. Thanking Yulian, she and Oksana lifted the crate through the doorway.

In the living room, Oksana's doctor friend was examining Babushka, holding a stethoscope to her chest. The doctor was a handsome man in his forties with silver-grey hair and chiselled cheekbones. Lily thought of Luka at the veterinary hospital and marvelled at Oksana's ability to get attractive men to do favours for her.

The women put the crate in the bathroom. 'They'll be fine here for a while,' Oksana told Lily. 'I've got a hospital cage set up for them in my apartment.'

When they returned to the living room, she introduced Lily to her friend.

'Lily, this is Doctor Pesenko.'

'She's still suffering shock,' he told them. 'I've given her an injection of B12, but I want to take some scans of her spine and chest. Can you bring her to my office the day after tomorrow?'

The three of them helped Babushka back into Lily's bed.

'There's something else,' Doctor Pesenko said when they returned to the living room. 'I couldn't get her name out of her, but when I rolled up her sleeve to give her the injection I found a serial number tattooed on her forearm.'

'You mean like one from a Nazi concentration camp?' asked Oksana.

Doctor Pesenko shrugged. 'There isn't a triangle or other symbol to single her out as Jewish. But it's possible she was sent to a camp if she lived in a village that was invaded by the Germans during the war.'

Lily glanced at Babushka, who was asleep now with Laika tucked under her arm. Everyone who had lived to that age had a story to tell, but Lily sensed that this old lady's tale was an exceptional one.

Even after two days, Lily and Oksana couldn't coax Babushka to tell them her name. When Lily had first met her in Pushkin Square and again at the building site, she had been articulate and alert. The shock of the bomb in the underpass seemed to have caused her to retreat into herself. She mumbled words that sounded as if they could be names of places or people but Lily couldn't catch them.

Each time the telephone rang, Babushka jumped as if she'd been given an electric shock. So it surprised Lily that Babushka showed no resistance when she and Oksana took her to Doctor Pesenko's surgery. She submitted meekly as the doctor weighed her, took her blood pressure and a blood sample, felt her neck and legs, and then listened to her chest before sending her with a nurse down the hall for an X-ray.

When she had gone, Doctor Pesenko invited Oksana and Lily to sit down opposite his desk. 'She'll need more tests, but everything so far indicates that she has a chronic heart condition that's been left untreated,' he said, taking his own chair. 'The most I will be able to do for her is give her medication to help alleviate the symptoms.'

'Do you mean her condition is terminal?' Oksana asked.

Doctor Pesenko nodded. 'I'm surprised she's kept going this long. She's malnourished, which doesn't help, of course.'

'How long do you think —' Lily broke off as she felt herself choking up. Babushka must have sensed that her health was worsening; that's why she had been so desperate for Lily to take Laika.

'She might have six months. She might have three days,' replied Doctor Pesenko. 'It's difficult to predict. I'm going to try to pull some strings and see if I can get her into a hospital — a State or charity one — for further tests and palliative care.'

The nurse came in with the X-ray results in a folder. 'I've left the patient lying down in the examination room,' she told Doctor Pesenko before leaving again.

Doctor Pesenko opened the folder, took out the X-rays and studied them. He put them on the light box so that Oksana and Lily could see.

'There is evidence of pulmonary congestion,' he said, pointing to the lungs. 'But there is something more unusual. You see, her heart is further to the right than it should be.'

'Why's that?' asked Oksana. 'Is it something she was born with?'

The doctor shook his head. 'I've only seen this twice before. In one instance the displacement was the result of a chest injury sustained in a car accident. The other was in a man who had been so badly beaten by thugs that his heart was punched out of place.'

'I wonder if something happened when she was in the concentration camp,' said Lily.

Doctor Pesenko wrote out several prescriptions and handed them to Lily. 'What are you going to do with her until I can find a hospital bed?' he asked. 'This woman is going to die and most likely in the near future.'

Lily sensed that Oksana was looking at her. She was under no illusions about how difficult it was to care for someone who was dying but she felt compelled to help Babushka. 'She can stay with me,' she told Doctor Pesenko. 'If Oksana doesn't mind?'

Oksana nodded. 'Of course not. Yulian is moving out of his apartment tomorrow. It's bigger than yours, Lily — you can use it until we can get a place for Babushka in hospital.'

'So we are conspirators,' said Doctor Pesenko with a gentle smile. 'Three people willing to help an old woman we know nothing about.'

'You know,' said Oksana thoughtfully, 'dying animals often come to me. I believe they are angels in disguise, because in caring for them I find that they always leave me a gift.'

NINE

Moscow, 2000

O rlov woke with a start. He glanced at his clock: it was four in the morning. A weight pressed on his chest as if he'd relived the darkness of his childhood while asleep. Now that he was reaching the end of his life, images from the beginning of it came back to him in dreams. He turned on his side to alleviate the discomfort in his chest. What was it? Indigestion? He barely ate anything these days. His gaze settled on the empty vodka bottle by the bed and he squeezed his eyes closed. Even the vodka wouldn't shut out the memory of the clackety-clack of the wheels of the train that took him, his older brother and his mother to disaster.

His father had fought in the White Army during the Civil War. When the forces loyal to the Tsar had been pushed back to Vladivostok and were on the brink of defeat, he'd sent word to Orlov's mother to bring the children and his parents to the east. There were plans for an evacuation to China. As an aristocratic family in 1922, they would be imprisoned or executed if they stayed in Moscow. But Orlov's grandparents refused to go, despite his mother's pleas. In the end, fearing for the life of

Orlov and his nine-year-old brother, Fyodor, she had boarded a train with them for Siberia.

The face of Orlov's red-headed brother arose in his memory. Four years older than Orlov, Fyodor had been his protector. Because of the war, the journey to Vladivostok took much longer than normal, with frequent stops at villages in between stations. In some of the places along the way, famine had hit so severely that the train was besieged by hundreds of orphans. The sight of their outstretched hands and the wail of their voices had frightened Orlov. He had never seen such misery. Even if the passengers on the train had given these children all the provisions they had, it would not have been enough to feed them all. In one village near Novosibirsk, Orlov saw groups of small children digging up roots in the forest and running away from any adults who came near. As a grown man, whenever he saw stray cats in the street he would remember those children. He had found it impossible to imagine that they didn't have parents to care for them. He didn't know then that Russia's homeless orphans numbered in the millions. And he'd had no inkling that he would soon be one of them.

The train Orlov was on with his mother and brother caught fire outside Chita. Those who survived the inferno fled to a village that had been hit by typhus. Orlov's mother caught the disease and died a week later. Fyodor had to give the priest every last rouble in their possession so that she could be buried with the proper rites.

'The priest said that Vladivostok has fallen to the Reds,' Fyodor told Orlov. 'Father is either dead or has already fled to China. Our only choice is to go back to Moscow.'

With no money for the fares, Orlov and Fyodor returned to Moscow by hanging on to the undercarriages of trains, along with other orphans who hoped to escape the famine by going to the big city. When they returned to their home, they found that their grandparents were gone and the house had been occupied by proletarian families.

A former servant took pity on them and admitted them to an orphanage. But when Fyodor laid eyes on the overflowing latrines and the emaciated faces of the children, he pushed Orlov out of a ground-floor window and they took to living on the streets. Their upbringing hadn't prepared them for such a life, and without Fyodor's ability to adapt quickly Orlov would have perished.

'Watch what those street urchins do,' Fyodor told Orlov, pointing to a couple of children who were hiding behind a planter in an outdoor cafeteria. As soon as a patron departed, they would descend upon his scraps and shove whatever they could into their mouths before the waiters came and chased them away.

Orlov and his brother survived the increasingly cold weather by burrowing into woodpiles or sleeping among the litter in garbage cans. For a while they found shelter in a crypt in Vvedenskoye Cemetery, until some older street children discovered their 'luxurious' accommodation and forced them out.

The Bolshevik government had made plans to get the orphans off the streets and into State institutions, but the problem was overwhelming for an administration recovering from a civil war. Appeals were made to citizens to adopt the children. When Fyodor learned of this, he took himself and Orlov to stand in the designated disused churches along with hundreds of other hopefuls, all trying to look appealing enough to attract genuine families and not those looking for cheap labour.

On several occasions couples had approached Orlov. 'What lovely dark curly hair,' said one woman to her husband. Orlov had heard another make a remark about his cute button nose.

'Go with them,' Fyodor would tell Orlov. 'Go and have a good life.'

But Orlov would cling to his brother's sleeve and refuse to be separated, and no one wanted this older boy with his wizened face and nervous twitch brought on by living on his wits.

Winter set in and food became scarcer. Fyodor found them some space in a tunnel at the train station. When morning came, hundreds of children crept from the tunnel or the crevices in the station's walls. Orlov developed a cough, and no matter how tightly Fyodor held him to his chest he couldn't keep his brother warm. Then Fyodor learned of a new orphanage that had opened a few houses down from where they had once lived. Some of the other children staying in the tunnel had gone there in an attempt to steal food and clothing so they could sell them on the streets.

'Did you have any luck?' Fyodor asked one of the boys when he returned.

'No! It's run by a retired Red Army general. That old Bolshevik was too smart for us.'

'Do you think he'll take Valentin?' Fyodor asked, indicating Orlov. 'And maybe me?'

The boy laughed. 'Getting too soft for the streets, are you?' He shook his head. 'I think they're already full, so there isn't much chance of the old general taking the two of you. I heard he runs the place like a military camp. But it did look clean.'

Orlov remembered the day that Fyodor had carried him on his back to the orphanage. He smuggled Orlov into the hallway and hid him in a closet.

'What are you doing?' Orlov asked his brother.

Fyodor put his finger to his lips. 'You stay here where it's warm, all right? I'm going to get some medicine for your cough. I'll be back soon.'

Fyodor embraced Orlov and kissed his cheeks before sneaking out the front door again. Orlov wouldn't see his brother again for twenty years.

*

The pain in Orlov's chest subsided and he went to the living room and stood by the window. Although his building contained two hundred apartments, everything was quiet. The sun was beginning to rise and he could feel the warmth of the day through the glass.

What a strange life I have lived, he thought. People have always called me lucky. Lucky that the old Bolshevik and his wife took me into their well-run orphanage; that the State gave me a good education; that I was selected for an elite air-force academy; that I survived the war; that I was chosen to be part of the most ambitious adventure mankind has ever attempted; that despite my age I survived a heart attack. But I'm not lucky. I'm cursed. He would have traded all his success in return for coming home with Natasha from the war; for having a family with her and growing old by her side.

Orlov strode to the bathroom. He filled the sink with warm water and swirled his shaving brush and razor in it. The citrus scent of the shaving soap he used to lather his face roused in him memories of summers past. He dragged the razor down his cheek in a long stroke and rinsed the blade in the water. An image came back to him from the war: he was shaving in his bunker and when he looked out the window he saw Natasha by her plane. She was sitting on a chair, her legs stretched out and her head bent back. Svetlana, her mechanic, was washing her hair for her, mixing hot water from the airplane's engine with the water she had in the bowl. Natasha broke all the rules. She was naturally blonde but she persuaded the medical staff to give her some precious peroxide each month so she could bleach her hair even lighter. She was vain about her appearance even in the midst of death and destruction. The women pilots and ground crew were required to cut their hair short, which made them look like boys. Natasha slept in curlers and wore her hair like a film star. Orlov, a stickler for order, should have despised her for her narcissism. Yet, despite all his attempts to discipline her, he'd secretly found it alluring.

He rinsed his face with cold water and patted his skin dry. He reached for his toothbrush and began to clean his teeth. The image of the two women stayed with him. He and Svetlana had shared an obsession for Natasha. Whenever the squadron left on a sortie, the mechanics used to return to their quarters to catch up on sleep, to play cards or to eat. Not Svetlana. She would pace the tarmac, her eyes never leaving the sky, until the planes returned. When Natasha landed, Svetlana first checked that her pilot was uninjured and then she checked the plane. The relief on her face when Natasha came back safely was palpable. She was like a loyal groomsman waiting for her master to return from the hunt. If Orlov came back from a sortie with bullet holes or damage to his plane, his mechanic, Sharavin, scolded him. When Natasha returned with battle damage, Svetlana would embrace her and say, 'You go rest. I'll see to the plane. It will be as good as new by morning.'

At first when he saw the women together, Orlov wondered if they were lovers. The intimate way they put their heads together and whispered sometimes made jealousy ripple through him and sometimes desire. Then he found out that Natasha and Svetlana had shared a friendship that went back to their youth, that was all. There had been a rift for a while, something had happened between them, but they'd been brought together again when they both volunteered for Raskova's women's air regiments.

Orlov had been transferred from his regiment soon after Natasha's disappearance. After the war, when he'd searched the records, he'd found Svetlana listed as missing in action presumed dead, along with half the pilots and ground crew. He'd grieved to hear that. The last days of the war in Orël Oblast had been brutal and he'd wished he'd been allowed to remain with his regiment.

Orlov rinsed his mouth and returned to the bedroom to dress. He had no idea why, even after retiring, he'd kept this strict regime of rising early and preparing himself for the day before breakfast. He put on a pair of pressed pants and a shirt with a collar. What day was it? He glanced at the calendar that hung on his wardrobe. Monday. Leonid and his family wouldn't be expecting him for their weekly dinner until Thursday. He would need to find something to occupy himself with until then. He went to the living room and stared at his bookshelf. Finally he decided to read Solzhenitsyn's *One Day in the Life of Ivan Denisovich* again and settled into an armchair.

He'd only just started when the sound of the telephone jolted him. He looked at it suspiciously then glanced at his watch. It was six o'clock. Who would be calling him so early? Worried that something had happened to Leonid, he picked up the receiver.

'Hello,' a male voice said. 'Valentin?'

'Yes. Who is this?'

'It's me, Ilya,' replied his friend. 'How soon can you come to Orël? Can you get the train tonight?'

Orlov was taken by surprise. One minute he had no plans and the next Ilya was asking him to travel four hours out of the city. He hesitated before asking, 'Is it something official?'

'No. Don't request a car. Don't tell anyone you're coming.'

Orlov had a sense that whatever he had been waiting for all these years was about to happen. But not the way he had hoped.

'Why?' he asked. 'What have you discovered?'

Ilya's voice was sharp with excitement. 'I've got a lead on Natalya Azarova. I think I know where she's buried.'

TEN

Radio Mayak, Moscow, 2000

Announcer: Our next guest is Professor Andreas Mandt of the University of Cologne. Professor Mandt's speciality is Russian–German relations and we've invited him to speak with us today regarding the war heroine Natalya Stepanovna Azarova, whose fighter plane was recently found in the Trofimovsky Forest, fifty-seven years after she went missing. Azarova's plane was recovered but not her remains, continuing to support claims that she was a German spy who faked her death to avoid arrest.

Good morning, Professor Mandt. It's a pleasure to have you on the programme.

PROFESSOR MANDT: Good morning to you, Serafima Ivanovna. It's a pleasure to be here.

ANNOUNCER: Professor Mandt, for many years now the Kremlin has refused to award Natalya Azarova the distinction of Hero of the Soviet Union — now Hero of the Russian Federation — based on the lingering controversy about her being a spy. What's your view on that?

PROFESSOR MANDT: I think it's an absurd theory that belongs to the Stalin era of paranoia. If, as the proposition suggests, Azarova had indeed been a spy for Germany it would have been excellent propaganda for the German war effort. If Azarova's identity as a spy could no longer be kept secret and she had managed to escape the country, then why didn't the German Ministry of Propaganda use her to demoralise the Russian people? Can you imagine? The Soviet Union's darling heroine, 'Stalin's pin-up girl' as she was often called, having actually been a spy working against her people all along? She could be quoted as having denounced Communism. But even if for some reason Nazi Germany didn't use that information against the Russians during the war, there would be no reason for the German government to continue to be quiet now. With improved relations between Russia and the West, they could put the matter to rest. The simple fact is they have no information to support the spy theory because it never happened.

ANNOUNCER: What you are saying makes sense. Supporters of Azarova argue that her kill record against the Luftwaffe was embarrassing to Germany. This brash young woman brought down some of their finest pilots. Revealing that Azarova had been persuaded to switch sides during the war might have helped redeem their pride in some way. The fact that the Germans said nothing does seem to weaken the spy theory.

PROFESSOR MANDT: Yes, that's my opinion too.

ANNOUNCER: The other possibility, of course, is that Azarova was captured by the German army, interrogated and then executed before being buried in an unmarked grave. But I suppose the German government could have also used her death as propaganda to demoralise the Russian people.

PROFESSOR MANDT: Oh no, I think that scenario would have been different. I don't think the German command would have admitted to capturing or killing Azarova back then.

ANNOUNCER: Really? What makes you say that?

Professor Mandt: The execution of their beloved heroine would have stirred the Russian people to fight harder. It would have worked against the Germans. Stalin would have called on every warm-blooded citizen to seek their revenge on the German army.

Announcer: Even if Azarova had given away valuable military secrets?

Professor Mandt: The Russian people would have said that she only gave those secrets away under torture.

Announcer: Yes, I can see how people would find it hard to believe that their revered heroine would have given information away otherwise.

Professor Mandt: You see that sort of hero worship with the cult of Stalin.

Announcer: That's true. People were so brainwashed to believe that Stalin was a saviour, the father of the Soviet Union, that even with all the evidence that's come to light regarding the millions of people who were murdered or who died in labour camps during his years in power, some remain convinced to this day that Stalin was a great leader.

Professor Mandt: Psychologists call that 'escalating commitment to a failing idea': as more evidence comes to light to refute a belief, the tighter the adherent holds on to that belief. But you know that Azarova suffered that condition herself?

Announcer: In what way?

Professor Mandt: She continued to believe Stalin was a hero even after he destroyed her family.

ELEVEN

Moscow, 1937–1938

I might have had a letter from Stalin supporting my acceptance into the Moscow Gliding School, but Sergei Konstantinovich, the chief instructor there, wasn't going to make things easy for me.

'How old are you?' he asked, staring at me over the piles of paper spread over his desk. His office was situated in an elementary school in Yuzhnoye Butovo.

'Nearly fifteen.'

Sergei rubbed his horseshoe moustache and shook his head. 'Tch, tch, tch, even younger than I thought.'

'I'm mature for my age,' I assured him.

His frown showed that he thought otherwise. 'You start with aeronautical theory,' he said, rising from his chair and guiding me towards the door. 'If you master that, we will see about gliding.'

'But I want to fly,' I protested as he pushed me into the corridor. 'Comrade Stalin said I could.'

'And I don't want you to break your neck. You start with aeronautical studies and then we'll see.'

The door shutting in my face told me that his word was final.

During winter, on the afternoons that I didn't have meetings for the Young Pioneers, I commuted to Yuzhnoye Butovo to join the other students of the Moscow Gliding School to learn about angles, direction of motion and how the density of air affected flight.

'Think of "lift" as Stalin and "drag" as the old Tsar,' Sergei told us. 'It is Stalin who makes you soar.'

It was a condition of my parents that I could only learn gliding if I kept up with my school work and piano practice. Even though I had to rise early on freezing mornings to fit in my study, my enthusiasm for what I was learning gave me the energy to continue. On Saturday afternoons, I was allowed to go with Svetlana to the cinema near Smolenskaya Square. Our favourite films were the ones about aviators: *The Motherland Calls* and *Tales of Aviation Heroes*. Afterwards we would stroll along Arbat Street and visit the studios where artists drew portraits. If there was something I hadn't understood in the flight theory classes, I could ask Svetlana to explain it to me.

'You will have to remember that flying a glider won't be like driving a sled,' she once told me. 'You won't be using the rudder pedals to steer the glider but simply by aligning its fuselage to reduce drag.'

As enthusiastic as I was, I couldn't have kept up all my activities to a high standard forever. I was going to have to make choices about what to concentrate on. In spring, what I truly wanted to do in life became clear-cut to me.

'All right,' Sergei announced to our class. 'We've had enough of theory. It's time to fly.'

Everyone rose from their chairs and cheered.

'Me too?' I asked.

Sergei squinted at me. 'You haven't grown. You're still the little doll you were when you arrived.'

He hadn't actually said no so I joined the others when they met early in the morning to launch the school's gliders from a high bank of the Moscow River. Launching a glider involved one student sitting in the cockpit while the rest of us, eight each side, ran forward while dragging the glider with all our strength using a rubber rope. Once the rope was stretched tight, the glider was catapulted like a rock from a slingshot and the pilot sailed the air for one or two minutes before bringing the glider to land.

Because of my size, Sergei Konstantinovich assumed I'd be useless to assist in the launching exercise. But gymnastics had given me reserves of muscle power and I used my compact size well. Once he gave in and let me help to launch a glider, he was astonished to see that I pulled best of all.

'Can I fly now?' I asked him.

'No. First you must watch what the older students do and then we will see.'

'For how long must I watch?'

'For one hundred flights, at least.'

Not all the pulls resulted in a launch. For every two or three successful pulls there was one in which the glider lifted only a few metres into the air and then crunched back to earth, accompanied by groans of disappointment from those who had pulled the rope and annoyed yelps from the bruised pilot. But watch and learn I did, until one day, when I'd almost given up hope of being allowed to pilot, Sergei pointed to me and then to the cockpit.

I placed my feet on the pedals and my hands on the control stick like someone about to ride a horse for the first time. I concentrated on everything I'd learned in my classes, from

Svetlana and from observation. I didn't want my first attempt to end with the glider nose down in the grass.

The other students dragged me forward. 'She's so light,' cried one boy. 'It's like there isn't a pilot in there at all!'

When the glider launched into the air, I gave a cry of delight. I was flying! For a moment, the whole world seemed quiet and still apart from the whirl of the wind. The air smelled pure and clean. I landed into the wind like a bird. While my landing wasn't smooth, I did manage to keep both wingtips off the ground. I looked up and saw the other students waving at me from the top of the river bank. They were cheering. Even Sergei was smiling. I knew then that to become a pilot was my destiny.

While I was enjoying learning to glide, the atmosphere in Moscow was growing darker and more apprehensive. Black vans appeared outside buildings at all times of the night. There were rumours of a mass grave of executed enemies of the people in Yuzhnoye Butovo, near the gliding school. But it was impossible to know what was the truth and what was the creation of overactive minds.

One day, our mathematics teacher, Olga Andreyevna, came to school sobbing. I heard her whisper to the music teacher, Bronislava Ivanovna, that her husband had been arrested the previous evening. The next week, Olga Andreyevna was gone too.

'Who would have thought mild Olga Andreyevna was an enemy of the people?' I said to Svetlana one afternoon while we did our homework together. 'The question that puzzles me is why these criminals don't try to run away and hide? Surely they know they're going to be arrested?'

Svetlana looked up from her textbook. 'Maybe they believe they are innocent. Or maybe someone denounced Olga Andreyevna and her husband out of spite. Mama says we must be careful what we talk about on the tram and while standing in line at the store in case something we say is misinterpreted and we're mistaken for criminals.'

I stood and poured us both some tea from the samovar before returning to the table. 'Mama says the same thing. And when he was last here on leave, I heard Sasha telling her to be careful not to complain about anyone or get into arguments with students who don't pay on time, because all sorts of lies are being told to the authorities by disgruntled people. But I think it's foolish for him to be worried.'

Svetlana picked up Ponchik and nestled her chin against his head. 'Why?'

'Because Comrade Stalin will know who is innocent and who is guilty. If anyone is arrested for something they didn't do, they'll soon be released.'

Mama and Lydia came into the kitchen. Mama poured some tea for Lydia, who sat down next to me and took off her shoes. I realised that she was wearing the dance slippers that had been given to me by Stalin.

'I hope you don't mind that we borrowed them,' said Mama, kissing me on the forehead. 'Lydia's own dancing shoes have fallen apart and she's having trouble finding another pair.'

'No, I don't mind,' I said. 'I'm happy to share my present from Comrade Stalin.'

Lydia raised her eyebrows. 'Comrade Stalin? You mean, thanks to Comrade Stalin we can all enjoy such bounty?'

'No,' I said, smiling. 'They were a gift from Comrade Stalin himself. After Papa and I attended the reception at the Kremlin for Valery Chkalov, he sent them to me.'

Lydia looked askance at her daughter. 'You didn't say anything to me about that.'

Svetlana looked away and I wondered why she didn't tell her mother about good things that happened to me. I boasted to Mama constantly about Svetlana's achievements. Lydia examined the shoes before handing them back to me. 'Svetochka, you have a science examination tomorrow and I expect you to come top of the class as usual,' she told her daughter.

Poor Svetlana. I suddenly understood why she didn't tell her mother about what I did. If I achieved something, she would be pushed harder to achieve something more impressive. But Lydia needn't have been so competitive. We all expected the best from Svetlana: she was destined to study at the Moscow Aviation Institute and make a name for herself. She was the brightest girl in our school. I wasn't doing as well as I used to in our subject tests but I didn't care. I was losing interest in school work anyway. All I wanted to do now was to fly.

The telephone rang. Zoya came into the kitchen to say that it was Pyotr Borisovich on the line, Svetlana's father. I'd met him a few times. He was a quiet and serious man; I'd never seen him smile. Svetlana said it was because he had an important job at the construction factory and worried a lot, but also because her mother was bossy and he'd got used to listening.

My mother picked up the receiver in the hallway before Lydia could reach it. 'Pyotr Borisovich,' she said in a flirtatious voice. 'Why don't you ever come to have dance lessons with your wife?'

I had put the same question to Svetlana once.

'Papa doesn't mind that Mama dances with the other Party officials when they go to functions,' she told me. 'He's content to be an ordinary factory manager and Party official. It's my mother who is ambitious for us to rise in life.'

As the arrests continued, even my light-hearted father grew anxious. I would hear him pace the floor for an hour before going to bed, and I blamed my mother for his agitation. Papa possessed a cheerful personality, while she was a worrier. Every time a car stopped outside our building at night, she would stiffen, expecting the worst. It was her jitteriness that was getting to Papa — and to me.

One evening I found her packing a bag with warm clothes, underwear, money, toothbrush and some toothpaste. I realised instantly what she was doing. She was preparing necessities for Papa in case he was arrested.

'You're inviting bad luck by doing that!' I scolded her. 'Comrade Stalin has only praise for Papa. He even gave him a toast at the reception for Valery Chkalov.' I took the bag from her and put the clothes back in the wardrobe. 'And Papa is no enemy of the people! His life's work is to give the Soviet people pleasure, which is exactly what Comrade Stalin wants him to do.'

Mama pursed her lips then said, 'It seems to me that it doesn't matter what you contribute to the Soviet Union if your family once served the aristocratic classes.'

One day I met my father alone in the living room. 'Papa, are you going to be arrested?' I asked him.

He placed the sugared fruits he had been examining on the side table. 'Natashka, darling!' he said. 'Have you been worrying about that? I had no idea! I thought you were having fun with your gliding lessons.' He took my hand and pulled me down onto the sofa next to him. 'Please don't be concerned for me,' he said, wrapping his arm around my shoulders, 'I may have seemed tense lately because of Pavel Maximovich.'

'What's wrong with him?'

Papa offered me a sugared fruit. I declined, but he took one and rolled it around his mouth. The scents of strawberry and melon reminded me of carefree summer days, and were at odds with the apprehension I was feeling.

'Despite the factory's high status, Pavel Maximovich can't get the supplies of cocoa beans and palm oil needed to keep up production,' he said. 'The factory didn't meet its targets for New Year's Eve. For the first time there were shortages of Red October chocolate.'

'But that's not his fault,' I said.

'Of course it isn't,' Papa agreed. He took out his handkerchief and wiped his fingers. 'But some of the workers see it differently. If Pavel Maximovich orders them to do anything these days they become difficult. The cooperative atmosphere at the factory is gone.'

Reassured by my father's explanation that he was concerned for the factory's chief manager and not for himself, I concentrated on my school work and glider lessons again.

Then one morning when I was having breakfast with my mother in the kitchen, Papa came home from the factory early. I gave a cry when I saw him. His clothes were dishevelled and there was blood on his sleeve. Mama stood up, her face twisted in horror. 'Stepan!'

Without looking at me, my father gestured for Mama to follow him to the living room. He shut the door behind them. I sat in the kitchen with Ponchik, too shocked to know what to do.

'It can't be true!' I heard Mama say in response to something Papa had mumbled. 'Pavel Maximovich cut his own throat? Was he so sure that he'd be accused of being a wrecker?'

'There are troublemakers at the factory who threatened to point the finger at him if they didn't get what they wanted,' Papa replied.

My parents were so agitated they had forgotten to speak quietly. I could hear every word they said.

'And you found him?' asked my mother. 'Just you?'

'Yes.'

'What did you do?'

Papa paused before he replied. 'I called the police and the NKVD came. They questioned me and told me that I wasn't to tell anyone. Not even you, Sofia. You must never repeat what I have told you. Tomorrow Pavel Maximovich's death will be reported in *Pravda* as a heart attack along with a warning for all Soviet citizens to make sure they keep up their exercise regimes.'

My mother gasped. 'They're covering it up! You must speak to Comrade Stalin! He is the only one who can protect you!'

After the death of Pavel Maximovich, my father went about as if he were in a trance. The strain became worse when a new manager was brought in to replace Pavel Maximovich.

'Don't come to the factory any more, Natasha,' Papa told me. 'The new manager watches me all the time. I find it impossible to work.'

I couldn't believe that anything bad would happen to my father, but trying to reason with my mother to remain calm was impossible. I stayed longer at my glider lessons or went to the aerodrome to watch the planes to avoid the tense atmosphere at home. I was taking advanced classes in glider flying now but my real ambition was to soar in airplanes to the far corners of the Soviet Union and be one of Comrade Stalin's eagles.

Then one afternoon Papa came home from the factory with a grin on his face. He looked himself again. Lydia was having elocution lessons with Mama, and I was doing my homework with Svetlana, when Papa walked into the apartment. He had two packages under his arm.

'Come, everybody,' he announced, nudging Mama into the kitchen and gesturing for Lydia to join us. 'I have good news!'

'What is it?' I asked him.

'Comrade Stalin telephoned me today. He said that he is personally ordering supplies for the factory so I can continue to work unhindered. He also insisted that we use the new State dacha on the river in Nikolina Gora this summer. You know the one — the villa with the pier and the long veranda.' Papa turned to Lydia. 'We would be honoured to have the Novikov family as our guests there,' he said.

Lydia's eyes flashed. She would have known that the dacha was used by high Party officials.

My father turned back to us. 'Then Comrade Stalin sent one of his bodyguards around with these packages addressed to the Azarov family.'

He placed them on the table and unwrapped one. It contained caviar, smoked fish, cheese, some dried peaches and a bottle of champagne from Abrau-Dyurso, the best wine-making region in the Soviet Union.

'Tonight we will have a party to celebrate.' Papa squeezed Lydia's arm. 'You must call your husband and ask him to join us.'

Lydia seemed confused as she eyed the food spread out on the table. Perhaps she thought I had made up the story about my dance shoes being a present from Stalin. She would have to believe his generosity towards us now.

Zoya led Lydia to the telephone and dialled her husband's number for her. We turned our attention to the other package.

'This one,' said Papa, 'came with the instruction that it was to be opened by my wife and daughter.'

'You open it,' Mama said, pushing the package towards me.

I unwrapped the brown paper to discover something large and soft wrapped in tissue paper. Mama's name was written on it. I handed it to her. She untied the string and pulled aside the tissue paper to reveal a fine wool shawl. She lifted it up and Svetlana and I gaped at its beauty: pink cabbage roses were printed on a sky blue background, and the fringe was gold. The shawl was elegant and would be perfect for summer evenings in Nikolina Gora.

The other item in the package was a black velvet box with a cardboard tag attached with my name on it.

'Perhaps it's a compass,' said Svetlana. 'Or something else to encourage you with your flying.'

'Open it!' urged Zoya.

The box smelled old and dusty. I lifted the lid. Resting on the cream silk lining was a sapphire brooch surrounded by tiny diamonds.

'Oh my!' Mama gasped. 'Stepan, can we accept such a valuable gift?'

Papa looked surprised when he saw the brooch. It was certainly something unusual. 'If it comes from Comrade Stalin, then we have to accept it … with gratitude,' he said.

'Comrade Stalin must be pleased with you, Stepan,' Mama said. 'He is being very generous with us.'

Her frown lines had disappeared and she looked as if ten years had fallen off her face.

I held the brooch in my hand and stared at it in wonder. The dance shoes had been the most beautiful thing I had owned — until now!

Lydia returned from the telephone, flustered. 'Pyotr said that Svetlana and I must leave. His mother has a bad cough.'

'I'm sorry to hear that,' said Papa, picking up the dried peaches and cheese and wrapping them in some of the tissue paper. 'Please take these for her. I hope she feels better soon.'

Lydia looked at my father with an odd expression on her face and ushered Svetlana towards the door. Before leaving, she turned and stared at us again as if about to make an announcement, but her lips trembled and she faltered. 'I know that dacha in Nikolina Gora,' she said finally. 'I've seen it in a photograph. It's very beautiful.'

'And we will all enjoy it together,' said Papa cheerfully. 'I hope your husband will be able to come and relax and leave his work worries behind for a while.'

Lydia nodded and put her arm around Svetlana, guiding her out the door.

Mama opened the bottle of champagne that Stalin had sent us and poured some for my father and herself. Even I was allowed half a glass. Then Mama put a record on the gramophone and she and Papa danced the tango to 'Wine of Love'. I placed the brooch on my desk in my room so I could admire it later.

Zoya called us for dinner and we sat down to eat.

'Lydia was not herself this evening,' observed my father.

'She was moved by your generosity,' Mama responded. 'She grew up in poverty. Her father and mother died when she was young and she had to fend for herself and her siblings. Considering where she's come from, Lydia's done well. Svetlana is a charming young lady.'

'I couldn't agree more!' I said, scooping some beetroot onto my plate.

'Alas,' said Papa, glancing at the clock, 'time for me to return to work. If Comrade Stalin is sending me supplies, I'd better start on new chocolate ideas for May Day.'

Papa was putting on his jacket when a knock sounded at the door.

'NKVD! Open up!'

We all looked at each other.

'Who are you after?' Mama called, moving towards the door. 'This is the Azarov apartment. You must have the wrong place.'

Before my mother could open the door there was a bang and the sound of splintering wood. The door fell inwards and three

NKVD agents rushed into the apartment. The tallest of them, a man with red hair and a moustache, grabbed my father and flung him against the wall. Mama and I screamed. Zoya ran out of the kitchen with a saucepan to defend Papa but one of the NKVD men pushed her away.

'There must be a mistake,' said my father, wincing with pain. 'I am Stepan Vladimirovich Azarov, chief chocolatier at the Red October factory. I'm on my way there now to receive supplies ordered by Comrade Stalin.'

The red-haired man reached into his pocket and ripped out a document. He shoved it into my father's face. 'There is no mistake. This is your arrest warrant. You are accused of being an enemy of the people. But first we will search the apartment.'

He dragged Papa to the living room and threw him on the sofa. The other agents pushed Mama, me and Zoya into the room after him. Mama clung to Papa and cried. It was then I noticed our neighbour, Aleksey Nikolayevich, shifting from foot to foot in the doorway. The NKVD must have forced him to act as a witness to the search and arrest.

For six hours we huddled together while the NKVD agents tore through our apartment like a hurricane, flinging books off the shelves and upending drawers. They seized the strangest of things as evidence: Mama's sheet music; recipe books; a camera; even the record Mama had put on the gramophone. I watched the red-haired agent write the items down in a notebook. He had long, elegant hands but they were calloused. I might never learn his name but I knew that I would never forget his hard, angular face and those cold eyes.

I heard the agents searching the room I shared with Alexander. Would they take the sapphire brooch and my dance shoes as well? Ponchik must have been hiding under my bed. He yelped when one of the men kicked him. I stood up but Mama tugged me back down. To my relief Ponchik came running to us and nestled by my side. What was to become of us? A moment ago we had been enjoying luxurious gifts sent to us by Comrade Stalin ... and now this? There must be a mistake. It gave me smug satisfaction to think that when Comrade Stalin learned about it, these men would pay dearly for treating us like criminals.

The red-haired agent returned to the living room and began searching it. He ordered us to stand up and then ripped through the sofa's cushions. Mama stifled a cry when he lifted the lid of her piano and slammed it down again. He opened the cabinet and saw the icon of St Sofia. My blood froze. Papa hadn't committed a crime, but worshipping icons was against the law. Forgive us, Comrade Stalin, I silently prayed. Despite everything I was taught at the Young Pioneers, the paradox of my faith had never registered itself so clearly until then. The agent stared at the icon before seizing it in both hands. I thought he intended to smash it on the floor but instead he winced as if he had been struck in the heart. The sound of the other agents returning to the room alarmed him. He flung the icon under the cupboard and said nothing about it. He didn't record it in his notebook.

The agents finished their work and forced my father to stand up. Where would they take him? Not to the Lubyanka, surely? My father wasn't a criminal! My mother would have to contact Comrade Stalin and Anastas Mikoyan, the commissar for the food industry, and let them know what had happened. My father would be released straight away.

Then, to my horror, I saw Mama take out a bag from the bottom shelf of the cupboard. It was the bag she had packed when she first began to fear Papa might be arrested. She must have repacked it. Why? Now he would look guilty! But I was too distracted by the agents marching my father out the door to be angry at my mother.

I followed the men down the stairs. A chill seized me when I saw the black van parked in the street.

'Papa!' I cried, grabbing his arm. 'Papa, they can't take you away!'

My father turned to me and I will never forget the look in his eyes. Papa, always playful, cheerful and childlike, was like a ghost. His skin was pale and his eyes were hollows, as if his soul had left him.

The red-haired man pushed me away. 'Go back to your mother,' he said. The door to the black van was slammed shut. The agents jumped into the front and the vehicle sped away.

'This will be sorted out and your father will be home later tonight,' a voice behind me said.

I turned to see the trembling figure of Aleksey Nikolayevich standing behind me. But even as I tried to console myself with my neighbour's words, I understood my world of family, comfort and privilege was at an end.

Mama wrote to Comrade Stalin and spoke to the secretary of Anastas Mikoyan regarding Papa's arrest. Comrade Stalin was away from Moscow, we discovered, but Mikoyan's secretary assured us that if my father could prove his innocence of the charges against him, he would be released.

Every day Mama and I went to the Lubyanka prison for news about my father. But the prison officials wouldn't reveal anything, nor would they accept the parcel of food we had prepared for him.

I used to despise the people I saw waiting outside the Lubyanka and other government offices. I had viewed them as collaborators and enemies of the people. Now I was one of them. These wretched souls, with their desperate expressions and the rings of exhaustion under their eyes, were the only source of information — and empathy — we had in our plight.

'Go to Butyrka prison,' a woman advised us one day when we were turned away yet again. 'Your husband might have already been questioned and sent there to await his trial.'

We thanked the woman for her advice. To our relief, Butyrka prison accepted our parcel, although the guards wouldn't confirm whether Papa was there or not.

'It's a good sign,' the woman waiting next in line assured us. 'If they accept the parcel, he is here.'

Mama and I looked up at the stark walls of the prison.

'He'll know that we are thinking of him,' Mama said, weeping. 'He'll know that we haven't forgotten him.'

My mother expected to be arrested at any time herself and she had good reason to fear it. I had learned that if a husband had been taken, it was almost guaranteed his wife would be detained shortly afterwards. The logic was that if she hadn't denounced her husband, she had failed in her duties to the State.

'No, Mama,' I told her when I found her packing a bag for herself. 'We are doing things differently this time. You are not to bring bad fortune on yourself. Instead of preparing for your arrest, we are going to get ready for Papa to come home.'

Some of our furniture had been damaged in the search, but no valuables had been stolen. The agents hadn't taken the sapphire brooch or my dance shoes as I'd feared they would. My mother and I fixed the apartment as best we could: mending ripped curtains, polishing away scratches on furniture, repairing Papa's favourite books. By keeping ourselves occupied, we pretended that things would return to normal and Papa would come home. Zoya continued to set his place at the table and Mama laid out his clothes for him every day. We were like children playing make-believe.

The magic must have worked in Mama's case — the NKVD agents didn't return to arrest her — but Alexander was discharged from the air force.

'Papa can't have been tried yet,' I protested when Alexander returned home to live with us.

'It didn't matter to my commanding officers,' Alexander replied bitterly. 'The mere idea that Papa might be an enemy of the people was enough reason to get rid of me.'

Nor was my brother the only one to suffer rejection after Papa's arrest. When I turned up at the gliding school to take my advanced examination I found Sergei Konstantinovich blocking the doorway.

'You can't come here any more,' he said. 'You put everyone who associates with you in danger. Don't you understand that?'

At school it was as if I had a disease. The teachers and pupils shrank away from me; they disappeared down corridors or into rooms when they saw me coming. Some of the bolder girls bullied me and wrote nasty things in my schoolbooks and stole things from my desk. They knew the teachers were afraid to stand up for me. I wished I had Svetlana by my side, but she had come down with scarlet fever the night my father was arrested and had to do her lessons at home. Only the music teacher, Bronislava Ivanovna, treated me as before and everyone knew that she was showing courage — and foolishness — to do so.

'Be strong, Natasha. Don't give up,' she'd whisper to me whenever I passed her in the corridor. 'You have too much talent to let them destroy you.'

There were no more special parcels of food and Mama's students stayed away. Lydia had to look after Svetlana so it was understandable that she didn't come. Without Papa's wages, money became tight. We lived on *kasha* and soup. Alexander went from factory to factory trying to find work but they all turned him away. The only job he could get was cleaning toilets at the metro station. Mama sold her gramophone and her jewellery to keep us.

'We are cursed,' she told Zoya. 'You must go away and find another family, otherwise you will fall with us.'

But Zoya refused. 'You've never treated me like a maid, Sofia, so I won't act like one. We are family now.'

In the end, Zoya became a lifesaver for us. As we no longer received special packages, we needed someone who could stand in line the whole day to secure food and other necessities. In other families, it was the babushkas who performed that task but both my grandmothers had died young. Zoya did her best but sometimes after waiting at the store for seven or eight hours, she might only return with sardines and potatoes. Still, that was better than nothing.

I didn't even consider going to the Young Pioneers meetings after Alexander told me what had happened to another boy whose parents had been arrested. When the boy refused to renounce his parents and spit on their portraits, he was stripped of his uniform and made to march home in his underwear. The other children taunted him and threw sticks at him. Later that day, the boy hanged himself.

We were allowed to deliver a parcel a month to Butyrka prison. When the next parcel Mama and I took was accepted it bolstered our spirits.

'Maybe Papa will be home soon,' I said to my mother. We returned to our apartment to find that the NKVD had been again and turned us out of our home. Our belongings were piled on the pavement and the apartment door was sealed. When I couldn't find Ponchik, I panicked. I thought that they'd trapped him inside and breaking an NKVD seal was a crime. But then Mama found him hiding under a blanket.

I picked him up and held him close to me. 'I'd die if anything happened to you,' I told him.

Mama sighed. 'Natasha, maybe Svetlana would like to have Ponchik. I don't know what's going to become of us. I don't know if we can keep him.'

The idea of being parted from Ponchik was unthinkable. He had been a gift from Papa. Besides, Lydia was allergic to animals; she would turn him out on the street. Mama must have seen the despair in my eyes, as she said nothing more on the subject.

We were allocated a room in a communal apartment, where the floorboards were painted red to look like carpet and the wallpaper was stained. Mama, Alexander, Zoya and I shared a kitchen, bathroom and toilet with three other families and a divorced couple who still lived together because they didn't want to give up their spacious room. The atmosphere was poisonous. The divorced couple fought constantly, and even though everyone had their own gas ring, shelf and kitchen table, the residents were forever accusing one another of stealing food.

At first we decided it would be better for us to eat in our room. But the way the other residents watched us was unnerving. Mama was sure they were scrutinising us for actions they could denounce us for in order to get extra space in the apartment. To avoid aggravating them, we decided to keep up the 'communal spirit' and ate in the kitchen despite the indigestion the tension caused us.

The partition walls were so thin that if we wished to talk privately we had to pull a blanket over our heads. We kept a picture of Papa hidden under the mattress Mama and I shared and we took it out every evening and set a plate of hard chocolate next to it. In the morning, we hid it again. Families of those accused of being an enemy of the people were supposed to erase all memory of the person and never mention them again. But how could we forget Papa?

When Mama was sorting through our clothes one day, she found a scarf she had borrowed from a neighbour in our old apartment building before Papa's arrest.

'Can you take it back on your way home from school?' Mama asked me. 'Slip it under the door and make sure nobody sees you.'

On my way home that day I did as Mama had asked. The seal on our old apartment was gone and there was a new doormat out the front. The air in the corridor smelled of fresh paint and floor polish. Some other family lived there now. Out on the street I was surprised to see Svetlana stepping out of a café. I had heard nothing from her since she had fallen sick. Our eyes met. 'Sveta!' I said, rushing towards her. 'You are well?'

She froze for a moment and then reached out her arms to me.

'When are you coming back to school?' I asked her. 'I've missed you!'

Lydia came out of the café and saw us. Her eyes narrowed as if I were a dangerous lion about to attack her daughter. She tugged Svetlana away. 'You don't talk to that girl any more!' she hissed at her. 'Do you understand? Do you want what has happened to her family to happen to us? Her father is a wrecker!'

Lydia sent me a ferocious look.

Svetlana struggled against her mother. 'It's Natasha!' she said. 'Natasha!'

Lydia slapped Svetlana across the face. Before her daughter had a chance to recover, she grabbed her around the shoulders and marched her like a prisoner down the street. Svetlana turned to look at me. The sorrowful expression in her eyes broke my heart. So I had lost Svetlana too. I tried to understand what was happening to me. It seemed that everyone else was alive but I wasn't any longer; I was looking at them all through a veil. 'Be strong, Natasha. Don't give up,' Bronislava Ivanovna had said. But how could I fight? I was still alive physically but I was dead in every other sense. I no longer existed as a member of society.

'You have to forgive Lydia's reaction,' Mama told me that evening. 'She was trying to protect Svetlana. Life has become horrible and insane. We've all turned into whisperers. We can no longer even trust our friends.'

I scrutinised my mother's face. 'Why hasn't Comrade Stalin answered us and had Papa released? He used to confide in Papa. Surely he knows he is innocent.'

Mama pursed her lips and turned away. 'Comrade Stalin is kept in the dark by his advisors, Natasha. You know he told your papa that he didn't trust the men around him. All this is going on without his knowledge. I will write to him again.'

At Mama's urging, and with Bronislava Ivanovna secretly paying my fees, I continued to go to school. Svetlana never returned, and I got used to passing girls in the corridor who had once been my friends and not saying anything to them. We didn't have a piano for me to practise on at home any more but Bronislava Ivanovna was convinced I could still apply for the conservatorium when I finished school. 'You have a beautiful singing voice, Natasha. Let's work on that.'

With my dreams of flying in tatters and no friends, I threw myself into singing to distract myself. As well as Russian classical songs, I learned songs by the jazz artists Leonid Utesov and Alexander Tsfasman, who were said to be Stalin's favourites. I wanted to prove that I was a good Soviet citizen. As all her students had abandoned her, teaching me gave my mother something to occupy herself with as well. The tension in the apartment subsided when Mama and I practised together. Even the divorced couple calmed down, and one day announced that they were expecting a baby together.

The following month, Butyrka prison refused to take our parcel. Mama swooned at the news. I reached out to support her, but I was on the verge of fainting myself. This was what we had been dreading.

'Don't fear the worst,' said a young mother with a child at her breast. 'They might be depriving him to get him to confess, or they might have tried him already. Go to the station. There is a train leaving for Kolyma today.'

With our legs trembling beneath us, Mama and I ran to the station. A train destined for the Far East was waiting there but the prisoners sentenced to the Kolyma labour camps had already been loaded. The windows were boarded up with only a gap at the top for air. It must have been stifling inside. People holding packages were going from carriage to carriage shouting their loved one's name. If there was an answer from inside, the guard would take the package to give to the prisoner. One woman received a note back from her husband and held it to her heart. Mama and I called out Papa's name several times but there was no answer.

When we returned home that evening we found the red-haired NKVD agent waiting for us on the street corner. He was holding a box. Mama and I froze, like deer caught in the sights of the hunter's gun.

The NKVD agent walked past us and handed the box to Mama without a word. We watched dumbfounded as he hurried away down the street. He hadn't come to arrest us.

We waited until we returned to our room to see what the box contained. Inside we found items from our apartment that hadn't been left in the pile for us: Mama's handmade quilt, a valuable clock, the sapphire brooch and dance shoes I had received from Stalin, and something wrapped in cloth. We opened the cloth to find the icon of St Sofia. On the back was scribbled in pencil: *Forgive me!*

Mama and I looked at each other. 'I wonder who he is,' Mama whispered. 'And why he ever became an NKVD agent.'

A few days later, I was combing Ponchik in the courtyard when I saw one of the apartment's residents, Ekaterina Mikhailovna, meet the postman. She sorted through the letters and found one that seemed to interest her. 'Sofia, there is something for you!' I heard her call out to my mother. I wondered who would be sending us a letter. Certainly not a friend; they had all deserted us. Perhaps Comrade Stalin had replied at last!

I picked Ponchik up and ran into the apartment. Ekaterina Mikhailovna was hovering outside our room but the door was closed. She scurried away when she saw me. I opened the door and found Mama on her knees. At first I thought she was praying but then I realised she was sobbing. I put Ponchik down and dropped to my knees beside her. Mama was holding the letter in her hand. It was typewritten and looked official.

My heart sank. Papa must have been found guilty. The people outside Butyrka prison had told us it was common for former friends and colleagues to testify against the accused if they thought it would advantage themselves in some way. What would happen now? Would Papa be sent to a labour camp like the prisoners on the train?

'Mama,' I said, putting my hand on her trembling shoulder, 'if Papa has been found guilty then we must see Comrade Stalin in person. We know that Papa is not a saboteur. He loved his work.'

Mama turned to me. Her eyes had a tormented look in them. 'It's too late,' she said.

'It's not too late,' I insisted. 'An appeal can be made. If Comrade Stalin isn't in Moscow, we must find out where he is and go there!'

The letter slipped from Mama's fingers to the floor. Something about the action made my stomach twist with fear. 'Mama?'

She put her hand on my wrist. It was ice-cold. I knew then that the inconceivable had happened even before my mother told me. 'Natasha,' she said, 'Papa was tried and found guilty. He was executed the same day. My darling, your father is dead.'

TWELVE

Orël, 2000

Orlov arrived at Kursky station with dozens of scenarios running through his head. Ilya hadn't wanted to reveal any more over the telephone; all Orlov knew from his call was that someone had buried Natasha. Who? Where? Did she survive the parachute jump, or did she injure herself and die? Or maybe she had survived the war, lived the rest of her years in a village and passed away an old woman? But in all the circumstances Orlov came up with, Ilya's use of 'buried' meant that the woman he had loved was dead. He had resigned himself to that possibility many years ago, but now that he was closer to finding out how she had died, he was terrified. He had lived in limbo for so long that the feeling of melancholic inertia it produced was familiar. What if the truth was worse than anything he had imagined? A shudder ran through him. He wouldn't allow himself to think of that.

He hurried past the stalls selling souvenirs — *matryoshka* dolls, fur hats, *khokhloma* spoons — and stopped when he saw a stall peddling Soviet memorabilia. His eyes narrowed as he took in the figurines of Lenin, the pieces of the Berlin Wall, the Soviet Union flag. These things were sacred once; ideals by which Russians had lived and died. Now they were relegated to the realm of kitsch and curios. He was about to turn away when he noticed the bust of Stalin. Could the younger generation make a joke of the devil too?

Orlov struggled past the tourists and other travellers to the first-class carriage. The train stewardess directed him to a seat by the window, opposite two young German businessmen. 'Hello,' they said in Russian and pointed to Orlov's overnight bag, using gestures to let him know that they would lift it onto the rack for him. It irked Orlov although he understood that they meant well.

When the men were all seated, one of the Germans took out a package containing slices of dark bread that smelled like molasses and a block of aged cheese. He cut the cheese and shared the meal with his companion, then offered some to Orlov, who accepted a piece of bread and cheese only because it seemed polite. Germans and their bread, he thought. The meals offered on Russian trains had improved in the last few years, but Orlov believed that it wouldn't have mattered if his travelling companions had been offered five-star cuisine; they still would have preferred their pumpernickel bread and salty cheese.

After their supper, the Germans returned to studying their laptops while Orlov tried to lose himself in the Solzhenitsyn novel he had started that morning. He looked over the top of his book at the Germans again. How strange a thing war is, he thought. And how easily animosity is erased when it's all over. I could have killed these men's grandfathers — shot them out of the sky or protected the bombers that blew them to smithereens — and yet here we sit, completely civilised. He looked out the window and his mind wandered back to the bronze bust of Stalin. Would somebody buy that and put it in their living room? Stalin was a madman who murdered millions of his own people.

Orlov had been in the air force when the crazed purges of the late 1930s began. He had watched in horror as his commanding officers fell one after the other. They had all been fine men, but had signed confessions, no doubt extracted under torture, stating that they had committed acts of anti-Soviet sabotage and spying. They had been executed or sent to labour camps. Stalin wasn't only vicious, he was a fool! Even during the German invasion, he continued to remove talented officers from the armed forces. At first, there might have been self-serving logic to the arrests: revolutions had often followed on the shirt tails of war and Stalin wanted to remove anyone who could threaten his power. But then things became frenzied. Every day, people were arrested and shot for nothing more than accidentally bumping a portrait of Stalin or wiping their backside with a piece of newspaper with his image on it.

'Listen, Natasha, there is something you should know ...'

Orlov was distracted from his memory of that fateful July afternoon by the drinks waitress pushing her trolley down the aisle. He purchased a bottle of Georgian wine for himself and the Germans.

'To friendship between nations,' he toasted them in Russian.

They had no idea what he'd said and toasted him back with '*Prost!*' Then they went back to their laptops and Orlov returned to his memories.

Nikita Khrushchev, whom Orlov got to know well when he was working on the space programme, told him that Stalin once said it was better to kill the innocent along with the guilty than to risk letting the guilty go free. The NKVD were given quotas during the purges, as if they were a factory, and when they couldn't fulfil those quotas they fabricated charges. Even the Bolshevik general and his wife who had run the orphanage where Orlov grew up disappeared in the purges. That general had been a Party loyalist and from the time Stalin came to power made the orphanage's children, including Orlov, stand and salute the portrait of 'their Great Leader' in the dining room every morning. 'It is because of Comrade Stalin that you have a roof over your heads. He has provided you with an education, warm clothes and a future. It is because of him that you are not dead,' the general had repeatedly told them.

Orlov often wondered why he himself had been spared. Despite the cult of Stalin he had been exposed to in the orphanage, he'd hated the man and the Communists. He had mouthed platitudes and kept his views to himself in order to survive. He had fought for Russia during the war, not Stalin. Stalin died in 1953, either of a stroke or poisoned by those around him, according to the differing views. The public mourning was overwhelming. People were crushed to death in the crowds that went to view his body. It was only when Khrushchev began his programme of de-Stalinisation that Orlov felt he could visit Natasha's mother without drawing attention to her. It was remarkable that she had survived after the arrest of her husband and with her missing daughter suspected of being a German spy. Orlov had found Sofia Grigorievna living in an apartment in the Arbat: one room, with a bathroom so small one could barely turn around in it and a kitchenette with enough space only for a sink and a café table. But the apartment was meticulously kept, with white antimacassars on the chairs, pink chrysanthemums in a vase on the windowsill and not a speck of dust anywhere. Orlov's eyes fell on the icon of St Sofia in the corner. His mother had once owned the same image. There was a portrait of a man — Natasha's father, he assumed — in a frame on a side table. Next to it was a photograph of Natasha with her brother, who was in an air-force uniform.

'Won't you please sit down, General Orlov,' Sofia Grigorievna said.

She had Natasha's fair colouring and doll-like features. But while her daughter's beauty had been vibrant, Sofia Grigorievna emitted the fragile dignity of a woman who had survived tragedy. All her family was gone, and the only living being she had to lavish her affection upon was the red-furred dog she lifted onto her lap.

'Natasha told me a lot about you,' she said.

Her grey eyes met Orlov's and he wondered how much Natasha had revealed to her mother. Then he realised that even if she knew everything, it wouldn't have made this meeting any easier.

'You were kind to write to me the details you knew of her disappearance,' Sofia Grigorievna continued. 'I have your letter still. I shall take it, along with Natasha's correspondence, to my grave.'

Orlov took this as confirmation that she hadn't had contact with her daughter since the war. Or was it? He decided to be more direct.

'Do you think that your daughter might still be alive?' he asked her. 'We have not found her plane ... or her body.'

Sofia Grigorievna's gaze moved to the pictures of her husband and children. 'I don't know. With my son, Alexander, I knew he had died the night it happened. But with Natasha ...' She shook her head. 'I simply don't know.' Looking back to Orlov she added, 'I am sure that if Natasha could have, she would have contacted you or me by now. Both of us know she wasn't a spy.'

They lapsed into silence. Out on the street there was the sound of singing. A group of old men and women were marching along with Stalin's portrait. There were those who believed that the Soviet Union couldn't survive without him. They listened to the singing and chanting for a while.

Sofia Grigorievna said suddenly, 'I'm glad that monster is dead. Aren't you?'

Orlov was taken aback. It wasn't the sort of statement people came out with, no matter what they truly thought. The Soviet Union was a nation of people who knew that a single utterance could cost them their lives. But he understood that her boldness meant she trusted him and he wanted to assure her that her faith wasn't misplaced. Something he hadn't considered telling her before came into his mind.

'Stalin signed your husband's death warrant,' he said. 'Did you know that all along?'

Sofia Grigorievna stroked the dog for a while before answering. 'When Stalin replaced Yezhov with Beria as head of the NKVD, hundreds of thousands of convictions were quashed and scores of people were let out of labour camps. For many it was proof that Stalin hadn't known about the NKVD's excesses and now he was making good.'

'Including Natasha? Even though it was too late for her father?'

Sofia Grigorievna placed the dog down on the rug and got up to close the window. 'I've always known who was responsible for my husband's death,' she said. 'The chocolate factory couldn't meet its quotas because the Soviet Union couldn't compete for ingredients with the Capitalist countries on the world market. When people don't have chocolate for New Year's Eve they blame the State. Well, you can't have that. Scapegoats must be found. The first was the chief factory manager, and when that didn't change anything, the axe fell on my husband.'

Natasha's mother had described things clearly but now Orlov was confused. He hesitated a moment before saying, 'Forgive me, Sofia Grigorievna, if I ask you too many painful questions but I'm trying to understand something. Did you never voice your opinions about Stalin to your daughter? You see, she worshipped him.'

Sofia Grigorievna didn't flinch. 'I think you understand very well, General Orlov. I let Natasha think that Stalin wasn't responsible for her father's death. I encouraged her in that belief. Why? Because my daughter had to survive in the Soviet Union. She already had her family background against her. How could I handicap her any further by making her hate Stalin? You know how headstrong she could be. Inflaming her would only have achieved her arrest and execution.'

Orlov recalled Sofia Grigorievna's explanation as he sat on the train to Orël. Even now, he was impressed by her wisdom. It must have been galling to hear her daughter praise the man who had been responsible for her husband's death, but she had borne it to protect the daughter she loved.

It was late when Orlov arrived at the hotel in Orël. There was a note from Ilya at reception saying that he would collect him at five o'clock the next morning. Where are we going, wondered Orlov.

He ate some smoked cod and bread for supper. Try as he might, he couldn't sleep. During the war, when sleep deprivation was a daily way of life, he had thought he would sleep forever when it was all over. But his post-war life had been plagued by the insomnia that came from a troubled mind.

The hotel was modern and the walls were thin. He could hear the restaurant's singer. Was she really singing that song or was it his imagination?

Wait for me, and I'll come back.
Wait in patience yet
When they tell you off by heart
That you should forget.
Even when my dearest ones
Say that I am lost,
Even when my friends give up,
Sit and count the cost,
Drink a glass of bitter wine
To the fallen friend —
Wait. And do not drink with them.
Wait until the end.

The lyrics were from a poem by Konstantin Simonov. It had been Natasha's favourite song during the war and the regiment used to ask her to sing it often. She had a beautiful voice and her interpretation of the song brought tears to everyone's eyes.

'If something should happen,' she'd once told Orlov after they'd made love, 'I'll wait for you no matter what because my waiting will keep you alive. I'll wait for you just as Svetlana always waits for me to return from a mission. It's because she waits for me that I survive.'

'I did wait for you, my darling,' Orlov whispered into the darkness. 'But now it seems you were dead all along.'

His mind drifted back to Sofia Grigorievna. He hadn't gone to visit her again after that first time but he'd used his influence to make sure she was well provided for until her death in 1960. She had been cremated, as was the new trend in the Soviet Union then. It occurred to Orlov now that he'd missed an opportunity by not asking her if he could read Natasha's letters. Perhaps there would have been some clue in them. But back then he'd still harboured the hope that he would find her in person. Now the truth was waiting for him, somewhere out there in the dawn.

'Where is she buried?' Orlov asked Ilya the next morning when his friend came to pick him up. He hadn't even said hello.

Ilya opened the door to his Skoda for Orlov. 'There is a village on the edge of the Trofimovsky Forest where a ninety-year-old woman says her father and uncle found the body of a female pilot in July 1943 and buried her in a family crypt.'

'A crypt?' asked Orlov in surprise. Family crypts were unusual in Russia, especially in the countryside.

'That's all I know,' said Ilya. 'I didn't want to investigate without you being there.'

'Why didn't you inform the Ministry of Defence? If there are remains there they'll want to run tests.'

Ilya stared at the road ahead. 'I didn't want to call them out until we're sure there is actually a body and we aren't simply listening to an old lady with a failing memory. But also because ... well, I thought that you should see her first.'

Orlov swallowed. He felt like he had a rock in his throat. 'So you think this could be it ... you think we've found her?'

Ilya reached across to the glove box and pulled out a map. 'I've marked the distance between the crash site and the village. If Natalya Azarova parachuted out of the plane she would have landed in one of the fields nearby. She is the only missing female fighter pilot who was active in that area at the time, and if a body is buried there it could well be hers.'

Orlov stared at the map. Did he want to be part of this process? What would be left of his beautiful Natasha now? Perhaps it would be better if Ilya and the Ministry of Defence handled this and simply gave him a forensic report. He looked at the birch trees that lined the road and remembered the plane they'd found in the forest. It was as if Natasha was calling to him, reeling him in like a fish. She'd had a strong will in life. Was it possible that her will had survived her physical death?

After a toilet and tea stop the two men took to the road again. Just over an hour later, Ilya turned the car off the bitumen road onto a dirt one. The farmhouses they passed, with their rickety wooden fences and vegetable gardens, looked the same to Orlov as they had during the war.

They drove through a gate and were greeted by a collection of boisterous farm dogs of all breeds and sizes. A man in a woodcutter's singlet waved to them, exposing his hairy armpit. Two blond boys with bare chests and buzz cuts ran towards the car.

'Hello!' said the man in the singlet. 'I am Dmitri Borisovich Mochalov. My grandmother is waiting for you in the garden.'

A woman wearing a kerchief on her head came out of the house and introduced herself as Fekla Petrovna, Dmitri's wife. Two other men in tracksuit pants and singlets, who Orlov took to be neighbours, joined them and the group led Orlov and Ilya to the back garden, where an old woman was waiting for them at a table, surrounded by chickens and more playful dogs. It was always a shock for Orlov to see someone close to his own age. He still had his hair, grey and thinned but still there, and his own teeth. Until his heart problem, his health had been good. This old woman looked ancient, with a sunken mouth and wrinkles so deep her nose and chin seemed to have disappeared into her weathered face. Her eyes were faded and watery, but she sat up straight with her hands on her knees and had an almost queenly pride about her.

Fekla pulled out chairs for Orlov and Ilya and sat down next to her grandmother-in-law. The others gathered around to hear the story. Dmitri stood directly behind Orlov and Orlov could feel the farmer's belly bumping into his neck. He cringed with the thought that Dmitri was sweating onions and meat through his skin.

'This is Olga Vadimovna,' said Fekla, putting her arm around the woman. 'In 1943 she was a mother of five young children. Her husband and brothers were away fighting. She ran the farm together with her uncle and father. She has never learned to read and has never taken interest in anything except her family and farm, but a few days ago she overheard Dmitri and me talking about the plane that was discovered nearby. That was when she told us her story ... about how her father and uncle found the body of a female pilot in the forest.'

Olga studied Orlov and Ilya with the suspicious expression elderly peasants bestowed on anyone from Moscow. But something about them must have overcome any misgivings and she began her story in a raspy voice.

'In the summer of 1943, the Germans occupied our village. All our produce beyond our basic needs was to be given to their army. Anyone who didn't comply was executed along with their family. Our neighbour was hanged with a piece of wire for keeping a cow in his barn so that he could give milk to his pregnant wife and two young children. The German soldiers raped the wife and then they tied her two children to her and threw a grenade at them.' Olga stopped for a moment, clenching and unclenching her fists, then continued.

You can imagine how much we hated the Germans. One day we were working in the fields when we heard the rumble of planes in the distance and machine guns firing. We looked up to see a Soviet plane fly over chased by three Messerschmitts. It made us furious to see the Germans attacking one of our planes. But the Soviet pilot wasn't going to be caught. The plane cut a jagged vapour trail across the sky as it dodged and weaved to avoid the bullets. Then the pilot turned the plane and headed back towards the pursuers, dividing them and shooting one down at the same time. We cheered as the enemy plane went down in flames. The Germans could have let the fighter go back to its own territory but they were determined to get it. The two remaining planes turned and pursued the Soviet pilot. We were forbidden to watch dogfights but we couldn't take our eyes off the battle taking place in the sky. The odds were against the Soviet plane, yet the pilot skilfully manoeuvred and again faced his attackers head on.

'That is no ordinary pilot,' my father said. 'That's why the Germans will not let him go.'

But the Soviet plane was doomed. It began to lose altitude and its guns stopped firing. 'It's either running out of fuel or ammunition,' guessed my uncle. The two remaining German planes closed in but the Soviet pilot wasn't going to go down without a final strike. We watched as he swerved to approach from the side and rammed one of the enemy planes, sending it spinning to the ground. There was just the one German plane left now, but the Soviet plane continued to lose altitude. It tilted nose down and hurtled towards the ground.

'Jump! Jump!' I screamed, although of course there was no chance of the pilot hearing. We watched to see if the hatch would open and the pilot parachute out but nothing happened.

'The pilot must have been shot,' said my father through gritted teeth. 'Or knocked unconscious when he rammed the other plane.'

Then we saw a figure emerge from the cockpit and fall towards the earth. I screamed in horror, but the parachute mushroomed and the pilot landed beyond the trees on the other side of the river. The plane hit the ground somewhere in the forest with a crash that echoed around the valley. The ground trembled beneath our feet. The remaining German plane circled and circled the area where the plane had gone down like a hawk searching for its prey. Then it rose again and flew away. We wondered if the German had seen the pilot parachute out but perhaps he hadn't. That's what we hoped.

My father wanted to go and find the pilot straight away. But my uncle stopped him. 'Don't be a fool,' he said. 'If the Germans catch you, you'll be shot. Wait until tonight. Those pilots are trained for survival. He'll know how to hide.'

'If he isn't injured,' my father lamented.

Olga paused and stared at the sky, memories animating her face. In her profile Orlov thought he caught a glimpse of what she had been like as a young woman, watching the battle in the air. Despite her age, Olga had been precise in her account. He was certain from her description that Natasha had been the daring pilot. Natasha was a woman when she lay in Orlov's arms, but in the sky she was a demon. Many of the male pilots, including Orlov himself, had been dismissive of 'Little Natashka' when she had been assigned to the regiment. Orlov had not objected to women in the air force altogether, as some of his colleagues had. He respected the women who were willing to risk their lives to save the Motherland. But while he believed women could capably fly bombers and hit military targets, he didn't think they had the killer instinct and cunning needed for pilot-to-pilot combat. Natasha had proved him wrong. After the Battle of Stalingrad, the men in the regiment had said, and not in jest, that they were glad Natalya Azarova was on the Soviet side: they would not want to fight her in the air. That was why the Germans had been determined to get rid of her.

Olga continued her story.

My father was grateful to the Soviet soldiers and pilots who were fighting to free us and he would have gladly forfeited his own life to save them. That evening he and my uncle packed a bag with the little bread we had and some vodka to take to the pilot, but as they were preparing to leave German soldiers stormed into the house. At first I thought they were after food, but by the way they overturned the beds and swept everything out of the cupboards before moving on to search the barn it was obvious they were looking for someone. It must be the pilot, I thought. I was glad because that meant he hadn't been caught yet. Then, to our dismay, some German officers arrived and took over the house for the night. My father and uncle had to delay their journey into the forest until the following evening.

While they were searching for the pilot, my aunt paced the kitchen. I put the children to bed and tried to distract myself by sewing. In the early hours of the morning there was a noise in the yard. We looked out the window to see my father and uncle returning. They were carrying something between them. 'It's the pilot,' I said to my aunt. 'He must have been hurt.'

But when my father and uncle came into the house, I realised that not only was the pilot already dead but that she was a woman.

'I couldn't leave her in the forest for the wild animals to finish her off,' my father wept. 'Look at her! She's just a young woman and she gave her life for us.'

They lifted the pilot's body onto the table. Her hair and face were covered in blood. I grabbed a cloth and began washing her face. Even with the wound on her forehead, I could see that she had been pretty. 'She looks like an angel,' my aunt commented. Even my stern uncle was moved. 'War is not women's business,' he said. 'They should be at home creating life, not taking it.' It was his way of expressing his sorrow. He didn't mean that the young woman had been wrong to defend her country, rather that it was wrong that circumstances should have brought her to have to do so.

We wanted to give the pilot a proper funeral but the village priest had been shot a week earlier for helping the partisans. My aunt and I removed the pilot's uniform and clothed her in my wedding dress, the only white item of clothing I had. We were uncertain about what to do next because the sun would be rising soon and it was too dangerous to be caught burying her. My aunt remembered the crypt in the cemetery. It belonged to a Polish family that had left the village long before the war.

My aunt ran ahead of us to make sure all was clear and then my father and uncle opened the crypt and placed the pilot's body on a shelf inside. I laid her leather helmet and gun, which my uncle had found beside the body, on her chest. Then we quickly crossed ourselves and rushed home to say prayers for her soul. Our intention was to leave her in the crypt and inform the Soviet authorities about her body if anyone came in search of her. But a few days later there was a fierce battle in the village as the Soviets fought the Germans to liberate us. My father and uncle both were killed. There were many more bodies then and much grief to deal with. The pilot remained forgotten until now.

Olga fell silent. Everyone seemed to be staring at the ground. The old woman's story had brought tears to their eyes. Orlov thought that he had never felt sadder or lonelier. No doubt when he passed away, there would be an obituary in the newspaper and a funeral with full honours. The President would make a speech. Natasha had been interred simply with love and devotion by simple farmers. Olga and her aunt had dressed her in the best clothing they possessed. Their gratitude for her sacrifice moved him greatly. It wasn't only words but true feeling.

Ilya took a photograph out of his pocket and showed it to Olga. Orlov saw it was a black-and-white picture of Natasha in her military uniform and flying helmet.

'Is this the pilot?' Ilya asked Olga.

Fekla took the photograph from him and held it up for the old woman, who squinted at it. 'Yes, I think it is. Or I think it could be. It was a long time ago and, you see, we didn't have electricity in those days, only lamplight, and her face was covered in blood.' Olga studied the photograph again with the expression of an elderly person who has seen too much tragedy. 'Yes, I am sure this is her. She was pretty like this young girl.'

'You say that her helmet and gun were found beside the body?' Ilya continued. 'And that she had a wound to the head?'

Olga nodded.

Ilya's and Orlov's eyes met. If the tight-fitting helmet was off then Natasha must have removed it herself. That meant she wasn't dead when she hit the ground. Did she shoot herself? Orlov knew that the women pilots had a pact with each other that if ever they were in danger of being captured they would commit suicide rather than be taken prisoner. Not only could they be tortured for information by the Germans but stories abounded of the pack-rape of female Soviet prisoners. That seemed the most likely explanation if Natasha's pistol had been beside her and not in her holster.

'What did you do with her uniform?' asked Ilya.

Olga thought for a moment. 'We burned it. We didn't want it to be discovered if the Germans searched our house again.'

'What about her identification?'

Olga looked confused and Ilya explained to her about the Bakelite capsule that members of the armed forces kept in their pocket with their name, home town and relatives written on a piece of paper inside.

Olga thought about it. 'Yes, there was such a capsule,' she said. 'We didn't know what it was, but we thought it might be important so I wrapped it in the helmet along with the gun.'

'Natasha wouldn't have been carrying her identification,' Orlov said.

Ilya looked at him, an eyebrow lifted quizzically.

'It was a superstition,' Orlov explained. 'Natalya Azarova believed that if she carried her identification capsule into battle, she'd be killed. She used to give it to her mechanic before she got into her plane. Her mechanic was like a sister to her and she'd put the capsule in her pocket alongside her own until Natalya returned.'

Ilya frowned. 'You've never mentioned that before, Valentin.'

Orlov grimaced. 'I had to argue with Natalya Azarova about every formality, but her belief was so strong that I turned a blind eye to that one. You can tell from the description of the battle what a skilled pilot she was, but she was as stubborn as a mule. I was strict about identification, but you have to understand that carrying it wasn't a formal air-force policy the way it is now, or as it was then with the German and British armies. It was left as a matter of personal choice.'

Ilya turned to Dmitri. 'Has anyone opened the crypt since the body was placed there?'

Dmitri shook his head. 'To the best of my knowledge, no. After the war the cemetery wasn't used any more. I can take you there now. You can see for yourself.'

The old village cemetery was a short walk from the farm through a field and a wood. It was shaded by lime trees, and overgrown grass rose up around the tombstones and the Russian Orthodox crosses. Some of the graves were marked out by iron fences that had rusted and sunk over the years. Towards the back of the cemetery stood a stone crypt with a copper domed roof that had gone green with age.

Dmitri's sons and neighbours had followed the group to the cemetery; even the dogs had accompanied them. Orlov remembered that people in the countryside did everything together. He was grateful, however, when the onlookers stayed respectfully outside the cemetery's gate. The crypt was now a site of investigation.

Dmitri walked ahead of Orlov and Ilya, beating the grass down with a stick, no doubt hoping to scare away any snakes that might be lurking there. But Orlov wasn't worried about being bitten. He kept his eyes on the crypt. Angel statuettes stood guard either side of the two steps that led to the iron gate. A bronze Catholic cross, tarnished and lopsided now, stood on top of the dome. It was an elaborate tomb for this part of the country. Olga had said that it had belonged to a Polish family who had gone from the region. Orlov wondered if they had left voluntarily, or if they had disappeared during the years of collectivisation, when wealthy landowners had their properties confiscated and were exiled to remote parts of the country.

The crypt's iron gate creaked on rusty hinges when Dmitri opened it. The wooden door beyond it was swollen with rot and wouldn't budge when he tried to open it. He asked Ilya for permission to break it.

'There appears to be no other way,' agreed Ilya.

Orlov thought Dmitri would return to his farm to get an axe. He gave a cry of surprise when the farmer took a step back before thrusting his shoulder into the door. The wood splintered but didn't give way. Stepping back again Dmitri kicked it. The door fell inwards with a crash and the men found themselves staring into the dim space of the crypt.

As Dmitri moved aside, Ilya entered the crypt but Orlov hesitated, bracing himself the way he used to do before he went into battle. Once inside the crypt, the air was musty and Orlov's eyes took a few seconds to adjust to the gloom. He squinted and saw in front of him a coffin with a collapsed lid. If there had once been a body inside, it was nothing but dust now. There was another coffin on the shelf above it, equally decrepit.

He turned and saw Ilya standing beside something. Orlov's knees buckled. Natasha was lying there on a stone shelf, dressed in white, her blonde hair cascading around her face. Her skin was as luminous as it had been when he last saw her. She turned to him and smiled with her full red lips.

Then he blinked and realised that wasn't what he was seeing at all. Lying on the shelf, shreds of cloth sticking to its ribs and hip bones, was a skeleton. Its arms were folded across its chest and underneath the hands was a piece of mouldy fabric and a rusted gun. Ilya took a torch from his pocket and illuminated the bald skull with its gaping mouth and yellow teeth.

'There are two holes in the skull,' he commented. 'It's in keeping with what Olga told us.'

Orlov barely heard him. It was taking all his willpower not to collapse to his knees. Everything pointed to the remains being

Natasha's, but according to Olga the pilot had been carrying her identification capsule; that left Orlov with some doubt.

Ilya shone the torch along the length of the skeleton: the spinal cord and limbs were intact. He brought the light back to the skull to examine the holes more closely. He touched the cranium and his hand brushed something that rattled. 'What's this?'

He shone the torch onto what at first looked like a bullet but turned out to be the identification capsule Olga had mentioned. Ilya deliberated over opening it. Unlike the stamped tags used by the German and British armies, the Soviet capsules weren't even airtight or watertight. On some recovery digs, Ilya and Orlov had opened the capsules to find nothing but dust inside.

Ilya glanced at Orlov. Even if they were to open it in ideal laboratory conditions, there was no guarantee that the paper inside wouldn't disintegrate.

Orlov had to know. Was this Natasha or not? 'Open it,' he urged.

His heart seemed to skip beats as Ilya unscrewed the capsule and used the tweezers on his Swiss army knife to carefully open the paper. It appeared to be intact. Ilya read the information and took a breath before turning to Orlov.

'It's hers. Natalya Stepanovna Azarova of Moscow. Daughter of Sofia Grigorievna Azarova.'

The blood rushed to Orlov's ears. It *was* Natasha's identification. Why had she taken it with her that day? Had she been so upset by what he'd told her that she had forgotten to give it to Svetlana? Or did she deliberately take it, intending to die on that mission?

He staggered out of the tomb, needing some air.

Dmitri, who was standing near the stairs smoking a cigarette, turned to look at him. 'Are you all right?'

Natasha had gone missing fifty-seven years ago but the grief that was gripping Orlov's insides was fresh. He desperately wanted to give in to the tears that were welling behind his eyes but he controlled his emotions.

'We've found her,' he said. 'It is indeed Natalya Azarova.' He felt faint and sat down on the steps.

Ilya came out of the crypt and put his hand on Orlov's shoulder. 'Well done, my friend. Your determination has paid off. You have done the honourable thing by your wingman. Now she can be buried with honours and any slur can be removed from her name.'

He turned to Dmitri and explained that they would seal off the crypt and inform the local police. Once he got back to Orël, Ilya would call the Ministry of Defence so that they could collect the skeleton. Dmitri left to tell his sons and neighbours, who were still waiting outside the cemetery gates, what had taken place. Their little village was about to become famous.

'Is that all?' Orlov asked Ilya, still not able to believe his long quest was finished. 'Won't the Ministry of Defence want to run forensic tests for absolute confirmation?'

Ilya took a cigarette from his pocket and lit it. 'A forensic anthropologist will be able to tell the age of the skeleton and how long it has been in the crypt. Natalya Azarova was a young healthy woman with no deformities. The skeleton confirms that. But as she doesn't have any relatives to check the skeleton's DNA against, they will have to use the circumstantial evidence and decide what to make of it. With the location of the plane, the identification capsule, the skeleton and Olga's testimony, we will have to hope that the Kremlin will agree to confirm that we have found Natalya Azarova's remains. That part will depend on the mood of the powers that be.'

Orlov looked away.

'Valentin,' Ilya said gently, 'we have found her. You know we have. Everything adds up.'

A pain was crushing Orlov's chest. He nodded. *Drink a glass of bitter wine to the fallen friend*: the words of Natasha's favourite song echoed around in his head.

Then Ilya said something that turned everything upside down again.

'I'm puzzled about one thing. When Olga described the pilot's body and said that the helmet and pistol were found next to it, I assumed Natalya Azarova had shot herself to avoid capture.'

The skin on Orlov's neck prickled. 'Yes, go on.'

'Well, I study airplanes and not people, but from what I can see the injuries to the cranium aren't consistent with a self-inflicted wound. The hole at the front of the skull is larger than the one at the back, and lower, suggesting she was shot at close range from behind by someone standing above her.'

Orlov jumped up. His mind was racing. 'An execution? But that makes no sense. A pilot would have information that the Germans wanted. She would have been taken to the commander of the nearest air-force regiment for questioning, not executed on the spot.'

'It makes no sense for the Germans to have shot her,' agreed Ilya, looking off into the distance. 'But the only person who can answer our questions is the person who killed her.'

THIRTEEN

Moscow, 2000

L ily added the rice to the sautéed mushrooms and onion and mixed them together. She took the dough out of the refrigerator, rolled it and cut it into small pieces, then flattened them with a rolling pin. Making her grandmother's mushroom *pelmeni* was one of her ways to relax. She was glad it was Friday night. She'd been shocked how, after Kate's death, things had returned to normal so quickly at the office. Scott was noticeably saddened, and had arranged to go to England to give the hotel's condolences at Kate's funeral, but apart from that everything carried on as normal. A bilingual temp from an agency had been hired to help the sales department with its administrative work. Mary didn't mention Kate again, and Richard, after a couple of days of being grief-stricken, was back to joking around the office and forwarding humorous emails. Lily found it impossible to believe that someone as popular as Kate could be so easily forgotten.

When the *pelmeni* were ready for cooking, she took three plates out of the cupboard and then set knives and forks on the dining table. Poor Rodney, she thought. He'd been so devastated by Kate's death that he'd returned to England, asking friends to close his affairs in Russia. He'd said he never wanted to return to the country that had given him many happy memories and then wiped them out with one horrific blow. Lily folded the serviettes. She knew that everyone expected Rodney, who was only twenty-six, to eventually find love again. She stopped mid-action when she remembered what Adam's mother had said to her at the funeral. 'You'll get on with your life, and in a year or two you'll meet someone else. But for our family, the grief will last forever.'

Shirley had been like a second mother to Lily, and together they'd tended to Adam through his illness. But after his death, Shirley couldn't bear the sight of her. It had been crushing to be thrust so coldly from Adam's family when she'd needed them most.

'Mrrr!' Lily looked down to see Mamochka sitting at her feet. This was the closest the cat had come to her.

Since they'd moved into Yulian's more spacious apartment, Mamochka had stopped hiding but she still didn't let anyone touch her. Now, she stretched out her paw towards Lily's foot. Lily reached down so Mamochka could sniff her fingers.

'Good girl,' she said. She knew it was a courageous step for Mamochka and didn't try to pat her. Trust had to be earned slowly.

Lily glanced towards the bedroom, where Babushka was resting on the bed with Laika. With the extra guests, Lily was glad that Oksana had let her use Yulian's vacated apartment. Like her own apartment, it was decorated in Russian froufrou style, with teal damask wallpaper and white laminated furniture, but the living room was four times bigger and had a sofa long enough for Lily to stretch out on when she slept on it.

'I have some raw beef for Laika,' Lily said to Babushka, placing the plate under the bedroom window, next to Laika's water bowl. 'Oksana is going to join us for dinner. She is so busy caring for sick kittens that she doesn't have time to cook for herself.'

Laika jumped down off the bed to eat her food. Babushka stared at the wall as if she hadn't heard anything Lily had said. Babushka was often lost in her own world, Lily had noticed. Was it simply age or something else?

There was a knock at the door. Lily assumed it was Oksana and was surprised to find Luka the vet standing in the hallway, casually dressed in a black T-shirt and jeans.

'Hi,' he said, 'I have some medications for Oksana's cats. She was in the middle of syringe-feeding a kitten and couldn't open the door so she asked me to leave them with you.'

Lily was so taken aback to see him that she took the package of medicine without saying anything.

Luka glanced at the table. 'You're about to have dinner. I won't keep you.'

It was bad manners in Lily's family not to offer food to someone who turned up at a mealtime. Although she hadn't been expecting extra company, she had to ask. 'Would you like to stay? I've made plenty of *pelmeni*.'

Before he could answer, Oksana appeared out of the elevator carrying a bottle of wine.

'How's the kitten?' Luka asked her.

'She ate well. She's asleep on a heat pad now. Thank you for not charging me for Artemis and Aphrodite, by the way.'

'My pleasure. You can put the money towards feeding the colony cats instead.' He turned back to Lily. 'Thank you for the invitation to join you for dinner, but I'm vegetarian and I don't want to impose.'

'You could never impose, darling,' Oksana told him, ushering him inside, 'and besides, Lily makes her *pelmeni* with mushrooms.'

Lily helped Babushka to the table and left Oksana to introduce Luka to her while she went to the kitchen to boil water for the *pelmeni*.

'She's a dear friend of the family,' she heard Oksana telling Luka. 'Lily has kindly lent her room, as I have no space in my apartment.'

Lily placed the *pelmeni* in the water. Oksana was sharp. She'd given an explanation that wouldn't raise too many questions.

Lily returned to the dining table and put out the wine glasses. 'But don't you find it creepy — hunting for the dead?' Oksana was asking Luka.

'Not at all,' he replied. 'My grandfather never came back from the war and my grandmother went to her grave still hoping he would return. I wasn't able to find out what happened to him, but after one dig I was able to give a man the control column of the plane his father had been flying when he was shot down in 1942. The man wept. "My father held this," he said. He thanked me for giving him a connection to the man who had died before he was born.'

'Your relic hunting is healing work then,' said Oksana, pouring everyone a glass of wine. 'You bring comfort to other human beings. It's no coincidence that your parents named you after the beloved physician in the Bible.'

Lily returned to the kitchen and dished out the *pelmeni* before adding dill and sour cream.

'Mmm, smells good!' said Luka when she placed his serving before him.

'Your uncle tells me that you are an excellent cook,' Oksana said.

Luka shrugged. 'He exaggerates, but I've learned a few things from my mother who is indeed a very good cook.'

Babushka picked up her fork. Lily was surprised when Luka stood to push the old woman's chair closer to the table. In Lily's experience, men with his exceptional good looks were often insensitive to others but Luka seemed the opposite.

Lily took her seat at the table. 'Can you salsa dance?' Oksana asked her. 'Luka goes out salsa dancing with friends a few times a week. You should go too.'

Lily looked at Oksana askance. She should know that Lily wasn't ready to go out dancing with attractive men.

'You only need the basic steps to enjoy yourself,' Luka said. 'It's up to the guy to do the rest. I can teach you.'

Lily smiled awkwardly. She'd gone to salsa lessons with Betty because Adam had thought that Latin dancing was 'too girly' for him. Now, the idea of lively South American music and people dressed in skimpy clothes didn't appeal to her.

Babushka put down her fork and turned to Lily. 'When he paid you attention, it was like the light in heaven was shining on you,' she said. 'But when he turned cold, you were truly in the dark.'

Lily waited for her to say something more, but her expression went blank again and she turned back to her food. Lily glanced at Oksana.

'Babushka gets a little confused sometimes,' Oksana whispered to Luka. In a louder voice she asked him, 'And how are Valentino and Versace doing?'

Lily was relieved that the interruption had taken everyone's minds off the salsa dancing.

'Oh, they're great!' replied Luka. 'They zigzag, step over, roulette and drag their toy balls like professional soccer players.'

'Who are Valentino and Versace?' asked Lily.

'Luka's cats,' replied Oksana.

When everyone had finished eating, Lily collected the empty plates from the table to take to the kitchen. Something dawned on her and she stopped short at the sink. Of course! Now everything made sense about Luka: the snappy dress sense; the dancing; the cooking; two cats named Valentino and Versace. He was gay! Oksana wasn't being insensitive at all. She was simply trying to get Lily to go out with people her own age.

Luka appeared in the kitchen doorway. 'I'm sorry that I have to leave so early,' he said. 'I'm giving a lecture tomorrow and I need to finalise my presentation.'

'Let me show you out,' said Lily, appraising him with new eyes. Of course! He was too perfect in every way to be straight.

'So would you like to come salsa dancing next week?' he asked, stepping out into the corridor. 'I can pick you up Thursday night at seven?'

'Sure,' said Lily. The invitation wasn't threatening now that she realised Luka wasn't interested in women. After all the generous help he was giving Oksana, she didn't want to come across as unfriendly. She waved as he disappeared into the elevator.

'Do you mind if I turn the television on?' Oksana asked after Lily shut the door. 'There's going to be something about the court case regarding the site in Zamoskvorechye. If it gets the go-ahead we'll have to somehow get those cats out of there sooner.'

'Of course,' replied Lily.

She washed and dried the dinner plates, put them back in the cupboard, then turned the kettle on to boil. The sound of the evening news programme came on as she made tea and arranged dried fruit and nuts on a plate. Then the volume faded. Lily placed a cup of tea in front of Babushka and went to help Oksana with the controls.

'The sound goes in and out sometimes,' she said. 'There must be a loose wire. It'll come back in a moment.'

The sound returned a second later and an image Lily recognised appeared on the screen. It was the black-and-white photograph of the female fighter pilot she'd read about in the *Moscow Times*, the one whose plane had been recovered.

'The Kremlin announced today that the body found in a village in Orël Oblast is in fact that of missing war heroine Natalya Azarova,' said the newsreader. 'Since the pilot went missing in 1943, controversy has surrounded her disappearance.'

The image changed to that of a middle-aged man in a beige jacket with the words *Ilya Kondakov: Airplane Archaeologist* highlighted on the lower part of the screen. Next to him stood a distinguished-looking gentleman in a military uniform with rows of medals on his chest.

'The dedication and persistence of General Valentin Orlov in searching for Azarova's plane and body is recognised today. It is thanks to his faith in the loyalty of his wingman that her name will now be cleared and her remains given a dignified burial.' The camera returned to the newsreader. 'According to the Kremlin's findings, after surviving a parachute jump from her damaged plane, Natalya Azarova was shot from behind at close range, which was a common military execution method at the time. However, German officials maintain that they have no record of Natalya Azarova ever being captured or executed. The commanding officer of the German air regiment stationed in the area at the time was killed in July 1943 when he was shot down by General Orlov. Therefore, while her plane and the body have now been recovered, who killed Natalya Azarova remains a mystery.'

Lily and Oksana were startled by the sound of china smashing. They turned towards the dining table. Babushka had risen from her chair, her face deathly white. Her teacup and saucer were in pieces on the floor.

'Oh God,' cried Lily, rushing towards her. She was certain the old woman was having a heart attack. 'Call Doctor Pesenko,' she said to Oksana. 'And get an aspirin from the bathroom.'

Lily attempted to get the old woman to lie down. But Babushka pushed her away with more strength than she expected.

'No, wait,' Lily said to Oksana. 'She's only weeping.'

Babushka dropped to her knees and tears poured from her eyes. 'Never make promises to each other, that's what everybody said. But we thought we were invincible.' She wept harder.

Oksana crouched beside her and held her by the shoulders. 'Listen!' she said, in the same gentle but firm tone she used with misbehaving cats. 'We've had enough of this game. Do you understand that you are very sick and that this young woman,' she indicated Lily, 'has taken you, a stranger, into her home? We want to help you, but you're going to have to give us your name. You need to tell us what happened to you. That would be the decent way to treat us after all we've been doing for you — and for Laika.'

The woman's weeping grew softer. Her mouth twitched as if she was trying to remember a word she hadn't spoken for years. She looked from Oksana to Lily.

'My name is Svetlana Petrovna Novikova,' she said finally. 'I was Natalya Azarova's mechanic during the war. I know exactly how she died.'

FOURTEEN

Moscow, 1939

My audition for the Moscow Conservatory went splendidly. I sang the 'Letter Aria' from *Eugene Onegin*, which was long and demanding, and some classical Russian songs. But afterwards I was called into the administrator's office to face a hostile board of examiners.

'Why have you wasted our time?' asked the chief examiner. He tossed Bronislava Ivanovna's letter of recommendation across the table. 'Your father was an enemy of the people,' he said. 'There are no places here for the children of scum.'

I wanted to reply that Comrade Stalin himself had said that the son does not pay for the sins of the father, but as Papa had been innocent I simply stood up and left.

It was humiliating that I, who loved the Soviet Union so much, should be regarded with suspicion and disgust. The time since my father's death had changed me. I was no longer the frivolous girl I had been at fifteen. The only way to claw my way back into society was to transform myself into the brightest citizen of all.

I applied for jobs at the steelworks and at the porcelain factory to improve my proletarian credentials but was rejected by both of them. I refused to give up. I heard that the Moscow aircraft factory was hiring workers. This time when I filled in the application and reached the section that asked applicants to declare if any relatives had been arrested for crimes against the State, I left the space blank. To my amazement, I was given a job as a riveting machine operator.

'Here comes the factory beauty,' Roman, the foreman, said one morning after I had been working at the factory for a week. 'I've never seen anyone look so fetching in overalls.'

Roman was in his twenties with blond hair and blond eyebrows. He even had blond hair on his chest and arms. I had noticed that several of the girls at the factory had eyes for him. I smiled flirtatiously and said, 'Thank you, Roman.'

I may have become serious in my mood but my appearance was more important to me than ever. It wasn't childish vanity or a desire to emulate Valentina Serova that made me pay attention to my grooming any more. It was a form of defence. With my hair bleached, my face powdered and my lips rouged, I could hide behind a powerful mask of womanhood. *Pravda* had said that the perfect Soviet woman was not only strong physically and mentally, but was feminine and attractive. If that was the ideal Soviet woman, I was determined to be her.

'Slut!' muttered Lyuba, who assembled engines, when I passed her.

Did Lyuba think that her greasy hair and dull skin made her a good Communist? Lenin might have agreed, but Stalin didn't. He had given a directive that good citizens should pay attention to their personal appearance and hygiene.

My mother and brother also refused to be crushed by our loss of status. Alexander became a plasterer and tiler for the new stations that were being built in the metro. He left for work each morning at four o'clock in his overalls and workers' boots. My mother obtained a position with the Moscow City Committee of Artists. The committee produced portraits of the Soviet leaders, which were hung in factories and offices and were also used as banners for parades. After Stalin told the committee leader that he liked the portraits my mother painted of him — she always gave him a benevolent expression and a divine aura — Mama was made a specialist in portraits of Stalin. She saw it as nothing but chance, but I was convinced that Stalin knew the artist was my mother. Because it was too late to save my father, demanding that his portraits be painted by her was his way of helping us. When I told Mama this, she quickly changed the subject. She was too humble to believe that she had been singled out for special attention. But I recalled the regard with which Stalin had treated Papa at the reception at the Kremlin Palace, and I knew it was true.

Thanks to the incomes we were earning, Zoya was able to continue to line up for food and other goods for us.

What crushed me was not being able to fly. As I riveted the inner wing assemblies of planes, I thought about the aviators who would operate them. The previous year, my heroine Marina Raskova, along with Polina Osipenko and Valentina Grizodubova, had broken another long-distance record when they flew from Moscow to Komsomolsk in the Far East. Stalin had awarded each of them with the Hero of the Soviet Union. They were the first women to receive the honour. How I longed to win such an accolade too. I imagined Stalin pinning the medal on me and how I would tell him that I still had the dancing shoes and sapphire brooch that he had given me.

My disappointment intensified when I saw a book poking out of Roman's bag one morning when he arrived for work. 'What's that?' I asked.

Roman gave me his usual bright smile. 'It's an instruction manual for parachute jumping. The factory has an aero club affiliated with it. You should join.'

My heart sank. 'I can't.'

'Why not?' asked Roman. 'You look fit to me.'

To join a club associated with the factory, especially a paramilitary one, I had to be a Komsomol member. The Komsomol was the youth division of the Communist Party. It wasn't compulsory to join, but anyone serious about being a good Soviet citizen and getting ahead became a member. As the child of an enemy of the people, the only way for me to become a member was to publicly denounce my father. Mama had once told me that I should condemn my father in order to enjoy the advantages of Komsomol membership. 'Natashka,' she had said, weeping, 'Papa would have understood. He is gone but you must survive. No, not only survive, you must thrive. Just because you criticise him with your words doesn't mean you deny him in your heart.' But no matter how strong my desire to succeed, I couldn't betray my father.

'You aren't afraid, are you, Natasha?' Roman teased.

I couldn't tell him that my reason for not joining was because I had lied — or least omitted the information — about my father on my work application form.

'Yes, I'm scared of heights,' I said.

'Bullshit!' Roman brought his face close to mine. 'I know why you can't join. You don't want to denounce a relative. Is that right?'

How had Roman guessed that? My heart beat faster. I was in trouble now. I regretted asking him about the manual.

'Forget it!' I said, hoping to end the conversation and get back to my work.

'You can join the Komsomol, Natasha, and you don't have to denounce anyone. I promise.'

I regarded him with suspicion. 'How's that?'

Roman grinned. 'Because I am the chairman of the Komsomol. I'll make sure that doesn't happen.'

Roman was true to his word. The day I joined the factory's Komsomol I wasn't asked any questions about my past. On the contrary, I was praised for the standard of work I produced. I said my oath of allegiance to the Soviet Union with true feeling, and when I was handed the membership card and saw that nothing further was expected of me, I beamed at Roman.

'Now we will go parachuting together,' he said, giving me a slap on the back.

I was more excited by the idea of going up in a plane than I was about jumping out of one. Those of us joining the factory's aero club were required to learn how to pack a parachute and to watch several jumps by experienced parachutists before we were allowed to participate ourselves.

When it was finally our turn to go up in a plane, Roman nudged me and nodded towards ashen-faced Lyuba. 'Not so tough now, eh?' he whispered.

It was obvious from the attention Roman paid me that he was flirting. He was an amusing and honest man, and I liked him but I didn't love him. If I was one of those women who could think shrewdly about marriage, he would have been a good match for me. His proletarian origins would have improved my status. But while I had learned to think shrewdly about many things, love was not one of them. If I was going to marry Roman, I needed to feel passion not just fondness.

The plane bumped and shook along the runway before lifting from the ground. Although most of my view was obscured by

Roman's head, being up high in the air and surrounded by blue sky made my heart leap with joy.

The aero club's hangars grew smaller and smaller until the plane banked and the instructor told us it was time to jump. Roman was the first to go, screaming at the top of his lungs as he threw himself into the air. I followed him.

I tumbled in a freefall and counted to three, as we'd been taught, before pulling the ring on the parachute. For a few heart-stopping seconds nothing happened and then my parachute opened and air hissed into it. The wind pushing at me and the view of the fields below lulled me into a sense of peace. I didn't realise how fast I was falling, even with the parachute, until I was close to the ground. The field seemed to suddenly rise up. I bent my knees to avoid injury but my landing was clumsy: I was dragged by the parachute with my limbs flailing until I could regain my footing. It was not an elegant end to the fall but I was confident I would get the hang of these landings.

The other parachutists dotted the sky and I waved to them before turning my attention back to the plane. The pilot was circling, preparing to return to the airstrip. The others in my group might be content to parachute out of an aircraft, but the experience of being in the air had reignited my desire to fly. In an act of boldness, I submitted an application to the club to train as a pilot. Roman wrote me a recommendation and I included my birth and education certificates. Then I had to take a medical examination, which involved nothing more than poking out my tongue for a doctor, submitting to a hearing test and reading an eye chart. I was pronounced fit enough to train. The next step was to appear before the credentials committee, which was made up of Soviet Air Force officers. They asked me to determine the latitude and longitude of various cities on a map. Then they gave me a geography quiz and asked questions from the flight theory textbook. I answered everything confidently.

'She has excellent recommendations from the aircraft factory,' one of the officers said to the others. 'It's good to have pilots who understand how their plane is made.'

The interview was progressing smoothly until one of the officers asked me about my family. Who was my father and what did he do? Memories of the scorn expressed by the Conservatory's examination board came back to me. I felt my lip quiver and I tried to deflect the conversation to my mother and brother who were involved in patriotic duties. 'If you are going to tell a lie then you have to stay with it until the end,' Papa used to say. Where would this lie take me? It was one thing to deceive a factory manager or even the Komsomol; quite another to lie to the military. To my relief, the interview was interrupted when one of the officers had to take a telephone call. When he returned to the room, the subject of my family seemed to have been forgotten.

'When can you begin training, Comrade Azarova?' asked the officer leading the committee.

'Right away,' I replied.

He closed my file and grinned at me. 'Then you can commence training next Saturday.'

So this is it, I thought. My dream is finally coming true.

Those of us who wanted to be pilots trained on U2 biplanes, which were used as crop dusters as well as for military purposes. The practical training involved sitting in the rear seat with the instructor in front, communicating through an intercom. While the instructor operated the controls, the student mimicked his manoeuvres by lightly touching an identical set of controls in the rear. I loved every moment I was in the air. I was never afraid of crashing; instead I was terrified of someone checking my records more thoroughly and throwing me out of the aero club.

But the months of flight theory and watching the instructor as he made turns, dives and climbs passed without incident, and before I knew it I was donning my Osoaviakhim overalls, helmet and goggles for my first solo flight.

The students lined up on the airfield and watched as a sandbag was strapped in where the instructor usually sat to balance the plane. Then the instructor called out. 'Azarova! To the aircraft!'

I was surprised to be chosen first, but I marched forward without hesitation and climbed into the cockpit.

'Now, do everything exactly as you have been doing with me,' the instructor said.

The mechanic filled the engine and pulled the propeller to prime the cylinders.

'Start your engine,' the instructor called to me.

The mechanic gave the blade a forceful turn and stepped out of the way as the propeller began to rotate and the engine came to life. Then he removed the chocks from the wheels and I taxied the plane to the runway. All the instruments seemed to rattle and vibrate more loudly than when I'd flown with the instructor.

I was given the signal to take off and as the plane lifted into the air and the ground receded, my view of the sky was clear. In that moment the sadness of the past couple of years lifted and I could feel my father's joyful presence. He would have been proud. I levelled out and drank in the beauty of the fields, farms and rivers, before performing the box pattern that was required for the examination and demonstrating my turns. Then I landed the biplane smoothly and taxied back to the hangar.

The instructor ran towards me and took hold of the wing, trotting along beside the plane. 'Well done, Comrade Azarova!' he said. 'Flying for you is as natural as walking.'

The comment went straight to my head. I was sure that I knew everything there was to know about flying now. But I would soon learn differently.

'Natashka, why do you never talk to me about your flying progress?' Alexander asked one day when I arrived home from the aero club.

'Oh, we only fly slow crop dusters,' I told him. 'It's just a bit of fun.'

'Flying, just a bit of fun?' Alexander cried. 'Since you were a child, you've been fascinated by it!'

I sat down next to him and stared at my hands. I had avoided telling Alexander about my progress because I didn't want to upset him. Before Papa's arrest he'd been an elite cadet for the air force. There was an aero club affiliated with the Moscow Metro, but Alexander didn't have someone like Roman to help him join it without denouncing our father.

Alexander guessed the reason for my hesitation. 'Please don't worry about me, Natashka,' he said. 'I like working on the metro. I'm building magnificent palaces beneath the city — ones that can be enjoyed by everyone.'

I nudged him affectionately. It was true that Alexander never complained about going to work, even though the long shifts gave him aches in his arms and legs. When the Mayakovskaya station was opened, he had guided Mama, Zoya and me around it with the pride of an artist showing off his best exhibition. The station was indeed 'a palace' with its elegant columns and arches. It was so ethereally beautiful and airy it was impossible to believe that we were deep underground.

'Alexander Deineka created the mosaics,' my brother told us, pointing to the ceiling. 'They depict twenty-four hours in the Soviet Sky.'

I marvelled at the images of planes and parachutists, but I couldn't forget that the station had been built to an unprecedented depth so it could be used as a bomb shelter if war broke out.

'I'm glad you are happy building your palaces, Sasha,' I said, standing up from the sofa. 'It's a lovely day. Let's go for a walk. We haven't done that for a while.'

Outside our building, I linked arms with my brother and admired his beautiful face. I thought he had never seemed more tranquil. I attributed it to his satisfaction in creating something everlasting with his hands, but later I would wonder if it was because he sensed what would happen next and was resigned to it.

Mama and I decided to go to the cinema that evening to see the film *Alexander Nevsky*. Zoya was away visiting her sister. We asked my brother to come with us but he had a shift on the metro. It wasn't his usual paid employment, but volunteer excavation work to complete a tunnel section to meet the new deadline set by Stalin. People thought I was brave for going up into the air in a wood and metal contraption, but Alexander descended into the darkness of the narrow underground shafts on icy ladders. Sometimes the metro workers had to climb down for fifty metres, and even pass each other on the way up or down. The film Mama and I went to see was about Prince Alexander who saved Novgorod from invasion by the Teutonic knights in the thirteenth century. Halfway through it, Mama turned to me and grabbed my hand. Her face was deathly white.

'He's gone!' she gasped. 'I can feel it!'

'Who?' I asked, not understanding.

'Alexander!'

At first I thought Mama was talking about the hero of the film but then she rose from her seat and clutched her face. 'I can't stand it! First Stepan and now Sasha!'

She began to wail and the other patrons turned to stare at us. I thought my mother had lost her mind. She was a nervous person and I wondered if the strain of the past couple of years had caught up with her. We didn't have enough money for a taxi so I had to struggle home with her leaning on me like a deadweight. I tried to get her to sit down while I made her a cup of tea but she kept standing up and pacing the floor.

'Sasha!' she wept. 'My firstborn! I will never forget the day I first held you!'

'Mama, calm yourself.' I placed the teacup on the table. 'I will go to the work site now and find Sasha. You will see that all is well!'

I hated leaving my mother alone in that state, but it seemed the only way to settle her would be to present her with the truth.

The night air had a biting chill to it and I wrapped my scarf around my head as I crossed the river and headed towards Pyatnitskaya Street. The new excavation work was taking place near there. An eerie atmosphere had fallen over the city: shadows leaped towards me from doorways and the trolley buses that passed me seemed to be travelling at unnatural speeds. I imagined myself returning to Mama to tell her I had spoken to Alexander's foreman and that he was fine. Poor Mama. She needed a rest. She got herself so worked up about those portraits of Stalin. I knew she wanted to do good work for him but it seemed to drain her.

I stopped in my tracks as soon as I smelled the acrid smoke. I knew that something was wrong then and ran towards the excavation site. A crowd had gathered around it. Policemen were pushing the people back to allow fire trucks through to join those that were already there. That was when I saw the flames leaping from the shaft.

'No!' I cried, falling to my knees.

The firemen were pumping volumes of water into the shaft but the flames shot higher into the air and dense halos of smoke engulfed the fire trucks and the crowd. I heard something I couldn't identify: the roar of the fire or screams? I didn't know. All I knew for certain was that no one in that shaft could survive such an inferno.

The horror turned my blood cold and broke something inside me. Mama's premonition had been right: my dear brother was dead.

FIFTEEN

Moscow, 2000

The first Lily had heard of Natalya Azarova was the article in the *Moscow Times* revealing that her fighter plane had been found. But one glance at Oksana's stunned face when Babushka revealed her identity and Lily realised that Natalya Azarova was of special significance to the Russian people, even those born after the war.

'You were the mechanic to Natalya Azarova?' Oksana asked Svetlana. 'And you know what happened to her?'

Svetlana glanced at Oksana warily and nodded.

'But people have been speculating about her disappearance for years,' said Oksana, placing her hand on Svetlana's arm. 'Why didn't you come forward and reveal what you knew?'

A look of mistrust shadowed Svetlana's face and she shrank from Oksana's touch. Oksana sighed and considered her with wise, compassionate eyes. 'If you didn't come forward,' she reassured Svetlana, 'you must have had your reasons. But if that knowledge is a burden to you and you would like to share it, we promise that nothing you say will go further than this room.'

The television sound went off again and the silence was heavy as Lily and Oksana waited for the old woman to respond.

Svetlana closed her eyes tightly, as if something caused her pain. But when she opened them again, she appeared to have gathered strength. She no longer looked pale and sick, but more like the woman Lily had first met in Pushkin Square: determined.

'Natasha and I had been school friends but we were separated after her father was arrested as an enemy of the people.' She looked at Oksana and then Lily. 'But perhaps Natasha should be remembered for who she really was,' she said.

Sensing something important was about to unfold, Lily turned the television off. She scooped up the broken cup and saucer and whisked them away to the kitchen while Oksana helped Svetlana up into a chair. Lily brought fresh cups of tea to the table.

'I will tell you what happened to her, but in order for you to understand, I need to tell you this story from the beginning,' Svetlana said. 'You have to know who Natasha was … and what she meant to me.'

Lily and Oksana nodded. The old woman held them in suspense for what seemed an eternity before she began her story in a slow, deliberate voice.

I was a student at the Moscow Aviation Institute when Germany attacked the Soviet Union in June 1941. I arrived for my classes the morning following the blitzkrieg to find students rushing about in the corridors and speaking to each other in high-pitched voices. Those with shortwave radios claimed that Minsk, Odessa, Kiev and other cities on the western border had been bombed. But there had been no announcement by Stalin, so the reports were impossible to believe.

'Vladimir, that can't be right!' I heard one student challenge another. 'Your French is poor. You have misunderstood. Comrade Stalin made a pact with Germany.'

'I'm not worried,' piped up another student. 'The Soviet Union has the largest air force in the world and more tanks than all the other countries combined. If the Germans have attacked us, they will be sorry.'

But Vladimir was insistent. 'I'm telling you, the mighty Soviet Air Force has been destroyed in a lightning attack on the airfields. The pilots didn't have time to camouflage the planes. They were destroyed like rows of dominoes.'

Those of us who had not heard the foreign transmissions for ourselves did not know what to believe. A few hours later, our teachers told us to gather around radios in the lecture halls. An important announcement was to be made by Molotov, the minister for foreign affairs.

'Today, in the early hours of the morning, without forwarding any grievances to the Soviet Union and without a declaration of war, the German armed forces attacked our country …'

'So it's true!' I gasped.

'Don't worry,' said Nadezhda, one of our Komsomol leaders, 'the German people are civilised. It's Hitler who is a brute. I'm sure if we explain to the German soldiers how they are being exploited by Fascism, they will not want to fight us. We are all comrades; all brothers and sisters.'

'Civilised or not,' said another student, Afonasy, 'with modern technology it's not going to be a long drawn-out war of attrition. It will all be decided in a matter of days.'

I looked from Afonasy to Nadezhda. I wanted to believe them but a sinking feeling in my heart told me that this catastrophe would be neither civil nor short.

Moscow transformed before my eyes. Only a few days earlier I had been to the cinema with some friends to see Valentina Serova in *A Girl with Character* and afterwards we had eaten ice-cream in a café. My mother had been packing for our holiday to the dacha, which we had planned to take as soon as I finished my examinations. Now everything was uncertain. Men between the ages of twenty-three and thirty-six were mobilised. Police and guards patrolled the streets, and buildings and statues were reinforced with sandbags. Queues, even longer than usual, formed in front of the shops, which quickly ran out of sugar, salt, matches and kerosene. Artists were called on to paint the streets so that they looked like rooftops, and fake aircraft and munitions factories were constructed out of canvas and wood while the real ones were moved east.

But for Muscovites the war seemed far away until reports of atrocities from the western border began to reach us: nurses shot while tending to wounded soldiers; prisoners of war taken with no intention of feeding them; villages razed to the ground with the inhabitants locked inside the buildings. Along with other students from the institute, I volunteered for civil defence. We learned that the German army was marching along the same route that Napoleon and his troops had taken when they invaded Moscow. The battle with Napoleon had been termed the Patriotic War; and now this new conflict was christened the Great Patriotic War. We travelled in trolley buses and then by foot to the outskirts of the city to dig anti-tank trenches, alongside elderly men and women and young children.

'We are not the genteel British nor the delicate French,' said Vladimir. 'We are Russians and we will fight with every last drop of our blood for our land!'

'Indeed,' said Marya, another classmate, 'Hitler regards us Slavs as an inferior race whom he can treat as he pleases. We, who have produced some of the world's greatest paintings, music and literature! This is the country of Tchaikovsky, Pushkin and Tolstoy, and he deems us to be sub-human!'

We all agreed heartily. We were indignant at the treachery of the Germans in attacking us and secretly ashamed of not being better prepared.

Our group of volunteers had been digging for several hours when we heard the roar of planes approaching. The call went up: 'Germans!' We had nowhere to hide except in the ditches we had dug and nothing to protect us but the spades, which we placed over our heads. Bullets riddled the ground around me like hailstones. My heart thumped in my chest. We heard the planes fly off into the distance but stayed in our ditches until we were sure they weren't returning. I looked at the other students' faces, knowing that I must have appeared as shaken as they did.

Our little group was unhurt, but an old man and a woman had been killed and several of the children were wounded. Nadezhda burst into tears.

'Why did they attack us?' she asked. 'We aren't soldiers!'

We were sombre on our way back on the trolley bus. One of the other volunteers told us that Marina Raskova, the famous pilot, was forming women's air regiments and had advertised for volunteers.

'I'm a pilot in an aero club but I don't want to be in the auxiliary services,' protested Marya. 'I want to go to the front and fight those bastards face to face.'

'This isn't the auxiliary services,' the volunteer said. 'These are regiments for frontline duty. Raskova has been given permission by Comrade Stalin to form exclusively female units. They aren't only calling for pilots, but also mechanics, cooks and office staff.'

I remembered the poster of Marina Raskova that Natasha had hung on the wall in her room. Had Natasha learned to fly as she'd wanted? Or had everything been barred to her? I hadn't seen Natasha since that awful day in the Arbat after her father had been arrested and my mother had forbidden me to speak to her. My parents transferred me to another school. For nights I cried bitter tears into my pillow. People had called us 'the twins'. Being separated from my friend and thinking of her suffering was unbearable.

'I'm going to volunteer for that regiment,' I announced. 'Where do I sign up?'

Marina Raskova was interviewing volunteers at the Zhukovsky Air Force Engineering Academy. Nadezhda, as the Komsomol's representative at the institute, wrote a recommendation for me. Not long afterwards I received a telegram summoning me to an interview and advising me to pack necessities. If I was selected for one of the air regiments, I would leave for training straight away.

I told my mother that I was going to stay with Nadezhda to work on a group project. She wouldn't have let me go otherwise. When I was younger my mother and I had been close, but she had changed. She was more concerned about her status in society than her own family now, and there was little that I confided in her any more. But she was my mother and part of me still loved her.

As I left the apartment, she was hanging blackout curtains with the maid. 'It's a pity that because of the Germans we have to take down our pretty curtains and hang these ugly things,' she said.

'Goodbye, Mama,' I told her. 'I'm off.' But she didn't hear me.

The academy had the unruly atmosphere of a girls' school on enrolment day. There were air-force pilots in uniform, civil air fleet pilots in flying suits, and students from the Osoaviakhim aero clubs wearing their helmets. Women who had never been near an airfield, as well as hockey and gymnastics champions, factory workers and secretaries also answered the call. I recognised Raisa Belyaeva who was a famous aerobatic stunt pilot.

Some of the candidates paced the corridors with their chins up and their hands behind their backs, while others clutched their flying gloves nervously. There among them, sitting on a chair and reading a copy of Tolstoy's *War and Peace*, was Natasha. She looked different from when I'd seen her last. Her face was sterner and she had a serious air. In the old days, she would have been chatting to the other girls, not isolating herself from the crowd with a book. But she still liked to stand out. She was wearing a dress suit with a pleated skirt and fitted jacket, and a polka-dot scarf tied around her neck. Her hair, blonder than I remembered, was curled under her crimson beret.

She glanced up, as if she had sensed someone was watching her, and I slipped back among the group. I was ashamed that I had not stood by her after her father's arrest. I couldn't bear for a reunion after all those years to be marred by a look of disdain on her prettily made-up face.

Marina Raskova and her selection committee interviewed the applicants individually. Most of the women wanted to be pilots, and fighter pilots especially, and were disappointed if they were assigned the roles of navigators. Pilots, in everyone's eyes, were as glamorous as film stars. The women who were given preference for the pilot roles were professional airwomen. Students from aero clubs were only considered if they had been recommended as exceptional by their instructors.

I heard Natasha's name called out and saw her rise to go into the interview room. I hoped that her dream of becoming a pilot would come true. An hour passed before she re-emerged.

'What role were you given?' the other girls pressed her. Natasha evaded their questioning but when they kept pestering she finally answered: 'They selected me for pilot training, most likely in the fighter regiment.' The girls regarded her with admiration. I was seized by an idea.

Wouldn't it be wonderful if Natasha and I were placed in the same regiment? But women from universities and institutes were being trained as navigators for the bombers. The fighter pilots flew solo and did their own navigation. And the mechanics' roles were being given to the girls from factories.

'Svetlana Petrovna Novikova.'

I entered the interview room. Although there were three other women in there, it was Marina Raskova who caught my attention. She was even more beautiful than she appeared in photographs in the newspaper, with her clear bright eyes and her dark hair neatly parted in the centre and pulled back in a bun.

'Before we begin,' she said, a pained expression on her face, 'you must understand we are not selecting women for summer camp. We are choosing women to fight for our country. Women who may be maimed or killed.'

Marina was softly spoken but exuded confidence. No wonder she was admired. I sensed that she also cared for our welfare.

'I understand,' I told her.

'Good! Because your qualifications are excellent and you are the first candidate we have interviewed who hasn't commenced by insisting that she be a fighter pilot.'

The woman next to Marina, the battalion commissar, said, 'We need navigators for the bombing regiments.'

I had to think quickly if I wanted to be placed in the same regiment as Natasha. 'But you see, I hoped to be a mechanic,' I said.

The commissar's chin rose. Marina Raskova regarded me curiously.

'I'm scared of flying,' I told them.

Marina bit her lip as if she were trying not to laugh.

'You do realise that you have applied to an air regiment?' the commissar asked. 'When the regiment moves airfields, the mechanics and armourers are flown by transport planes.'

'I will be fine when moving airfields,' I said. 'But every day, several times a day in a plane ... I'd get airsick.'

The women exchanged glances. I could tell that they were impressed by my qualifications and didn't want to lose me.

'Does this have anything to do with Natalya Azarova?' Marina asked me.

The mention of Natasha caught me by surprise.

'I thought so,' she said. 'You see, Natalya spent half her interview time praising you and your ability to fix things. We need navigators but good mechanics are also worth their weight in gold, especially in the fighter regiments where the turnaround time is vital.'

So Natasha had seen me after all.

That evening, after we had been assigned rooms for the night, I found Natasha writing a letter to her mother. She lifted her eyes and, far from giving me the look of disdain

I had been expecting, she stood up and threw her arms around me.

'I'm so happy to see you again,' she said. 'I heard that they selected you to be a mechanic!' So Natasha wanted to be with me as much as I wanted to be with her.

We reconciled after all those years with no recriminations. Just as I had never forgotten her, she had never stopped thinking of me. There was much to catch up on and we wanted to talk more, but the political officer ordered lights out and told me to go to my own room.

The following day, we were issued with our uniforms. The military pilots, like Marina Raskova and her chiefs of staff, already had smart uniforms, but as the decision to create women's air regiments had been made at the last minute, no special provisions had been made for us. We were taken to a room and issued uniforms that had been made for men. Peals of laughter filled the air as we donned trousers that hitched up higher than our breasts and jackets with sleeves that dangled past our knees. We were even given men's underwear! One girl modelled a pair of long johns with a fly opening while the rest of us rolled around the floor laughing. The worst thing, however, was the boots. They were gigantic. We stuffed newspaper into the toes but still we could only shuffle instead of walk.

'How are we ever going to march?' Natasha whispered to me.

That night we sat in our rooms with scissors, needles and pins, doing our best to make our uniforms fit. Many of the girls tried to adjust the pants by shortening the legs, but ended up with the crotches of their trousers down near their knees. Natasha, who was good at sewing, showed the other girls how to cut and resew the trousers so they fitted, but there was only so much we could do before lights out.

The next evening, those of us who had been selected marched to the station to catch a train to our airfield in the east. The platform was crowded with people evacuating Moscow as the Germans came nearer. They must have despaired at the sight of us. We shuffled along with our greatcoats trailing behind us, like unwieldy gowns. We lacked military discipline and chatted like schoolgirls departing for a picnic.

The trip to Engels took nine days. We sat in the icy rail cars according to our place in the regiment: pilots, navigators, mechanics and auxiliary staff. The train had to wait several times in the sidings to allow the passage of soldier transports heading west. Whenever we were allowed to stretch our legs, Natasha and I would find each other. Sometimes we read *War and Peace* together and sometimes we huddled up against each other in the weak autumn sunshine. Natasha wrote letters to her mother but also, I noticed, to a man named Roman whom she said was fighting at the front. I wondered if he was her fiancé but was reluctant to ask. Was that the change I had noticed in Natasha? Had she known physical love? It was only when we were stuck at one station for hours that I had a chance to ask her about Alexander. Tears came to her eyes when she told me that he had been killed in a shaft fire.

'I wish I'd been there for you!' I said.

Natasha grasped my hands in hers. 'We will always be there for each other from now on. Always!'

We arrived at Engels at night. Everything was dark in the town because of the blackout. Even the Volga River was invisible. The cold air bit at our faces, reminding us that winter was on its way. The burly garrison commander at the airbase, Colonel Bagaev, showed us to our dormitory. 'Sleep well,' Marina instructed us, 'for tomorrow you begin a new life, which will be very demanding. You must study hard and persevere because your examination will not be in a great hall but on the field of battle.'

We were exhausted and got ready for bed as soon as Marina left us. Uniforms were discarded and out came nightgowns and bed socks. Some of the women brushed each other's hair and helped braid it. One girl took out a doll from her knapsack and sat it on the end of her bed, while another spread out a tapestry to work on until lights out. Natasha pinned her hair into curls and massaged cream over her face and hands. I suddenly understood the magnitude of what we had signed up to do. We were just girls, most of us weren't even twenty yet. For many of us this was the first time we had been away from our families — and we were going to take on the mighty German Luftwaffe.

We were in the military now, but when the order came the next day to cut our hair to five centimetres all over, we were horrified.

'You can go to the barber or do it yourself,' Colonel Bagaev told us. 'But I want to see you on parade this afternoon with your hair short and your boots polished.'

Natasha had shoulder-length hair but the rest of us still had our maiden's braids, which we pinned up on top of our heads. 'Why can't we leave it in braids?' asked one girl, who had beautiful hair the colour of honey. But we soon learned that an order in the air force was an order and we had to obey. Some of the girls kept their braids to send to their mothers.

Natasha cut my hair. She snipped it short at the nape of my neck and left longer strands around my ears and crown. 'Pin those parts back,' she said, wetting my hair and slicking the longer strands down. 'Comb them forward when you are off duty so you don't look entirely like a boy.' Although I wasn't happy about having my hair so short, she had managed to make me look fetching!

Natasha took obvious pride in her movie-star waves. When it was my turn to cut her hair, she held the mirror in her hand and gave me instructions on every strand I touched. Instead of five centimetres all over, she made it ten and then put her hair in rollers. 'When it's curled, it will be five centimetres all over,' she said.

The other girls, who had already shorn their hair, looked at her enviously. 'Why didn't I think of that?' asked one of them.

I had no idea how long curled hair took to set. I only hoped Natasha didn't intend to go out on parade with her hair in rollers. She didn't. But she did wear her lipstick and perfume. Marina noticed but didn't say anything. Perhaps she realised that Natasha, like herself, was a person who paid attention to detail.

The training at Engels was a three-year course condensed into six months. The pilots spent fourteen hours a day in combat training as well as studying theory. The mechanics worked equally hard. We learned to repair, maintain and refuel planes in freezing winter conditions, which the windswept plain of the airfield readily provided. Some of the parts were in narrow cavities, so we had to remove our padded jackets to reach them and work in our field shirts or overalls. Our arms turned numb and we would slap them to get the circulation going again. Sometimes the bolts were frozen and scorched our fingers. To prepare us for battle conditions, Marina would sound the alarm in the middle of the night and we would have to leap out of bed and assemble outside. The first time it happened, Natasha didn't have time to take the rollers out of her hair. Marina made her march around the airfield in the biting wind. The punishment didn't stop Natasha curling her hair; she learned to use pins to style it instead of rollers, which she could hide flat underneath her cap if called out in a hurry.

Most of the male instructors were good to us, but one of the flight instructors, Lieutenant Gashimov, was antagonistic to our pilots. He did not believe that women should be trained to fight on the frontline. When he learned that Marina had used her influence with the Kremlin to secure Yak-1s for the fighter regiment and the latest Pe-2 bombers, he was livid. 'There are experienced male pilots waiting for planes and we are giving new ones to a bunch of women who will turn back at the first sight of a German!'

When student pilots complained to Marina about Lieutenant Gashimov undermining them, she told them, 'When I was at the military academy some of the men used to speak over the top of me or refuse to address me according to my superior rank. I learned that trust in myself rather than complaining conveyed an inner power that was disconcerting to those men. The bombers I have secured for the regiment require three people to operate them — the pilot, the navigator and a gunner. We will also require more mechanics. There isn't time to train more women for these roles so you are going to have to get used to giving men orders and, if they don't like it, too bad.'

The Yak-1 was a single-seat monoplane and, compared to the biplanes that the women had trained on, very fast. Marina supervised the candidates she was considering for the fighter pilot roles, including Natasha. No one was allowed to do more than take off and land for the first session. Only after they had mastered that were they allowed to circle the airfield. When Lieutenant Gashimov saw that the pilots weren't daunted by the Yak's speed, he became even more hostile towards them. He'd swear at the pilots, although Marina had forbidden the men at the airfield to use foul language in front of us, and did his best to reduce them to tears. He even went so far as to call Natasha a 'painted-up tart'. Instead of being upset, Natasha, in her blithe way, showed she was amused by his insult, which infuriated him further.

When the women began combat training on the Yak, Lieutenant Gashimov went hard at them from the first day, giving them no chance to practise their manoeuvres. He stayed in close on their tail and didn't budge until they were forced to make the sign of the cut throat and land. He did everything he could to demoralise them.

'I'm going to teach him a lesson,' Natasha told me.

The way that Natasha could manoeuvre a plane was exceptional. She might be flying the same aircraft in exactly the same conditions as another pilot, but she had the reflexes of a cat. When a cat doesn't want to be held it wriggles in all directions to free itself, and that's what Natasha was able to do in the Yak. One training session, when Lieutenant Gashimov was trying to harass her into landing, she flew upwards and went into a spin, manoeuvring so that she was behind him. Wasn't Lieutenant Gashimov surprised! He tried everything he could to shake Natasha off his tail but she stuck to him like glue and forced him to land.

When they were both on the ground he tore strips off her. 'What the hell do you think you were doing up there? If you can't follow a command you don't belong in the air force!'

Marina, who had seen the whole episode, strode out onto the airfield. 'She did exactly what we would want her to do in a dogfight!' she reprimanded the lieutenant. But he could not be calmed. It wasn't only Marina who had seen the exercise but every man on the base.

'It might be one thing for her to fly a plane,' he shouted before storming off, 'but she can't shoot to save her arse! This is a war not a circus show!'

Indeed, while Natasha was a natural pilot, her shooting skills were below standard. There was no point being a fighter pilot and performing all the aerobatics involved if you couldn't bring the enemy down. The pilots practised by aiming at a drogue, but Natasha often missed the target completely.

'I hate it when it's Natasha's turn to shoot,' said the pilot of the plane that flew the drogue. 'I'm scared she's going to miss the drogue entirely and hit me instead!'

The day was drawing close when Marina and the chiefs of staff would have to select the pilots for the fighter regiment and I was sure that Natasha practised in her sleep. One day after another disastrous gunning practice, Colonel Bagaev came up with an idea. He fetched a cushion from the hangar, which he placed on the pilot's seat.

'Try again,' he said to Natasha. 'You're so small I don't think you're sitting up high enough to aim properly.'

Natasha hit her targets perfectly, and after that she always flew with a cushion.

It wasn't only Lieutenant Gashimov who gave us a hard time. The wives of the officers stationed at Engels made a complaint that Natasha, with her coquettish appearance, was distracting their husbands.

When Colonel Bagaev told Marina about the complaint she was furious. 'Comrade Azarova is going to risk her life to protect those women. They can be quiet or go to the front themselves!'

When the other girls learned what the wives had said about Natasha, a group of them made a delegation to Marina to demand an apology from the women.

'No one works harder than Natasha,' they said. 'While the rest of us are in bed she is still up studying.'

Natasha couldn't have cared less what the officers' wives thought of her, but when she learned about the delegation she was touched. She stopped isolating herself with her books and letters and began to socialise with the other girls more. She would sometimes entertain us by playing the piano and singing. She had a beautiful voice. I realised then just how much being ostracised as the child of an enemy of the people had damaged her. She had stopped trusting people.

'Sveta, you must promise never to tell anyone that Papa was accused of being a saboteur,' she said to me one day. 'A friend lied for me so I could join the Komsomol. Because I was a member, the aero club didn't search my records, assuming they'd already been thoroughly checked. It's not anywhere on my papers. If anyone found out I would be arrested.'

'Of course, Natashka,' I assured her. 'I would never do anything to hurt you.'

'I know.'

I watched her walk away and my heart sank. You see, I carried a dark secret of my own.

The selections were made and our group was divided into three regiments. When I saw Natasha's name on the noticeboard, listed as a fighter pilot in the 586th regiment, my heart leaped with joy. She had not come from a prestigious military background or an elite flying school and yet she had been given the role that everyone craved. I was overjoyed to see that I was listed as her mechanic.

So our three regiments left for the front: the 586th fighter regiment with the sophisticated Yak-1 Soviet-made fighter planes; the 587th day bomber regiment with modern Pe-2 bombers; and the 588th night bomber regiment with Po-2 biplanes. I felt sorry for the 588th regiment with their antiquated wooden planes: the Po-2s were slow, with an open cockpit and they easily caught fire. But it was the night bomber regiment that was to become the most celebrated and feared of all. They attacked at night, flying low and cutting their engines to glide silently over the enemy before dropping their bombs. The Germans were terrified of these night raiders and astounded when they discovered the stealthy assassins were women. They called them the *Nachthexen*: the night witches.

Svetlana stopped and gazed at the table, lost in her own thoughts. Lily and Oksana were leaning forward in their seats; they didn't want the story to end. But it was clear that Svetlana's tale wasn't one that could be rushed or told in one sitting. They would have to be patient and not tax her.

'We'll help you to bed,' said Oksana, gently squeezing Svetlana's arm. 'As a child I read about Natalya Azarova and my parents took me to visit the small museum in the Arbat run by the school teacher. But you have brought her to life for me. You have made me see her as flesh and blood, a real person.'

Svetlana smiled faintly. 'Yes, Natasha was once a real person,' she said.

SIXTEEN

Stalingrad, 1942

Captain Valentin Orlov manoeuvred his fighter plane over the outskirts of Stalingrad, hiding himself in the smoke that enveloped the city. The air reeked of scorched earth, munitions powder and something putrid that Orlov didn't want to think about. To the west he saw German Junkers with their fighter cover dropping bombs onto already burning buildings. Some Soviet fighters engaged them, attempting to break their formation, then withdrew. The Luftwaffe dominated the skies now. They had reduced Stalingrad to rubble. Orlov grimaced at the sight of the charred and dismembered bodies that littered the streets. He wasn't sure who he hated more: Hitler for giving orders to destroy the city, or Stalin for forcing the citizens to stay and defend it.

Orlov's wingman had been killed in his bunker when their airfield was bombed a few days ago, and to engage the enemy alone under the present conditions would be suicide. Frustrated, he turned back to his airfield.

Reducing his engine power on approach, Orlov saw the ground crew moving three Yak-1s into the earth and wood hangar. New planes or new pilots? After the losses they had suffered at Stalingrad, the regiment needed both.

He landed and taxied towards the hangar. Once Sharavin, his mechanic, arrived to take the plane, Orlov climbed on the wing and jumped to the ground. There was no sign of any new pilots; perhaps the planes had been ferried to the airfield.

Orlov went to the commander of the regiment's bunker and knocked on the door. Colonel Leonid Smirnov was sitting at his desk, his shoulders hunched as he stared at some documents that the chief of staff, who was standing next to him, had obviously handed over. The colonel looked up when he heard Orlov and scowled.

'Comrade Captain Panchenko,' he said to the chief of staff, 'tell Comrade Captain Orlov what you have just told me.'

Captain Panchenko moistened his lips before speaking. His large bulging eyes seemed to protrude further when he conveyed the message. 'We have new pilots and they have brought their mechanics with them.'

To Orlov that should have been good news, but he could tell by the sour expression on Colonel Smirnov's face that somehow it wasn't. 'Novices again?' he asked.

The last pilots sent to the regiment were ground artillery soldiers who'd been given thirty hours of flight training. At the risk of being shot for disobeying orders, both Colonel Smirnov and Orlov had refused to send them into combat. Instead, they'd used their planes and put the men on ground duties until they received further training. The situation in Stalingrad was desperate, but while Stalin might be demanding that anyone who could hold a gun should defend the city, neither Orlov nor his commander believed in throwing away lives for no purpose. That common belief was one of the things that made them friends.

'No,' answered Captain Panchenko. 'These are qualified pilots. They served in Saratov, defending the railway lines and troops from enemy attacks. One of them has an Order of the Red Star for bravery and another is an experienced night fighter.'

A night fighter? Orlov was impressed. To fly and attack at night required nerves of steel. You had to trust your instruments on the position of your plane, and your instinct and night vision for the location of the enemy. Even returning to the airfield was dangerous. To avoid enemy attack they weren't lit and pilots were only permitted to flash their landing lights once to see the runway. Someone of that skill would be invaluable to the regiment. Why then did Colonel Smirnov look so unhappy? Were the new pilots political prisoners bent on redeeming their honour by getting themselves killed?

'What's the catch?' Orlov asked Captain Panchenko.

'They are women.'

Orlov looked from Captain Panchenko to Colonel Smirnov then back again. 'Are you joking?'

'No,' replied Captain Panchenko. 'They have been sent to us from the 586th regiment. The communications are out. They arrived here the same time the message did.'

'Shit!' Orlov wasn't a chauvinist. He considered women, particularly Russian women, capable. They made excellent engineers, scientists and surgeons. He knew that women pilots were undertaking heroic efforts in medical and troop transport. But support and defence weren't what was required in Stalingrad. This was no place for women. It was a bloodbath.

'I'm sending them back, of course,' said Colonel Smirnov. 'But we can use their planes tomorrow. Have you chosen a new wingman?'

'With all due respect, Comrade Colonel Smirnov,' said Captain Panchenko, 'these are Marina Raskova's pilots and crew. It will be insulting to them to be refused. You'd better explain it to them in person. I sent them to the mess bunker. They are waiting for you there.'

'Yes, of course,' said Colonel Smirnov, looking annoyed. He glanced at Orlov. 'You're good with the ladies, Comrade Captain. Why don't you explain it to them?'

Colonel Smirnov and Orlov made their way across the airfield together. Orlov knew he'd been duped by his friend. The colonel was married to a young woman who was expecting his child; he knew as much about women as Orlov did. As they walked, Orlov considered how to explain the situation to the pilots. Should he give the order to them firmly or soften it to spare their feelings? If the night fighter had survived the war this long, she couldn't be a terrible pilot. But defence and attack were two different things. The Soviet Air Force in Stalingrad was using new tactics now: instead of flying in defensive formations and getting picked off by the Germans as a result, they were experimenting with more aggressive strategies. Orlov had been transferred to the regiment on the understanding that it was to be developed into a core of elite pilots who would be what was termed 'free hunters'. Instead of only responding to attacks, they would also roam the sky and decide on their own targets.

Orlov and the colonel entered the mess bunker. The female pilots and their ground crew stood to attention. If their belted field tunics didn't make it so obvious that these were shapely women, Orlov would have thought they were children. They were tiny!

'Yes, yes, please be at ease,' said Colonel Smirnov, waving his hand. He nodded to Orlov.

'I'm afraid there has been a mistake,' Orlov began. 'You see, this is a men's regiment. We have nowhere to accommodate you.'

One of the pilots, who had dark Georgian features, spoke up. 'Comrade Captain, we served with men in the 586th. We don't expect special treatment. A curtained-off area in any of the bunkers will be adequate.'

The 586th Fighter Regiment, which was commanded by Major Tamara Kazarinova, included a squadron of men, Orlov recalled that now. But unprepared for that argument, he continued with his original train of thought. 'Women in the regiment will cause too many problems for the men.'

The colonel had been right when he described Orlov as being 'good with the ladies'. But that was civilian ladies: Moscow women who wore dresses and walked little dogs on fancy leads. For some reason, face to face with women in military uniform, Orlov couldn't get to his main point. The women remained attentive but seemed perplexed. Obviously they had worked alongside men in the 586th regiment. What specifically would be the problem here?

'Women and men are made differently,' he continued, 'for different things.'

Colonel Smirnov looked askance at Orlov. His expression seemed to say that if Orlov had any point to make then he should get to it.

Sensing he was failing, Orlov tried again. 'Women are made for bearing babies.'

The women remained expressionless, except the little blonde one, Orlov noticed. Was that a smirk on her face? Was she laughing at him?

Orlov could see that his superior was regretting entrusting him with this task. 'Listen, I'm not going to beat around the bush with you,' the colonel told the women. 'Stalingrad is not Saratov. It's Armageddon. We've lost some of the finest pilots here and I'm afraid women are not up to what is required.'

The women looked shocked at his patronising tone. The Georgian frowned. Colonel Smirnov nodded to Orlov to take over again.

'You can sleep in this bunker tonight,' Orlov told the women. 'I will arrange for your transfer to another regiment tomorrow.'

There, it's said, he thought. All I have to do now is get Captain Panchenko to organise the transfer …

'Permission to speak, Comrade Captain?' the little blonde pilot piped up.

Orlov stared at her. It was the politest he'd been addressed since the start of the war but still he sensed trouble brewing.

'Permission granted.'

The pilot stepped forward. 'Comrade Captain, when Major Kazarinova sent us here, we made a pledge to uphold the honour of our regiment, to fight courageously and to return victorious. If you send us back without trying us, it will be a great insult to Major Kazarinova.'

The pilot was right, of course. But this was a matter of life and death; Major Kazarinova's opinion was irrelevant. Orlov found the way the pilot stared at him provoking but he wasn't about to be swayed by a pretty face. He turned to Colonel Smirnov.

'Perhaps we should at least give them a try,' agreed the colonel.

Orlov couldn't believe what he was hearing. The battle-hardened colonel wasn't able to say no to the little pilot? But something about the determined set of her jaw gave Orlov the impression that she was used to getting her own way.

'Tomorrow morning we will test one of you to see if she is up to the task of being Comrade Captain Orlov's wingman,' continued the colonel. 'If she fails, you will all go back. Do you understand?'

He indicated to Orlov to make his pick. It was merely a concession: Orlov knew that the colonel had no intention of keeping the women in the regiment. He was annoyed that he was being forced to waste his time.

'Which one of you is the night fighter?' he asked.

As soon as Orlov posed the question, he sensed that he would regret it. All the women's eyes turned to the blonde pilot.

Oh shit! thought Orlov.

'Sergeant Natalya Azarova at your service, Comrade Captain,' she said.

Orlov met Sergeant Natalya Azarova on the airfield the following morning. They walked in silence towards their awaiting Yaks. Natalya studied the sky. Orlov was surprised to find her more restrained than he had anticipated. She seemed to be mentally preparing herself for the task ahead. From his first impression he'd been expecting a presumptuous pain in the arse. Natalya's mechanic was fussing over her plane like a mother hen, topping up the fuel, checking the brakes and rudder, and wiping the windscreen and canopy until there wasn't a single speck of grime. Sharavin leaned on Orlov's Yak and winked at him.

'This is a training exercise,' Orlov said to Natalya, 'but it's dangerous up there in the sky. We don't know what we might encounter. Stick to my tail and don't do anything else unless I order you to.'

'Yes, Comrade Captain,' she answered him.

Natalya's mechanic jumped down from the plane and helped her with her parachute harness. The two women were both so pretty and petite that Orlov didn't see how anyone could take them seriously as air-force personnel. Natalya was wearing make-up and an expensive-looking sapphire brooch on her lapel. Had she been fighting all this time and never been reprimanded for breaches of uniform? He turned towards his aircraft and noticed Colonel Smirnov and the other pilots and ground crew lining up on the side of the airfield to watch. He turned back to Natalya.

'Listen,' he said, conscious that all eyes were on them, 'I have to go hard. I have to show you how difficult it will be to fly here and we won't even have the gunfire and noise of real combat. But if it gets too much for you, pull out. Don't get yourself killed out of pride.'

Natalya's eyes met his and she smiled. 'Did you ever consider the possibility that I might surprise you?'

There it was! The brazenness he'd picked up on.

'This is no joking matter!' he said. 'The lives of your fellow pilots and the fate of the Motherland depend on you being able to do your job! I hope you realise that by making us go through this farce you are wasting fuel and time!'

Orlov turned his back to her and donned his parachute harness, then strapped himself into the cockpit. He did his pre-flight checks and tested the brake pressure and rudder. When the flare went off to indicate clearance to take off, he signalled to Sharavin to remove the chocks from his Yak's wheels. He checked to make sure that the cocky little pilot was ready too. She was: the canopy pulled shut, helmet and mask on.

They taxied to the runway and turned into the wind. Natalya positioned herself behind him, slightly to the right. He opened his throttle and then raised his hand and lowered it: the signal to take off. The two pilots accelerated down the runway, their wheels coming up, and took to the air like two birds in flight. Orlov checked around him for enemy planes. The smoke from Stalingrad had eased and the only cloud cover was high in the sky. At least their view was good.

He levelled off and kept a steady course, hoping to lull Natalya into complacency and get her distracted by the terrain. Maybe he could leave her behind first go and that would be the end of this silly game? When out on a mission, a pilot had many things to fear. Apart from being killed outright, there was the chance of being wounded, set on fire, running out of fuel or ammunition, or suffering a mechanical failure. Orlov had enough to think about without worrying about a woman being up in the air with him. He'd always managed to take care of his wingmen in the air but, if attacked, he'd trusted them to be able to fight back. He realised that that was what he'd been trying to express to the women pilots the previous night: it was a man's natural instinct to protect a woman and that would jeopardise the new strategy of offensive action.

Without any radio instruction, Orlov swerved right. He checked behind him. Natalya was on his tail. So she wasn't a daydreamer. He grabbed the stick and performed a roll and then a spin. Natalya stayed behind him like a persistent mosquito. He threw everything he could at her: tight turns, fast rolls and dives. Yet each time he checked, she was holding her position. A lesser pilot would have spun out of control.

'All right then,' Orlov said. He stroked the stick forward, diving down hard. His eyes bulged and his head banged against the canopy as the negative Gs pressed him against his harness. He plummeted down at full power. Natalya tore right after him. Orlov imagined that she was the enemy and did everything he could to shake her off. She's better than I expected, he thought with dismay. He pitched the plane's nose forward and flew upwards so fast he was pressed back against his seat. He glanced back hopefully. No, she was still there. He levelled and thought about what to do next.

Natalya's small voice came over the radio transmitter. 'Comrade Captain.'

Ah, at last, thought Orlov, she's ready to give in.

'Comrade Captain! Nine o'clock high.'

Orlov strained his eyes to look into the sun. A black shape — no, two — were speeding towards them from that direction.

Messerschmitts! Orlov wondered how Natalya had seen them before he did.

The Germans approached so fast they overshot the pair, giving Orlov the second he needed to think.

'Follow me!' he shouted into the receiver. 'We'll break them up, then you take one and I'll take the other.'

The Germans turned and came in for the attack.

Orlov didn't have time to worry about protecting Natalya now. She was either with him or she was dead. He swallowed hard and switched his gun control to FIRE. Using a technique he had practised with Colonel Smirnov, he approached the Messerschmitts head on, like a knight charging forward on his horse in a joust. He hoped Natalya's nerve would hold out.

The aircraft raced towards each other, their engines screaming. The Messerschmitts filled Orlov's windscreen, but at the last moment they split. Orlov yanked his plane into a turn and pursued his prey. He had to trust that Natalya, even if she couldn't take down the other plane, would at least prevent the pilot from attacking him. Orlov managed to pull up on the port side of the Messerschmitt and sent a burst of fire into its armour. He saw the hits run along the side of the plane and was pleased when black smoke poured from it. The plane lost height. The pilot bailed out, but his parachute caught on the tail and he went down with the aircraft, his limbs flailing in his efforts to escape. At the beginning of the war such a death would have horrified Orlov, but he had steeled himself against human suffering. It was another German gone as far as he was concerned, and many Russian women and children had died worse deaths.

He whipped his head around, searching for Natalya and spotted her. She was sitting on the other Messerschmitt's tail as doggedly as she had been on his a few minutes before. Then

Orlov saw the skulls and crossbones painted on the German's fuselage. More than thirty! They represented the Soviet planes that the pilot had shot down. Natalya was pursuing an ace! He was flinging himself about, trying to shake Natalya off and evade her gunfire. Orlov could predict what would happen next: she'd run out of ammunition and the ace would turn on her. Sure enough, the Messerschmitt's pilot wrenched the plane into an aerobatic turn. In a few seconds he'd be behind Natalya and giving her a dose of her own treatment.

Orlov's blood froze, even though he knew he had to act quickly. But in the blink of an eye it was over. Natalya had fired a shot into the cockpit at the exact moment when the ace was most vulnerable. The noise was deafening as the plane went into a vertical dive.

Orlov couldn't believe what he'd just witnessed. He moved astern of Natalya's plane. Her eyes were visible over the top of her mask. He couldn't see her mouth but he was sure she was smiling. She waggled her wings at him and Orlov was so relieved they were both alive that he was almost tempted to waggle his wings in return. Instead, he circled the area where the planes had gone down to confirm their kills before heading back to the airfield. They had taken down two enemy aircraft on the first sortie of the day. Normally, after such a triumph, Orlov would have performed a victory roll over the airfield before landing. But he wasn't in the mood for messing about and went straight down. When he climbed out of the cockpit his legs felt unsteady. His uniform was saturated with perspiration.

'Well, that was a nasty surprise,' said Captain Panchenko, approaching him. 'We saw some of what went on up there. Glad to have you back.'

Sharavin slapped Orlov on the shoulder and nodded at Natalya's plane approaching the airfield. She came down smoothly and gunned her engine over the uneven patches on the runway so that she landed with the grace of a dancer. When she came to a stop, her mechanic leaped on the wing and opened the cockpit. She unhooked Natalya's harness and lifted her under the arms out of the cockpit. The other female pilots and crew rushed to Natalya to congratulate her. Orlov watched her relating the details of the fight to her comrades. You wouldn't think from looking at her animated face that a short while ago she had killed a man. She reminded him of a child who had just ridden on a Ferris wheel and was begging to go again.

He walked towards Colonel Smirnov. There must be a way out of this tricky situation. Natalya was an excellent pilot but she couldn't possibly stay in the regiment. Orlov didn't like to speak to anyone after a mission until he refocused his mind. He didn't need some female wingman gabbling to him each time they landed.

'Comrade Colonel, what do you say to that?' he asked his friend.

The colonel cocked his eyebrow. 'What I have to say, Comrade Captain, is that it seems you have a new wingman. Like it or not, we could use a pilot like that. Now let's test the others.'

Orlov and Colonel Smirnov hadn't wanted the women pilots, but in the end they were glad they had come. The other flyers and ground crew from the 586th proved themselves to be as worthy of an elite regiment as Natalya, and the colonel had them all promoted to junior lieutenants.

The Georgian pilot was named Alisa Khipani. She had earned the Order of the Red Star after she and her leader were called out to engage a pair of fighters and found themselves facing a squadron. The fighters were protecting bombers that were headed to a railway station. The junction was crowded with Soviet troops and if the bombers reached their target it would result in a massacre. Rather than turn back, the women split the squadron and frightened off the bombers. The feat cost Alisa's leader her life and left the Georgian pilot with burns to her legs that put her in hospital for two months.

The third pilot, Margarita Filippova, was from Leningrad. The regiment had been depleted and demoralised but Margarita's energy made up for ten men. 'Of course we are going to beat the Germans!' she would say with conviction. 'We just have to figure out how to do it!'

Dominika Bukova, who was the mechanic for both Alisa and Margarita, was also a morale booster. In only a few days she learned the names of everybody in the regiment along with those of their wives and children. 'Come on, let's get to it,' she would say when she saw the ground crew first thing in the morning. 'Let's get this war finished so we can go home to our families.'

Natalya's mechanic, Svetlana Novikova, was more sensible than her pilot. Orlov discovered that she had studied at the Moscow Aviation Institute and there was little that she didn't know about planes. He would have swapped Sharavin for her gladly.

As for Natalya, who insisted everyone call her Natasha when they weren't on duty, Orlov thought that Captain Panchenko summed her up perfectly when he said, 'She has everything to excess: skill, talent and charm. She's also a pest who is used to getting her own way. She belongs on the stage, not in the air force.'

Colonel Smirnov disagreed. 'In my experience, the best fighter pilots aren't the measured and calm personalities but the unpredictable ones.'

For all her flamboyance, Orlov noticed that there was a serious side to Natasha too. While she sang and played the piano for her comrades, she wasn't gregarious in the same way Margarita and Dominika were. She was friendly but she wasn't intimate with any of the other women except Svetlana. Natasha spent her free time writing letters or taking solitary walks around the airfield. Contrary to what Orlov had feared, she wasn't loquacious after a mission either. Like Orlov, she hurried to get her reports out of the way so she could throw herself onto her bunk for whatever sleep she could snatch before the next sortie. Natasha was a paradox: attractive to others but essentially a loner.

Her behaviour gave Orlov the impression she had something to hide. So what? he countered. Didn't he have secrets of his own? He certainly never made his noble origins known, nor his disdain for Stalin.

The women stayed in a dugout bunker, to which the colonel appointed a sentry. He'd made it clear that the female personnel were off limits for amorous advances. 'They are professional airwomen and crew. If you want any funny business, go somewhere else,' he'd told the regiment. The only male permitted to visit the bunker was Orlov himself, because he had to discuss missions with his wingman. Alisa and Margarita flew together.

He was respectful of the women's privacy and spoke to Natasha in the doorway, never going inside. Yet he started to notice aspects about his behaviour that disconcerted him. Why was it that before going to see Natasha he felt compelled to check whether he was closely shaved and his uniform was straight? Stalingrad wasn't a place for airs and graces. Even Colonel Smirnov, usually a stickler for appearance, stomped around in dusty boots and pants with mud-stained cuffs. When Orlov had told the women that their presence would cause problems for the men, he had meant the *other* men in the regiment. Even after Natasha had downed the German ace and the women had been welcomed into the regiment, he had considered himself impervious to her charms. But whenever the pilots and crews were called together for a meeting, he was conscious of where Natasha was sitting. He realised he was becoming infatuated with her, but couldn't understand why. In Moscow he'd had affairs with renowned beauties and none had affected him the way Natasha did.

Then something happened that he was certain would cure his attraction. It was pouring with rain one day when Orlov went to see his wingman. Margarita opened the door to the bunker. 'You're not standing outside to catch your death in the wet, Comrade Captain. Come in! We have a fire going here and I will make you a cup of tea.'

Although the bunker was fashioned out of the same wood and earth as the men's bunkers, the women had made theirs homely. A portable stove stood in the centre and rugs covered the floor. They'd hung pine branches from the ceiling to freshen the air, and a jar of wildflowers was set on an upended box. Natasha and Alisa — the only others in the bunker at the time — were sitting on their beds: Alisa attending to some needlework and Natasha writing a letter. Alisa's bed was covered with an embroidered quilt, while Natasha had a pair of silver dance shoes next to hers. They stood to attention when they saw Orlov.

It was the first time Orlov had seen Natasha without make-up and he was struck by how young she looked. Then he caught sight of the portrait of Stalin that hung above her bed. He pursed his lips, filled with a rage that he found hard to contain. How could she be so stupid? Natasha presented as an independent thinker and yet she worshipped the monster like the rest of the masses. The hell the Russian people now found themselves in was Stalin's fault. Colonel Smirnov, who had friends in high places, had confided in Orlov that Stalin had been so adamant that the Germans would never attack the Soviet Union he had forbidden his generals from taking the most basic precautions. The generals, terrified of purges that would see them and their families sent to labour camps, had no choice but to obey. As a result the aircraft at over sixty bases were destroyed within hours of the Germans attacking. Without air cover, the ground troops, when finally mobilised, were annihilated. Stalin, looking for someone to blame other than himself, had the commander of the Western Army, who had repeatedly warned of an impending German attack, tried for treason and shot. That was the kind of hero Stalin was!

Orlov was so infuriated by the picture that he made up the ploy of remembering something he had to do and left. Afterwards, he behaved coldly towards Natasha. He sent her to the guardhouse three times for breaches of uniform, and in her absence flew with a male pilot who wasn't half as good. He knew he was being irrational and he hated it. Why did he despise Natasha's adoration of Stalin so much when he'd endured in silence the whole country's delusions until then?

The next time he flew with her and they downed two enemy planes together, his feelings towards her softened again. She's been indoctrinated to worship Stalin like everyone else, he reasoned. He remembered his days at the orphanage when the children had to salute the portrait of Stalin in the dining room. Hadn't he been one of them? Then there was the oath he'd sworn to 'the Great Leader' when he'd joined the air force. He wondered if it was his own duplicity that had made him react so violently to Natasha's view of Stalin; and also perhaps because he expected so much of her now.

Orlov was dismayed to discover that his feelings for Natasha had returned with a greater intensity. They were like a fever one thinks has been overcome but which flares up again. It seemed to him that his heart, accustomed as it was now to constant danger and cold-blooded killing, beat faster whenever Natasha was near. A simple glimpse of her smile sent waves of warmth rippling through him. *Don't be stupid!* he wanted to shout at himself. The only time he could remain indifferent to her effect on him was when he was in the air. By a supreme force of will, he had trained himself to think of Natasha as another man when they went into combat. He'd learned to trust her like one.

One day, when they were returning from a mission and walking across the airfield together, the sound of planes approaching sent a chill through Orlov. He could tell by the pitch of the engines that these planes weren't their own. He and Natasha looked back in the direction of Stalingrad to see German fighters coming in to attack. Orlov managed to push Natasha into one of the mechanics' trenches and cover her with his body before bullets sprayed the ground where they had been walking moments before. They were showered with pieces of dirt. The raid damaged a hangar and set fire to two planes which had landed after Orlov and Natasha and which the ground crew hadn't managed to move in time.

The enemy planes passed and didn't return. Orlov stood up and dusted himself off. Natasha sprang to her feet. When she saw Svetlana emerge from the hangar unhurt, along with the other mechanics, she was noticeably relieved.

She turned to Orlov. 'That attack was more terrifying than any I've experienced in the air! In the sky I feel like a powerful eagle, but down here on the ground I was like a helpless ant. We pilots are much better off than the artillery. What those poor souls suffer!'

Her face crumpled and Orlov feared that she was going to cry. He hovered near her awkwardly. If she had been an ordinary woman, he'd have taken her in his arms. But what did one do with a fellow pilot?

One of the planes that had been hit exploded, sending flames and pieces of metal into the air. Orlov realised that he should be with the others, helping to stop the blaze spreading, but he didn't want to leave Natasha there alone. He tried to think of something to comfort her.

'When these things happen,' he said gravely, 'the important thing is to stay calm.'

Natasha lifted her beautiful eyes to meet his. Her mouth twitched and she bit her lip before covering her face with her hands. Orlov was horrified that somehow he'd made things worse. Her shoulders were shaking and she was making a strange muffled sound. He kneeled down next to her.

'Do you need a medic?' he asked her. 'Were you hit by debris?'

Natasha took her hands away from her face. Her cheeks were tear-stained but she wasn't crying. She threw her head back and laughed. 'The important thing is to stay calm!' she repeated, slapping her legs with mirth. 'Comrade Captain, sometimes I don't know what to make of you!'

She tried to keep a straight face, but burst into peals of laughter again. Her laugh was musical and infectious. Orlov chuckled without understanding why what he'd said was so amusing, but the harder she laughed, the more he laughed too. They sat together amid the destruction, laughing like two drunks on New Year's Eve. Natasha's cheeks were flushed and her eyes sparkled. It was then Orlov realised that his infatuation had changed and that he loved Natasha even without quite knowing her.

SEVENTEEN

Stalingrad, 1942

Dear Mama and Zoya,
It has been some time since I've had an opportunity
to write to you more than a few lines. But it's raining
today and the Germans are staying away so I am here
in our bunker with the other girls and a little stove to
keep us warm. To tell you the truth, when you informed
me about Roman's death in Voronezh, I was saddened
and found it difficult to talk to anyone. I rallied myself
for our missions, but when I returned all I wanted was
to go to sleep or to take a walk. As you know, Roman
was kind to me. Rightly or wrongly, before we left for
the war we promised each other that if we survived we
would marry. I wasn't in love with Roman but he was a
good man and perhaps we could have made a happy life
together. Now, when we fly missions to cover ground
troops, I remember him and do my best to protect the
men.

Having Svetlana here is a comfort to me. Knowing
that she looks after my plane gives me confidence in

the machine that takes me into battle each day. The
mechanics have a harder life than the pilots. They must
check and make ready again each plane when we return
from our sorties — sometimes six or more times a day —
and then they must repair the planes at night with only a
torch to guide them. We women pilots and crew share an
underground bunker, but as it gets colder the mechanics
have to ensure that the engines don't freeze overnight. So
now Svetlana sleeps in a trench near the planes with the
other mechanics and with only a canopy to protect her
from the elements. When I greet her in the morning I see
that she has ice in her hair!

What a friend I have in Svetlana! With her
qualifications she didn't need to come to the front but
she did so to be with me. Her mother writes to her here,
I know that, but she never sends Svetlana anything.
Perhaps Lydia Dmitrievna is in difficult circumstances.
Could you send me the quilt from my bed to keep
Svetlana warm and those slim gloves I have in my
drawer? She has scabs on her hands and perhaps the
gloves will allow her to reach the awkward parts of the
engine while protecting her skin. What a pair we will
make then: me with my hair in curlers and Svetlana
wearing evening gloves to fix the plane! What will
Captain Orlov say?

I haven't told you about my squadron leader yet.
Captain Orlov is the handsomest man I have ever met:
tall, with broad shoulders, a strong jaw, brown eyes
and chestnut hair. But he is so serious! Of course, the
desperate situation we find ourselves in at Stalingrad is
no laughing matter and we are all more sombre than
we might otherwise be, but Captain Orlov speaks in the

*same grave tone whether he is talking about the soup,
Pushkin's poetry or informing us that our squadron is
about to take on fifty enemy aircraft. His solemnity gives
me the giggles, which is awkward, as he has no sense of
humour and the harder I try to control myself the more I
find myself laughing.*

*Mama, you asked me in your last letter if I am
frightened when I go into combat. I am terrified when
I sit in readiness-one on the runway. As we wait in our
cockpits, my stomach churns and my heart pumps so
fiercely I almost faint with the dread. There are times
when my teeth chatter so loudly I'm sure the whole
regiment can hear them. Will this next sortie be my
last? Will I ever see you both again? But as soon as
the order to take off is received and I move the plane
down the runway, a sense of calm washes over me. I
deaden all feeling inside and concentrate. I become like
a machine and focus only on the mission, not the fear
or the consequences. To go into this state I have rituals.
In readiness-two, I apply lipstick, powder and perfume.
It's my war paint, my way of saying to the enemy: I
am ready to face you! I do not allow myself to think
of the Germans as people; never as somebody's father,
brother or husband. To do so would be fatal. I remind
myself that I would not be killing Germans if they had
not invaded the Motherland and slaughtered innocent
people. Before we attack, I cross myself and commit
my soul to God. Captain Orlov does not understand
these rituals. Several times now he has ordered me to
the guardhouse for breaches of uniform regulations.
He has also reprimanded me for the items I keep in the
cockpit — the little icon you sent me, my lipstick and my*

powder compact and mirror. He thinks my cosmetics are purely vanity, and even if I tried to explain he wouldn't understand.

The guardhouse is not a pleasant place. You have to hand in your belt — so you can't harm yourself with it — and sit there in solitary confinement. The guards let me sing at least, although I do so quietly so as not to get them into trouble. Even when I use the toilet, they are supposed to go with me and keep their eye on me. But the guards here are gentlemen and always look away. What you have to get used to in a war!

Even though the punishment for a breach of regulations can be several days, Captain Orlov comes and gets me after a few hours. You see, I fly as his wingman, and although he wasn't happy when I was first given that position, I think he now feels safer with me than any other pilot. We have shared some kills together and I have also scored two solo kills so far in dogfights since arriving here. When Captain Orlov orders me out of the guardhouse, he hopes that I will be contrite and not wear cosmetics any more. But when we go to readiness-two, Svetlana sneaks me my make-up and the pattern starts all over again.

I haven't been sent to the guardhouse lately though, and here is what I think has happened. It's a nuisance for Svetlana each time I am sent into solitary confinement because she has to adjust the pedals of my plane so a male pilot can fly it, and then she has to adjust them back again for me. I am sure that she has expressed her unhappiness, and now it seems Captain Orlov has given up on reprimanding me. You see, I am a good soldier — I always win!

When our regiment commander, Colonel Smirnov, saw the sapphire brooch that I wear he didn't admonish me. He simply asked if I didn't think the brooch was too precious to take into combat. I answered him, 'I'm precious and I'm going into combat!' He laughed at that. (You see, Colonel Smirnov has a much better sense of humour than my squadron leader!)

Anyway, if the rain clears up tomorrow we are sure to be busy and I'd better get some sleep. A kiss to the both of you!

Love, Natasha

PS: Mama, I know that you are sad about losing Ponchik. But our doggie lived to a good age and was so dearly loved! Please find yourself another stray from the metro in memory of Ponchik, Papa and Sasha. Those unfortunate creatures must be so hungry and afraid now. Take one of them into your heart. Dogs are loyal and never treacherous, unlike people!

EIGHTEEN

Moscow, 2000

It was Saturday morning and Oksana had come back to Lily's new apartment first thing after feeding her cats to hear the rest of Svetlana's story. She had brought the three small kittens she was looking after, and placed them in their enclosed basket on the sofa.

Svetlana looked from Lily to Oksana and needed no prompt to continue.

I knew that Natasha was in love with Valentin Orlov even before she did. As for Valentin, his feelings for Natasha were obvious no matter how he tried to hide them. One day he flew a mission with Colonel Smirnov, Natasha and three other pilots, to accompany a squadron of bombers that were going to destroy German supply lines. What should have been a routine mission turned into a dogfight, with our fighter pilots outnumbered twenty to six. One of the Yaks went down in flames, and a dive bomber was disabled and had to make an emergency landing. Despite this, the mission was accomplished and the German planes were forced to flee. But in the chaos our fighters were separated. Valentin, running low on fuel, was the first to return to the airfield. He waited on the runway for the others to arrive. Colonel Smirnov returned next and then the other two surviving pilots. There was no sign of Natasha.

'Did anyone see anything?' Valentin asked the others. 'Besides Maksimov going down?'

'I saw her take some hits along her fuselage,' replied one of the pilots, 'but no smoke or flames. She appeared to be holding her own.'

Colonel Smirnov telephoned divisional headquarters to find out if there was news of a downed pilot but they had nothing to report. The tension grew as all of us — Valentin, Colonel Smirnov, the pilots and crew — stared at the sky hoping to catch sight of Natasha's plane returning. As time wore on, Valentin couldn't disguise his feelings. His face was white with anguish. I was on the verge of collapsing myself. Of course, we had been through this many times. Pilots didn't return from missions; that was the course of things. We buried them or had memorials for them. When Natasha and I were with the 586th fighter regiment in Saratov, it was distressing to wake up in the bunker and see the undisturbed beds of comrades who had been killed the day before. Their half-finished sewing, letters and drawings reminded us that our own lives could be cut short at any moment. Natasha told me to never imagine anything bad happening to her. She believed that what you pictured vividly in your mind would come true. To avoid bad luck she even refused to take her identification capsule with her. She gave it to me to look after before she flew a mission. Despite my promises not to imagine the worst, each time she left for a sortie I would pace the runway anxiously until she returned. Had my fears caused Natasha's death? I couldn't bear to think of life without her.

One of the armourers turned to me. 'Listen!' he said. 'Is that your engine? It is, isn't it?'

I strained my ears and heard the faint hum of a plane's engine. Each of us mechanics knew the sound of our plane as intimately as a mother recognises the cry of her baby. Natasha's plane appeared from the west. The relief that ran through all of us was palpable. Colonel Smirnov slapped Valentin's shoulder. Valentin allowed himself a chuckle. The rest of us clapped and cheered. We watched Natasha approach the airfield. There was a dip to her wing, which indicated damage to the plane. She touched down and we waited for her to taxi to the end of the runway but her plane came to an abrupt stop. Had she run out of fuel? We grew quiet with apprehension, waiting for the plane to start moving again. But it didn't.

Sensing something was wrong, Valentin and I raced down the runway. Valentin, with his long strides, reached the plane before me. He leaped on the wing, which was riddled with bullet holes. The windshield was shattered. Valentin ripped open the canopy. Natasha lay there, slumped back in the seat. Her face was deathly white and her uniform was soaked in blood. She'd been hit in the shoulder and must have lost consciousness as soon as she'd landed her plane.

Valentin tore a strip of material from the front of his shirt and folded it into a dressing pad to apply pressure to the wound. 'Get the medics!' he screamed to the other pilots and crew who were running to see what had happened.

Two orderlies were dispatched from the hospital bunker and sped down the runway with a stretcher. Valentin unhooked Natasha's parachute and harness and lifted her out of the cockpit, cradling her in his arms. 'Natasha!' he said softly to her. 'Natasha, come on!' He placed her on the stretcher and ran beside it, keeping the pressure on her shoulder as the orderlies hurried to the hospital bunker. I ran after them.

The nurse cut open Natasha's sleeve and examined the wound. 'She'll need surgery and a transfusion,' she said. 'We'll stabilise her then get her to a hospital.'

Valentin didn't take his eyes off Natasha's face. He wasn't behaving like a squadron leader concerned about one of his subordinates. The desperate look on his face was that of a man who sees his beloved in pain. As the nurse cleaned Natasha's wound and bandaged her arm, Natasha regained consciousness and noticed Valentin by her side. At first she seemed puzzled and then she smiled. That smile told me all that I needed to know. I felt so many things in that moment: happiness for Natasha and Valentin that they could still experience love in the middle of all this horror; but also fear for them. It was accepted wisdom that at the front no one should make promises; they should wait until after the war. When life could change in an instant, promises only brought suffering. In the end, my fears were well founded.

The kittens started to move around in the basket and meow. As captivated as Lily and Oksana were by Svetlana's story, they took a break for Oksana to mix up some formula.

Lily realised that she and Svetlana hadn't had breakfast. While Oksana was busy with the kittens, Lily toasted some rye bread and served it with cottage cheese and sliced tomato. When she handed Svetlana her plate, the old woman seemed lost in thought. Lily sat down next to her. Oksana put the kittens back, but before she rejoined them her mobile telephone rang.

'It's Doctor Pesenko,' she said, looking at the number. After a few minutes of conversation, she ended the call and indicated for Lily to come with her to the kitchen. 'Doctor Pesenko has found a place for Svetlana,' she said, 'a good one. It's an aged care facility that will be able to give palliative care.'

The day before, Lily would have been relieved by the news. She'd been worrying about what she'd do if Svetlana took a turn for the worse. Oksana had enough on her hands with the colony cats and orphaned kittens.

'So soon?' she replied. 'But Svetlana's just started talking to us. We still don't know whether she has any family.'

'I've got someone checking on that,' said Oksana. 'Meanwhile Doctor Pesenko has persuaded the administrator to accept her by giving my details as her caregiver.'

'When do we take her there?' Lily asked.

'Doctor Pesenko is at the facility now. He wants us to come straight away. We can't miss this opportunity — there are very few places like this in Moscow. Most Russians care for their elderly relatives at home.'

Lily set aside her impatience to hear the rest of Svetlana's story and helped Oksana pack a bag for her. They put in the nightdress Lily had bought for her and a dress Oksana had obtained, along with toothpaste and other necessities. Lily fastened a collar and lead on Laika, assuming that she could come along too. During the drive to the facility, Lily noticed Svetlana staring out the window. Is she thinking about Valentin and Natasha, Lily wondered. She remembered Valentin Orlov from the television: a man who had never stopped searching for the woman he loved. Finally he'd found her but she was dead. Natasha and Valentin's love story didn't have a happy ending.

Doctor Pesenko greeted them at reception and helped them to register Svetlana Novikova. When they went inside to the rooms, Lily was relieved to find that it wasn't so different from the nursing home where Adam's grandmother lived in Sydney. Everything was clean and freshly painted, and the common room had a television set and comfortable armchairs. Yet the pictures on the walls and the vases of flowers couldn't hide the fact that for everyone who came here, this was the last stop. The tiled floors, metal hospital beds and locked bedside cabinets were typical of medical institutions, but it was the shrivelled human beings that inhabited the place, with their shocks of white hair and gaping mouths, that marked it as an institution for the old and the dying. Lily watched Svetlana, but the old woman didn't seem to have registered the change of location.

Svetlana was assigned to share a room with a woman who was so wasted away that Lily kept glancing over at her to make sure she was still breathing. A plump nurse with brown curly hair entered the room.

'This is Polina Vasilyevna, the matron,' said Doctor Pesenko. 'I'll leave you in her capable hands and check again on our patient tomorrow.'

Polina tugged the curtain across between Svetlana and the other woman and placed Svetlana's belongings in the locker. 'We've got a shelf here for mementoes and photographs,' she said, pointing to a glass cabinet on the wall. She glanced at Laika and smiled. 'And pets are welcome to visit as long as they have a certificate of health from a veterinarian.'

Oksana nodded and Lily knew she would get Doctor Yelchin to take care of Laika's certificate. Svetlana lay on the bed and said nothing.

'It's natural to be unsettled at first,' Polina said, patting Svetlana's hand. She turned to Lily and Oksana. 'We're about to serve lunch. Why don't you stay with her for that? Then when you come tomorrow you'll see that she's more at ease.'

Later, when the two women returned to the car, Lily felt a knot form in her stomach. 'Svetlana started to trust us and we've bundled her off here,' she told Oksana.

Oksana put her hand on Lily's arm. 'Sweetheart, she'll settle in and we'll come and see her every evening. She's seriously ill and you wouldn't have been able to care for her yourself. Also, don't forget that we don't know where she was living before. It was probably somewhere a lot worse. She's safe and comfortable and she's got what she most wanted — someone she trusts to look after Laika.'

That night, Lily lay in bed back in her own apartment with Pushkin snuggled against her on one side, snoring peacefully, and Laika on her other side. The dog was restless; she kept nudging Lily's arm.

'It's all right,' Lily assured her. 'You're safe and your mistress is being taken care of. You'll see her again tomorrow.'

Lily thought of Svetlana lying in her hospital bed with a stranger sleeping next to her. She reminded herself of Oksana's words: she had done the best she could. Since the fall of Communism, the average life expectancy for a woman in the Russian Federation had fallen to seventy-one. Based on what Svetlana had told them so far, Lily guessed her age to be about seventy-eight. Despite having spent some time in a concentration camp and having a damaged heart, she'd already beaten the odds.

'She's tough,' Lily told Laika. 'She'll be all right.'

The following day, Lily and Oksana put Laika into the jeep and set off to visit Svetlana. 'She's still quiet,' Polina said, leading them to Svetlana's room, when they arrived. 'But her vitals are good. Doctor Pesenko examined her this morning and praised you both. She's in better health than he expected.'

Svetlana was sitting up in her bed. She looked glum, but when Lily held Laika up to her, she brightened instantly.

'Hello,' she said, kissing the dog. 'Do you like your new mistress? You must be a good girl for her.'

'Come, let's explore this place,' said Oksana.

When the old woman didn't object, she drew Svetlana off the bed and out of the room. They walked to the recreation room, where several residents were playing chess or watching tropical fish dart back and forth in a giant tank. Some women worked together on a jigsaw puzzle. From the lively chatter that came from their side of the room, Lily gathered they were a friendly group, still in possession of their faculties.

'I hope you like puzzles,' Oksana said breezily.

Svetlana showed little interest in any of the activities, and when the trio returned to her room she lay back on her bed and closed her eyes. There would be nothing more about Natasha and Valentin that day, the younger women could see.

It was the same on the succeeding three nights. Svetlana seemed distant and uneasy, despite the reassurance Lily, Oksana and the staff offered.

'I expect she'll open up again when she gets used to the place,' said Oksana.

'I hope so,' said Lily. 'She has me intrigued.'

On Thursday evening, when Lily was getting ready to visit Svetlana, Oksana came to the door. 'I hope you haven't forgotten you're going out salsa dancing tonight,' she said.

'Oh, yes!' Lily had indeed forgotten. She glanced at her watch. Luka was due to pick her up in half an hour. She hesitated. Did she really want to go? She'd much rather see Svetlana than go out dancing but Oksana wouldn't hear of it.

'Go get ready!' she said, taking Laika's lead. 'I'll visit Svetlana tonight. You need to get out and live like a young person.'

Oksana's right, Lily thought while she took a shower and put on fresh make-up. In Sydney she'd had a busy social life and now she lived like a recluse. But each step forward felt like betrayal. It was as if she and Adam had been on a train journey together and he'd suddenly got off while she'd continued onwards. She wanted the train to stop and go back to where she'd left him, but of course that was impossible.

Luka arrived wearing a blue satin shirt and dark flared pants. 'You look beautiful,' he said to Lily, admiring the black ruched dress she was wearing. He opened the door of his car with a flourish. 'Your chariot awaits you!'

Lily laughed. Perhaps it was a good start for her to be going out with an attractive man in a pressure-free arrangement. She realised that she'd missed male company.

The salsa club was in the basement of an office building in central Moscow. Lily followed Luka into the dimly lit interior and saw that the dance floor was crowded. From the profusion of accents it was apparent the patrons were a mix of Russians and expats — Brits and Americans mostly, but also some Turks and Germans. They were dressed more casually than was the norm when going out in Moscow: jeans and tank tops — although in the case of the Russian girls, the jeans were labelled Armani and were paired with Manolo Blahnik shoes.

Luka steered her through the crowd and brought her to a stop in front of four people sitting on lounges under an artificial palm tree. 'Hi, guys,' he said. 'This is my Australian friend, Lily.'

A pretty girl with black hair and a long nose stood up. 'I'm Tamara and this is my boyfriend, Boris,' she said pointing to a young man in a Lacoste shirt.

The other two were an English girl, Jane, who was in Russia working for an IT company, and another Russian named Mikhail, who was a dentist.

The band got louder and Lily couldn't hear anything Luka said, so they gave up talking and just danced. He was a good lead, putting her on the correct foot and taking care not to spin her into the path of other dancers. The music was festive and Lily found herself having much more fun than she'd expected.

Afterwards, Luka invited everyone back to his apartment. He lived in the Meshchansky district. One look at his sleek Scandinavian furniture and Lily regretted not having done anything about the tacky décor in her own apartment.

'Come in, everyone,' Luka called to his friends, who were walking down the corridor from the elevator. 'Please, Lily,' he said, indicating an egg chair, 'have a seat. I'm going to throw something together in the kitchen.'

Luka's living room was lined with ceiling-to-floor shelves filled with books and objets d'art. One wall was dedicated to studies of Russian history, while the other shelves held books on animal physiology — which Lily would have expected — as well as books on art and poetry.

Two panther-like cats emerged from the bedroom. 'Hello, Valentino,' said Tamara, picking up the all-black one and giving him a cuddle, which, from the blissful expression on his face, he enjoyed. 'You look muscular and boyish but you're a softy,' Tamara told him.

The other cat, Versace, who was black with white whiskers and tuxedo markings, made a beeline for Lily's lap. Lily stroked his silky fur and Jane leaned over to scratch his chin. Luka came out of the kitchen with a platter of bruschetta. He smiled at the women fussing over the cats.

'Valentino and Versace always go for attractive women. They aren't stupid!'

'How long have you had them?' asked Mikhail. 'I don't remember them being here last time.'

'They were hiding then,' said Luka, bending down to stroke Versace. 'Lily's friend Oksana gave them to me. They were strays from the street. You wouldn't think so looking at them now.'

'No,' agreed Jane. 'They're so handsome!'

Versace nuzzled Lily's stomach and purred. If he was once a feral cat, she thought, there's hope for Mamochka.

'I've got a dog too,' Luka told Lily. 'He's a Samoyed mix. I keep him at my parents' place. They have a garden and my mother has time to walk him every day. I'd have more animals if I had more space. Is it true that in Australia everyone lives in a house with a big garden?'

Lily smiled. 'Not everyone, but that is the Australian dream; although these days it's more like a big house with barely any garden — unfortunately for our wildlife.'

Luka poured everyone a glass of wine then returned to the kitchen to whip up some *blini*. Lifting Versace from her lap, Lily gave him to Jane to cuddle before following Luka. The kitchen was white with pale wooden counters. One wall was taken up by framed sketches of animals.

'Did you do those?' Lily asked. 'They are so lifelike.'

He nodded. 'I draw the ones that I can't save. They inspire me to study more and become the best veterinarian that I can be. And by remembering them, I keep their spirits with me.'

Touched, Lily turned away to collect herself. With his animal work and relic hunting, Luka was clearly someone who believed he could make a difference to tragic situations. She herself had once been like that. But since Adam's death, she'd lost faith in her ability to change anything. She tried to — by helping the old women in the underpass and the colony cats — but she didn't have a sense of optimism about her actions. Perhaps that was why she was becoming drawn to Luka. She needed a friend who could remind her what hope felt like.

'Your apartment is fabulous,' she told him. 'With your interest in relic hunting I expected you to have guns and helmets on display.'

Luka cracked eggs into a bowl and added milk and flour. 'I don't keep that stuff. It goes to the relatives or to a museum or stays where it is.' He nodded his head in the direction of the living room. 'But I take photographs and make sketches. I've got albums on the shelf underneath the coffee table. I'll show you later if you like.'

Lily saw an opportunity. 'I've been following the news story about the recovery of Natalya Azarova's plane and remains. It all sounds fascinating.'

'Indeed,' said Luka, smiling at her. 'But with Natalya Azarova it's difficult to separate the romanticised accounts from the reality, as it is with all heroes. I was on the recovery dig for her plane. A friend of my uncle's invited me.'

'Really?' Lily sat down on a stool. She would have liked to talk to him about Svetlana, but it wasn't her secret to share.

Luka heated a griddle pan and ladled some of the *blini* mixture over its surface. 'He's a professor at Moscow University and interested in the cult of national heroes. He wrote a book on Natalya Azarova. I've got it there on my shelf. I'll lend it to you.'

Luka flipped the pancake with a spatula. 'He's updating it for a new edition. He's been given access to previously confidential files. Natalya Azarova's father was the chief chocolatier of the Red October factory. He was executed as an enemy of the people, but who denounced him has never been made public before.'

Lily felt a tingle run down her spine. 'Is that so?'

Luka must have noticed her reaction. 'I can get us together for coffee if you like — or dinner. Yefim loves to talk about his research. He'd be thrilled that someone all the way from Australia is interested in his work.'

'I would love to meet him,' said Lily. She couldn't believe her luck. Since Svetlana had made her startling confession, Natalya Azarova had become a subject of absorbing interest to Lily. Now she was going to meet an expert on her.

She helped Luka carry the platter of *blinis*, with their feta cheese and marinated bell peppers and eggplant accompaniments, to the living room.

'So, Lily, how did you meet Luka?' Tamara asked. Lily explained about the colony cats, and everyone nodded approvingly.

'He's a great guy,' said Mikhail. 'We went to school together.' Lily glanced at Luka. He *was* a special person. Apart from being handsome and showing impeccable taste, he was talented, intelligent and kind. She glanced over to the shelves for a telltale photograph of a boyfriend but she couldn't see one. Surely he has someone who appreciates how great he is, she thought. Then she remembered that Moscow wasn't like Sydney. Gay people couldn't be open here without the risk of abuse or physical attacks. Perhaps he did have someone but they played it low key and didn't go dancing together.

The gathering was friendly and they asked Lily about life in Australia. Boris was interested to know about the beaches and about the venomous snakes and spiders. When Lily had told her Australian friends that she was going to work in Russia they'd reacted as if she was hauling herself off to the Wild West. 'Russia is a dangerous place,' they'd said. Lily now realised that there were Russians who viewed Australia in the same way.

When it was time to leave, Luka took Yefim's book from the shelf and handed it to Lily. 'I'll call him tomorrow and find out when he's free.'

Luka dropped Lily off at her apartment. Before she got out of the car he kissed her on her cheeks. 'It's been a great night, Lily. Would you like to come out with us again? I think my friends liked you.'

'Sure,' said Lily. 'I liked them too.'

As she changed into her nightdress and brushed her teeth, Lily thought about how going out with friends was like picking up a book again after a long interval of not reading it and trying to recall the threads of the story. Only she still wished Adam had been there to enjoy the night with her.

She climbed into bed with Pushkin and Laika and looked at the cover of Yefim's book. His last name was Grekov and the book was titled *Sapphire Skies: Natalya Azarova, Russia's War Heroine*. She looked up Svetlana's name in the index and saw that she wasn't mentioned until Natasha was posted to Stalingrad, and then only briefly as her mechanic. Lily realised that she knew more intimate things about the pilot than even the foremost authority on the subject. It seemed Yefim was unaware that Svetlana and Natasha had been childhood friends. In the chapter that recounted the day Natasha went missing, Yefim claimed that Svetlana had disappeared too, gone in search of her pilot:

> *Novikova didn't have permission to leave the camp and could have been shot as a deserter. But the other mechanics let her go, and didn't inform the new commander of the regiment, Captain Valentin Orlov, because they were sure that she'd turn back. Anything could have happened to her, but it is doubtful that Novikova found Natalya Azarova. She most likely never made it behind enemy lines before she was caught and shot, or stepped on a mine and was blown to bits.*

She might even have been eaten by a bear or a wolf.
According to her comrades she wasn't a survivor like
Natalya Azarova.

'Well, he's wrong on two counts,' Lily said to Laika. 'One, your mistress is most definitely a survivor. And two, she did find Natalya Azarova. How else could she know what really happened to her?'

Lily closed the book and turned out the light. She had to be patient and wait until Svetlana was ready to tell that part of the story.

NINETEEN

Moscow, 1943

The doctors at the military hospital tended to my shoulder as best they could, then sent me by train to Moscow for more surgery. It was then I heard the news: Marina Raskova had been killed when her plane crashed in a snowstorm. The woman who had inspired me and who had turned me into a fighter pilot was dead.

A nurse from the hospital in Moscow accompanied me so I could file past Marina's urn with the thousands of other citizens who came to the Civil Aviation Club to pay their respects. I hadn't believed it was possible for my heroes to die. But as the war went on, die they did. Marina's ashes were later placed in the Kremlin wall, near Polina Osipenko's grave, the co-pilot on their historic flight in the *Rodina* and who had been killed in a training accident along with Anatoly Serov, the husband of my film idol, Valentina Serova.

A week after my surgery, I was allowed to go to my mother's apartment to recuperate. Mama now lived in the Arbat district again with a red-furred puppy she'd named Dasha. She'd found her wandering the street, half-starved and with sores on her feet.

It was only when Mama had settled me into an armchair with a blanket over my legs and sat down herself that she told me Zoya was dead. She had been killed in an air raid in the last week of January 1942, when I had been training in Engels.

'We were in the apartment with the other residents when the air-raid alarm sounded,' Mama explained. 'We all rushed to the cellar but the building collapsed on us. Ponchik and I were the only survivors.'

I was stunned by the news and couldn't speak. I had been writing to both my mother and Zoya from the front. All this time I had thought she was alive.

'Mama,' I finally managed to say, 'you told me about Ponchik and Roman, but not Zoya. Why?'

Mama rubbed her arms. 'At first I couldn't bring myself to believe she was dead. I kept thinking that I would wake up and there would be Zoya, cheerful as ever. But then I had other reasons too.'

Mama stood up and opened the drawer of a bureau near the window. She handed me a scrapbook of newspaper articles, similar to the one I'd kept as a teenager of my favourite aviators and film stars.

'Zoya was like a sister to me,' she said. 'I knew that if you thought I was alone in Moscow, you wouldn't be able to concentrate on what you were doing.'

I opened the scrapbook, curious to see what my mother had been collecting. The articles were about me — stories in *Ogonek*, *Izvestia* and *Pravda*. Reporters came to the airfield from time to time wanting to interview me. Colonel Smirnov told me to be circumspect. I answered the reporters' questions and let them take photographs of me near my airplane, not thinking much of it and assuming they were paying similar attention to other women in frontline roles. Now, as I turned the pages of the scrapbook, I saw that I was being held up as a role model for girls, just as Marina Raskova had once been for me. I looked at my mother. She had tears in her eyes.

'Papa, Sasha and Zoya would have been so proud of you!' she said. 'You've restored our family's good name!'

I could see that the scrapbook meant a lot to my mother, so I didn't express my true feelings, but I was horrified. When I was younger, I'd dreamed of becoming a famous aviator. Papa's death had changed that. All I wished now was to defend the Motherland. Being famous meant that people wanted to know everything about you and I'd been able to become a pilot because I'd kept my past secret. Marina Raskova had been given the first State funeral of the war. Stalin had been a pallbearer at the funeral of Polina Osipenko. But even though I was the first woman in the world to become a fighter ace, Stalin hadn't uttered a word about it. Not once in any of the articles did he refer to me as one of his eagles. Stalin knew that my past was best forgotten. He always understood everything perfectly. It was thanks to his genius that the tide of the war was turning.

Moscow had been in danger, but the Germans failed to capture it, and its citizens had been spared the horror of the blockade suffered by Leningrad, or having their city destroyed like the people of Stalingrad. Still, it had been a narrow escape and Muscovites were now making the most of life. Mama and I strolled along the streets with Dasha and looked at the people crowding the cafés and listening to jazz or dancing.

The heating in Mama's apartment was unreliable but it was nice to snuggle with her on the mattress she spread out each night on the floor, with Dasha curled up at our feet. I woke up to the smell of coffee — mixed with acorn flour to make it last longer — and fritters made from potato skins. When my shoulder was better, we wrapped ourselves in our warmest coats and went to the cinema to watch Valentina Serova in *Wait For Me*, a film about a woman who never gives up hope that her husband will return to her, even after his plane is shot down by the Germans. We learned the song 'Wait For Me' and sang it with gusto at every opportunity.

These were simple pleasures and I relished them. At the same time, I worried that tasting civilian life again would make me too soft to return to the front. Sometimes the peace and quiet unnerved me and I longed to be in my Yak in the sky, fighting the Germans again. One day I came home from a walk with Mama and Dasha to discover a letter had arrived for me. It was from Captain Orlov himself. At first I thought something must have happened to Svetlana and my hands trembled, but the letter did not contain bad news at all.

Dear Natasha,

I have received a report from the hospital in Moscow that your surgery went well and you are now recovering at home. I am glad to hear it. Svetlana tells me that you have a wonderful mother and no doubt you will thrive under her loving care.

We miss you here at the regiment. The tide is changing in our favour. I'm not sure how much news you are getting in Moscow, but Hitler's Sixth Army has surrendered and Stalingrad is ours again. Of course, there is much work to do and it seems likely the Germans will push towards Kursk and that will see us deployed there in the not too distant future.

I also have good news on a more personal level. Colonel Smirnov will not be pleased if he learns that I have informed you of this ahead of him — so please act surprised when he does — but as your squadron commander I am delighted to tell you that on returning to the regiment you are to be presented with the Order of the Red Star Medal for your exceptional service in the defence of the Soviet Union and also the Order of the Red Banner for valour during combat. Colonel Smirnov has arranged for you to be promoted to the rank of senior lieutenant and you will be commanding your own squadron — though I hope from time to time you will do me the honour of flying as my wingman again on missions of grave importance.

We have received our upgraded planes. The new models have much improved rearward visibility and better gunsight and control systems. I know you were attached to your airplane and I did it the honour of thanking it for its service to you before it was taken away.

Thinking of you and looking forward to seeing you again.

Yours faithfully,

Captain Valentin Orlov

I had often thought of Captain Orlov while I had been in Moscow. He had been attentive to me the day I was injured. The tone of his letter told me something I had begun to suspect: that under his cold and proper exterior lay a warm spirit. Even though there wasn't a declaration of love in the letter, there was much more than a commander's concern for his wingman. I was so happy that I read the letter over and over until I knew it by heart.

I showed it to Mama. She was quiet for a long time before she spoke to me. 'Natasha,' she said, then hesitated. I assumed that she sensed the same thing I had and I expected her to warn me to be prudent. To fall in love when the world was in the throes of madness could only lead to heartbreak. But she did not.

'Natasha,' she said, 'seize every moment you can to be happy.'

In March, I was declared fit enough to return to my regiment. Mama came with Dasha to see me off at the station. She wore her hair in a fetching chignon, with a dusky pink scarf around her throat and matching gloves. She looked so pretty.

'When I return,' I told her, 'we're going to see many more films together and I'm going to grow my hair long again and wear it like yours.'

I kissed Mama's cheeks and patted Dasha. It was a simple parting and one filled with the confidence of my safe return. I waved to Mama and blew her a kiss from the window as the train pulled out of the station. 'Wait for me!' I called to her. How was I to know that I would never see her again?

The train took me from Moscow to an airbase near Saratov, from where I was transported back to my regiment by a supply plane. Colonel Smirnov was out on a mission when I arrived, so I went to the mess bunker to see who I could find. None of the weary-looking pilots and crew that were eating there was familiar to me. I ran to the sleeping bunker I had shared with the other women and was relieved to find Alisa taking a rest. She jumped up when she saw me. 'Natasha!'

I looked around the bunker. Margarita's bed and her belongings were gone.

'She was killed last week,' Alisa said quietly, the pain of losing her comrade heavy in her voice. 'Her plane exploded. There wasn't anything of her left to bury.'

I threw my bag down and sat on my bunk. Margarita was gone? She had kept us cheerful during the darkest days. Her plane had exploded! Still that was better than catching fire and burning slowly — that was the worst way to die.

'And the others?' I asked.

Alisa understood who it was I was anxious about. 'Svetlana is fine. Captain Orlov is out on a mission with Colonel Smirnov.'

I ran to the hangar to see Svetlana. We embraced fiercely and she filled me in on what had happened since I had been away. The Soviet Air Force had gained supremacy over Stalingrad and now the Germans were being more aggressive in their tactics. Their new strategy was to outnumber us in air combat and nearly half the pilots in our regiment had been killed or wounded.

When we heard the planes returning to the airfield, Svetlana and I went outside to greet the squadron. Valentin spotted us and performed a victory roll which blew off my cap. If any other pilot had flown so close to the ground, they would have been put in the guardhouse for a week.

'You've changed him,' Svetlana said. 'He's different because of you.'

When the planes landed and the pilots alighted, Valentin turned to me and our eyes met. It was as if nothing else existed; it was only Valentin and me in the whole world. Then Colonel Smirnov distracted him with a question and the spell was broken, but the fluttering sensation in my heart remained.

That evening, Colonel Smirnov threw a party in my honour. Everyone had been saving their chocolate, sugar and milk rations so the cook could bake a cake for my return. Colonel Smirnov played the piano while the rest of us danced. Because the women were outnumbered, some of the men partnered with each other. Valentin danced only with me and no one interrupted us. The happiness I felt was at odds with the reality that we were fighting against an increasingly desperate enemy who had annihilated so many of our comrades.

'Why didn't you tell me about all those we had lost in your letter?' I asked him.

'I didn't want you to worry,' Valentin replied. 'I wanted you to get well and come back.'

The regiment asked me to sing the latest song from Moscow and I sang the one from the film I had seen with Mama.

Wait for me, and I'll come back.
Wait with all you've got.
Wait, when dreary yellow rains
Tell you, you should not.
Wait when snow is falling fast,
Wait when summer's hot,
Wait when yesterdays are past,
Others are forgot.
Wait, when from that far-off place
Letters don't arrive
Wait, when those with whom you wait
Doubt if I'm alive.

Valentin's eyes were on me and I knew the song was for us. As long as we loved each other and expected the other one to survive, neither of us would die.

Afterwards, Colonel Smirnov ordered us all to bed, as we were flying out to a new airfield the following day. I settled into my bunk, but after tossing and turning for half an hour, I decided to take a walk outside to clear my head. I slipped out of bed, wrapped my coat over my nightdress and tugged on my boots before going outside. I approached the sentry and told him I couldn't sleep and wanted to stretch my legs.

'Thank you for informing me,' he said with a touch of irony in his voice. 'Otherwise I would have shot you.'

The moon was full and the air was fresh as I walked around the airfield. There was no longer the smell of smoke that had choked the atmosphere around Stalingrad when I was first transferred here from the 586th. I thought about Valentin and how handsome he had looked as we'd danced together.

'Natasha.'

I turned to see him standing behind me.

'Did you enjoy your party?' he asked.

'I did.'

Valentin smiled with a tender expression in his eyes. 'Are you glad to be back here ... with me?'

I wanted to tell him that I returned safely because I'd known that he was waiting for me but I couldn't get the words out. Instead I stepped towards him. He embraced me and kissed me softly, then with deepening passion. For a moment neither of us moved, then he stood back and took my hand. There was a hut next to the runway where the pilots would wait on the days the weather was too inclement for us to sit in our planes. He led me there. My body felt weightless and our steps were languid.

The hut was dark except for the glimmer of moonlight that seeped through the gaps in the walls and the window. Valentin closed the door behind us and took me in his arms. My heart pounded. His warm breath on my neck made my knees go weak. He moved away again, taking off his overcoat and laying it on the floor. Then he removed his boots before reaching down and taking off mine. I slipped my coat over my shoulders and gave it to him to lay on top of his.

'Here we are, Natasha,' he said, taking me in his arms again and lowering me onto the coats. He lay beside me and unfastened the buttons on the front of my nightdress then caressed my breasts and stomach. Everything he did sent tingles of desire through me. Aroused with yearning, I untucked the shirt from his trousers and ran my hands over the soft bare skin of his back. He smelt fresh, like lemons.

In one fluid movement he sat up and tugged his shirt over his head, sending his neat hair in all directions. I reached up and smoothed it down again, giggling as I did so.

'Still laughing, beautiful Natasha?' he whispered, unbuckling his pants and pressing his naked flesh against mine. Every part of me burned when he moved over me.

I held his face in my hands knowing that I would never love another man the way I loved Valentin.

TWENTY

Moscow Times, 4 September 2000

*The Defence Minister announced today that the war
heroine Natalya Azarova, whose remains were recently
discovered in Orël Oblast, is to be given a funeral with
State and military honours. The funeral is to be held in
the newly consecrated Cathedral of Christ the Saviour.*

*According to Professor Yefim Grekov of Moscow
University, who has written a book on Natalya Azarova,
the granting of a State funeral, and a Russian Orthodox
one at that, is a sign of the massive changes that are taking
place in the country. 'Choosing the Cathedral of Christ the
Saviour for Natalya Azarova's funeral ceremony is highly
symbolic,' he claims. 'Last month the Russian Orthodox
Church canonised Tsar Nicholas II and his family,
eighty years after they'd been brutally executed by the
Bolsheviks. The Church declared them to be martyrs, even
though during the Soviet period the Tsar and his family
were considered criminals. Now Natalya Azarova, whose
memory was once sullied by the suspicion that she was a
foreign spy, is to be honoured in the highest possible way.'*

The original cathedral was built to give thanks to Christ for saving Russia from Napoleon. Under Stalin, the beautiful church was demolished with the intention of building a 'Palace of the Soviets' in its place. Due to geological problems and a lack of funding, the palace was never built and the site was turned into a public swimming pool. After the fall of the Soviet Union, the Russian Orthodox Church received permission to rebuild the cathedral in all its glory and over a million Muscovites donated money to the project.

'It is quite extraordinary,' says Professor Grekov. 'In a country riven with economic and social problems, wars and terrorism, symbols of the past have become more important than ever. The government anticipates that a beautiful heroine from the Great Patriotic War is exactly what the Russian people need to inspire them again.'

Natalya Azarova's body will lie in state for five days, under the watch of a guard of honour. The public will be able to pay their respects during this time. As the remains are skeletal, the coffin will be closed, but the sapphire brooch she received from Stalin — and from which her call sign, Sapphire Skies, was derived — will be displayed on a cushion on top of the coffin. Also displayed will be her Gold Star medal, recognising her as a Hero of the Russian Federation, the honour that was denied her for so many years.

Lily showed the *Moscow Times* article to Oksana.

'I'll check with Doctor Pesenko,' Oksana told her, 'but Svetlana seems well enough to go to the funeral. I'm sure she would want to.'

But when Lily put the question to Svetlana that evening a troubled look clouded the old woman's face. She remained quiet for so long that Lily began to worry that she was feeling unwell again. When Svetlana finally spoke her voice was heavy with grief.

'Natasha loved the Motherland and its people. She fought and died for them alone. I'm glad that they now know she didn't forsake them and she was never a German spy. But as for everything else, the hypocrisy of it is disgusting.'

Hypocrisy? That wasn't a sentiment Lily had expected and she wondered what Svetlana meant. Was she angry that the government had refused to recognise Natasha as a national heroine for so many years and might only be doing it now for political reasons? But Svetlana said nothing more and Lily didn't want to push her.

'I think if she doesn't at least watch the funeral broadcast, she'll regret it,' said Oksana on the way home. 'They were like sisters. I'm going to speak to Polina and see if we can use a private room at the hospital that has a television set.'

'Good idea!' said Lily. 'The funeral's scheduled for Friday week. I'll take the day off work so I can watch it with you.'

Oksana said good night to Lily in the elevator but telephoned her apartment half an hour later. 'I've got some news that I couldn't wait to tell you,' she said.

'What?'

Oksana drew a breath. 'I've just finished speaking with my contact who's been trying to find out where Svetlana lived before she came to us. He's met with nothing but dead ends. As you discovered in Professor Grekov's book, Svetlana Novikova was listed as "missing in action presumed dead" in 1943. The survivors of the three women's air-force regiments get together every year on the second of May in a park in front of the Bolshoi Theatre. Svetlana has never attended or set the record straight. Even her parents believed that she'd been killed in the war right up until their own deaths in the early

1970s. The Svetlana we know has been living under a false name, which she hasn't disclosed to us. I suspect she doesn't want to go to the funeral because someone — one of the other women who trained at Engels with her or Valentin Orlov — may recognise her.'

'I did wonder about that,' said Lily. 'Why would she have wanted everyone to continue thinking she was dead?'

Oksana clucked her tongue. 'My guess is that she is afraid of something. I only hope that she'll tell us one day soon what that something is.'

'I have a lot of respect for the elderly who lived through the war,' Polina told Lily and Oksana on the day of the funeral. 'Natalya Azarova must be an important figure for them.'

Polina had allocated the women a private room in the hospital and provided them with tea-making facilities and cut sandwiches. Oksana helped Svetlana into an armchair and propped her up with cushions. 'Listen,' she said, stroking Svetlana's hair, 'we are going to watch the broadcast of Natasha's funeral because, while it might bring back painful memories, it will help you say goodbye. You will regret it if you don't. The way you've described Natasha to us, we can see how deeply you cared for her.'

Svetlana looked into Oksana's eyes and didn't make any protest. Lily turned on the television. Natasha's coffin was surrounded by bouquets of roses, carnations and asters. Priests in white cloaks sprinkled holy water and intoned prayers. Lily couldn't take her eyes off Valentin Orlov, who stood alongside the President and the Prime Minister. He was stony-faced and solemn, but now that Lily knew his story she sympathised with the heaviness he would be feeling in his heart. Wasn't the fact that he'd searched for Natasha all these years a testament to his undying love?

Behind General Orlov stood the men and women veterans of the air force and other dignitaries. The President gave the eulogy, saying that Natalya Azarova represented a generation of heroic young men and women who gave their lives for Mother Russia. Many of the veterans wept as he spoke. Lily knew that no matter how much she learned about the war, she would never fully be able to imagine the horror those people had lived through. It was beyond comprehension.

Heroes were no longer interred in the Kremlin wall, and after the ceremony the coffin was driven in a black Mercedes hearse to Novodevichy Cemetery. The streets were lined with people throwing red carnations before the procession. To Lily's surprise, while there were many elderly people among the spectators, most of the crowd were her age or younger. It seemed the newspaper report was true: Natasha was bringing the nation together.

Before her coffin was placed in the ground, she was given a three-volley gun salute and a squadron of air-force planes swept overhead. A military band played the Russian national anthem. Even if Lily had never met Svetlana and learned the intimate details of Natasha's life, she would have been moved by what she was seeing on the screen.

When the broadcast finished, Svetlana sat motionless in her chair, her fists curled in her lap. Lily glanced at Oksana. Perhaps making Svetlana watch the funeral hadn't been a good idea after all. She remembered how after Adam's death, before she sold their beach cottage, she kept looking at things that had belonged to him: his surfboard; his clothes in the wardrobe; the signed T-shirt from Kelly Slater, the famous American surfer. She'd hoped that by staring at Adam's possessions, she could desensitise herself to the sadness. But it never worked. Perhaps there were certain kinds of pain that remained raw forever.

Svetlana started to cry. 'All these years I thought ...'

Lily rubbed Svetlana's arm and waited for her to continue, but she didn't. Perhaps sharing the truth would be the final closure for her, not the funeral.

'Svetlana, you said that Natasha would have been disgusted by the hypocrisy. I don't think you meant the church, because Natasha was a believer. I also don't think you meant Valentin or her comrades, because they've clearly never forgotten her. Whose hypocrisy were you referring to?'

Svetlana straightened herself and emotion animated her again. It was like watching a flat tyre being pumped up. 'The hypocrisy of the State,' she hissed. 'The utter hypocrisy of the government.'

'Ah,' Oksana said. 'Because they wouldn't give Natasha the benefit of the doubt all these years even though she sacrificed her life for her country?'

Svetlana shook her head. 'No,' she answered sharply, 'because it was the government that killed her.'

A shiver ran down Lily's spine. 'What do you mean?'

Svetlana raised her eyes to Lily's and enunciated every word clearly. 'It wasn't the Germans that executed her. Government agents killed her mercilessly without a trial. The President and Prime Minister may not be aware of that, but someone in the government must know the truth. It will be there somewhere, tucked away in their files.'

Lily froze. She was now privy to information that could get her into trouble. Russia was more open than it used to be but possessing that sort of knowledge still put her and Oksana in danger. But she couldn't stop at this point. She had to know what had happened.

'The government killed Natasha?' she repeated. 'But, Svetlana, why would they have killed one of the Soviet Union's best pilots in the middle of a war?'

TWENTY-ONE

Kursk, 1943

In the spring of 1943, the German forces prepared for an attack on Kursk, a city south of Moscow. They called in air units from France and Norway as well as from parts of the Russian front. The Luftwaffe wanted to regain their supremacy in the skies, but the Soviet Air Force was now a foe to be reckoned with. We were experienced in combat and our factories were producing planes rapidly and of improved design.

As a squadron commander, one of my roles was to train the new pilots who joined our regiment. I chose for my wingman a sergeant by the name of Filipp Dudko. I had perfected two manoeuvres: one was a climbing spiral that I used to evade attack; and the other was a snap roll that tricked a pursuing plane into overshooting and so becoming my victim. I needed a wingman who could stay with me no matter what I did. Filipp had quick reflexes, but something about him concerned me. Once, when we were on patrol, I spotted German Focke-Wulfs strafing a supply road. I led the squadron to a higher altitude so we could swoop down on the enemy aircraft. Our attack resulted in a fierce dogfight. Filipp kept my rear covered and we were able to scatter the planes. I was pleased with his performance, but when the squadron returned to the airfield and the pilots recounted the fight, Filipp was puzzled.

'Was there a fight?' he asked. 'I thought it was an impromptu training exercise.'

He hadn't seen the enemy planes.

'It's a common problem with inexperienced pilots — and even experienced ones,' Colonel Smirnov assured me. 'Dudko will develop the ability to see approaching planes with practice. At least he didn't get himself separated from you or move into your firing position. You've made a good choice with him.'

There weren't bunkers at our new airfield, which had been hurriedly built in anticipation of the push, and we were billeted in a village that had been liberated from the Germans. The house where Svetlana, Dominika, Alisa and I were staying was next door to where Valentin and Colonel Smirnov were billeted. I could see Valentin's room from the attic of the house and sometimes I climbed up there to wave to him. Once, as a joke, he made signals to me using a mirror. But Colonel Smirnov caught him and threatened to throw him in the guardhouse. Valentin and I were in love but we were in the middle of a war. There were rare moments when we snatched a swim together in a river or made love, but most of the time our minds were engaged in fighting the enemy. I wanted to defeat the Germans quickly so that we could return to Moscow and begin a new life together.

The house where we were billeted was owned by a woman named Ludmila who treated us with kindness. She put flowers in our room and gave us more food than the air force paid her for. She was fascinated by the idea of women combatants and when Alisa and I returned to the house at the end of the day she would ask us about our missions. If either of us had shot down a plane, Ludmila would want a blow-by-blow account of the fight. Nothing pleased her more than the idea that we'd killed Germans. At the same time she would fret, 'They shouldn't have sent young girls like you to the front.'

One day, when Svetlana and I were about to go to the bathhouse to clean up, Ludmila called to us. 'Come, I want to show you something.' She led us to a house on the outskirts of the village. 'My sister lives here,' she informed us, knocking on the door.

A woman younger than Ludmila answered and introduced herself as Rada. I thought that we were there to collect eggs or berries, but Rada had another reason for inviting us into her home. She showed us into the kitchen where the fire had been lit. Sitting by it was a young woman. Her head moved erratically from side to side and her tongue hung out of her mouth. In the apartment building in the Arbat where I had lived with my family, there had been a boy like that; he'd been born with the umbilical cord wrapped around his neck.

I expected Rada to ask us if we could obtain something for the girl — clothing, medicine, some item of food not available in the village. Instead she reached up to a shelf and handed us a framed photograph. It was a picture of a young girl about sixteen years old; a true Slavic beauty with high cheekbones and long blonde hair.

'That was Faina before the war,' Ludmila said.

Rada wiped her hand over her face. 'My beautiful Faina, my beautiful girl,' she said, her voice breaking.

Svetlana and I looked to Ludmila for an explanation.

'When the Germans occupied our village they would take Faina to the woods,' Ludmila said. 'Rada used to try to hide her but the Germans threatened to kill the whole village, children and all, if she wasn't surrendered. Even on the day of their retreat, the Germans couldn't leave Faina alone. They raped her and then bashed her head with a rock.'

The story made me sick to the stomach.

Ludmila pointed to the pistols that Svetlana and I wore on our belts. 'Promise me something, my courageous daughters. If either of you is ever in danger of being captured, you must shoot yourself rather than be taken prisoner by those monsters.'

Faina's story made Svetlana morbid. In our room that evening she asked me, 'Could you do it? Could you kill yourself?'

I didn't tell her that I'd come close to having to do so a few days earlier when my plane was shot down and I'd had to crash-land in German-held territory. I just managed to pull myself from the wreckage when I heard trucks and voices heading in my direction. Fortunately for me, Filipp had seen me go down and landed his plane next to my wrecked one. I'd squeezed myself onto the floor of his cockpit and he'd whisked me away before the Germans arrived.

To steel their nerves and intimidate the enemy, the pilots in our regiment liked to paint emblems on their planes. The high-scoring aces painted crosses on their cowlings to represent the kills they'd made, while others painted tiger stripes or jaws with sharp teeth. One of the pilots offered to paint a sapphire on my fuselage but Colonel Smirnov forbade it.

'The German command knows who you are, Comrade Lieutenant. Believe me! German men do not like to be bested by women and there is a high price on your head. Keep the advantage of anonymity on your side. Your talent as a pilot is more useful to the Motherland than your celebrity.'

It wasn't only the Germans we had to fear. Each regiment had attached to it a political officer. Their role was to make sure that everything we discussed was in keeping with Communist ideology and no one was voicing 'incorrect opinions'. When I was with the 586th regiment, the political officer was a woman. Although she disseminated Communist material and gave classes in ideology, she was also concerned about how we coped with separation from our families. In Stalingrad, we'd had a male political officer who, while not concerned with our emotional states, wasn't particularly attentive to our beliefs either. At our new airfield, the political officer was a man named Lipovsky and I didn't like him. He watched everything I did. 'You are old enough to progress from Komsomol membership to full Communist Party participation,' he told me one day. 'Why have you not done so?' Potential Party members had their backgrounds checked thoroughly. If I were to apply for Party membership, my father's record would be uncovered. Fortunately, Colonel Smirnov intervened.

'Let her focus on the war first,' he told Lipovsky. 'You can see that she fights like a good Communist for the Motherland. When the war is over, she can think about politics.'

With Lipovsky lurking around, I had to be careful. I was discreet about my little icon of St Sofia, which I kept hidden in my pocket. I crossed myself before take-off only when I was sure that Lipovsky wasn't looking. I couldn't afford trouble.

In the middle of July our regiment was moved closer to Orёl to assist the Soviet ground forces' advance on German lines. Every inch of land was fiercely contested. We kept pressure on the enemy. One day we would gain air supremacy, then the next day the Germans would win it back. We flew so many sorties a day that I felt like a coiled spring that was being pulled tight. Valentin and I had hardly a moment together. Sometimes we would snatch a kiss and then part with a smile that said 'after the war'.

Colonel Smirnov called the regiment together one evening to tell us that the Germans had brought to the battle one of their best aces, the Black Diamond. He was an efficient killer with over ninety victories to his name.

The colonel explained his technique to us. 'The Black Diamond avoids dogfights,' he said. 'He uses the element of surprise and moves perilously close to his target before firing, preventing the pilot from taking evasive action. Of course, I don't encourage the newer pilots to adopt the Black Diamond's technique. Debris from the plane you've destroyed can catch you too. The Black Diamond has gone down a few times, but only because he's been hit by debris. He's never been downed by one of us.'

One day Filipp and I were flying on patrol with Alisa and her wingman when we spotted German Junkers accompanied by fighters heading towards our troops. We had the advantage of altitude and I instructed Alisa and her wingman to engage the fighters while Filipp and I attacked the bombers. I couldn't protect Filipp forever. He needed combat experience. I ordered him to get into the firing position and to take aim at the outermost Junker. I saw he kept his nerve and waited until he was in a good position before firing. He hit the Junker, which burst into flames and broke apart. Flaming debris spun to the ground.

'Don't stare at it,' I told him over the radio. 'Watch your back.'

I passed above the bombers and turned around, intending to help Filipp make another strike on the Junkers. Something made me look rearwards. Approaching from behind was a Messerschmitt that hadn't been part of the fighter formation. Where had he come from? Out of the sun? I knew who it was. I was glad Filipp wasn't with me: he would have missed seeing the Black Diamond for sure. Unfortunately for the German ace, he had chosen for his target a pilot who had spotted him in plenty of time.

I turned my plane hard before he was close enough to take a fatal shot and swung around behind him. The hunter was now the prey. 'So you don't like to fight, Black Diamond?' I said. 'You like to have it your way.'

The Black Diamond threw himself around the sky with me on his tail. I was determined to down him. The Black Diamond sensed that too. He tried to lure me over the frontline and closer to the ground, where I'd be vulnerable to anti-aircraft fire.

I pushed my plane to maximum speed, lined the Black Diamond up in my sights and hit my gun button. The bullets sprayed along his fuselage. At first I thought they hadn't penetrated the armour but then smoke began to pour out of the engine and the Black Diamond's plane went into a dive.

I flew upwards to avoid fire from the ground and circled to see what had happened. The Messerschmitt was heading for a field a short distance over the line. Why doesn't he bail out, I wondered. Then I realised that the Black Diamond intended to save his plane and land it. At that speed he'd surely be killed.

To my astonishment he landed without it breaking up. I circled again and saw him climb out of the cockpit, unhurt. But there weren't any troops to protect him where he had landed. He watched me swooping towards him and, with no escape possible, straightened himself, presenting his chest to take my fatal bullets.

At the beginning of the war, downing an enemy plane was enough of a victory. Now the war was a bloody battle where every factor counted. But as I approached, I saw that the Black Diamond was a handsome man. Not in an Aryan way; instead, he was tall and dark like my brother, Alexander, had been, with a broad chest and hefty legs like tree trunks. He lifted his hand to his forehead and saluted me. I switched on the FIRE button, but I couldn't press it. I held the Black Diamond's gaze for a moment, then I returned his salute and climbed high into the sky.

The shock of the encounter wore off when I returned to the airfield, and the magnitude of my blunder hit me. Valentin had returned from another mission and he and Sharavin were examining the damage to his plane. I taxied alongside them. Valentin's Yak was riddled with bullet holes and the tail badly dented. It was a miracle he had made it back to the airfield. I didn't know if I had been unable to shoot the Black Diamond because of his resemblance to my brother or whether simple weariness had clouded my judgement. But I realised that in not finishing him off, I had left a dangerous beast roaming in the forest; one that could kill my beloved Valentin.

When I wrote out my report, I didn't claim the Black Diamond as a victory, although to have done so would have earned me another medal and much glory. When Alisa asked me about the plane I had pursued, I told her that it had got away.

My error in judgement had left me with much to worry about. Only the previous week news had come to us that some inexperienced pilots of Pe-2 bombers had accidentally attacked our own ground troops. Those responsible had been shot as traitors. I'd known that those pilots hadn't betrayed the Soviet Union. Most likely they'd made navigational mistakes because they weren't used to the intensity of combat. If anyone had seen me spare the Black Diamond — nearby ground troops, talkative peasants, a pilot on another mission — and Lipovsky found out, I'd be shot too.

*

Early the following morning, I was called into readiness-one and sat in the cockpit of my plane with Svetlana next to me on the wing. The heat of the day hadn't reached its peak and we took turns reading to each other from *Anna Karenina*, although we skipped the parts where the characters ate lavish meals. We missed Ludmila and her cooking. At our new base we were back to eating in a mess bunker and sometimes, when the fighting was intense and it was difficult for supplies to reach us, we had soup with bread for all our meals. Lately, we had only had bread and soup once a day. It was not enough sustenance for us to maintain the strength we needed for fighting. Our airbase was surrounded by fields of sunflowers that had gone unharvested, and the pilots and mechanics alike would gather the seeds in our breaks for the cook to add to the bread. We collected mushrooms and berries too, but it was risky to venture into the forest in case of mines.

I looked up from the novel for a moment and surveyed the sky. Valentin had left on a sortie with Colonel Smirnov and six other pilots to cover ground troops during an advance. By reading I could keep my mind off worrying about him. I wished that I'd gone as his wingman that morning. I could protect him from the Black Diamond if he was up there. And if for some reason I didn't see the German in time, I would cover Valentin with my own plane and take the bullets for him.

The din of engines interrupted my thoughts, and Svetlana and I turned to see the planes returning. These days, to come back from a mission was triumph enough and I waited to see if the planes would do a victory pass over the airfield. But they landed straight away and from a high altitude. Something was wrong. I counted the planes: seven. One was missing. Whose?

I wasn't supposed to leave my plane when I was in readiness-one but alarm bells were ringing in my head. I loosened my parachute and jumped down from the cockpit, straining my eyes to see the numbers on the planes. It was Colonel Smirnov's Yak that hadn't returned.

Valentin struggled out of his cockpit and staggered towards the hangar. He said something to Sharavin that made the mechanic's shoulders slump.

'Valentin!' I called, running after him.

He turned, his face deathly pale. 'Leonid ... Colonel Smirnov ... he went down in flames.'

Everything became hazy. I couldn't speak. The look of despair in Valentin's eyes was unbearable.

'He fought to the end, Natasha,' he said. 'He aimed his plane for a German transport truck on his way down. I heard his screams on the radio as he was burning alive. He begged me to look after his wife and his infant son.'

A feeling, like a cold shadow, swept over me. 'Valentin, did a fighter shoot him down or was it ground fire that got him?'

Valentin held my gaze. 'It was the Black Diamond. The Black Diamond killed Colonel Smirnov.'

Valentin was made regimental commander and I was in a dilemma. The fighting had grown even more intense and Valentin needed every bit of his mental and emotional strength to focus on the task. Should I tell him about the Black Diamond in an attempt to alleviate my conscience, but risk him making errors in judgement that could cost other lives? I decided not to, for the same reason that I'd never told him about my father's arrest and execution. Sometimes ignorance kept you safe. If I was arrested, at least Valentin could say that he didn't know about my past or the Black Diamond. It wasn't guaranteed to save him — but it might. I had no choice but to stay quiet.

Yet I was doomed.

I realised it one evening when I was heading towards my bunker after the last sortie of the day. Walking through a field of sunflowers to reach it, I caught a glimpse through the stalks of a black car on the other side and a man standing next to it, watching me. Our eyes met and my blood turned to ice. I knew the first time I saw him that I would not forget his gaunt face, red hair and cold eyes. It was the NKVD officer who had arrested my father.

As we stared at each other in recognition, I was tempted to fall to my knees and beg him to have mercy. If I must die, then let me die for the Motherland and not for crimes against the State. But when he turned away and climbed back into his car, I knew it was finished. My arrest warrant had been signed and my execution was imminent.

TWENTY-TWO

Moscow, 2000

After Natasha's funeral, Orlov sat in a restaurant on Kutuzovsky Prospekt with his son, Leonid. Lost in his own thoughts, he hardly took in the orange interior or the cuckoo clock that chimed every fifteen minutes, or the smells of tobacco smoke and pork that lingered in the air. After fifty-seven years he had completed his quest: his beloved Natasha was buried and her honour restored. His work in space exploration was finished, his wife was dead, his son was a grown man. What was left for him now but to await his death? He wasn't afraid of it. Orlov often thought that he had lived too long and should have died in the war like Natasha and Leonid Smirnov.

His son, sensing Orlov's need for silence, ordered him beetroot salad and fish soup, and the grilled salmon with mashed potato for himself. He then occupied himself with reading the menu as if it were a fascinating novel.

Orlov turned over in his mind the last twenty-four hours before Natasha had disappeared, as if he might discover some fresh clue that he hadn't recalled before. The death of Colonel Smirnov had hit him hard but he hadn't allowed himself to grieve. He had an enemy to fight and a regiment that was now dependent on his leadership. There had been no time to rest as he coordinated attacks with other units, then flew missions himself. He'd hardly seen Natasha in those last days. She was one of the few surviving combat pilots with experience and he had relied on her to lead the most dangerous sorties.

The evening before she'd disappeared, Orlov had received an unexpected visitor. Spent from the day's fighting, he had returned to his private bunker and switched on the light. The stature and moustache of the man who had been waiting in the dark weren't familiar but the red hair and troubled eyes were. Orlov thought he was seeing a ghost. It was Fyodor, a man now, but unmistakable to Orlov, who had loved his brother.

'I've done all I can to protect you,' Fyodor told him. Orlov was too overwhelmed by the return of his brother to make sense of his words. It had been twenty years since he had seen Fyodor. What had happened to him in that time?

'When you push the Germans back into their own country, don't return over the border,' Fyodor told him. 'Get out. Do you understand what I'm saying? Don't return to the Soviet Union. Take your fiancée with you.'

'My fiancée?'

Fyodor leaned against Orlov's desk and pulled the stub of a cigarette from his pocket. He lit it and offered it to Orlov. When Orlov declined, Fyodor took a few puffs before extinguishing the cigarette again.

'Natalya Azarova,' he said. 'Don't think we don't know. We know everything.'

'We?' asked Orlov, sitting down on his bunk. His head was spinning.

'The NKVD,' replied Fyodor.

Orlov's cool-headedness returned. So his brother was an NKVD agent? His gaze moved to Fyodor's hands. They were trembling. His brother hadn't come to reminisce about the past.

'Stalin has wavered over signing an arrest warrant for Natalya Azarova many times,' Fyodor continued. 'He authorised her father's execution without batting an eyelid, but he had a soft spot for her and left her alone. I don't know why. He doesn't show pity even for his own family. Natalya slipping through the cracks after her father's death might have been overlooked, but for her to reappear as an ace pilot and heroine of the war is a provocation.'

Fyodor explained: 'Her father was the chief chocolatier at the Red October factory. A harmless man who was in no way an enemy of the people. He was collateral in Stalin's war of paranoia.'

Orlov had sensed that Natasha possessed a secret. But now the portrait of Stalin she hung above her bed was even more mystifying. Didn't she know that Stalin was responsible for her father's death?

'Surely the NKVD isn't planning to arrest her now?' Orlov asked his brother. 'She's one of the top pilots of the air force! This regiment will go to pieces without her!'

Fyodor looked at him and sighed. 'If only logic were part of it. But the Kremlin takes a different view. Children of enemies of the people aren't supposed to amount to anything. Imagine if Natalya Azarova were to publicly announce that she is the daughter of a saboteur!'

Orlov rubbed his face. It was madness. Pure madness. Here they were on the point of defeating the Germans and Stalin was concerned about whether people were going to embarrass him or not.

'Nothing will happen now,' Fyodor said. 'Natalya Azarova's picture is pasted in the scrapbook of every schoolgirl. Stalin can't afford to dishearten the Soviet people. But after the war ... well, none of you heroes will be spared. I've been in Stalin's inner circle long enough to know how he operates. You are competing with him for glory and he'll get rid of you all. He's already marked out Marshal Zhukov.'

'Zhukov!' Orlov stood and paced the floor. 'Stalin should be kissing Zhukov's arse! Every citizen saw that we were going to be attacked by Hitler's forces sooner or later, but it came as a complete surprise to our great leader! If it wasn't for Zhukov turning things around, the Germans would have finished us off by now!'

Fyodor grimaced. 'Look, Valentin, the only person who will be credited with winning this war will be Stalin. The only heroes allowed will be dead ones.'

Fyodor picked up the jacket and hat he had left on Orlov's desk.

Orlov frowned. 'You're leaving?'

'I have to. I took risks to come here so listen to my advice.' Then, as he had done the day that he'd left Orlov at the orphanage, Fyodor embraced his brother and kissed his cheeks. 'When you get over the Soviet border, don't come back,' he repeated. With those words, he again departed from Orlov's life.

After Fyodor's visit, Orlov recalled, he wanted to rush to Natasha's bunker to warn her. He had no reason to stay in the Soviet Union; he would escape with her across the border when they entered Germany if that would keep her safe. But he was halted by an order from the air-control HQ. The entire regiment was to be ready for combat in a few hours. Things sounded ominous. Orlov spent the rest of the night marking maps with Captain Panchenko.

The following morning, he appointed Alisa leader of Natasha's squadron and took Natasha as his wingman. He was acutely aware that he could be killed in the next couple of hours and he had to tell her what Fyodor had said.

The Germans didn't attack in the morning as expected. What were they waiting for? The pilots sat in readiness-one in their planes on the runway, becoming tired and thirsty as the day grew hotter. The control sticks burned their hands when they touched them. They must move to a hut on the side of the runway, Orlov decided. It meant they would have to dash for their planes when they were called to combat, but he saw no point sending his pilots into the skies dehydrated and with white spots before their eyes when the time came.

In one way the delay was a stroke of good fortune because it would be easier to speak to Natasha in the crowded hut than it would be out on the runway. The regiment was used to Natasha and Orlov putting their heads together and talking softly. Orlov sat down next to her, ready to begin his explanation, but he was distracted by her obvious unease. Her fists kept opening and closing and there were dark circles under her eyes.

'Are you unwell, Natasha?' he asked her. 'I can take Bogomolov with me instead.'

Natasha flinched at the suggestion she should be replaced. 'No.'

Then for some reason Orlov could not comprehend, she started to talk about Stalin and the time she'd met him. Orlov should have kept his cool and heard her out, but he too was agitated. 'Listen, Natasha,' he said. 'There is something you should know. Stalin personally signed your father's execution order.'

Natasha's face crumpled and a look Orlov had never seen before came into her eyes. She drew away from him and into herself. He immediately regretted his haste but what else could he have done? He had only a brief opportunity to destroy her misplaced faith in that madman. But it was too late for him to explain more. The order for combat came. They had to scramble.

Sharavin and Svetlana were waiting for them on the runway by the planes. They helped them into their parachute harnesses and into their cockpits. Orlov tried to catch Natasha's eye but she wouldn't look at him. She turned to say something to Svetlana but the flares went up. They headed down the runway as a pair and lifted into the sky. It was the last battle they would fight together.

'You loved her, didn't you?'

Orlov glanced up to see Leonid staring at him. The waitress arrived and placed their food before them. Orlov stalled for time by picking at his salad. When Natasha didn't return, he'd searched for her frantically. He would have gone on searching even at risk to himself if the political officer, Lipovsky, hadn't interfered and had him transferred to a regiment fighting in Romania. He looked at Leonid. His son was a grown man. No, more than a grown man, Orlov realised: he was ageing. Yet Orlov couldn't separate his adult son from the boy he'd wanted to protect. He shifted uncomfortably, his natural aloofness and his wish to be kind to Leonid warring within him. If he wasn't prepared to tell Leonid the truth now, when did he intend to do so? Then he realised that Leonid hadn't asked a question; he'd made a statement.

'How long have you known?' Orlov asked him.

Leonid smiled with a tenderness that stabbed Orlov's heart. 'Papa, I've always known.'

Orlov's lip quivered. He was uncomfortable with Leonid's sympathy. He did not deserve it.

'Your mother was a good woman,' he said. 'And your father was the best man I've ever met. I wish you could have known him.'

'You're the only father I've known,' Leonid said.

'Yes, I suppose that's true.' Orlov opened the serviette, which had been folded like an opera fan, and placed it on his lap. 'A poor excuse for one,' he muttered. 'I was always working.'

The men fell into silence as they ate. Orlov thought about his brother again. For years he had thought Fyodor must have defected to the West, or that he was still with the secret police protecting him, because Orlov was never arrested. Then, when Orlov was selected to train pilots for the space programme, he was given access to his brother's file. He discovered that in 1943, not long after Fyodor had visited him at the airfield, his brother's body was found floating in the Moscow River. In his pocket was a list of the people he'd arrested over the years, with the words 'Forgive me' written next to each. Stepan Vladimirovich Azarov's name was on it. With Fyodor's death, Orlov lost the last member of his family.

'Khrushchev wasn't insane like Stalin, but he was ruthless,' he said. 'When your mother's cousin defected to the United States and wrote critical things about the Soviet Union, Khrushchev wanted revenge. He persecuted other members of the family.'

'Khrushchev liked you,' said Leonid, repeating the story his mother must have told him. 'So you married Mama to save her — and me.'

Orlov sighed. He was like a prisoner in his own head. He was full of remorse and yet he'd done the best he could at the time. He had helped Yelena financially after the war and made attempts to be a father figure to Leonid, but her critical situation needed decisive action. Natasha had been missing for ten years by then. Orlov had never let go of the hope that she would return to him, but he thought she would understand why he'd had to marry Yelena and adopt Leonid. He couldn't bear for Colonel Smirnov's wife to end up in a labour camp and his son sent to an orphanage. But it hadn't been easy. He had found it difficult to be physical with Yelena, although she was still a young woman and must have yearned for affection. He felt unfaithful to Natasha and as though he was betraying Leonid's father.

'I've wasted my life,' Orlov said.

Leonid looked surprised. 'You were one of the developers of the space programme. You made the impossible happen. You are a fighter-ace hero of the war —'

'What do those things matter?' Orlov interrupted, pushing aside his soup. 'I was a terrible father and an inadequate husband. I was never there for either of you.'

'You're hard on yourself,' replied Leonid. 'You risked your position to save us. Yes, you were often away working in a job that you weren't allowed to talk about, not even to your family. But there were good things too. You always spoke gently to Mama and kindly to me, you took me on adventures in the woods around our dacha, and you encouraged me to do well at school.'

'Dear God, Leonid! A nanny could have done those things for you! I wanted to ... be more involved but I felt paralysed.'

'Maybe as a child I wished you had been around more, but now I'm a father myself I understand. No matter what good parents we hope to be, we will always have our own human frailties to deal with. You did your best. You lost your family in the Civil War, you were brought up in an orphanage, you only knew military life, you fought in a war where twenty-seven million of your countrymen died, including the woman you loved. Considering all that, it's amazing you turned out to be so decent!'

Orlov looked at Leonid incredulously. Who was this fine, compassionate man? Was this little Leonid all grown up? Orlov appraised his son with new eyes.

'You are all Yelena,' he said. 'I'm glad you had each other. If what I did kept the two of you together, then maybe I didn't waste my life after all.'

Leonid drove Orlov back to his apartment. They were silent on the journey, but when Leonid parked outside the building and opened the door for his father he said, 'Irina wants you to come to live with us. I'd like that too.'

Orlov waved off the suggestion. 'Leonid, I'm eighty-three years old. Your family doesn't want some useless old man hanging around.'

'*Your* family,' said Leonid. 'And yes we do. Nina and Anton often talk about you. They would both like to know you better.'

Orlov was bewildered that Leonid could be so generous to him. He didn't intend to take up the offer, but something in him wanted to hug his son, to thank him for his forgiveness.

After Natasha disappeared he had never confided to anyone that he had loved her, although of course Yelena guessed it. He was grateful Leonid had allowed him to admit it. Somehow it made him feel Natasha was alive again.

He stepped forward to embrace his son, but old habits prevented him from showing affection and he stopped short as if he'd walked into a wall. Instead he reached out his hand, took Leonid's arm and squeezed it.

TWENTY-THREE

Moscow, 2000

Lily sensed that she'd opened a Pandora's box with her question to Svetlana. But she just didn't know what would unfold because of it.

Svetlana's eyes turned dark. 'Why would the government have killed one of the Soviet Union's best pilots in the middle of a war?' she repeated with a bitter smile.

'Stalin was a monster. He could treat you with such warmth one moment and the next sign your arrest warrant without a second glance. His favourite game was to make his victims fear that they were about to be arrested and then shower them with gifts and favours. Then, having lulled them into a false sense of security, he would send the NKVD to arrest them. He did that to Natasha's father, who was a kind and generous man. When Stalin paid someone attention, it was like the light in heaven shone upon them. But when he turned cold, that person was doomed.'

Svetlana exhaled a long rattling breath. Lily didn't like the sound of it. Oksana took her hand. 'Don't go on now. Rest. We can talk about this later — and only if you want to.'

But Svetlana now couldn't be stopped. Her story was bursting out of her.

When Natasha didn't return from her mission and there were no reports of a Soviet plane being downed on our side, I couldn't stand idly by. I went to look for her.

'What are you doing?' Sharavin demanded when he caught me packing a knapsack with food and supplies.

'I'm going to find Natasha.'

'Don't be stupid!' he told me.

I knew Captain Orlov wouldn't give me permission to leave the airfield so I didn't ask him. I could have been shot as a deserter. Sharavin only let me go because he didn't think that I would have enough courage to get past the Russian sentries, let alone the German guards. He expected me to return in a few hours. But I was determined to find my friend. I moved across the frontline, avoiding both the Russian and German patrols. I met a partisan group operating in the German territory and when I told them who I was searching for they willingly helped me.

We travelled the rest of the night, and when morning came they took me to a safe house while they made inquiries among the villagers about any Soviet plane to fly over or be shot down. The villagers told them that indeed a Soviet plane had come down, in the vicinity of the Trofimovsky Forest. The partisans had much to do in preparation for the Soviet advance, so they assigned a peasant to help me on my search.

'Be careful,' the villagers warned me. 'You're not the only one looking for a Soviet pilot. Several farms in the area have been searched by the Germans.'

The peasant and I were making our way through the forest at dusk when we heard voices. Something was going on in the trees ahead of us. The peasant held me back.

My eyes sought out a group of people not a hundred metres away from us. I saw a kneeling figure dressed in a Russian Air Force uniform and realised it was Natasha. A man in civilian clothes stood behind her, pointing a gun at the back of her head. I rose up to scream but the peasant pulled me down and covered my mouth with his hand. A single shot rang out into the night air and the men moved quickly away.

I struggled from my companion's grip and ran towards Natasha, but in my panic I slammed into a low branch and knocked myself out. I came to after a minute or so, but I'd hit my forehead so hard that I was nauseous and confused. The peasant lifted me over his shoulder and I passed out again. The next thing I knew, I awoke in a house in a nearby village.

'Listen, the NKVD has executed Natalya Azarova,' the peasant told me. 'There are Russian spies operating all over the enemy territory. You can't trust anybody. Her body wasn't there when I checked this morning. They must have come back and removed her, or the Germans found her.'

When I realised that Natasha was dead, and that she had been murdered by the Soviet government, my strength drained away. I knew why the NKVD had killed her. Someone had found out that her father had been executed as an enemy of the people. There were thousands of people with that record in the armed services but they weren't famous fighter aces venerated by the Soviet people. Natasha had to be eliminated. When neither her body nor her plane were found, it was easy to discredit her by insinuating that she'd been a German spy.

*

Oksana was staring at Svetlana open-mouthed. 'But then what happened to you?' she asked.

Svetlana's eyes filled with tears. Laika rested her head on her mistress's knee as if to comfort her.

'After Natasha's death, I couldn't return to my regiment,' she said. 'I couldn't bear to work for the Soviet Air Force or to be a mechanic for another pilot. If I was going to be part of the war effort, then it was going to be for the people and not for the government. I stayed with the partisans and they gave me the identity of a village woman, Zinaida Glebovna Rusakova, who had died a few years earlier. I helped them by smuggling messages and repairing equipment. The Russians were advancing rapidly by now and the Germans were becoming even more ruthless. Our group was betrayed by a village spy. The leaders were hanged and I was arrested and sent to Auschwitz.'

Auschwitz! In her mind, Lily saw skeletal figures, furnaces and piles of clothing. She didn't have to ask what had happened to Svetlana there. She could only wonder how anyone survived the place.

Oksana tightened her grip on Svetlana's hand. 'Thank you, dear woman, for sharing this very sad story with us. It's been a draining day for you and I think you should rest. As Lily and I promised, we will keep your story to ourselves. Thank you for trusting us with it. I hope in some way it helps you to know that there are people who know the truth.'

On the way home, Oksana and Lily stopped off at the building site in Zamoskvorechye to feed the colony cats.

'Parts of Svetlana's story don't ring true,' Oksana said to Lily when they got back in the car. 'While it's plausible the partisans helped her to find Natasha, it's too much of a coincidence that she and the peasant discovered her at the moment the NKVD carried out its execution.'

'I was thinking the same thing,' said Lily. 'But the pain in Svetlana's voice was genuine. Something happened but maybe not the way she described.'

Back in her apartment, Lily mulled over Svetlana's story while cleaning the kitchen and sorting her washing. She noticed Laika watching her. 'What about you?' she asked, looking into the dog's eyes. 'Do you know something I don't?'

She was jolted back to reality by the telephone ringing. She picked up the receiver. 'Hello?'

'Lily? It's Luka. The hotel said you'd taken the day off so I thought I'd try you at home.'

'I wanted to see the funeral of Natalya Azarova this morning. The book you lent me was fascinating.'

'Well, that's a coincidence,' Luka said. 'I told Yefim about your interest and he said he has some new information from the files. Would you like to join us for dinner? He lives in the Bogorodskoye district and I know a good Georgian restaurant there. I can pick you up.'

Lily felt instantly alert. 'What time?'

As Lily and Luka entered the restaurant, Lily hoped Yefim would tell her something that she didn't already know. She had finished his book in three nights. It was engagingly written, but Lily had heard the story from someone who had known Natasha personally. Could Yefim have found anything new in the Kremlin files? Was the government really so much more open these days?

The restaurant's interior was rustic with wooden tables and stone walls. Yefim was waiting for them in a booth in the corner. Lily took a liking to him straight away; with his smiling face, dishevelled hair, and the fleshy body of someone who spent a lot of time in libraries, he gave the impression of being intelligent yet approachable. Whether or not he could tell her anything new about Natalya Azarova, she sensed their conversation that evening would be interesting.

'You speak Russian perfectly,' Yefim said to Lily after Luka had introduced them and they'd made small talk about Australia and Russia. 'I was worried I was going to have to struggle with my poor English.'

'My parents are Russians who were born in China,' Lily explained. 'They went to Australia after the Communist takeover. I spoke English at school, of course, but at home we spoke Russian.'

They ordered a Georgian salad, stuffed eggplants and red beans with coriander and garlic.

'The *khachos khinkali* are very good here,' Luka told them.

Lily looked at the menu and saw that *khachos khinkali* were dumplings filled with ricotta and mint. 'They must eat well in Georgia,' she said. 'That sounds delicious!'

'Lily read your book about Natalya Azarova and watched the funeral on television today,' Luka said to Yefim after the food arrived. 'Did you discover anything new in the Kremlin files?'

'Yes and no,' replied Yefim, heaping some beans onto his plate. 'The Soviets destroyed information as they pleased but the Kremlin archivist was helpful and I believe she handed me everything that was available on Natalya Azarova. She also gave me the file on her father, Stepan Azarov. The most intriguing thing was what I learned about Natalya Azarova's mechanic during the war — Svetlana Novikova.'

Lily's heart skipped a beat.

'And what was that?' asked Luka, passing the eggplant dish around.

'She and Azarova went to school together before the war. Their families knew each other.'

Lily let out a breath and tried not to show her disappointment. She wasn't at liberty to reveal anything she'd learned from Svetlana but there was a childish part of her that wanted to say, 'I could have told you that!'

Yefim took a sip of wine before continuing. 'It was Novikova's father who denounced Stepan Azarov to the NKVD. He accused Azarov of praising foreign countries and mocking the Soviet system of production. He even insinuated that Azarov was spying for France.'

Time stood still for Lily. 'Stepan Azarov was arrested because of Novikova's father's report?' she asked.

'Oh, it gets worse than that,' said Yefim. 'After Azarov was arrested and his family was evicted from their apartment, Novikova's family moved in. The apartment was a reward for Azarov's denunciation. Natalya and her family had to live in communal housing.'

Lily struggled to absorb the new information. Svetlana hadn't said anything about that, but she had said that she had a dark secret: it was clear what that was now.

'Yefim,' Lily began, thinking about how to ask her question without giving away something that wasn't in his book, 'I imagine the relationship between a pilot and their mechanic is very close in a combat situation. Do you think Natalya Azarova ever found out what Novikova's family had done?'

Yefim shrugged. 'I don't know. I doubt it, don't you? Could you be friends with someone whose family had destroyed yours?'

For dessert, Yefim recommended walnut cake accompanied by fresh mint tea. Lily's thoughts raced around in circles. What Svetlana's parents had done cast a strange interpretation over everything Svetlana had said about her friendship with Natasha.

It also highlighted the niggling doubt Lily had about whether the NKVD had really killed Natasha. Perhaps Yefim would know something about that.

'It's still a mystery who actually killed Natalya Azarova, isn't it?' she ventured. 'Did you find anything in the files that told you more about her death?'

'No,' he replied. 'But I tend to agree with the Ministry of Defence's conclusion that she was shot by the Germans.'

Again Lily was careful how she framed her next question. 'Is it possible that Natalya Azarova was killed by the NKVD?'

Yefim stared at her before breaking into a smile. 'So you have read the article by Vladimir Zassoursky and his conspiracy theory? He claims that the three planes that chased Natalya Azarova into enemy territory were captured Messerschmitts flown by Russian agents.'

The waitress set out their tea and cake slices on the table. Yefim waited for her to leave before adding, 'In any other country that might be a laughable theory, but Russia has a history of bizarre political assassinations. Personally, however, I don't believe that's what happened in Natalya Azarova's case.'

'Why not?' Luka asked.

Yefim took a sip of tea. 'There is no doubt that Azarova was being watched by the NKVD. But everyone was being watched by the NKVD in those days. Famous pilots like Natalya Azarova, Valery Chkalov and Alexander Pokryshkin were deified by the Soviet population. While that could be seen as a threat to Stalin, Natalya Azarova wasn't so big a target that she'd be worth that kind of elaborate operation.'

'Isn't there a theory that Valery Chkalov was bumped off after displeasing Stalin? Also that Yuri Gagarin died after his plane was tampered with on the order of a jealous Leonid Brezhnev?' asked Luka.

Yefim grinned. 'Yes, there are many conspiracy theories, but I think they stem from the idea that we don't like to believe that our heroes sometimes make stupid mistakes. There were branches of the NKVD that were assigned "black work" that left no paper trails. But think about what a strategic operation it would have been to kill Natalya Azarova in combat. You'd have to train three Russian pilots to fly German planes and then send them into enemy territory. We now know from the eyewitness report that Natalya Azarova downed two of those planes before she bailed out herself. It would have been much easier to poison her soup.'

Yefim and Luka shared a laugh. It was obvious that they enjoyed discussing the topic. But to Lily it had personal significance. She'd grown fond of Svetlana and now she wasn't sure what to believe.

'That third plane — what about that?' Luka asked his friend. 'Natalya Azarova was a prize target yet there are no military reports of a German pilot claiming the victory of downing her.'

Yefim sat back and patted his stomach. 'I guess that is why I am a boring academic and not a Hollywood director. I stick to the facts. The most plausible explanation of why that German pilot didn't claim the victory is because he never made it back to his base. The day that Natalya Azarova went down was one of the worst days of the war — confusion and exhaustion reigned. While there is no report of a German pilot claiming victory over Natalya Azarova, there are three reports of German Messerschmitts being downed by friendly fire.'

As Lily and Luka made their way to the car after saying goodbye to Yefim, Lily tried to sort out her thoughts. Why hadn't Svetlana told them that her father had denounced Natasha's father? Svetlana had hinted at a rift between herself and her mother. Maybe that was the cause of it and she hadn't mentioned it because she felt guilty.

Luka opened the car door for Lily, then went around and got into the driver's seat. 'You sure have been doing your research on Natalya Azarova!' he said. 'I'm impressed.'

He turned the key in the ignition. 'You should come on a dig with me next summer. You meet some great people: a lot of history buffs and some nutters too. You know the types — grown men who play with toy soldiers.'

'If I'm here next summer, I might,' Lily said. 'I understand your interest in relic hunting much better now.'

Luka glanced at her. 'Are you thinking that you'll go back to Australia before then?'

She shrugged. 'I don't know. I miss my parents and my friends. On the other hand, I'm not sure I'm ready to go back yet and my boss wants to extend my contract.'

Luka pulled out into the traffic. 'Oksana told me about your fiancé, Lily. I'm sorry. That must be hard.'

They passed the Elektrozavodskaya metro station, which was next on the list of stations Lily wanted to visit. She wondered if she would forever associate the Moscow Metro with her solitary weekends.

'I don't seem to be making much progress with the grief,' she confided in him. 'I still wake up hoping that none of it ever happened and then I have to spend the rest of the day living with the fact that it did.'

Luka reached over and touched her shoulder. 'Don't let anybody rush you or tell you what's right or wrong to feel,' he said. 'I deal with many people who feel ashamed about grieving over their dog or cat. I tell them that the loss of an animal companion is as real as that of any family member or close friend, and to not let anyone belittle what they're going through. In a way grief is beautiful.'

Lily turned to him. 'Grief is beautiful?' She thought it was the most dreadful feeling possible. At best she viewed the world through a haze, and at worst everything looked black.

'It means you've loved another with all your heart,' Luka said. 'What's the use of being alive if you've never loved like that, not even once?'

A sentiment like that would normally have reduced Lily to tears. But to her surprise instead of thinking about Adam she found herself thinking about Valentin Orlov. She remembered his stony face on the television. What a price he paid for loving Natalya Azarova.

The next morning Lily went to tell Oksana what she'd learned from Yefim about Svetlana. From the meowing coming from inside Oksana's apartment, she knew the cats were waiting for their breakfast.

'You're just in time to help,' Oksana said, when she opened the door.

The cats' morning meal was a chicken and vegetable stew that Oksana cooked up on weekends and stored in the freezer. She warmed the defrosted stew on the stove, spooned it into wide bowls and mixed supplements into it.

Lily placed the bowls on a tray and headed to the cats' room, which was the largest in the apartment. She opened the door to see thirty expectant faces looking at her. To house so many cats and keep things in order, Oksana had arranged plastic chairs around the room, with a cushion on each seat and another underneath the legs so each chair served as a double-storey bed. Most of the cats Oksana rescued went up for adoption on the Moscow Animals website, but she kept the older ones or those who had lost an eye or an ear, as it was much harder to find them homes. The cats that knew the routine gathered around the door, nearly tripping Lily over, but the newer arrivals waited cautiously on their chairs and stared at her. The sight always made Lily laugh: it was like walking into an audience of felines waiting to be entertained.

'Here we go, kitties,' Lily said, placing the bowls on the floor.

She checked the water dishes, and the litter trays, which were out on an enclosed balcony. The trays were children's wading pools filled with pellets Oksana made herself by soaking and drying shredded paper. 'If I feed them like clockwork they do their stools like clockwork,' she'd told Lily. Oksana was scrupulously organised with her animals. None of the neighbours complained about her cats because there were never any bad smells or fleas.

Lily looked around at the orderly room and the climbing ladders and platforms. Oksana had once said that caring well for thirty cats wasn't much different from caring well for ten. Lily loved cats but she didn't want to test that theory out.

After the cats were fed, they returned to their cushions and groomed themselves. Lily and Oksana washed the bowls and saucepan then sat down for a cup of tea in the kitchen.

'I met Luka's friend Yefim last night,' Lily told Oksana. 'He said Svetlana's father was responsible for the arrest of Natasha's father. He denounced him.'

Oksana gasped and put down her teacup. Lily could see that her friend was as stunned as she had been the night before. 'Something's certainly not right,' Oksana said finally. 'And I've been doing some investigating myself. After Svetlana told us that she'd taken the name of Zinaida Rusakova, I asked a friend in the police department if there was an address for an elderly woman by that name in Moscow. He found one. Interestingly enough, she's been reported by a neighbour as missing, though of course nobody has done anything further about it. We can go there now, if you like, and visit Svetlana afterwards. We'll leave Laika in your apartment.'

The address was for an apartment building in Kapotnya, near the oil refinery. Lily looked up at the five-storey building. It was made out of prefabricated concrete panels, like many buildings that had been hastily constructed during the housing shortage of the 1950s, and now stood dilapidated, with peeling paint and broken drainpipes. A rusted Lada, stripped of its wheels, sat in the courtyard. Svetlana's apartment was on the ground floor. It had bars on the window and the net curtains made it impossible to see inside.

'Who are you looking for?'

Lily and Oksana turned their eyes upwards. An elderly woman wearing a kerchief on her head was addressing them from a first-storey window.

'We're here on behalf of Zinaida Glebovna Rusakova,' Oksana answered. 'She's in hospital. We believe someone made a missing person's report. We came to tell them that she's unwell but she's being looked after.'

'Ah, Zina!' said the woman. 'I made that report. Just a moment. I will come down.'

A short while later she appeared at the door to the courtyard. 'Come in,' she said. 'I'm so happy to hear that Zina is alive. She hasn't been well this past year. I thought she might have dropped dead in the street and nobody knew who she was. What about her little dog, Laika?'

'She's with me. I'm looking after her,' Lily said.

The woman's relieved expression showed that she was pleased to hear that.

'I'm Oksana Alexandrovna Fyodorova and this is Lily Nickham from Australia,' Oksana explained to the woman.

'Thank you for reporting her missing. Too many elderly people become ill with no one to look out for them.'

'I'm Alina Markovna Barsukova,' said the woman. She held up a key and directed them down the corridor. 'I can show you Zina's apartment. I cleaned out the food to prevent rats but everything else is as she left it.'

The sight of bandages under Alina's dress saddened Lily. It seemed Alina shared her grandmother's affliction of ulcerated legs as well as her name.

The apartment Alina showed them into was bare but clean, with a single bed in one corner and a kitchenette in another.

'We share the bathroom down the corridor,' Alina explained. 'This place is falling down around us. Zina and I and some of the other residents put our names down for better housing but we've been on that list for ten years. I understand there are plans to tear this building down now yet nobody has told us where we're to go.'

Apart from the rose-patterned bed quilt and a red polka-dot apron with lace around the edges that hung on the armoire, the room was bare. A couple of dog-eared books — *War and Peace* and *Anna Karenina* — sat on the floor by the bed, next to two dishes that might have been Laika's food and water bowls. No pictures adorned the walls and no photographs or bric-a-brac gave away the identity of the apartment's occupant. There was no television, radio or telephone, either. What did Svetlana do with herself when she was alone?

Lily turned to Alina. 'How long has she lived here?'

'She was allocated this apartment in 1963, a few years after I arrived here. She worked at the refinery.'

'Do you know anything about her life before that?' Oksana asked.

Alina shook her head. 'Zina would never speak about her past. In fact, she hardly spoke at all. She was the quietest person in the world. She never had visitors and she never went to see anyone, not that I know of anyway. Her greatest joy came from her little dogs. She took them in as strays from the metro. Laika is two years old. The doggie before that was named Mushka and the one before that was Pchelka.'

'They're the names of dogs the Soviet space programme sent into space,' Oksana said. 'The ones who didn't come back.'

Alina shrugged. 'I don't know why she gave them those names. I always thought it was sad.'

Lily opened the armoire but it had only a couple of worn dresses inside; she and Oksana had already bought better ones for Svetlana.

With nothing else to see, Lily and Oksana took the books and apron with the intention of giving them to Svetlana. They offered the quilt, clothes and other items to Alina to give to someone in the building who might need them.

'Could you take something to Zina for me?' Alina asked.

'Of course,' replied Oksana.

Alina went to her apartment and returned with a bunch of pink carnations wrapped in newspaper. 'Tell her that everyone here misses her — especially her beautiful singing,' she added with an impish smile.

'Her singing?' asked Lily.

'Yes,' said Alina. 'She didn't sing often but when she did it was wonderful. She has such a melodious voice. I don't think she had any idea that the rest of us were listening.'

Oksana and Lily thanked Alina again and headed towards the car. Oksana was opening the door when Lily stopped in her tracks. She brought her hands to her face. Her head was spinning.

'What is it?' asked Oksana. 'Are you unwell?'

She had such a melodious voice. Lily's thoughts were flying. Pieces of things Svetlana had told them were coming together, but not in the order Svetlana had given them. She remembered the items they had seen in the apartment. The pretty quilt and the apron on the armoire, Tolstoy's books by the bed. Then she recalled the way Svetlana had spoken about Stalin: *When Stalin paid someone attention, it was like the light in heaven shone upon them. But when he turned cold, that person was doomed.* Those were the words of someone who had experienced Stalin's treachery first hand. 'Oh my God!' said Lily, leaning against the car. 'Why didn't I see it before?'

'What is it?' asked Oksana, moving towards her.

'That's not Svetlana Novikova in the hospital bed,' Lily told her. 'That's Natalya Azarova!'

Oksana looked shocked, but then understanding dawned on her face. 'You're right. But whose body did they find?'

Lily took a breath. 'I believe that was Svetlana Novikova … and that Natalya Azarova killed her.'

Polina was on duty at the hospital. 'Thank goodness you're here,' she said when she saw Lily and Oksana. 'I left messages on both your answering machines. Svetlana hasn't been at all well today. She won't eat or drink and she refuses to tell me what's wrong. I believe she's upset about the funeral. If she doesn't drink something soon, I'll have to put a drip in her arm. In her condition, becoming dehydrated is especially dangerous.'

The old woman was alone in her room when Lily and Oksana entered. She wouldn't look at them and kept her eyes fixed on the window. Lily was afraid to speak at first. What if she said that they knew she was Natalya Azarova and it made things worse? But Oksana nudged her and so Lily moved around to the side of the bed near the window where Natasha was forced to notice her. Whatever she had done, Lily couldn't help feeling pity for the poor worn-out human being in front of her.

'I know who you really are,' she whispered. 'I know that you are Natalya Azarova.'

The old woman didn't respond. Lily put her hand on her shoulder and gave it a gentle squeeze.

'I also know that you killed Svetlana Novikova,' she said. 'Was it because you found out that she'd betrayed you?'

Natasha's gaze shifted and she looked into Lily's face. Her mouth moved painfully and tears came to her eyes. 'I did kill Svetlana,' she said. 'But not for the reason you suggest. Svetlana *never* betrayed me.'

TWENTY-FOUR

Orël Oblast, 1943

After I had seen the NKVD officer watching me, I didn't think things could get worse. But they did. Much worse.

I ran towards the command bunker, intending to warn Valentin that I was about to be arrested, but he was in his plane on the runway with the rest of his squadron. Sharavin was standing next to him, ready to move the chocks from his wheels. Svetlana was working on my plane, which had taken some hits on my last sortie. I would tell her.

I headed towards the hangar but was stopped by Lipovsky. 'Where are you going in such a hurry, Comrade Lieutenant? You can't gossip with your mechanic now. She has to assist with the other planes as well as yours.'

I was of equal rank to Lipovsky and his pompous tone was out of order. But I couldn't afford to make trouble.

'Here,' he said, handing me a wad of envelopes. 'The mail has arrived. Make yourself useful and take these back to the women's bunker.'

Personal letters were checked and censored by Lipovsky and their distribution was highly confidential. Was he getting pleasure out of treating me like a subordinate and making me deliver the mail? Perhaps it was Lipovsky who had reported me to the NKVD. I took the mail and was thankful to find none of the other women were in the bunker when I arrived. I planned to write two notes: one to my mother and one to Valentin. I would entrust them to Svetlana.

I placed Alisa's mail on her pillow and sorted through the rest of the pile. The sloped feminine hand on the envelope addressed to Svetlana was that of her mother. The return address brought me to a standstill: *Apartment 23, 11 Skatertny Pereulok, Moscow*. It was where I had lived with my family before my father was arrested. My mind turned to fog. How could Svetlana's family be living in our former apartment?

The fog cleared. People who denounced their colleagues or neighbours, I'd learned, were often rewarded with the accused's possessions. I'd heard of a professor at Moscow University being given the head of the department's position after he had denounced his superior, and an opera singer 'inheriting' the furs belonging to the wife of the company's director after her accusations saw the both of them sent to a labour camp. Why shouldn't a traitor be rewarded with an apartment she coveted for doing the same? Lydia's strange behaviour on the evening of Papa's arrest was now plain. She'd known what was coming. Or had she been unnerved when she saw the brooch Stalin had so falsely sent?

She had got what she wanted. I remembered the new doormat and the smell of fresh paint and floor polish I had noticed when I'd returned the scarf Mama had borrowed from our former neighbour. My thoughts turned black. It no longer mattered if the NKVD were about to arrest me because everything that I had lived was a lie. Svetlana, to whom I daily entrusted my life, was a traitor to me and my family.

I thought that when Svetlana returned to the bunker I would slap her, but instead I stood rooted to the spot and said coolly: 'My father was executed — and for what? Because your mother wanted our apartment?'

Svetlana's gaze fell to the letter that I held in my hand. The colour drained from her face and her shoulders slumped. She sat down on her bed and put her hands over her eyes.

'And you had the gall to pretend you were my friend!' I went on.

'I didn't know. I didn't know what my mother had persuaded my father to do.'

'You didn't know?' My voice was hoarse. 'You lived in our apartment — in our home — and you didn't know?'

Svetlana dropped her hands into her lap and looked at me. Her eyes were tear-filled. 'Not at first. My mother said it was a coincidence: that they'd applied for a better apartment and happened to get yours because it had become available. But of course it was obvious.' She clenched her hands. 'I was so ashamed of her ... so ashamed of my own mother!'

Svetlana pleaded for me to understand but I couldn't feel anything for her. All I could think about was Papa. He had been dragged from our home, imprisoned and then killed. How could I forget that look on his face when he was arrested? The Novikovs had done that to him!

I wanted to lash out at Svetlana, to shove her and punch her, but she looked defeated and would have collapsed at the first blow. Instead I threw the letter at her and fled into the night.

I sat in one of the sunflower fields, anger ripping through me. My mother had been generous with Lydia. My father had said that he would take the Novikov family to the dacha in summer. In return, she had put us in hell! I thought of

Lydia living in that lovely apartment while my mother sat alone in a tiny place without her family. The fact that the betrayal had happened years ago and I had only just found out, made everything worse. I wanted to hate Svetlana but I couldn't. It had been Lydia's doing. As I sifted through things in my mind, I began to see why, with all her qualifications, Svetlana had come to the front to work as my mechanic. She felt the shame that her mother didn't. I stood up, intending to return to the bunker to sleep for a few hours, but Captain Panchenko announced over the loudspeakers that the regiment was to assemble immediately. Valentin described to us the seriousness of the day ahead. The Luftwaffe was amassing armadas of aircraft to halt our advance.

'The fighting will be fierce,' he said. 'I want to take this opportunity to say how honoured I am to have been your commander.'

Valentin's squadron and mine — to be led on this occasion by Alisa — along with the others, waited in our planes all morning but it seemed that the Germans were holding off their attack. I kept looking over my shoulder around the airfield, wondering where the NKVD agent was lurking. He was taking his time to arrest me. The sun was scorching and the controls burned my hands when I touched them. My throat was parched. Svetlana and the other mechanics took shelter beneath the planes' wings. It was a convenient way for Svetlana and me not to face each other. 'We can't keep sitting out here,' Valentin said. He directed all the pilots to wait in a hut by the runway. When we joined them, he studied me with concern. 'Are you unwell, Natasha?'

He wanted to replace me with another pilot but I refused. How I loved my precious Valentin! I'd been so shocked by what I'd discovered that I hadn't written the notes for him and my mother. If I was killed or arrested, Valentin would be told that Papa had been executed as an enemy of the people. He would wonder why I'd kept that from him. I needed to explain to him what a good man my father had been. I thought that if I told him about attending the reception at the Kremlin for Valery Chkalov, Valentin would realise the high esteem in which Stalin and the other commissars had held Papa. He had created hundreds of new types of chocolate. His joy in life was to give people pleasure. He'd had no interest in destroying the Soviet Union.

'I met Stalin once,' I began. 'I thought it was the most exciting day of my life. I was fourteen years old.'

Valentin's expression changed in an instant. He grimaced as if he'd tasted something bad. 'Listen, Natasha, there is something you should know. Stalin personally signed your father's execution order.'

I felt as if I'd been struck on the head. For once I could see things clearly. My mother had written to Stalin many times but had never received a reply. Whatever arrows Svetlana's parents had shot at my father, Stalin could have overturned the accusations with a stroke of his pen. But he hadn't. I didn't know how Valentin even knew about Stalin and my father's death, but I was certain that he was right. It was as if he had yanked down a curtain and I saw Stalin for who he was unblinkered by my foolish veneration.

I wanted to run to Svetlana to tell her that I forgave her. But the call came to scramble. A frantic message from the frontline told of massive formations speeding towards our troops.

Valentin and I sprinted to our planes, followed by the other pilots. Svetlana was waiting by mine to help me with my parachute. I handed her my identification capsule but she kept her eyes averted from me. There was no time to reconcile now.

The sky had been clear in the morning, but in the afternoon clumps of dense cloud had formed. Three squadrons took off for the first sortie: Valentin's crack quartet, of which I was one; Alisa's covering quartet; and a reserve group led by Filipp. We taxied together, turned to the wind, opened our throttles and lifted into the air. The familiar vibration of my aircraft calmed me. There was nothing to think about now except fighting.

When we reached the frontline it seemed that the sky was a mass of planes. I counted sixty Junkers covered by ten Focke-Wulfs and twenty Messerschmitts. The first Junkers of the formation were diving in attack. The roar of the bombers' engines and the whines of those of the fighters were deafening. 'Stay in tight formation,' Valentin ordered us over the radio.

He led our quartet to attack the bombers while Filipp steered his group to engage the fighters.

Valentin closed in on a Junker and let forth two bursts of fire. The first killed the rear gunner and the second set one of the engines ablaze. The aircraft was loaded with bombs and exploded into a fireball that rocked my plane. Alisa shot down a Focke-Wulf that was close to my tail. It gushed smoke and spiralled to the ground.

The crack and covering squadrons took turns in attacking the Junkers. There was crossfire, terrifyingly close at times. Tracers whizzed past me. Planes were going in all directions but I kept my eyes on Valentin. No matter what, I had to protect him.

Two more Junkers broke apart and fell to the ground. A Focke-Wulf on fire plunged between us and I pulled away to avoid being taken down with it. I lost sight of Valentin. A Messerschmitt appeared under me and I moved it into my sights. Something hit my plane. It was either debris or bullets but in the chaos I couldn't tell. Everything shook and for a moment I thought I was finished. But the gauges read normally. I pressed the gun button and claimed my fighter. The plane flipped and went down belly up.

I spotted Valentin and moved back into position. Our quartets had driven the Junkers away from their target. We'd lost two of our fighters but I'd seen one of the pilots bail out on our side of the front. Filipp's plane was shot full of holes but seemed to be operating. At least we had helped our troops. It was up to them now to advance.

Valentin's voice came over the transmitter. 'All right, back to the airfield now. Well done!'

It was the most ferocious battle we had fought in together and yet Valentin sounded as calm as ever. 'Doesn't anything faze you?' I radioed back to him, but he didn't respond. My transmitter must have been damaged. He couldn't hear me although I could hear him.

The airfield came into sight through the clouds. A sense of relief washed over me: now I could reconcile with Svetlana and explain to Valentin about my past. If I could do those two things, I no longer cared what the NKVD might do to me.

Out of the corner of my eye I saw shapes in the clouds. Had one of the quartets moved out of formation? Then I saw them again. No! Three planes. Messerschmitts!

I tried my transmitter again but it was no use. The German planes burst through the clouds and headed straight towards Valentin. Even if he had seen them he wouldn't have had a chance. He'd already begun his descent. His landing gear was down and he'd tapered off his speed. He was at too low an altitude to bail out and survive. I increased my speed and flew parallel to the lead pilot. I dipped my wing as if I was having trouble controlling my plane. My mask covered most of my face but he would be able to tell I was a woman. He might even guess who I was. Colonel Smirnov had said that there was a high price on my head. The pilot took the bait and followed me as I turned away from the airfield and in the direction of the front. To my surprise, the other two pilots did too; neither stayed behind to finish off Valentin. They couldn't have been ace pilots if they were so easily distracted, but I was glad they had fallen for my trick.

I flew through the clouds with the three enemy planes on my tail. I knew with multiple pursuers to never fly straight but keep turning and attacking. But my main concern now was leading them away from Valentin and the airfield. I had blundered with the Black Diamond and I didn't intend to fail this time.

The clouds thinned and disappeared. Below lay open fields with forest beyond. I didn't have to look at my map to know that I was over enemy-held territory. It was time to engage the fighters. I turned and flew full power towards the three Messerschmitts. The centre pilot opened fire and tracers flashed past my cockpit. I knew that if I wavered, I'd be shot up. Captured German pilots had revealed to us their airmen considered Slavs fatalistic and prone to suicidal tactics. They also knew that we had the NKVD at our backs if we failed in our missions. That belief gave me the upper hand. They did exactly as I hoped: they lost their nerve, opening up their formation like a fan. I hit one plane with my cannon and it dropped to earth, trailing smoke behind it. I was clear now to retreat to our side of the frontline. I glanced at my fuel gauge: I might have just enough to make it.

But the two other Messerschmitts weren't prepared to let me go. They turned and followed me. I could lure them low to the trees, but on this side of the front I was in danger of anti-aircraft fire. If I was going to go down, better to do so in those remote fields I'd seen than in the middle of the German army.

I turned and made another pass. I pressed my gun fire button but it clicked. I was out of ammunition and my fuel was too low to keep fighting. The Germans would realise that and catch me in the pincer manoeuvre they were so fond of and force me to land. I had one final trick up my sleeve. It had a high fatality rate, which was why only the most desperate used it. Those who survived were awarded the Order of the Red Banner.

I approached one of the fighters from the side, shearing off part of its wing and piercing its fuselage with my propeller. The plane wobbled and went nose down, but I had ruined my chances of crash-landing. My Yak lurched. I pulled back on the control but it was like a piece of string in my hands. I had no choice but to bail out now.

I tore off my mask and headphones and reached for the canopy. It was stuck and I struggled with it as my plane began to plummet. Finally I managed to rip the canopy open. Blinded by the rushing wind and battered and buffeted by the air around me, I struggled to lever myself against the cockpit rim. Suddenly I was sucked out. The plane fell away from me. I was sorry that I hadn't been able to save it. It plunged into the forest with a loud rumble and a lightning flash.

Then I remembered where I was and pulled the ring on my parachute. I clipped a tree on my way down and swung before hitting the ground at an awkward angle and briefly knocking myself out. When I came to, I saw the remaining German plane circling above. Had he seen me jump?

I lay still until the plane departed then sat up. It was a miracle that I'd survived the jump apparently in one piece. I felt my arms and legs and everything seemed all right except for a sharp pain in my side. But when I tried to stand up, pain seared through my legs. I sat down again and yanked off my boots. My feet were swollen and purple. I had either broken them or torn ligaments. I ripped the bottom off my shirt and bound my feet tightly, then gingerly put my boots back on.

I touched my belt and realised that I'd lost my pistol when I exited the plane. If the pilot had seen me he would alert the ground forces to my location. I prayed the partisans would reach me before the Germans did.

There was a grove of trees nearby and then a forest across another field. I could hide in the grove for now and then move to the forest after nightfall.

I hobbled towards the grove. Every step was agony. I hid myself in the undergrowth and picked my insignia and decorations off my uniform. If I was captured they would give away my identity. I folded my insignia inside my papers and buried them under the tree I was leaning against. Then I felt around my buttonhole and realised I'd also lost the brooch that Stalin had given me. I was glad to be rid of it now; it was a symbol of treachery. Not only was that monster responsible for Papa's death, but he was to blame for my brother's fate too. None of those metro volunteers would have been killed if Stalin had not set that impossible deadline. Without my rose-coloured glasses I saw everything clearly.

When darkness fell, I made my way towards the forest. I stumbled, fell, crawled and got up again until I reached the trees. I held on to a trunk to spare my feet having to bear the weight of my body. In the distance I could hear bursts of machine-gun and artillery fire. The front was moving closer. Maybe I could hide myself until the Soviet Army recaptured the forest.

Suddenly, I heard the hum of motorcycle engines and dropped down into the grass. A patrol of Germans passed right by me. The sight of them made my heart race. I had to go deeper into the forest. Each time I moved, I set myself the small goal of reaching the next tree; and at each rest stop I thought of something that gave me pleasure to help me regain my strength. I heard music and imagined dancing with Valentin; I saw myself reading Tolstoy to Svetlana; I pictured Mama arranging flowers in her apartment, with Dasha asleep on a pillow beside her; I thought of delicious *pelmeni*, sweet-smelling flowers, pretty dresses and perfume.

Finally, in too much pain to move any more, I curled up against the base of a pine tree and stared at the starry sky. I was aware of every rustle and animal sound in the undergrowth around me. It was summer and the bears, lynxes and wolves would be active. But I wasn't as afraid of them as I was of the Germans. Predatory animals killed when they were hungry or to protect their young. They didn't kill their own kind en masse in an orgy of greed and evil. And I recalled Ludmila's words: *If either of you is ever in danger of being captured, you must shoot yourself rather than be taken prisoner by those monsters.*

I tried to stay awake but fell asleep sometime before dawn. I dreamed that a figure stepped out of the early morning mist and put a pistol to my head. I woke with a start but there was no one there. The forest was devoid of human sounds, but the woodpeckers and quails were busy looking for food. I watched the sky brighten. When I tried to stand, I stumbled and fell. The pain in my feet and side was worse, but I couldn't stay in the forest. I had to find help.

Somewhere nearby I heard the trickle of a stream. I crawled on my hands and knees towards the sound. When I found the water, I plunged my hands in and cried with relief. I drank great scoops of it, then, gritting my teeth, I removed my boots and soaked my swollen feet. Half an hour later I began moving again, using the method I had tried the day before — tree to tree, rock to rock.

Later, I saw Junkers tear across the sky accompanied by fighters. It was hard to believe that only a day ago I had been in a plane going out to meet them. I thought about my Yak, buried somewhere in the forest. Would anyone find it? If I died here would anyone find me?

Eventually I became feverish and could walk no further. I burrowed into the undergrowth, hoping that an hour or so of sleep might give me the strength to move again. I woke a short while later, all my senses alert. Two rabbits were running through the undergrowth. I heard footsteps … human footsteps. I thought I was dreaming again but then two figures appeared from the trees. One of them saw me and gave a cry. I thought I was finished but then I heard a woman's voice.

'Natasha!'

Svetlana! Was this real or was my fever making me hallucinate? I tried to stand but collapsed. I looked up and saw Svetlana standing above me. Behind her was a young boy, maybe ten years old.

Svetlana threw her arms around me. 'I knew I would find you!'

'How did you?' I asked her, still unable to believe she was really there. 'Have we taken Orël?'

Svetlana shook her head. 'No, not yet. I crossed the frontline in the dark and avoided the enemy. The partisans helped me locate where you went down. They sent this boy to help me find you. He knows the forest well.' She glanced at my feet. 'Are you hurt?'

'I injured my feet when I jumped,' I told her. 'I can't stand on them for long.'

Svetlana turned to the boy. 'Help me carry her.'

The boy grabbed my legs while Svetlana slipped her hands under my arms. But when they lifted me it felt as if my ribs were coming apart and I couldn't breathe. I cried out with pain and they placed me on the ground again.

'We won't make any progress that way,' Svetlana said. 'You're too badly hurt. We're close to a road and village here and we'll be noticed unless we move quickly.' She turned to the boy. 'Can you get help? Is there anyone in the village you trust?'

The boy's eyes darted from Svetlana to me as if he were sizing us up. He was gaunt and nervous, not at all like a boy that age should be. I was sorry that life had made him that way.

'I'll get help,' he told Svetlana. 'You wait here with her.' And he disappeared into the forest again.

'Who is he?' I asked Svetlana.

'An orphan who lives with the partisans. They had to blow up a bridge to stop the Germans getting supplies, so they sent the boy with me. He's wild but he apparently knows every inch of this forest.'

'Can we trust him?'

It felt like a harsh question to ask about a child. But this was war. You had to be careful of everyone.

'The partisans use him as a guide,' Svetlana replied. 'So I'm sure we can.' She kneeled behind me and rested my head in her lap. 'Natasha, will you ever forgive me?'

I reached up and touched her face. 'I'm sorry I became so angry. None of it was your fault. None of it! It was Stalin who signed my father's execution order. It was he who betrayed Papa. Perhaps your mother's accusations didn't help, but Stalin could have easily rejected them.'

Svetlana removed my leather flying helmet, which I hadn't realised I was still wearing, and placed it on the ground beside her. She stroked my throbbing forehead. 'You would have been proud of me, Natasha. Sharavin didn't expect me to persevere. But I made it past the frontline. I pushed any dark thoughts from my head, as you've always told me to do. I kept repeating, "Natasha is alive and I will find her."'

I smiled at her. 'I've always been proud of you, Sveta.'

She leaned over to pick some bilberries from a nearby bush and fed them to me one by one. 'Valentin has been searching for you. Perhaps the partisans will be able to get a message to him somehow.'

She stopped and looked around her. I had heard it too: something in the distance. I sat bolt upright despite the pain in my ribs. Engines. I could smell exhaust fumes. Svetlana had said we were near a road but we must have been closer than I'd realised. Then the sound of trucks was replaced by voices. They were shouting orders. Dogs barked. Had the boy alerted the whole village? Did they have to make such a racket? Then I heard the voices more distinctly: they were speaking in German. My blood turned cold.

I looked around. I couldn't escape, but Svetlana could still run. Then I realised the voices were coming from all directions. We were surrounded. Had the boy alerted the wrong person in the village by mistake? Or had he deliberately double-crossed us in return for some advantage?

I turned to Svetlana. There was terror in her eyes. I knew what she was thinking. To be captured by the Germans and abused at their hands wasn't a future we could endure. We knew the only course we had now.

Svetlana swallowed then took the pistol from her belt. 'I used three of the bullets to scare off a wild boar,' she said. 'There must be three left.' She handed the gun to me. 'I'll never be able to do it, and I can't watch you die,' she said, her voice trembling. 'Please … me first and then … you.'

I choked back tears. How could I destroy my dearest friend? But what other choice did we have? We knew what awaited us at the hands of the Germans and in a few minutes the choice would be taken from us. I grabbed the gun from Svetlana.

She fumbled in her pocket, then handed me the identification capsule that I'd given her before my last flight. 'So if our comrades ever find us, they will know who we are,' she said.

I slipped the capsule into my pocket. Using the tree for support, I raised myself to my feet. 'Please turn around,' I told her. I couldn't shoot her if she faced me.

There were only three bullets in the gun. The worst thing would be to botch the job and not kill her cleanly. I pointed the barrel at the back of Svetlana's head, then hesitated, unsure of my decision.

'I love you,' I said.

'I love you too,' she replied.

The voices and barks grew louder. I saw German soldiers coming through the trees. One shouted out: he'd spotted me. They started running towards us.

'Now, Natasha,' Svetlana pleaded. 'Please, now. I am ready.'

My heart pounded in my chest. An image of Svetlana and me running home from school flashed through my mind. 'God forgive us,' I said, tormented by the unspeakable act I was about to commit. I pulled the trigger. The shot rang out and sent a flock of grouse into flight. Svetlana slumped forward. Her body quivered for a moment then stopped.

Now she was gone, I longed to follow her. I lifted the pistol to my temple and pulled the trigger. Nothing happened. I pulled it again. Nothing. The next thing I felt was a blow from a fist to my head, which sent me sprawling to the ground.

The world went black.

TWENTY-FIVE

Moscow, 2000

Tears poured from Lily's eyes. Natasha had killed Svetlana out of love, not retribution. Lily understood the strength that would have taken. In Adam's final days, as he lay bathed in sweat and weeping, she had sat alone with a pillow scrunched in her hands, wondering if she was strong enough to hold it over his face and end the suffering that was not alleviated by the measured doses of morphine his nurses administered. But she couldn't bring herself to do it. When he fell into a coma and faded away, Lily realised she'd been spared crossing a line from which there was no return.

'I had accused Svetlana of betraying me,' said Natasha, 'but she had a pure soul. Svetlana believed that I would stay alive if she imagined it so. She even trusted me with her death. It was I who betrayed her.'

'You killed her out of mercy,' said Oksana.

Natasha squeezed her eyes shut. 'I didn't follow her in the end.'

'But you couldn't have,' said Lily. 'Your gun jammed.'

Natasha grimaced and lifted her hand to her chest. 'After that ... I could have found a way. Svetlana could not have lived without me. She loved me too much. But I chose to live without her.'

'You can't blame yourself for that,' said Oksana, pouring a glass of water from a jug on the bedside table. 'It's the human instinct.' She held the glass to Natasha's lips and helped her take a sip.

Lily waited until Natasha seemed ready to continue before asking, 'What happened after the Germans captured you?'

The old woman stared at the ceiling. 'Perhaps my consolation is that I spared Svetlana from the nightmare that was to come. She couldn't have endured it.'

I regained consciousness on the floor of a storage bunker. The air was hot and reeked of sacking and gunpowder. It was dim in the room and everything was hazy. My head throbbed and so did my ribs and my feet. My neck was stiff but I managed to lift my head to look for Svetlana. Then I remembered what had happened. My throat thickened and I thought I was suffocating.

A German guard was standing near the door. When he saw that I was coming to, he called to another guard outside. I heard the words '*die Mechanikerin*'. Then he turned back to me and shouted in Russian, 'Stand up!'

The command brought me to my senses. My heart skipped a beat but I couldn't move.

'Stand up!' the guard shouted again, jabbing my hip with the end of his gun.

I brought my legs under me and slowly straightened myself up.

'*Die Mechanikerin*,' the guard repeated to the man outside and I realised he was talking about me. Why did he think I was a mechanic and not a pilot?

The guard outside shouted something and the one next to me pointed his gun at me again and jerked his head. My feet were still too painful to bear my full weight and I stumbled when I tried to walk. The guard grabbed my arm to support me and led me out the door and onto an airfield. Every step was torture and bile rose in my throat. Pilots, mechanics and armourers all turned their heads to look at me. To find myself on an enemy airfield, surrounded by German airmen and their ground crew sent chills through me. Some of the men seemed curious while others glared at me. But among those stares were a few that conveyed pity and that surprised me.

The command bunker was underground. A map of the front took up an entire wall. Near it, an operator was listening to Soviet radio transmissions. My ears picked up the crackled voices of the Russian pilots. The call signs weren't those of my regiment but the sound of fellow fighters heading into battle made me realise how far away I was from Valentin now. I may never see him again, I thought. My captors were probably planning to interrogate me and then shoot me — or worse.

There was a man sitting at a desk writing on some papers; I assumed he was the commander. He looked up when the guard announced me and I recognised him. It was the Black Diamond. He was as handsome up close as he had been at a distance, only now I could see that his trousers were crumpled and his chiselled face was darkened by stubble. He pointed to a chair and said something to the guard in German. The guard dropped me into the chair and left.

The Black Diamond stared at me for a long time, then picked up the identification capsule from his desk and played with it in his hand.

'We both know that you are not the mechanic,' he said in educated Russian. He had a strong, theatrical voice and only the slight touch of an accent.

I glanced at the capsule and understood what had caused the mix-up. In the panic of being surrounded, Svetlana had given me hers by mistake. Because I had taken the insignia off my uniform, apart from the capsule, there had been no way to identify me.

The Black Diamond pursed his lips. 'I think it's best that you keep that cover. We have orders that all Soviet female combatants be shot on capture. Field Marshal von Kluge despises the idea of Russian women killing German men.'

I stiffened. It was typical German arrogance. They expected Russian women to stand by while they slaughtered our families. As disgusted as I was, I refrained from responding in case the Black Diamond was trying to trick me into giving him information.

'There isn't much I can do for you now,' he said, lowering his voice so the operator couldn't hear him. 'I've requested for you to go to a prisoner-of-war camp where most of the inmates are British and American soldiers. They might be able to help you. I should warn you that Germany has a policy of starving Soviet prisoners to death. But even if the High Command obeyed the Geneva Convention, your own leader, Stalin, refuses to allow Red Cross assistance to any Soviets who are captured.'

I didn't need any more evidence to convince me that Stalin was a tyrant but I still couldn't be sure how much of what the Black Diamond said was true. Perhaps he was trying to scare me into talking.

'Why don't you say something?' he asked, sounding exasperated. 'You don't know how you've terrorised my pilots. When the radio operator reported that you were in the sky, it was hard to get the men to fly. Even senior pilots were scared of you. You are the only person to have shot me down.' He stood and moved closer to me. 'Listen, I'm not going to interrogate you if that's what you're thinking. Germany has made a mess of things and we're not going to win this war. There's nothing I can get from you that is going to save us. But there is one thing I would like to know. Why didn't you kill me when you had the chance?'

That, I didn't understand myself. Apart from his resemblance to Alexander, perhaps I'd seen him as another human being. Or maybe I'd spared him because I admired his courage and skill.

When I didn't answer, the Black Diamond sighed. 'What a pity that the war has put us on different sides,' he said with a wry smile. 'You are very beautiful ... and determined. We could have married and run a flying school together.'

Despite the horror of my situation, the Black Diamond's ridiculous comment made me smile. He intrigued me. He was handsome, charismatic and spoke refined Russian. He came across as a decent human being. If he hadn't killed Colonel Smirnov, I would not have regretted sparing his life.

The radio operator called out to the Black Diamond: he seemed to have discovered something on the transmitter. The Black Diamond picked up the microphone on his desk and made an announcement that was carried to the airfield by loudspeakers. He moved to the door and called out to the guard who was waiting to take me back to the store room, then turned to me.

'Listen, I'm going to order the guard to bring you a meal. I also want the medical orderly to look at your feet. Don't refuse our help out of foolish pride. It might be the last assistance you get and the journey to Germany is a long one.'

Germany! I wasn't going to Germany. It was bad enough to be a prisoner, but to be taken away so far from Mama and Valentin was unthinkable.

I cooperated with the medical orderly when he examined my feet, smothered them with a pungent balm and bound them tightly. I ate the black bread and potatoes the guard brought me. But I didn't do those things because I was afraid or grateful; I did them because I was gathering my strength in order to escape.

As I ate, memories of my last moments with Svetlana came back to me: her frightened face; the sound of her voice as she told me that she loved me; the jolt of the gun in my hand when I ended her life. But I had to push them away. I couldn't think of Svetlana any more. I couldn't even grieve for her. It wasn't that I didn't love her but that I had loved her so much. When I'd held the pistol to my head I had been prepared to die with her. But now that I'd survived, I no longer had that wish. I couldn't think about her death and go on living. And I had made the decision to survive so I could return to Mama and Valentin.

Escaping while I was still near my regiment was the most desirable scenario and the guards knew that. I spent several nights in the store room with them watching me like a hawk. They made no allowances for my sex when I used the toilet and kept their guns on me the whole time. Another woman might have tried flirtation but I couldn't bring myself to do that. Then one morning I was taken out of the store room and put on the back of a truck. The pain in my feet had lessened and I was sure that I could run if I had to. I scanned the landscape as we drove, memorising landmarks so I could find my way back once I'd got free. But the guard who travelled with me was also vigilant. The punishment for letting a prisoner escape must have been severe.

The truck came to a stop at a railroad junction. A group of Red Army prisoners was sitting in the scorching sun, supervised by German soldiers. The guard pushed me from the truck and marched me towards the men. The prisoners looked dejected. Had they given up so easily? I was forced to sit down and one of the men glanced up at me. His face was bruised and he had a wound to his arm that needed attention. I stifled a cry when I recognised him. It was Filipp.

A cattle train approached the junction. While the guards were distracted I moved closer to him.

'What happened to you?' he whispered. 'I thought you were dead.'

'I ran out of fuel and ammunition — I had to jump. You too?'

He nodded. 'I took a bad hit.'

The train's brakes squealed and it came to a stop. The engine pulled eight wagons, two of which had booths manned by soldiers clutching machine guns. My chances of escaping looked slimmer by the minute. A guard opened the door to one of the wagons and the prisoners were ordered inside. Filipp helped me up and we sat together near a small window. It was stifling inside the wagon and we hadn't been given any water. My throat was parched and I was sweating as if I were in a sauna.

After the guards slammed the door shut, I told Filipp about the Black Diamond and what he'd said about the way Germans treated Soviet prisoners of war.

'We have to escape,' I said. 'But we'll have to do it in the dark.'

'The Black Diamond is dead,' Filipp said as the train started to move. 'Captain Orlov shot him down the day before yesterday.'

The mention of Valentin made my heart ache. Svetlana had said he was searching for me. I hoped that he wouldn't do anything foolish. He couldn't save me now. All I wanted was for him to survive the war so that one day we could be together again. I remembered the joke the Black Diamond had made about he and I getting married and running a flying school. I was sorry he was dead. That brief coversation had made me like him. But if it were a choice between him and Valentin, I was glad my lover had been the victor.

I peered at the landscape moving past the window. It was open farmland now and all of it in enemy territory. 'How are we going to escape?' I asked Filipp.

One of the soldiers cleared his throat and held up a penknife. 'We'll cut a hole in the door and lift the bolt.'

So the soldiers hadn't given up at all. They'd merely been acting that way to fool the Germans.

The soldier used the penknife to pierce the door, then filed the metal to create a larger hole so he could slip his hand through. I told the others not to watch him in case our anxiety made the penknife break, but the screech of the metal set my teeth on edge. The tension made the air in the car even hotter. I could barely breathe. When the blisters on the soldier's hands started to bleed, he passed the knife to another man.

We all took turns filing the door until the train slowed and came to a stop. We heard the guards shouting and other harsh voices answering. We glanced at each other: had someone noticed us cutting the door? I squinted through the window. A group of German soldiers stood outside the car talking. If they saw the cut in the door we were finished.

I heard more voices but they were those of women and children. I craned my neck and saw that hundreds of people carrying suitcases and bundles of belongings, were being loaded onto the train. There were only eight cars. How were they going to fit?

'They've stopped to pick up more passengers,' I whispered to the others.

'Passengers?' echoed one of the prisoners. 'This isn't a passenger train.'

'They must be forced labourers,' said Filipp.

The train began to move and we resumed filing the hole. Our only chance to escape would be at night and we had to work quickly. The train was travelling rapidly for wartime and I was terrified we'd be in Poland before we got out.

'Listen,' I told Filipp, 'don't wait for me. Save yourself. I hurt my feet when I jumped from my plane and I don't know how fast I'll be able to run.'

He frowned at me.

'I mean it,' I said. 'You're not my wingman any more. If you survive and I don't, find Valentin and my mother and tell them what happened to me. Tell them that I never stopped thinking of them.'

Filipp nodded then looked away. 'You'll survive,' he said. 'You are the bravest woman I've ever known. After the war, Comrade Stalin will personally name you Hero of the Soviet Union twice over.'

After what Valentin had told me, I doubted that.

*

Late that night, we succeeded in cutting the hole in the door. One of the soldiers snapped through the wire that held the bolt shut.

'We'll go in order of rank,' he said. 'You first, Comrade Lieutenant Azarova.'

I gaped at him. How did he know who I was?

'Your picture hung on the wall of my bunker,' he said with a sheepish grin.

He opened the door and the night air rushed inside. I peered into the darkness, petrified. Trees flashed by. We were passing through a forest. Jumping from a moving train was more frightening than parachuting from a plane. If we waited for the train to slow down there was a greater chance of the guards seeing us. But if I hit a tree or went over a ravine I'd be killed. Yet there was no other option: I leaped into the night.

Pain jolted through my feet when I hit the ground. The momentum carried me onto my side and I rolled down a slope and crashed into a tree. The impact winded me and I gasped. I didn't see the other men jump but there was shouting and the train squealed to a stop. Machine-gun fire split the air. The Germans had reacted faster than we had anticipated.

I dragged myself behind the trees and kept my head low. Spotlights shone around the area. Guard dogs barked. Then there were more shouts and gunfire. I pushed myself as flat against the ground as I could. Someone ran past me. A light caught him. Filipp! There was a rattle of machine-gun fire and he was shot full of holes.

The air went silent. I heard the wagon door slam shut and wondered if the soldiers had given up searching and were getting back on the train. Then I felt a weight on my back.

A boot. Someone dragged me to my feet by my collar and pushed me back up the slope. A German guard. When we reached the track, he boxed me around the ears and punched me in the stomach. I collapsed to my knees, sure that he was going to shoot me, but instead he wrenched me up again and dragged me towards another wagon.

A soldier standing by the door tugged it open and a foul stench rolled out. A mix of urine, sweat and fear. In the flash of the soldier's torchlight I glimpsed terrified faces: women, children, old people. I was shoved inside the crowded car and the door was slammed shut. A few moments later the train moved again. I could no longer see the people around me but I could sense their wretchedness. Who were they and where were we going?

The journey took four days, which we endured without food or water. I learned that the people in the carriage were Ukrainian Jews on their way to a work camp. On the third day a child died. The guards had to prise the child's corpse from the mother's hands. Her wails pierced my heart. The only way I could cope was to rest my head on my knees and think of nothing.

The day after, we passed through a station. My heart sank when I saw the sign: *Kraków*. My worst fears were realised: we were in Poland. A while later, the train came to a halt with a long, low whistle. The doors were slid open and German soldiers ordered everyone out. I waited for the others to leave before lowering myself from the wagon to the ground. I searched the sea of faces for any of the Red Army soldiers I had been with before our escape, but there was no one. I was the only survivor.

'Poor Filipp,' I muttered. An SS officer in a neatly fitting uniform and polished boots glared at me. Something seemed to irritate him and he indicated that I should stand to the side while the other passengers were divided according to their sex. As I was the only prisoner of war in the group, I wondered if that was what had annoyed him. Perhaps I was supposed to have been taken to a transit camp in Germany instead of here.

I spotted men and women in striped uniforms working in a field beyond the barbed-wire fence. There were watchtowers at regular intervals manned by guards with machine guns. Other guards patrolled the fence line with dogs. They must be determined to keep these people imprisoned, I thought. An odour that made my stomach heave reached my nostrils: the stench of burning flesh and hair. I'd smelled it many times over the battlefield but it was much stronger here. I glanced around for the source of the smell and noticed a red-brick building behind some trees. Smoke was drifting from its chimney. A sense of foreboding washed over me.

One of the guards indicated that I should join the women who didn't have small children. Women with young children and those who were pregnant were ordered to the left, along with the elderly. The rest of us were told to line up in single file.

Arbeit macht frei: work makes you free. I had no idea what those German words meant when I entered Auschwitz-Birkenau that day, nor that I had passed into a living hell run by monsters. I was selected to work in the storage area, sorting the goods that had been stolen from the Jews and other prisoners when they were brought to the camp. Every day I picked through muslin-wrapped cheeses, jars of preserved vegetables, canned fruit and sweets. The depot was nicknamed 'Canada' because of all the riches that were stored there — jewellery, clothes, shoes, household goods, as well as food; it was considered one of the preferable jobs in the camp. The women who worked there were permitted to grow their hair, unlike women in other areas of the camp who were shorn from head to foot. Our uniforms were better and so were our barracks.

'You can eat some of the food,' said the kapo who supervised me and the other women in the section. 'The guards will turn a blind eye. Just don't take anything back to the barracks. That will earn you a beating.'

'Why do we get treated better here?' I asked Dora, who worked with me and was teaching me basic German.

She shrugged. 'I don't know. The mental torment might be enough.'

I didn't understand what she meant until one day a train arrived from Czechoslovakia. When the passengers had disembarked, I saw that the pregnant women, young children and old people were being herded towards the red-brick building that I had glimpsed on my arrival. I carried on with my work but kept returning to the window to see what was happening. Then I heard screams and cries. I felt sick to my stomach. Were the people being beaten?

Sometime later I heard motors start up, like those on ventilators in factories. Smoke rose from the chimney. When the kapo saw the smoke he ordered us to shut the windows, even though it was hot inside the storehouse. I obeyed his order but as I did so I saw through the glass two prisoners pushing a cart with naked corpses on it. One of the dead was a woman. An umbilical cord dangled from between her legs with a fully developed baby attached to it. I dropped to my knees.

'You'll learn not to look next time,' Dora said when she found me vomiting into a piece of cloth.

Even the horrors I had seen in Stalingrad did not compare to what was going on in Auschwitz. Innocent people were being gassed to death. I thought incessantly of escape after that, but soon realised it was futile for someone who worked inside the camp. The Forbidden Zone was wide and vigilantly patrolled and I'd be shot before I could reach the wire.

'Listen,' Dora told me one day, 'stay strong and don't risk your good fortune in being allocated this work. Most of us ended up here because we have relatives in the work-assignment office who arranged it for us. It's awful, but the guards here don't starve us and they don't send us to the gas chamber if we do what we're told. According to you, the Russians are pushing the Germans back. Well, hold on until they get here.'

I saw that Dora was right. It was a Soviet pilot's duty to try to escape if captured, but I also had a duty to my mother — I was all she had now — and a duty to Valentin because he loved me and would be waiting for me. Working in the storehouse section was the reason I survived two winters at Auschwitz while other prisoners, reduced to living skeletons by a lack of food and from overwork, died in their thousands.

'Are you noticing the changes?' Dora whispered to me one day.

I was. The number of trains arriving each week was decreasing and the selections had stopped. Food rations began to improve in quality and quantity. Fewer people were being killed randomly or for minor offences.

'They're getting desperate,' Dora said. 'They *need* our labour now.'

I dared to allow myself the hope that the changes meant the front was drawing closer.

In late autumn, some of the crematoriums were dismantled; and then one night in early January, when I lay in my bunk shivering from the cold, I heard a sound that made me sit bolt upright. Planes! I knew from the pitch of the engines that they were Ilyushins: Russian bombers. Had I imagined it? I looked around. Other women were sitting up; they'd heard them too. After the planes came the boom of artillery and the crackle of rifle fire.

'The Russians are close,' one woman whispered.

The following day, dozens of German armoured vehicles rumbled past the camp. The Nazis were fleeing.

Dora and I were transferred from sorting food to packing clothes, suitcases, shoes, spectacles and other stolen goods for dispatch to Berlin. The guards ordered us to hurry but the snow hampered the speed at which we could push the wheelbarrows and carts from the bunkers to the trucks. My feet were wet and frozen, and the last thing I wanted, now that the Red Army was approaching, was to die of pneumonia.

An explosion ripped through the air as another crematorium was blown up. On one of my runs a prisoner stopped me and whispered that she'd seen SS officers throwing hundreds of documents and registration books onto bonfires.

'They're destroying the evidence,' she said. 'They know what they've been doing is abhorrent.'

'But what about us?' I asked her. 'We're eyewitnesses to their crimes. What do they intend to do with us?'

Anticipating that there would be some desperate act by the Nazis before the Red Army arrived, Dora and I stowed away food and prepared a hideout in one of the storage bunkers.

A few days later, Russian bombers destroyed several bunkers, including the food depot. Fortunately Dora and I had been loading a truck at the time and weren't inside the depot. We rushed to inspect the damage and were relieved to see our hideout bunker still standing.

The SS soldiers ordered prisoners out of their barracks, even though the temperature had fallen seventeen degrees below zero. Those who didn't move quickly enough were beaten. In the confusion Dora and I, along with another woman from our bunker, slipped away to our hideout. From the commotion we heard outside it was clear something terrible was happening.

'They're going to make all able-bodied prisoners march west, to Germany,' the woman claimed.

I stared at her in horror. The idea was madness. Even the strongest prisoners weren't up to that in the extreme cold. They were inadequately clothed and many of them didn't have shoes.

We remained hidden in the storage bunker, huddling together for warmth. I heard Soviet planes engaging with the Germans near the camp and imagined Valentin up there in his Yak fighter coming to rescue me.

Early the following morning the lights outside the bunker went out and darkness fell over the camp. I crawled to a window but I could only see the flames of dozens of bonfires. We ventured out, hiding behind abandoned barrows and crates in case the Germans were still about. All around us lay the frozen bodies of women who hadn't been well enough to march. The SS had shot them. They've made a bad job of hiding the evidence of their atrocities, I thought.

There seemed to be no guards around and parts of the barbed wire around the camp had been cut. Was it a trick? I squinted at the guard towers, trying to see if any soldiers remained there. But they appeared to be abandoned. Were we truly free at last? I wanted to believe it but was anxious that this was only a lull before another storm hit.

'I'm going to the men's camp,' said the woman who had hidden with us in the bunker. 'I want to find out what happened to my husband and son.'

We couldn't stop her. In her shoes I would have done the same thing. But Dora and I thought it was wiser to go back to our hiding spot. We were right. At first light SS soldiers arrived in trucks. They spread throughout the camp, dragging sick patients out of bunkers and forcing them to stand in the snow. Dora and I clung to each other when we heard soldiers breaking into the storage bunker where we were hiding. We covered ourselves with piles of blankets but the soldiers had brought dogs and we were sniffed out.

'Out! Out!' the soldiers screamed, beating us with the butts of their rifles.

We were forced to line up with the other women from the camp in rows of five. Jewish women were placed in the front rows, the rest of us behind them. The blood drained from my face. They were going to execute us, row by row. I glanced up, willing the Soviet Air Force to arrive. But the sky remained empty.

The soldiers formed into their murder squads. The woman next to me, a Polish resistance fighter, started to pray. From the rhythm of her speech I knew that she was reciting the Lord's Prayer. I crossed myself.

From behind the soldiers came a rumbling sound: vehicle engines. A convoy of German armoured cars pulled up.

An officer leaped out and rushed towards the commander of the firing squad. A heated discussion took place, and a few moments later the commander gave an order and the soldiers turned on their heels and boarded the trucks that had brought them here. Then they drove off towards the road to join the convoy.

We prisoners looked at each other. We were still alive despite such a close encounter with death. Several women fainted.

'We'd better find some food and drinking water,' Dora said.

We hurried as fast as our thin bodies could carry us to the main camp, checking over our shoulders for guards, but no one appeared. Some of the prisoners had already raided the SS storage cellars and were astounded to find piles of warm clothing and food left behind in the Nazis' haste to depart.

Dora grabbed a coat, a pair of boots and some bread. 'I'm not taking any chances,' she told me. 'I'm leaving now!'

For me, the best decision seemed to be to stay in the camp and wait for the Red Army. I embraced my companion of the past eighteen months, knowing that I would never see her again.

Red Army soldiers arrived at the camp the following day. We gathered around the fences and watched them.

They were horrified when they saw the state we were in. Several of them tugged open the gates. 'You are free!' they shouted. 'You are free! You can go home!'

We staggered towards them, embracing and kissing them. I stumbled towards one soldier and fell at his feet. 'Thank you!' I cried, hugging his legs. 'Thank you for coming for us!'

The soldier's eyes filled with tears. 'Comrade, you are Russian?' he asked, bending down to help me up. 'Of all the horrors I have seen … Comrade, what have those monsters done to you?'

The Red Army brought with them doctors, nurses and volunteers, and the stone buildings of the main camp were turned into hospital wards. The nurses tended to the sick, while the volunteers, many of them Polish people from the surrounding countryside, handed out clothes from the storage rooms. I had borne the cold so long that the coat, boots, underwear and dress I was given felt luxurious.

Now that we were free, I wanted to return to my regiment — which was my first duty — and then make contact with my mother. It was raining and the snow was turning to mud but I was determined to leave Auschwitz as soon as possible. The soldiers said that the government was setting up repatriation points for Soviet men and women who had ended up in Poland or Germany as prisoners or forced labourers. They told me there was one in Katowice, thirty-three kilometres north-west of Auschwitz. The food volunteers gave me a package of cheese, bread and dried fruit for the journey.

I headed towards the gate, shoving my hands in my pockets to keep them warm. My fingers touched something inside. I took the object out: it was a ticket for a cinema in Budapest. The discovery drove home to me that I was wearing another woman's coat; a woman who had met her end in the gas chambers. Something in my mind jumped. I heard screaming and lifted my hands to my temples. I saw the dead woman in the cart and her miscarried child. My feet felt as if they were sinking into the ground. The buildings around me no longer seemed solid but vibrated before my eyes.

A soldier near the gate turned and looked at me. I

collapsed to my knees and he rushed towards me. 'Wait!' he said, helping me up. 'You'll freeze to death.'

He took me back to the hospital barracks, informing one of the nurses what had happened. The nurse took my pulse and my temperature, then made me remove the coat so she could feel my arms and legs.

'What made you think that you'd have the strength to walk to Katowice?' she asked. 'You're malnourished and dehydrated. Stay here another week and rest. Then you can go.'

Over the next few days, I helped the volunteers in the kitchen by peeling potatoes and chopping cabbage for the vats of soup they made for the hospital patients, staff and soldiers.

'It's just as well the nurse stopped you from heading out on your own,' one of the cooks told me. 'They are driving some of the hospital patients to the railway station this afternoon to evacuate them to Katowice. You'd best go with them. The army unit stationed here is well disciplined, but there are other units that are roaming the countryside and raping any women and children they find. Their officers can't seem to bring them under control. They target mainly German women for revenge, but they've also raped Russian women and Jewish women liberated from the Nazi camps.'

The cook's news filled me with dismay. Being in Auschwitz had confirmed that I'd fought on the side of right in this war. But the behaviour of these Russian soldiers meant that we were brutes now, just like the Nazis.

The trucks in which we were driven to the station were crowded and uncomfortable, but the volunteers made sure each person had plenty of food and water.

'Eat only small amounts,' a nurse reminded a male patient

who was no more than skin and bones. His eyes were enormous globes in his head. 'If you eat too much or too quickly your digestive system won't be able to take it,' she warned him.

As we exited the main gate, I glanced back at the ironwork sign that I had seen that first day: *Arbeit macht frei*. I looked at the emaciated man the nurse had spoken to and felt sure that whatever life threw at me, it could never be worse than what we prisoners had endured at Auschwitz. What could be worse than the very depths of hell?

TWENTY-SIX

Katowice, 1945

In Katowice we were met by Polish Red Cross volunteers and billeted in public buildings. Inside the school, where I was to stay with other former inmates of Auschwitz, we were led to a dining hall and given soup to eat. It was nothing like the foul-tasting muck at the camp. The soup was flavoured with onions, pickle and dill and I relished every piece of carrot, potato and parsnip in it. Mama made a similar dish and the taste reminded me that I would see her again soon.

While we were eating, some women arrived. They explained that they were Polish Jews who had been hidden by sympathetic neighbours in Katowice. One woman showed me a picture of a mother with two young children. 'Did you see my sister and her boys at the camp?' she asked in German, which was the common language between us all now. 'She was given up by a work colleague.'

I took the photograph from her and studied it, then shook my head and handed it back. How could I tell her that her sister and her nephews were surely dead? I didn't have words for what I had witnessed at Auschwitz. When later I took a bath I soaped myself vigorously, scrubbing behind my ears and between my toes, as if I could cleanse off the horror. But when I dried myself, it seemed that the stench of burnt flesh still clung to me. I was distressed that I might never be rid of the smell.

The following day a doctor examined me, and afterwards I was interviewed by a Red Cross official. She was assisted by a Russian interpreter. The woman was brisk and efficient in her manner but the interpreter made me uncomfortable. When he spoke to me his lips curled back, exposing his yellow teeth. It gave me the impression of a dog about to attack.

The official took down the number that was tattooed on my arm. 'The guards destroyed most of the registers before they fled Auschwitz,' she said through the interpreter. 'You have to tell us who you are.'

I hesitated. I had been a number for so long that I'd almost forgotten my name and who I was along with it. The memory of the NKVD officer staring at me across the sunflower field came back to me. Was it better to go on pretending I was Svetlana? But I was not as scared of the NKVD as I had once been. Now that the Soviet Union was on the brink of victory, I doubted that they would persecute me when I had fought for the Motherland and had ended up in Auschwitz for my trouble.

'I am Natalya Stepanovna Azarova.'

I gave my rank and regiment details. My name meant nothing to the official, but the interpreter frowned. 'I want to rejoin my regiment,' I told them. 'I can be useful to the Soviet Air Force when they enter Berlin.'

The interpreter translated my remark for the official but it seemed to me that he added some comment of his own.

'I admire your courage,' the official told me, 'but according to the doctor's report you are suffering from malnutrition.

The Soviet government has ordered all prisoners of war to be sent to Odessa for repatriation. The train won't leave for another week, however, so why don't you take the opportunity to recuperate here? The medical officer in Odessa will be able to judge if you have improved enough by then to rejoin your regiment.'

I was disappointed at not being returned to combat immediately but disobeying the order to go to Odessa would have been regarded as desertion.

At the end of the interview, the official gave me a notebook and a pen. As soon as I returned to the dormitory I wrote letters to Mama and Valentin. I didn't tell them that I had been in Auschwitz, only that I'd been captured. I poured out my love for them, and wrote out the words of 'Wait For Me' for Valentin.

When I boarded the train for Odessa the following week, I was buoyant with joy. I would soon be back among my people and flying again! The other Russian women in my carriage were mostly nurses who had been captured, or civilians who had been taken to Poland to work in the labour camps for the German Reich. There were a couple of tank drivers but no other pilots.

A young woman sat down next to me and introduced herself as Zinaida Glebovna Rusakova. We started talking and I learned that she was from Moscow too. She had been in her final year of medical school when the war broke out and had enlisted as a field doctor.

'I was captured when the Germans encircled the Soviet Army in Vyazma,' she told me. 'I was kept in a prisoner-of-war camp until I was brought to Poland to work in a German armaments factory.'

'You were captured in 1941!' I exclaimed. 'How did you survive so long?'

Zinaida leaned towards me and whispered, 'The prisoner-of-war camp was pure hell, but at the armaments factory we weren't treated badly. I ate better there than I had when I was growing up in Moscow!'

I was taken aback by Zinaida's story. It made me wonder whether I might have ended up in a camp like hers instead of Auschwitz if I hadn't tried to escape. 'The thing that kept me going,' Zinaida continued, 'was that I made sure every twentieth shell I produced was a dud. That way I was still assisting the Motherland.'

I was filled with admiration. Zinaida could have been hanged or burned alive for doing that. I'd seen it happen to inmates in Auschwitz who had tried the same thing. She reminded me of Svetlana in many ways: she had the same bright, cultivated energy.

The memory of Svetlana's death came back to me. I'd had to shut it out in order to survive, but now it returned like a nightmare. My heart ached and I excused myself to go out into the corridor so I could shed the tears I should have cried back then. But even though I wept my heart out, I felt no relief. I tried to recall the good things about Svetlana — her pretty face, the sound of her voice, her gentle touch, but they were blurred. I'd lost the essence of my friend when I'd shot her. How could I ever live with myself?

As the train moved through the Ukraine, I was sickened by the destruction I saw. Entire villages had been reduced to ruins. The people who remained were living in holes in the ground, like rabbits in burrows.

The women and I were travelling in passenger carriages but attached to the train were some cattle cars like the ones the Germans had used to transport prisoners to Auschwitz. When we stopped, I saw men climbing out of those cars to stretch their legs and go to the toilet, always under the watchful eyes of the guards.

'Who are those men?' I asked Zinaida.

'They are soldiers who were captured by the Germans and agreed to fight on their side in special Russian units,' she replied. 'They will certainly be tried as traitors when they're repatriated, but I guess it was either that or starve.'

Although Odessa had been bombed and parts of it lay in ruins, the station was decorated with garlands of flowers and a band played the Soviet anthem when we alighted from the train. There was a giant portrait of Stalin with a message written underneath it: *Our great leader, Comrade Stalin, welcomes his children home.* I stared at the portrait and recalled my last conversation with Valentin when he had told me Stalin had personally signed my father's execution order. Now, as much as I hated Stalin, I could never show it. I had to think of Mama. We were directed by soldiers to walk to the port on foot. A New Zealand warship had arrived from Marseille and Allied soldiers were supervising the disembarkation of troops of Soviet soldiers.

The passengers from our train were led towards a warehouse. Outside it, Soviet officials examined the passenger lists from both the train and the ship. We were divided into two groups. The first group of repatriated men and women, including Zinaida, were ordered to enter the warehouse. As part of the second group, I remained outside. I had an eerie flashback to the selection process at Auschwitz, but in my anticipation of getting back to my regiment I pushed the memory away.

'What's going on?' an Allied officer from the ship asked one of the officials in Russian.

'Don't worry,' the official told him. 'We are dividing people into groups to make the processing easier.'

The Allied officer nodded and shook hands with the official before returning to his ship.

A truck arrived from the station with the belongings of those who had come by train. It was a shabby assortment — mainly bundles of clothing and other personal items. Everything I owned I now carried in my pocket: the notebook and pen the Red Cross official had given me, and the toothbrush, toothpaste and comb I'd been issued with in Katowice. The possessions were dumped in a pile. A soldier came along with a can of petrol and poured it over the goods before setting them alight. Those of us who saw what happened gasped but nobody dared protest. I searched my mind for an explanation. The only one I could think of for this callous act was that many of the camps had been plagued by typhus-carrying lice. Fire was the only way to destroy them.

Two Ilyushin bombers appeared and circled over the harbour. The sound of their engines was deafening. What were they doing? I heard a sound like a volley of gunshots. Feeling uneasy, I looked around, but nobody else seemed to have noticed.

About half an hour later the planes left and two men wheeled a mobile sawmill into place next to where we stood. The piercing scream of the saw hurt my ears. Was there some purpose in creating this noise? Then the doors to the warehouse opened again and our group was ordered inside.

I was following my companions when an official grabbed my arm. 'Natalya Stepanovna Azarova?'

I nodded.

'Come this way,' he said.

He led me along the length of the warehouse towards a waiting car.

'What is the meaning of this?' I asked.

'I have orders that you are to be sent directly to Moscow,' the official said. 'I know nothing further.'

The driver opened the door for me. Before getting in, I noticed four men flinging what at first I thought were sacks onto a truck. Then I realised that they weren't sacks. They were bodies. The men misjudged the distance with one corpse and it toppled to the ground. Its head flopped back and its eyes stared straight at me. I recognised the face and my blood turned cold: it was Zinaida.

As soon as I was put on the train to Moscow I knew a hero's welcome was not what was in store for me. The train compartment was divided into wired cages. Several prisoners shared the other cages but I was placed in one by myself, with nothing more than a plank bed. The window was barred and had been painted over so I couldn't see outside.

When we arrived in Moscow, my fellow prisoners were bundled into a prison truck but I was shoved into a baker's van with gold lettering on the side: *Bread, Rolls & Cakes*. I had seen hundreds of these types of bakery vans around Moscow before the war. Now I realised that they hadn't been carrying bread at all. It explained why the food stores were always empty and the prisons so full.

As the van bumped and jerked along the streets, I heard the sounds of Moscow around me: the rattle of the trams;

car horns; construction workers calling out to each other. After a short while the van stopped and I was ordered out. I found myself in the courtyard of a massive building, which felt oddly familiar. Then I realised I was in the Lubyanka, the headquarters of the NKVD. It was where my father had been taken the night he was arrested. Two guards armed with machine guns escorted me inside. I was thrown into a brightly lit cell with green walls and a parquet floor. The window was boarded up. The only furniture was an iron-framed bed and a slops bucket that gave off the sickly sweet odour of carbolic acid. There was nowhere for me to sit except on the bed, but as soon as I approached it a square window opened in the door and a guard looked in at me.

'Stand up!' he whispered. 'No sleeping!'

Why was he whispering? The window closed again and I waited, expecting something to occur, but hours passed and nobody came to the cell. All I could hear was the sound of my own frantic breathing. Papa's face flashed before me. Everything that was happening to me had happened to him. The thought that my cheerful, playful father had suffered the mental anguish that I was now enduring made me weep.

Sometime later, the guard opened the door. A man wheeled in a trolley on which sat a silver serving platter covered by a dome. Was I being brought some sort of elaborate dinner? The man lifted the dome to reveal two pieces of black bread and a mug of hot water.

Although I hadn't eaten for days, my nerves had destroyed my appetite. I forced myself to swallow the food and water. When I'd finished I sat down on the bed.

The guard immediately entered the cell and whispered, 'Get up! No resting for you!'

'Why are you whispering?' I asked him.

'Shh!' he said. 'It is not permitted to speak loudly here.'

I assumed that I wasn't allowed to rest because I was about to be interrogated. I paced the floor but still nothing happened. Finally, a long time later, a different guard opened the door and ordered me into the corridor. I was taken down several flights of stairs to a basement where a woman in a military uniform ordered me to take off all my clothes and lay them on the table. She went thoroughly over each item, snipping the buttons off the dress with a pair of scissors, emptying the pockets and feeling along the seams. She threw my brassiere and stocking garters into a bucket, then cut the elastic out of my underpants and set it to one side along with my coat, stockings, boots, hat, gloves and scarf. She made me remove my hairpins so she could search through my hair.

'Now get dressed,' she said.

I pulled on my slip and tied a knot in my underpants so they wouldn't fall down. Without the buttons I couldn't fasten my dress so I held it closed with my hand. I waited for the woman to give me back the other items but she didn't. In my dishevelled state I was marched to another room where I was photographed and had my fingerprints taken. After that I was returned to my cell.

It was cold in the cell without my coat and boots. I lay down on the bed and curled up into a ball. The guard appeared at the window in the door and whispered that if I was going to sleep I had to keep my face turned to the light. I rolled onto my back and fell asleep. I was jolted awake by a bloodcurdling scream. I sat up. What sort of animal had made the sound? A few seconds later the howl sounded again and I realised it was a man crying out. He screamed again, just once, then made no other sound. A few minutes later the guard came into my cell. 'Hurry!' he whispered. 'The interrogator is ready.'

I was marched along a corridor with my hands secured behind my back. Without the buttons, my dress slipped open and I couldn't hold it closed as before. There were several minutes of going up and down stairs and along corridors, and all the while I was terrified I was going to be tortured like the man I had heard screaming. Then I was pushed into the same cell I had just come from.

The pattern of not allowing me to sleep, or disturbing me when I did, continued for what seemed like weeks but may have only been days. I lost all sense of time. My food continued to be served in the same elaborate way but was always a starvation ration: black bread and a cup of hot water; two spoonfuls of porridge and a cup of hot water; soup that was often nothing more than a cabbage leaf floating in hot water. The bread was fresh and the porridge was tasty, but it wasn't enough. Then one night the guard woke me and whispered, 'Time for your interrogation.' I expected to go through the same farce of walking up and down the stairs and corridors to no purpose other than to frustrate me. But this time I was led down a different corridor and into a spacious room where a man was waiting for me behind a desk. The room was lavishly decorated with carved table lamps, Bessarabian rugs and gold curtains. A portrait of Stalin hung on the wall and a fire gave off a warm glow.

'The prisoner is ready for interrogation,' announced the guard.

The man behind the desk was around thirty years of age and wore a major's uniform, but his pudgy face and pot belly told me that he hadn't fought on the frontline. His gaze fell to my breasts. I rearranged my dress to cover myself.

'Please sit down,' the major said, indicating a mahogany-and-velvet chair opposite his desk. 'I trust you have been treated well?'

He didn't wait for an answer and nodded at the guard to dismiss him. A few minutes later a woman came in with a tray of tea things and *pryaniki*. The honey and nutmeg aroma of the cookies made me even more aware of how hungry I was.

The major poured tea into a cup and placed it in front of me. 'Lemon? A cube of sugar? Jam?' he asked me. 'Some *pryaniki*?'

Although I was starving, I shook my head. Surely this was a trick.

'Why am I here?' I asked. 'Why have I been arrested?'

The major took a sip from his own cup and stared at the ceiling for a few moments, giving me a view of his double chin. Then he turned his attention back to me. 'To confess your crimes,' he said.

His voice was gentle and encouraging, like a lover. It sent shivers down my spine.

'I am Natalya Stepanovna Azarova,' I told him. 'The pilot. I was downed over enemy territory in Orël Oblast after running out of ammunition and ramming a Messerschmitt with my own airplane. I was captured by the enemy, and although I tried to commit suicide and also to escape I did not succeed in my attempts. I was transported to Auschwitz where I remained until it was liberated by the Red Army on the twenty-seventh of January. I haven't committed any crime that I am aware of. I never *surrendered* to the enemy. I fought with everything I had.'

The major lit a cigarette and inhaled deeply. 'What did you do at Auschwitz?'

'I was put to work sorting food and clothing.'

The major turned his penetrating gaze on me. I suddenly felt guilty. But surely sorting clothes in order to receive food for survival wasn't aiding the enemy?

'We have plenty of time in the Lubyanka,' he said. 'We never hurry. At first it barely hurts and you wonder what all the fuss is about. And then ... well, if you continue with these lies you will find out.'

I tried to appear calm but my heart was racing. 'Everything I've told you is the truth!' I said.

The major rose from his seat and stood above me. 'Lies! Lies! Lies!' he screamed. His face was so close to mine that I could smell the vodka-scented sweat of his skin. 'You are Zinaida Glebovna Rusakova and you worked for the Gestapo!'

'That's wrong!' I replied. 'Zinaida Glebovna Rusakova was a passenger I met on the train from Katowice to Odessa. She was shot when we arrived at the port!'

'Do you know the punishment for spying, Zinaida Glebovna?' the major asked me. A thread of spittle clung to the corner of his lip and his forehead was covered in sweat.

'I told you, I'm not Zinaida Glebovna!'

Zinaida had said she'd worked in a labour camp in Poland. Either she'd been lying or the major was. I remembered Zinaida's friendly manner and was certain she hadn't worked for the Gestapo.

The major took a strand of my hair between his fingers. 'You have long hair. You haven't wasted away to skin and bones. You don't look like someone who has been in Auschwitz. You look like a well-fed German whore. Where did you get that dress?'

Was it worth even replying, I wondered. The more I argued with the major the further I seemed to be dragged into his game. Was he trying to make me believe that there'd been a mix-up and I'd been arrested in Zinaida's place? But to what purpose? There was probably no logic to the interrogation. It was nothing more than sadism.

I had spent eighteen months in a concentration camp, and two years before that fighting in a brutal war. I was physically and mentally exhausted. I pulled up the sleeve of my dress to reveal my Auschwitz tattoo. 'What is it you want from me?' I asked. 'If you are convinced that I worked for the Gestapo why didn't you put a bullet through my head in Odessa? If it's information about the Germans you want, I have nothing to give you!'

The major returned to his chair and put on a pair of spectacles. He opened a folder on his desk and rummaged through its papers as if he'd forgotten me. Then he looked at me over the rim of his glasses.

'You think it's going to be as easy as that?' he said coldly. 'Yes, you will be killed — eventually — but you're going to have to *work* for your death. You are going to pay back the Motherland for your crimes against her. Where Auschwitz failed, Kolyma will succeed.' Kolyma? That was a prison colony in the Arctic Circle. Nobody came back from there! 'In Kolyma you will become thin and your skin will turn black,' said the major, emphasising each word. 'Your teeth will fall out and your organs will shrivel. But not before you have worked with the last drop of your blood to atone for your crimes. We'll keep you alive long enough to do that.'

'I am not a criminal!'

The major went back to looking through his folder. He pulled out a piece of paper and placed it in front of me.

'Sign this,' he said. 'It's your confession.'

My situation was hopeless, I knew, but I couldn't give in to these ridiculous accusations.

'I will not sign it!' I said. 'I told you: I am Natalya Stepanovna Azarova. I am a decorated fighter pilot. I fought for my country! Did you?'

I expected my taunt to infuriate the major but he didn't react.

'I would stop pretending that you are Natalya Azarova if I were you,' he said. 'Don't you know that Natalya Azarova deliberately flew into enemy territory so she could join the Germans? She was a daughter of an enemy of the people, but she lied to get a job at an aircraft factory and then lied to the Komsomol in order to become a member. She even lied to the great Marina Raskova and the Soviet Air Force. She's already been stripped of her medals.'

I was too shocked to say anything more. So that is what the Soviet people would be told: that I was a spy and a traitor! How could justice prevail as long as Stalin was leader?

The major took some papers out of the folder and made sure that I got a look at them. They were the letters I had written to Mama and Valentin in Katowice. Letters that I now knew they would never receive.

'Besides,' said the major, throwing the letters into the fire, 'if you *were* Natalya Azarova, you would sign the confession.' He grinned. 'Natalya Azarova would remember that she has a mother who lives in the Arbat. And … oh yes, a fighter pilot for a lover. His name is Valentin Victorovich Orlov, I believe.'

I understood then that everything was lost. The NKVD knew perfectly well who I was. My beloved Motherland was in the hands of lunatics. 'Yes, Natalya Azarova would sign her confession,' continued the major, 'if she didn't want something … *dreadful* to happen to those she loved.' He pushed the paper closer to me and handed me a pen. 'Remember to sign it by your real name, Zinaida Glebovna.'

My hand wavered over the document. If I didn't sign it, the NKVD would still kill me, and Valentin and Mama would certainly be doomed. Signing it was the only chance I had of protecting them. My hand trembled as I formed the letters of my false signature. When I had finished, the pen slipped from my fingers and clattered to the floor.

The major opened the curtains to reveal a view of the square below. The snow had melted and the sky was a magnificent blue.

'Look at Moscow one last time!' he said, spreading his arms wide. 'Say goodbye. You won't be seeing it again. Twenty years' hard labour without the right of correspondence.' That was my sentence? In signing the confession Natalya Azarova had ceased to exist and I was as good as dead.

TWENTY-SEVEN

Moscow, 2000

Natasha was about to continue with her story when Polina came in pushing a mobile drip.

'Ah, I see she's been drinking some water,' she said, pointing to the half-empty jug on the bedside table. 'I called Doctor Pesenko and he recommended giving her intravenous fluids anyway.'

Polina set about preparing to insert the catheter into Natasha's arm. Lily was aware that she and Oksana had been with Natasha for nearly two hours, a much longer visiting time than was usually allowed. She wanted to hear the rest of Natasha's story, but the nurses had a schedule to keep, and Natasha's health came first.

'We'll come and see you tomorrow,' Lily said, patting Natasha's hand. 'And I'll bring Laika.'

The dismay on the old woman's face stung Lily. She sympathised. How could the telling of Natasha's life story be interrupted at this crucial point, like a video put on pause for a toilet break?

On the way out of the hospital, Oksana's mobile phone rang. While she took the call, Lily thought about what Natasha had told them. It had been a rollercoaster ride and her head was spinning. She had come to Russia to connect with a country that was part of her heritage and had got much more than she'd bargained for.

Oksana ended the call and looked at Lily. 'That was Antonia. She went to feed the cats this afternoon at the Zamoskvorechye building site and a woman from the apartment block opposite threw a bucket of water over her. She also found several dead kittens. Their heads had been crushed, probably with a brick.'

'That's awful!' said Lily. 'Does Antonia think it's the same woman?'

Oksana shrugged. 'Possibly. We deal with this all the time. People see stray cats as vermin.'

Lily knew the Moscow Animals volunteers had been speeding up their trapping programme with winter approaching, but the difficult thing was finding people who could care for the cats. Oksana had recently found a home for Max and Georgy, and Lily expected that she'd miss the kittens when they went to live with their new owner.

'I can take more cats into my apartment,' she said.

Oksana shook her head. 'I can't impose on you like that. You've been generous enough as it is.'

'Yes, you can,' said Lily, grinning. 'I want to be a crazy cat lady like you!'

Oksana laughed. 'What are you up to tonight? Do you want to come trap some cats?'

'There's nothing I'd rather do!' Lily replied.

She wasn't entirely joking. After listening to Natasha's harrowing story, she didn't want to be alone, and Oksana would understand exactly how she was feeling.

At the building site, Oksana set up the new box trap she'd invented in the hope of outsmarting Tuz, a ginger tom who had figured out how to remove food from a trap without stepping on the trigger plate and getting caught. They needed to trap him urgently because he was one of the toms impregnating the females and adding to the cat population.

'It's going to take patience,' Oksana told Lily. 'It's not easy to fool street-smart cats like him, and Antonia has already fed the colony. Normally we don't give them food on the day of the trapping so the cats are hungry enough to take the bait.'

To work the box trap, Lily and Oksana had to sit some distance away holding the string that set off the trap. While they were waiting for the cats, a woman appeared at the fence.

'You're trespassing!' she told them. 'I'll call the police.'

Oksana went over to explain to the woman what they were doing. From their conversation it became apparent to Lily that this was the woman who'd thrown the bucket of water over Antonia and possibly killed the kittens. She'd expected the woman to be a crazy old biddy, but she was smartly dressed in linen trousers and a tailored blouse, and looked to be in her mid-forties. What a bitch, Lily thought, indignant on behalf of all the volunteers who were trying to help the animals.

'We're with an authorised animal group and we're removing the cats,' Lily heard Oksana say. 'Leave us to do what we have to and then you won't have any more cats to worry about, okay?'

The woman pursed her lips and stormed off.

'People like that disgust me,' Oksana told Lily when she returned to her spot. 'They have no compassion at all.'

It was two in the morning before any of the cats ventured near the box trap. By then Lily had resorted to wiggling her toes and fingers to keep the blood flowing. The first cat that approached was a tortoiseshell that looked like Mamochka and might have been one of her daughters. But she only inspected the trap from the outside before scurrying away.

Tuz was the next cat to appear. To the women's astonishment, he went straight inside the box trap. Oksana pulled the string and the door closed. Tuz spun around in terror and Lily felt sorry for him, but she knew he would be better off after Luka had desexed him, and Oksana had found him a new home.

In his panic, Tuz darted straight from the box trap into a cage with only a poke from Lily. Oksana shut the door.

'All right, Tuz, my friend,' she said, about to throw a blanket over the cage to calm him down, 'off to a new life for you!'

'Stop! Don't move! Get down on the ground with your arms and legs spread!'

Torchlight shone over them and Lily and Oksana turned to see two policemen scaling the fence and running towards them.

'Shit!' said Oksana.

'Get down!' yelled one of the policemen, pointing his gun at them.

Lily wasn't about to argue. She lay next to Oksana and felt one of the policemen grab her arms and pin them behind her back. It was surreal. She'd never even so much as received a parking fine in Australia and now she was being arrested?

The policemen hauled the women to their feet and pushed them towards the fence. After they'd all climbed back over, they handcuffed Lily and Oksana and led them towards the police van. Oksana tried to explain about Tuz: that he couldn't be left exposed in a cage like that; he needed to be let out. But one of the policemen told her to shut up.

The sound of the van door slamming shut on them unnerved Lily. She was living Natasha's story. Were she and Oksana about to be taken to the Lubyanka?

'So explain to me again what you were doing,' said the burly sergeant.

Lily glanced at the clock on the wall. It was four o'clock on Sunday afternoon and she and Oksana had spent the whole day in a stinking cell along with a chain-smoking prostitute. The women had been permitted to make one call each, and Lily had phoned the Australian embassy's emergency line. The official who'd responded had said he would contact her employer, but so far there'd been no word from the hotel. Oksana had used her call to contact Luka so he could provide evidence of their work with animals, but his receptionist had informed her that he was out on an emergency call. She'd also asked the guard to call the hospital where Natasha was, to explain that they would not be able to see her, but he'd just shrugged as if to say it wasn't his problem. When the prostitute was let out she said to them, 'I'll get my things back and then I'll telephone the hospital for you.' True to her word, she'd returned a few minutes later to tell them that the nurse on duty had said that Natasha was fine and had been sleeping most of the day.

'I'm a committee member for Moscow Animals,' Oksana explained to the sergeant for the second time. 'My colleague here is a volunteer. We've been rescuing stray cats from the building site and re-homing them. We're trying to get all the cats out before winter sets in.'

The sergeant looked at the policemen who had arrested them. They stood by the door, arms folded, faces stern. 'You didn't find anything on them? Narcotics? Dope?'

The policemen shook their heads. The sergeant gave a weary sigh and turned back to Lily and Oksana. 'An informant from an apartment opposite reported that she saw you selling drugs.'

Lily thought of the woman who had confronted Oksana. Then she thought of Tuz, terrified and trapped in a cage with no food or water. That woman would probably do something terrible to him. It made her want to cry.

The sergeant clucked his tongue. 'At the very least I'll have to charge you with trespassing.'

There was a flurry of activity outside the door and Lily's heart lifted when she heard Scott's voice asking to see her. He was shown in, and the police sergeant explained what had taken place. Scott's skin was glowing and he was wearing a plush tracksuit. He looked like he'd come from the gym.

'You've been arrested for rescuing cats?' he asked Lily, raising his eyebrows.

Lily felt foolish, as if she'd been arrested for riding a unicycle nude down Tverskaya Street, holding a bunch of balloons.

'No, for trespassing,' said the sergeant.

'Because she was rescuing cats?' asked Scott.

The sergeant looked exasperated. It wasn't a good sign.

Another policeman came in carrying the cage with Tuz in it. The tomcat was snarling and swiping like a lion at a circus. Lily was relieved to see him still alive.

'We found this at the site,' said the officer, placing the cage on the floor. 'But no drugs, not at the site nor in the suspects' car.'

Oksana put her jacket over the cage to calm Tuz. 'You must always cover them,' she scolded the policeman, 'or they panic so much they can injure themselves on the wire.'

'You're not wrong,' said the policeman. 'This one pissed all over the car.'

Lily suppressed a smile. Undesexed male cat urine? It was going to take weeks for that smell to fade.

Scott bent down and lifted a corner of the jacket to look at Tuz in the cage. 'So this is one of the cats you were rescuing, is it, Lily?' He went to poke his finger through the wire to pat Tuz.

'Please don't,' said Lily. 'These cats aren't used to humans. They need to be desexed and socialised before they can be handled like ordinary pets.'

She realised that everyone in the room was staring at her, and the feeling of being nude on a unicycle grew stronger.

'So does this cat need a home?' Scott asked.

'We have a serious problem here,' the sergeant interrupted. 'These women have been arrested for trespassing. One of them is a foreigner and an employee of yours.'

'I've already left a message for our hotel lawyer,' Scott said, giving Lily an encouraging wink. 'We'll organise representation as the embassy advised me to.'

The sergeant sucked in his breath and looked even more infuriated. Lily realised that Scott didn't understand what the officer had been hinting at. Arresting her and Oksana had been a waste of time and would make the police look foolish. The sergeant wanted to be recompensed, not to become embroiled in messy paperwork and with lawyers. She wondered how to tell Scott that a bribe was what was called for.

As she was trying to come up with a way to take Scott aside and explain, another man was shown into the room. It was Luka. He sent Lily and Oksana a serious look then addressed the sergeant.

'I believe there has been a misunderstanding and I would like to correct it as quickly as possible,' he said firmly, keeping eye contact with the man.

He pulled an envelope from his pocket and placed it on the desk along with a bottle of vodka. The sergeant's mood improved when he saw the envelope was well padded and the vodka was premium label.

'Well, these things occur,' he said with a gruff laugh. 'No harm has been done. We can send everyone home now and not give it too much thought.'

'I believe there are more cats at the site that need to be rescued,' Luka said, keeping his gaze on the sergeant.

Lily watched in amazement. Luka had always been so gentle and considerate; she hadn't imagined he could also be stern and determined, bold enough to stare down the law.

'Well, we won't be arresting these two again,' the sergeant said, indicating Lily and Oksana, 'and we'll warn the woman who reported them to stay away from the site.'

With the matter resolved to everyone's satisfaction, Luka picked up Tuz's cage and led Oksana and Lily out to his car. Scott followed, looking impressed by Luka's decisive action.

'Do you need a lift too?' Luka asked him, opening his car doors for the women.

'Oh, no, thank you,' Scott answered when he realised Luka was talking to him. 'I drove.'

'Thanks for coming, Scott,' Lily said. 'I'm very sorry for the trouble.'

'Not at all,' he replied, still looking distracted.

Oksana got into the front passenger seat while Lily sat in the back. Luka secured Tuz's cage next to her with the seatbelt.

'I don't like resorting to bribes,' he said, 'but sometimes it's the only way to get out of a tricky situation. As we say in Russia, "Let's put a candle before God and a present before the judge."'

He settled in behind the wheel and handed Oksana a key from his pocket. 'I'm sorry, I only got your message an hour ago. I had two animal emergencies today. All the other traps at the site were empty. I put them in your car and locked it. I'll drive you there now.'

'The police left the key in the ignition?' asked Oksana incredulously. 'I'm amazed it wasn't stolen.'

Luka was about to pull away from the kerb when Scott knocked on Oksana's window. Luka lowered the glass so they could speak to each other.

'Listen!' Scott said, his eyes shining with excitement. 'When you ladies next go trapping cats, can I come too?'

It was six o'clock in the evening by the time they picked up the traps, and too late to visit Natasha on a Sunday night. Luka took Tuz straight to his practice to desex him.

'He's had enough stress in that cage all day,' he said. 'We'd better do it now so we can get him settled into a larger cage.'

He arrived a while later at Lily's flat with Tuz still drowsy from the anaesthetic and transferred him to a hospital cage Oksana had set up in Lily's living room.

'If you aren't worn out from your brush with the law, would you like to come to the cinema with me tonight?' Luka asked the two women. '*Man with a Movie Camera* is showing. It's a late session, so we'll make it in time.'

'Not me,' said Oksana. 'I'm exhausted. But Lily ought to go — it's a Russian classic.'

'Sure,' Lily said. She'd been wrought up by the day's events and needed to relax before she could sleep. 'I'll just take a quick shower. I've heard of that film but I've never seen it.'

'You'll love it,' said Oksana, giving her a wink.

The cinema was in one of the skyscrapers known to foreigners as the Seven Sisters, built in Stalin's preferred mix of Baroque and Gothic styles. It had the musky odour of an antiques store, and the ticket seller resembled a café intellectual from the 1920s in his turtleneck sweater and beret. Lily stopped to look at the framed posters of coming attractions, including *Dark Eyes* with Marcello Mastroianni and *Dreams* directed by Akira Kurosawa. She hadn't been to see an art-house film since her university days. Adam had loved action films and going to the cinema with him usually meant watching something like *Die Hard* or Arnold Schwarzenegger's latest release.

'I hope you enjoy the film,' said Luka. 'The director is Vertov — he was at the forefront of the Russian avant-garde. The film was made in 1929.'

Lily and Luka took their seats in the cinema, along with a group of students and some elderly Russian women. The lights dimmed and the opulent red curtains swept back to reveal the tiny screen.

'It's a silent film,' Luka whispered. 'The cinema's giving it an orchestral soundtrack tonight.'

Within minutes, Lily found herself hypnotised by the images on the screen. The film showed Soviet citizens in various Ukrainian cities from dawn until dusk. Machines and the way people interacted with them became 'art' before her eyes. The film didn't show the suffering of the peasants in the countryside, or give any indication of how machines would be used to destroy life in the near future. Instead, it burst with vitality and a sense of optimism. It was exactly the sort of film she needed to see after the weekend she'd had.

When it ended, she turned to Luka. 'That was one of the most beautiful films I've ever seen!'

'Many of the cinematic techniques Vertov used were experimental for the day — double exposure, jump cuts, tracking shots and so on,' he explained.

They headed towards the cinema café in the foyer, found a table and sat down.

'You were great with the police sergeant today,' Lily told Luka. 'I think you even impressed my boss with your *savoir faire*. Have you had many run-ins with the law?'

'No,' laughed Luka. 'And you?'

'That was my first,' Lily told him. 'Thank you for saving us, by the way.'

'No problem,' he said, reaching out and touching her hand briefly. 'I'll always come to your rescue.'

Lily looked down at her menu, embarrassed. It was a nice sentiment for Luka to express but it was something Adam would have said. He had promised to always be there for her and now he wasn't.

Lily found it difficult to concentrate at work on Monday. She wanted the day to be over with so she could go to the hospital and see Natasha again. She hoped that the old woman wouldn't be angry and clam up on them. No one knew how much time she had left and Lily sensed it was important to her that somebody knew the truth about what had happened.

'My thoughts are simple and concise.'

Lily glanced up to see Scott standing next to her desk. Oh God, she thought, what's my affirmation? Then she remembered it was Monday so she'd be getting a new one for the week.

Scott handed her a slip of paper.

'Thanks,' she said, taking the paper and clipping it to her document holder. *I have direction and purpose. I always know exactly where my life is going*, the affirmation read.

How did Scott so consistently manage to give her affirmations that were incongruous to how she was feeling? But instead of being annoyed she was amused. From the way that he had rushed to the police station to help her it was obvious that his intentions were good.

'I like cats,' he announced. 'My wife and I used to volunteer at an animal shelter in Washington. I miss having a cat of my own.'

Their conversation was cut short by Lily's telephone ringing. Scott returned to his office. She watched him go, surprised that she was beginning to feel fondness towards him.

When five o'clock came, Lily tidied her desk and checked her diary for the following day's appointments. Then she rushed home to pick up Laika and meet Oksana. Before she left the apartment, she changed the litter tray and food dishes in Tuz's cage. When Oksana had first brought Mamochka to Lily, the female cat had thrashed around in her cage, but Tuz sat calmly in his covered box. Maybe he's figured out he's better off here, Lily thought.

'How was the film?' Oksana asked her when they got in the car.

Lily settled Laika on her lap. 'I enjoyed it,' she said.

Oksana started the engine and pulled out onto the road. 'Luka's great, isn't he? I've known him since he was a boy,' she remarked after a while.

Lily nodded. 'Yes.'

'Do you like him?'

'Of course I do.'

'Well,' said Oksana, when they searched the hospital car park, 'he seems to like you.'

Lily frowned. 'I don't understand what you mean. He's gay ... isn't he?'

Oksana stared at her as if she'd just confessed she was an alien from outer space. 'Where did you get that idea?'

Lily shifted uneasily. Where *had* she got the idea? 'He's cute, he dresses well, he can cook, he likes to dance ... he has cats named Valentino and Versace.'

'I gave the cats those names!' Oksana said. 'Luka didn't want them to get confused if he renamed them.'

'Oh,' said Lily.

Oksana's mouth twitched and she started to laugh.

'Look,' said Lily, trying to defend herself, 'it's not my fault. Australian men don't wear satin shirts and wiggle their hips when they dance.'

An image came to her of Adam and his friends with their shirts untucked, bouncing around the dance floor to Midnight Oil. But her comment only made Oksana laugh more.

'Luka got married ten years ago,' Oksana said, becoming serious again. 'He wanted a family, to be a young father and all that. He'd known Inna since university, and she seemed to want the same things. But two months after the wedding she decided she'd rather be single. He hasn't looked at anyone since then.'

Lily remembered the remark Luka had made about rescuing her and the way he'd touched her hand. 'I hope I haven't misled him!' she said. 'Especially if he is still shy of relationships after his bad experience.'

Oksana glanced at Lily. She looked amused. 'Why don't you relax and enjoy yourself,' she said, 'and see where things take you? I don't think there is a better man than Luka and you spend far too much time alone.'

Natasha was sitting in a chair by the window. She looked forlorn, but her expression brightened when she saw Laika. Lily expected her to reproach them for not coming the previous day as they'd promised. She was surprised when the old woman turned to them with a thoughtful expression and said, 'For a long time I thought I had lost all recollection of Svetlana. I pretended I was my friend because I was afraid to say who I was. But in talking about her with you, she has come back to life. It's like my friend is here with me again. Thank you.'

Oksana and Lily sat down on either side of the old woman and each held one of her hands. Laika settled near her feet.

'Are you ready?' Natasha asked them.

Lily and Oksana nodded.

Natasha looked at Lily. 'I trusted you with Laika and I wasn't wrong. And I know that I can trust you with this. Please keep your promise that everything I am telling you will never leave this room.'

TWENTY-EIGHT

Kolyma, 1945

Along with hundreds of other prisoners, I was crammed into a train made up of cattle cars similar to those the Germans had used to transport their victims to Auschwitz. We too were starved and refused water on the month-long journey east, and those who were too old or too young did not survive. Their bodies were dumped on the side of the tracks to be finished off by wild animals.

The women in my car were political prisoners like me. On the journey, I learned what their 'crimes' had been. A concert pianist who had studied in Paris was charged with 'counter-revolutionary' activity, as was a woman who had worked in a dress store in Moscow and had served the wife of a foreign diplomat. There was a ballerina who had accepted flowers from an American admirer, and a housewife who had been charged with anti-Soviet agitation for naming her puppy Winston after the British Prime Minister.

'What did you do?' asked the woman next to me, whose name was Agrafena. She was grey-haired with intelligent brown eyes and had once been a university professor.

'I was a prisoner of war in Poland,' I told her, which was as close to the truth as I could get now that I was supposed to be Zinaida Rusakova. 'I've been charged as a terrorist.'

She shook her head. 'No, your crime was to have found yourself in a foreign country. Stalin is terrified that anyone who has been outside the Soviet Union will spread the truth that even in the midst of a war, they *do* live better in the West.'

'And you?' I asked her. 'What's your crime?'

'I told a joke about Stalin.'

'It must have been a bad one!' I exclaimed.

Agrafena shrugged and smiled wryly. 'No, it was a good one. For a bad one I would have got five years. But my joke cost me ten.'

To reach the various camps in Kolyma we were packed into the hold of a steamer and taken across the Sea of Okhotsk. Five days later, green-faced from seasickness and covered in each other's vomit, we arrived in the port of Magadan. The wind blew so hard that we had to brace ourselves against it. It was heavy with salt, which stung our eyes and skin and formed strips of white lace on the shrubs and fences. A huge banner featuring Stalin's face flapped in the breeze: *Glory to Stalin, the father, the teacher and best friend of all Soviet people*. The sight of it nearly destroyed the last shreds of strength I had left. I recognised it as one of the portraits my mother had painted. I understood now why her work wore her down so much: she must have known that Stalin was responsible for Papa's death.

We were made to kneel while the guards counted us. If there were any escapees, the guards would be arrested themselves so they counted and recounted us. They took so long that many people fainted, and those suffering from intestinal ailments had no choice but to soil themselves.

After the roll call we were made to walk in rows of five past two guards. Having lost my boots in the Lubyanka, I'd had to fashion shoes out of rags. I felt every stone and pebble as we were marched up a steep hill into the town.

More banners lined the main street: *Glory to Stalin, the greatest genius of mankind*; *Glory to Stalin, the greatest military leader*; *More gold for our country, more gold for our glory! Welcome to Kolyma!*

'They don't only destroy us,' Agrafena muttered. 'They expect us to be grateful for it!'

When we reached the camp, we were sent to a bathhouse and made to strip in front of male guards. Each of us was issued with half a bucket of water to wash our filthy bodies. In the meantime, our clothes were taken away to be boiled and deloused, then piled in a damp heap on the floor. The underwear and dress I'd been given at Auschwitz were the only possessions I had, and I wanted to hold on to them. I found my slip first; the silk had puckered from the heat but at least it wasn't torn. Then I saw my dress and was relieved to find it was still in one piece.

A hand grabbed my arm. I turned to see a woman wearing only a bra and underpants staring at me. Her enormous breasts were tattooed, as were her shoulders and arms. A cigarette hung from her lip. She sneered at me, revealing her crooked teeth. 'That's my dress,' she said with a pronounced lisp.

'You're mistaken,' I replied.

'It's mine now,' she growled, making a grab for it.

I snatched the dress away and she lunged towards me.

'Political scum!' she hissed.

Two other women joined in the taunts. 'You piece of shit!' one of them said. 'You're not even a Soviet citizen any more!'

The other prisoners backed away, sensing there was going to be a fight. I didn't care who these women were; they weren't going to get my dress. Who knew what lay ahead? I might need to trade the dress for some necessity.

'Give it to her,' Agrafena whispered behind me. 'It's not worth your life.'

One of the woman's companions passed her a piece of glass. The woman made a slashing movement towards my face as if she intended to take out my eye. I ducked. The other women in the bathhouse screamed.

The guards, who had been talking amongst themselves, looked up.

'Settle down!' one of them shouted. 'Or there won't be food for any of you tonight!'

'Back off, Katya,' another heavily tattooed woman told my attacker. 'She'll keep for later and I'm hungry.'

Katya stared at me then turned away.

Agrafena pulled me towards the wall and helped me into my dress. 'Be careful of that one,' she said. 'She was in the same prison cell as me and she's been sent here for a terrible crime.'

'What?' I asked.

'She used to entice children from the street and sell them to paedophiles. Some of those poor innocents were butchered.'

I was horrified. 'What's her sentence?'

'Three years.'

I looked at the woman who had been arrested for naming her dog Winston. She was speaking with a machinist who had been condemned to Kolyma for being late for work. Both women had been given sentences of eight years.

Stalin had turned the world on its head.

After a period of quarantine we were examined by a doctor, a middle-aged woman with dark hair and pale skin. She checked my throat, ears and eyes and felt my skin to assess my muscle and body fat. She pinched my legs, then read my papers carefully before writing something on them. I prayed she would assign me to work in a kitchen or hospital, but knew that my sentence meant I was destined for one of the worst jobs.

After the medical examination, our clothes were taken away from us and we were issued shapeless dresses and shoes with soles made of used tyre treads. I realised how futile the argument with Katya over my dress had been. We didn't even have names any more; we were addressed by the numbers sewn onto our uniforms.

When we were assigned to our barracks I was relieved that Katya and her gang were sent to different quarters. Agrafena and I remained together, but any reprieve I felt disappeared when we opened the door to the wooden building and saw what lay before us. Along the walls ran two tiers of plank beds with more bunks in the middle of the room. Most of them didn't have pillows or mattresses. The floor was nothing more than stamped earth and the place reeked of mildew and sweat. But it was the four prisoners lying on their bunks that most upset us. It was obvious why they weren't out on work assignments: their limbs were grotesquely swollen and their skin was covered in pus-infected boils. In Auschwitz such prisoners were called *Muselmänner*. In Kolyma I would soon learn that they were called *dokhodyagi*: the living dead.

'Come on, move along!' An old toothless woman entered the barracks and organised the newcomers with the enthusiasm of a summer camp leader. Her clothes were rags but she had a colourful scarf wrapped around her head.

'You! Here!' she said to me and indicated an upper bunk at the far end of the barrack. Agrafena was assigned the space next to me.

That evening we were served soup made of spoiled cabbage leaves, potatoes and herring heads. The coarse black bread that came with it tasted as though it hadn't been properly baked. There were no bowls or spoons provided. The seasoned prisoners brought their own, fashioned from old tins or pieces of wood. Agrafena traded a scarf for two sets and gave one to me.

'Make sure you keep them with you at all times,' a woman across the table warned us. 'Otherwise they'll be stolen.'

When I lay in my bunk that night fighting off the mosquitoes, I thought of the *dokhodyagi* only a short distance away, fouling the air with their foetid breath and rotting flesh. Would I end up that way too? Maybe it was better to find a way to kill myself now, while I still had the strength. But in the morning, my resolve to survive returned. With the cup of water allotted to me, I cleaned my teeth with the sleeve of my uniform and washed my face and neck with the tarry soap that had been distributed at the health inspection. I looked up to see Slava, the toothless woman who was in charge of our hut, smiling at me.

'You shouldn't use your soap all at once like that,' she said. 'Halve it and trade the other half for something else you might need.'

'Thank you for your advice,' I said to her. Perhaps surviving a war and surviving in a camp were two different things. The first involved not giving in to fear, and the second involved not giving in to despair. 'Is there anything else I should know?'

Slava grinned. 'Plenty!' She bent down and picked up a cigarette stub. 'You see, a new prisoner discarded that. You can collect stubs like this around the camp and trade the tobacco. It doesn't matter if you start with nothing. A smart person can turn nothing into something.'

From her appearance Slava might have been a peasant in her former life, but her cunning made me wonder if she'd been a thief.

'What did you get arrested for?' I asked her.

She adjusted her scarf. 'I was once a governess in a noble family and after the Revolution that was enough of a reason to arrest me. I was released in 1932 but I had nowhere to go, so I stayed here. They pay me a small wage and the work isn't difficult.'

Breakfast was the same unappetising soup of the night before. On my way back to the barracks, I noticed a man sitting on a wooden fence staring at me. He had a crooked nose, hooded eyes and an unkempt beard. His biceps were as big as his thighs. He wasn't wearing a shirt and every part of his torso was covered in tattoos. The way he looked at me made my skin crawl. I didn't feel safe until the evening, when the guard locked us all into our barracks and I was surrounded by other women. I was soon to learn it was false security.

I was woken by a bang as the door to the barracks was flung open. A beam from a flashlight searched the room. I lifted my head and saw faces leering in the doorway. At first I thought I was dreaming but then a scream pierced the air. Two men dragged a woman by her feet from her bunk and carried her out the door. The light disappeared and the woman's cries became muffled. I could hear men grunting and wondered what was happening. Some sort of interrogation? I slipped from my bunk and moved towards the window.

'Get back to bed!' ordered Slava in a harsh whisper. 'Do you want what is happening to her to happen to you?'

I ignored her and made it to the window. By the light outside the barracks, I could see that the woman was pinned down by several men.

'They're raping her!' I cried. 'Get the guard!'

I rushed to the door and banged on it. Suddenly I was knocked backwards. I felt a hand over my mouth and the weight of bodies holding me down. At first I thought the men had caught me too but then I realised it was my fellow prisoners who were restraining me.

'The guard's in on it, you stupid bitch!' one of them said. 'Now shut up or I'll slit your throat!'

The women sat on me until the grunts and jeers from outside stopped and the men dispersed. Agrafena came and helped me back to my bunk.

I waited for the door to open and for the violated woman to return. But she didn't return, not even in the morning when the bell rang for us to get up. I stared at the empty bunk and tried to think who she was. Then I remembered a young girl I had seen when I'd arrived at the camp and who occupied that bunk; she didn't look any older than seventeen.

When we marched to the washrooms in the dim morning light I reeled in horror. The girl was lying on the ground in a pool of blood. Her mouth was open as if in a silent scream and her eyes stared blankly. She was dead. I looked around to see the other women's reactions, but only the recent arrivals showed any distress. The others averted their eyes and walked past the body as if it wasn't there. When we returned from the bathhouse the girl was gone.

The atmosphere at breakfast was subdued but nobody mentioned the girl. When we returned to our barracks that evening, the same guard as before locked us in. I lay awake the whole night trembling with fear, but nothing happened.

'Did anyone report the murder to the administrators?' I asked Slava the next morning. 'Are those men going to be punished?'

She stared at me, then sighed. 'You have to learn to live and let live here. Some of the men are beasts, and what happened has happened before and will happen again. You can't save anybody but yourself. You are young and pretty — you'd better get yourself a camp husband.'

'A what?'

'One of the men,' she explained. 'Choose one and offer yourself to him. Not one of the politicals — that will only make you a greater target. One of the criminals. If the other men know that you belong to him, they won't touch you. Nikita would be a good choice. I noticed him watching you the other day after breakfast.'

I stared at her in disbelief. Was the only way to protect myself to become the whore of someone like the fierce-looking man with the tattoos?

I saw Nikita again when I passed the repair workshop on my way back to the barracks. He and some other men were playing cards. For the criminals the camp appeared to be only a change of location: they did what they liked and went wherever they liked.

'Hey, Rasputin!' one of the men said, nudging Nikita. 'There's your girlfriend!'

Nikita stared at me in that intense way again. I could see why the criminals called him Rasputin: he did bear a resemblance to Tsarina Alexandra's disastrous monk.

A gang of women marched past on their way to the fields. I stared at their lined faces and shorn heads. There was nothing womanly about them: starvation and hard work had robbed them of their breasts and hips. The men paid them no attention when they passed and an idea came to me. I rushed to the camp's barber.

'What can I do for you?' he asked.

I removed my scarf and let down my hair. Many of the women transported with me to Kolyma had been shaved all over, like the women in Auschwitz, but I'd managed to avoid that. I'd prevented my hair becoming matted by combing it every day with my fingers.

'Ah, I see,' he said, giving me a stool to sit on and picking up a pair of scissors. 'Such a pity ... but it's better — the lice won't trouble you so much.'

I closed my eyes and didn't open them again until the last strand of my hair lay on the floor around my feet.

I was assigned work with a lumber gang. On the first day we assembled in the faint morning light near the camp gate, where our brigadier, a former train robber with a mouthful of gold teeth, took the roll. I was dismayed to see Katya in the group. She was wearing the dress that we had fought over in the bathhouse and paraded her victory before me.

'Well, haven't you changed in only a few days,' she said, looking at my shorn head.

I wondered how she was going to work in that dress or in the red leather shoes she wore with it.

Another lumber gang assembled behind us and I was disconcerted to see Nikita there. He didn't appear to recognise me and I was relieved. A piano accordionist and guitarist — prisoners also — played music while we collected our saws, axes, shovels and sacks. 'Work is honourable, glorious, valiant and heroic!' they sang.

Because we were carrying tools that could be used as weapons, the guards were armed and vigilant. They kept their guns pointed at us as we marched past the gate.

The head guard shouted, 'Keep to your rank and look

straight ahead! A step to the right or left will be regarded as an attempt to escape and we will shoot without warning!'

We marched five kilometres to our worksite, where we were put into pairs. I was placed with another woman, much taller than I was. Luckily for me she knew how to fell trees — cutting from three sides to make the trunk fall into an open space. We worked in rhythm to fulfil our norm. Our bread ration was dependent on achieving that quota. I was fortunate to be partnered with someone who was physically strong, even though I had to work hard to keep up with her. We spoke as little as possible, even during our meal break and on the way back to the camp: we couldn't afford to waste one ounce of energy.

While being in the forest was better than working in a mine, I didn't like lumbering. It hurt me to cut down the majestic trees. I winced each time we hacked into the trunks with our saws and axes. But the trees got their revenge. One day my partner and I misjudged which way a cedar would fall. A thick branch struck her and crushed her skull. It was an awful way to die and yet all I could think about was my bread ration. What would happen to me now? When I came to my senses, my cold-bloodedness horrified me.

My fellow prisoners had no such concerns. They acted quickly, stripping my fallen comrade of her shoes, pants and underwear before the brigadier had even been informed of her death.

With everyone else paired up, the only person left for me to work with was Katya and she did nothing. The next day, as soon as we reached our worksite, she was busy in the bushes, pleasuring our brigadier or one of the guards. She told the brigadier that I could fulfil her norm as well as mine, but even he saw that it would be impossible. Instead I was to work on my own to fulfil a reduced norm. I only had to cut down the occasional tree then; most of the time I was sawing branches off felled trees or stacking the wood for hauling.

As we settled into our routine, we were accompanied by fewer guards and sometimes none at all. The brigadier kept the gang in check; and where could a prisoner escape to in such a wilderness anyway? I felt secure in this arrangement until one day I struggled to keep up with my norm and returned to the camp later than the others. It was then that I crossed paths with Nikita. He looked as ferocious up close as he did at a distance, but he wasn't as ugly as I'd first thought. His beard was misleading and I realised that we could even be the same age. He peered at me through the twilight and recognised me. I turned to walk in another direction but he grabbed my arm.

'Wait,' he said. 'I want to talk to you.'

His voice surprised me. It was rough but not uneducated. From his appearance the most I'd have expected from him was a grunt.

'I want to talk to you,' he repeated. 'Not now because I have to get back. But sometime.'

I was struck dumb. A polite request for a conversation wasn't what I'd been anticipating. Nikita nodded as if we'd made a firm agreement, then he released my arm and strode off towards the camp.

Although cutting my hair seemed to protect me from unwanted attention, I still kept up my guard. The criminals assaulted old women and men too; they even raped each other. But there was a greater threat to our survival up here in the Arctic: winter.

'Come on, what's the temperature?' we pestered the prisoner whose duty it was to check the thermometer.

It was four o'clock in the morning and we were assembled in the snowy yard waiting for roll call to commence. We jumped up and down and slapped our arms and legs. The clothing we'd been issued was inadequate for the climate. The chill tore through my padded jacket and I had no warm scarf to protect my head. I rubbed my face and ears to prevent frostbite. A woman in my barracks had lost her nose that week: it had come off in her hand. The image of it wouldn't leave my mind and I was frightened that the same thing would happen to me.

'It's only minus 40,' the prisoner reported.

We let out a collective moan. Work wasn't called off until the temperature fell to below minus 45 degrees Celsius.

The roll was called and we walked off to our worksite. I slipped in the snow and pulled myself up quickly; not because I was afraid of the guards but because I didn't want to freeze. The cold and starvation were the real threats now. The food we were given wasn't enough to sustain us and the soup poured into our bowls for our daytime meals often froze before we could eat it.

One evening, Agrafena was chewing a piece of bread when she winced and touched her mouth. Blood ran down her hand. Our eyes met. A bleeding mouth was the first sign of scurvy. Over the next few weeks, I watched Agrafena decline. Her skin broke out in boils and she suffered constantly from diarrhoea.

'You must go to the hospital,' I told her.

Agrafena worked in the camp laundry. I only saw her at night because those who worked in the camp didn't have to get up as early as the lumber gangs did. The following morning I helped Agrafena to rise at the same time as me and took her to the hospital. The staff were only allowed to admit two patients a day so getting there first was important. But when I returned in the evening I found Agrafena lying in her bunk.

'They said I wasn't sick enough to be exempted from work,' she told me. 'I don't have a fever.'

I looked at her pale face and the suppurating sores on her neck. How sick did she need to become before they'd put her on anti-scurvy rations? She needed vitamin supplements, or at least carrots and turnips. If I didn't do something to help her, Agrafena would die. While working in the forest I searched for berries or mushrooms to feed her, but everything lay under a thick layer of snow. Then one evening when I was walking back to the camp, I saw Nikita striding through the snow ahead of me. He was wearing military boots, a scarf and padded gloves. Of course, criminals knew how to get everything. I quickened my pace to catch up with him.

'Nikita!'

He turned and glared at me with wild eyes. I took a step back, frightened. 'What?' he growled, showing no recollection of our last conversation.

'You wanted to talk to me?'

'What is it you want?'

There was no small talk in Nikita's world. I got straight to my point. 'Do you know how I can get some supplements? My friend has scurvy. They won't take her into the hospital. They say she's not sick enough!'

Nikita's lips curled into what looked like an unpleasant smirk. I'd been foolish to approach such a dangerous man in the forest alone.

'Yes, I can get those supplements for you,' he said. 'Everyone who works at the hospital owes me something.'

Part of me was relieved but I was also aware of what he would expect in return. When I'd first come to the camp the idea of trading my body was unthinkable, but desperation changed everything. I looked at him, not sure how to proceed.

'I have syphilis,' he said.

The blood drained from my face. In order to save Agrafena I had given myself a death sentence.

'I don't expect anything from you,' he said. 'I only want to know what you did before the war.'

I was surprised at the request. 'Why?'

'In my barracks we gamble on what the political prisoners did before they were arrested, then we bribe a guard to confirm who's right. I'm famous for never being wrong.'

My toes were turning numb from the cold but I had to hear what Nikita was going to say. I guessed criminals were good at being able to read people so they could swindle them.

'According to your records you were a medical student,' he continued. 'There's no way that's right. So either you altered your records or the government did. Which one?'

My breath froze in my throat. 'What do you think?'

Nikita grinned. It was the first time that I'd seen his teeth; except for the two front ones, all of them were gold. 'Definitely not a medical student. If you were a student, you'd look at things like a short-sighted person does because you were used to staring at books and notes. But you've got a deliberate way of walking and you squint at the horizon a certain way. My guess is that you were a pilot.'

I couldn't believe it. Either Nikita was a genius at reading people or this was a trick and he'd found out who I was some other way.

'I can't say,' I told him. 'It could cost my life.'

He nodded. 'You don't have to. I can see I was right. Come on, let me carry you back to the camp. You're turning blue.'

He bent to allow me to climb onto his back. His torso was so wide that my legs barely made it around him. When we reached the camp he walked straight past the guards with me still on his back and they said nothing.

He put me down and grinned at me again. 'Let everyone know that you are with me. That way the other men will leave you alone.'

The piggyback ride brought back memories of my brother, Alexander. 'I would make a terrible criminal,' I said to him. 'I didn't read you correctly at all.'

A few nights later, one of the female criminals slipped a bottle of powder into my hand while we were lining up to get our soup. 'It's from Nikita,' she said.

I looked around for Agrafena but she wasn't in the meal hut. I quickly finished my supper and headed back to our barracks. I found her in her bunk, struggling to breathe. I mixed the powder Nikita had sent me with some water and held it to her chapped lips.

She shook her head. 'It's too late for me. You take it. Save yourself.'

I wrapped my arm around her to keep her warm, but it caused her pain so instead I put the pieces of sacking I used as an extra blanket on top of her. Agrafena's eyes were dimming; she wouldn't last until the morning. How had this happened? How had the clever university professor become one of the *dokhodyagi*? I knew the answer to that. But I would never understand *why*.

Agrafena turned her face to me. 'Would you like to hear it?' she asked.

'What?'

'The joke I told about Stalin.'

I nestled closer to her. 'All right.'

She smiled. 'Stalin is dying and isn't sure if he wants to go to heaven or hell. He is given a tour of each. In heaven he sees people playing harps and singing. In hell he sees people eating, drinking and dancing. Stalin opts for hell. When he dies, he is led through a labyrinth and into a great hall where people are being burned on stakes and lowered into boiling cauldrons. Two of the Devil's henchmen grab him and drag him towards some hot coals. Stalin protests, "But on the tour, I was shown people enjoying themselves!" "That," replies the Devil, "was just propaganda!"'

Agrafena died in the early hours of the morning. Her uniform and underwear were too soiled and threadbare now for even the most desperate criminal to scavenge. But she had bequeathed me her mittens. They were in better condition than mine but I didn't wear them. I kept them hidden inside my mattress: something to remember her by.

Winter in the Arctic Circle lasts nine months. As time wore on I could no longer make my norm and the reduced food ration was further draining my strength. Our gang lost three prisoners in one week. Two of them dropped dead where they stood in the forest. The third walked towards the forbidden zone of the camp despite the warnings of the guards. He was shot. There were no prisoners strong enough to replace those we had lost and the camp commandant accused the brigadier of sabotage by not taking care of his team. Now the whole gang had a group norm to fulfil, including the brigadier and Katya.

The brigadier hated me now and often beat me. 'Work, you lazy slut! Or we'll all suffer!'

One day, when I was sawing the branches off a tree and shivering violently from the wind chill, my saw slipped from my hand. I reached to pick it up but I couldn't bend. The muscles in my legs stopped trembling and my arms and shoulders stiffened. My hand was a claw and when I tried to move my fingers they wouldn't straighten. My breath echoed in my head. I felt like a clock that was winding down. I'm freezing to death, I thought.

I struggled against it and tried again to reach for the saw. Failing that, I strained to call for help but I had no voice. Exhaustion overcame me and I collapsed backwards into the snow. At first I was terrified. I wasn't supposed to die: Valentin and Mama were waiting for me. But then a sense of peace came over me. I accepted my fate. I had done all I could to survive, but Kolyma had won, as the major who had interrogated me had said it would. As the last vestiges of heat left my body, I felt myself lighten as if I were about to float away.

'Get up, bitch!'

Something sharp hit me in the side but I didn't feel any pain. The brigadier's red face came close to mine. He was screaming. 'Get up, you lazy bitch! Get up!' He pulled me up by my coat, shook me and slapped my face. But as soon as he let me go, I fell back into the snow.

I gazed up at the trees. *I'm sorry*, I told them. *You are so beautiful. I had no right to kill you.*

I heard Katya laugh and smelled vodka on her breath when she bent down to look at me. 'Let's see how long it takes you to die, hey? Don't linger now, you piece of shit!'

She looked warm in a deerskin coat and high boots, impervious to the cold that was killing me.

'Let's take her clothes,' she said to the brigadier. 'She'll die quicker that way.'

'No!' said the brigadier. 'I've lost too many prisoners to the cold. We'll make it look like the tree fell on her.' Even though our lack of food and adequate clothing was not his responsibility, he was supposed to notice if one of his charges was freezing to death.

From the corner of my eye I saw the brigadier move a short distance away from me. Then he ran towards me, leaped into the air and landed with his two feet on my chest. My heart stopped for a second and pain shot through every part of my body. Inwardly I was writhing in agony but I couldn't move.

The brigadier stepped back, ready to jump on my chest again. I closed my eyes. Why couldn't he let me die in peace? But this time I heard shouting and blows. Suddenly my body was lifted from the snow. Somebody had picked me up, but who? I tried to open my eyes but I couldn't.

TWENTY-NINE

Kolyma, 1946

No one expected someone who had suffered a crushed chest as well as hypothermia and malnutrition to survive. My death certificate was filled out in the hospital file; all it required was the doctor's signature and date and time of death. But while patients with lesser injuries died around me, I didn't. When Doctor Polyakova, who had examined me when I first arrived in Kolyma, ordered me to be moved to the side of the ward where the patients who were expected to recover were situated, I asked her who had plucked me from the snow when I'd lost consciousness.

'Another prisoner,' she replied. 'He's been dropping off bread and sugar for you, but as you haven't been able to eat it I've been giving it to the other patients.'

It was Nikita who had saved me. A few days later, he came to see me and handed me two books: *Anna Karenina* and *War and Peace* by Tolstoy. The books were stolen, of course, probably from another prisoner. He pulled up a stool and sat beside me, staring at my face intently. The nurse gave him a disapproving look but said nothing.

'You know, you look how I imagine my little sister would if she'd reached your age.'

Now I understood the true reason for his interest in me.

'What happened to her?' I asked him.

'She died of typhoid fever.'

Nikita's rough outer appearance did not reflect the inner man at all. I sensed he was struggling to reconcile some pain in himself.

'Was it during the famine?' I asked, wondering if he had come from a peasant family.

Nikita shook his head. 'No. My family was well off. My father was an engineer. He was arrested as a saboteur in 1929 and executed. My mother was thrown into prison and my sister and I were sent to an orphanage. That's where she died.'

We had more in common than I'd realised. 'Did your mother survive?' I asked him.

Nikita knotted his fingers and stared at his hands. 'Every day I waited for my mother to come and collect me. While the other children played, I sat by the gate watching for her. One of the women in the orphanage realised what I was doing and told me, "Your mother is an enemy of the people! You must forget her. If she comes back for you, you must chase her away and tell her that you won't go with her." Every day that bitch said the same thing to me. She brainwashed me. A year later, my mother did come back. She wasn't young and pretty any more. She was thin with lines on her face. But she smiled at me with the same expression of love as always. "I've come to take you home, my darling," she said. There were tears in her eyes. She must have known about my sister. "No!" I screamed, picking up a rock and throwing it at her. "I won't go with you! I hate you! You're an enemy of the people!"'

Nikita stopped and drew a breath. 'I can never forget the look on my mother's face when I told her that. It was as if something in her died. Later, when I was older and I tried to find her, I learned that she'd hanged herself. I've always felt that I killed her.'

'Of course you didn't,' I told him. 'The government did.'

We lapsed into silence. I expected Nikita to say more about his mother and sister but he didn't. Instead he stood up.

'I'm being transferred tomorrow,' he said. 'I don't know where.'

'I hope somewhere better.'

He shrugged. 'Who knows?'

I looked at the books he had given me. Although I was happy to have them, I hoped their original owner was dead. I didn't want to deprive someone of what might have been their only pleasure.

'My two favourite stories,' I said.

'I told you I was good at understanding people,' Nikita said.

As I watched my strange guardian angel leave the ward I sent him a blessing. A few days later, I learned from one of the nurses why Nikita was being sent to another camp. He'd had three years added to his sentence for killing the brigadier who had attacked me.

'We have to find something for you to do,' Doctor Polyakova told me. 'Can you sew?'

I nodded. I knew she was trying to help me. I could no longer work in a lumber gang, and the review commission had decided I wasn't sick enough to be released. If Doctor Polyakova couldn't find work for me I would be sent out into the fields. I told her that I sewed well, and after that the nurses brought me sheets and prison robes that needed mending.

At the end of spring, a guard came to the ward and called out my number. 'With things,' he added.

I glanced at Doctor Polyakova, who rushed to find me a prison dress and some shoes. 'With things' was a command that could mean a number of scenarios, from being released to being shot.

In my case it meant being transferred to one of Kolyma's few women-only camps near Magadan. On arrival, I was taken by a guard into a factory where about forty women sat at long tables and operated sewing machines. The forewoman introduced herself as Ustinya Pavlovna Kuklina.

'Now,' she said, leading me to a seat and plugging the sewing machine's cord into a socket, 'have you used a machine before?'

'My mother's,' I told her. 'A long time ago.'

Ustinya picked up a piece of fabric and placed it under the needle. 'The machines here have bigger motors than domestic machines and sew faster, but the principles are the same. You'll get the hang of it. Use this piece of fabric to practise on.'

She explained that the factory made uniforms for the prisoners and guards and also garments for the free population of Kolyma. My job was to sew the cuffs of the shirts and pants. As I got to work, a couple of the women nodded at me. It was clear that this camp had a better atmosphere than my previous one. No one looked like they were starving or sick.

When we stopped for our daytime meal, I thought there'd been a mistake when I was handed not one but two slices of bread. The woman sitting next to me, Radinka, smiled at my astonishment.

'Ustinya is a free worker, not a prisoner,' she told me, 'so she's not afraid of the camp commandant. She told him that the factory can only meet the quotas if she has healthy workers.'

Not only were the working conditions and food better, but the barracks were clean and free of lice and bedbugs. We each had a mattress and a pillow, and there were curtains on the windows. No doubt the better conditions were the reason why the prisoners were in good spirits and even had the energy to entertain each other in the evenings. Several of the women were excellent storytellers and another amused us with her mimes. No one spoke about their personal lives.

'To talk about our families and children is pointless,' Radinka explained to me. 'To do so only creates despair. We understand each other. We're all in the same situation.'

'Zina, perform something for us,' said a woman named Olesya to me one evening. Zina was the diminutive of Zinaida, which everybody in the factory, including Ustinya, used to address me. 'Do you sing?' she asked.

'I can sing,' I said. 'But it's a long time since I have done so.'

'Well, get rid of the rust,' she said with a kind smile.

The other women murmured their encouragement and so I cleared my throat and sang a song about the Dnieper River, which had been popular with my regiment. When I finished, the women clapped.

'You should have gone to the Conservatory,' another woman named Syuzanna said. 'Your voice is beautiful.'

That night I lay on my bunk and thought of all the things I might have done if Stalin hadn't signed my father's death warrant. I clenched my hands into fists, trying to contain my anger. At the same time, I knew that I could be as angry as I wanted but it wouldn't change a thing. I had been given an opportunity to survive and I must make the most of it.

Valentin's face appeared before me. 'Wait for me,' I whispered as I fell asleep. 'Wait for me and I'll return.'

Life in the sewing factory had a monotonous rhythm to it but for a prisoner with a sentence as long as mine it was better that way. I still wasn't allowed to correspond with anybody, and I coped best when I emptied my mind and refused to reflect. For seven years I lived that way — rising, washing, working, eating, sleeping, like a mechanical doll.

Then one day in the spring of 1953 a guard came to the factory and, with a grave expression on his face, handed Ustinya a piece of paper. I watched her eyes scan the note. Her cheeks paled.

'Please stop the machines!' she said and moved to the front of the workroom to address us.

The whirring of the sewing machines came to a halt. Ustinya's hands trembled as she read the statement: 'Dear comrades and friends. The Central Committee of the Communist Party of the Soviet Union announces with profound sorrow to the Party and all workers of the Soviet Union that on the fifth of March at 9.50 pm Moscow time, after a grave illness, the Chairman of the USSR Council of Ministers and the Secretary of the Central Committee of the Communist Party of the Soviet Union, Joseph Vissarionovich Stalin, died.'

The announcement was met with silence. Everyone contained their response because of the guard. Yet the excitement was palpable. The monster was dead! Radinka rested her face on her arms and wept. It wasn't grief for Stalin that made her cry. She was mourning her former life and the family she had lost. The rest of us began to weep too.

When the guard left, satisfied that we had reacted appropriately, we were able to express our true feelings. Syuzanna danced across the room. The rest of us cheered and embraced each other.

'You are going to be freed, I'm sure of it!' Ustinya said as she moved among us and kissed our cheeks. 'The nightmare is over!'

Things changed dramatically in Kolyma in only a matter of weeks. Thousands of people were granted amnesty and released: the elderly; pregnant women; prisoners accused of economic crimes or with sentences of less than five years; and people under eighteen. Convoy after convoy passed by our camp on their way to the port.

Over the next two years, the releases continued in fits and starts. When it was announced that amnesty would be given to all servicemen and women charged with treason and collaborating with the Germans, I allowed myself to be hopeful. Officials came to the camp and prisoners were released, but I was not called to appear before them. Ustinya wrote letters on my behalf to the authorities, citing my good behaviour and work ethic, but I suspected there were special reasons why I wasn't being released.

In 1956 Khrushchev denounced Stalin's excesses and hundreds of thousands of political prisoners were released, yet I remained in Kolyma with a handful of other prisoners. Perhaps Khrushchev had been party to my arrest and releasing me might expose him. Then in 1960, as I was beginning to fear that I might be buried in Kolyma forever, the camp commandant summoned me to his office.

'Congratulations,' he said. 'Your case has been reviewed. You are free to go if you sign these two documents.'

After all these years of torturous waiting, I was free to go? I read the documents the commandant placed before me. One was my official release form. It had been signed and dated two years earlier. What had been the reason for the delay in summoning me? Perhaps nothing more than bureaucratic bungling had cost me two years of my life!

I studied the other form. It was an agreement that I would never reveal anything that had happened to me from the time of my arrest in Odessa to the last day of my imprisonment. If I broke the condition, I would be re-arrested and returned to prison.

I glanced at the camp commandant. Did he know I wasn't Zinaida Rusakova? Whoever had worded the statement did. To sign the form meant that I would have to go on pretending to be someone else.

I hesitated but then thought: what does it matter what people call me? I am being allowed to return to Moscow, and nowhere in the statement does it forbid me from seeing my relatives or former acquaintances.

I was twenty-three years old when I came to Kolyma and I was now thirty-eight. I thought of my beloved Valentin and Mama. If pretending to be Zinaida meant I could go free, I would do it.

After the boat trip back across the sea from Magadan, I waited at the station for the train that would take me to Moscow. The other passengers on the platform were mostly free workers, but some were prisoners from the labour camps of Kolyma too. They still wore their prison jackets, with the numbers removed, and foot rags, and their shorn heads and spindly limbs were a sure indication of where they had been. Ustinya had insisted that I sew a dress for myself before leaving the factory. It was grey cotton and nowhere near as lovely as the outfit I would have liked to return home wearing, but it was better than a prison uniform or rags. My shoes were the clumpy lace-ups that Doctor Polyakova had given me when I'd left the hospital. They had holes in the bottoms now, so I'd made cardboard insoles to stop the stones piercing my feet.

Rain began to blow in from the sea and I, along with the other passengers, rushed into the waiting room to escape the weather. Inside there was a ceiling-to-floor-length mirror and the women gathered around it to fix their hair and straighten their clothes. I joined them and gave a start when I saw myself: a mousy-looking woman with frown lines on her forehead. I wanted to turn away but couldn't. I wasn't hideous. Frostbite hadn't gouged out pieces of my face nor had scurvy deprived me of my teeth. Yet the lustre of my youth had vanished. I was like a tarnished wedding band. I wanted to cry. But then I remembered Mama and Valentin were waiting for me. It will be all right, I told myself. Love will restore you.

It took me a month to reach Moscow and I was as hungry on the journey as I had been on the way to Kolyma. I'd been given a ration of bread and a small amount of money when I'd left the camp, but it was barely enough to buy eggs and tomatoes from the peasant women at stations along the way. If Ustinya hadn't given me a parcel of nuts, pickled cucumbers and salted fish I might not have survived.

I arrived at Moscow's Yaroslavsky railway station in early June, worn out from the journey. When I emerged into Komsomolskaya Square, I was deafened by the onslaught of noise. The streets were full of cars and buses and the air was acrid with exhaust fumes. I found the congestion frightening, although the people around me seemed unaffected.

A policeman who was directing traffic turned and stared at me. There was no reason to arrest me, my papers were in order, but I was afraid of such men now. I bent my head and tried to keep pace with the crowd, attempting to look like I belonged. But returning to Moscow after all these years was like arriving on a foreign planet. I was used to the silence and routine of the camp.

The new trams rattled along too fast for me and I decided to make my way to the Arbat on foot. There were no watchtowers in the streets or guards with guns and yet I felt afraid. Despite the heat, I hurried along as if I were being pursued by a pack of bloodthirsty hounds. The lack of posters bearing Stalin's face was noticeable. Posters boasting of the Soviet Union's achievements had taken their place. They showed farmers harvesting bumper crops; muscular athletes; smiling factory workers; housewives feeding their children delicious-looking food. One poster intrigued me: the picture was of a handsome square-jawed man gazing into space and cradling a rocket with two dogs inside. *The way is open for man* the caption read. What did it mean?

I passed a café that played strange music that grated on me. Old men and women still wore the same drab clothes, but the young girls looked pretty with their bouffant hairstyles and headbands. I was admiring one girl's pointed shoes when a young mother passed by pushing a pram. I sat down in a doorway, overcome by the realisation of all that I had missed out on — marrying Valentin, starting a family, wearing nice clothes, and having fun. Instead, I had spent my best years in prison camps.

I reached the courtyard of Mama's apartment building and looked up to her window to see the white lace curtains flapping in the slight breeze. I braced myself for the tears that would pour down our cheeks when she realised that I had come home. My legs trembled as I climbed the stairs. When I reached the door, I hesitated before ringing the bell, aware that I was about to re-enter the life I had left behind.

I pushed the button. The sound of footsteps came from inside and the door swung open. The first objects I saw were Mama's chair and the bureau under the window. But the woman who stood in the doorway with rollers in her hair wasn't Mama. She looked me up and down. Her presence in my mother's apartment was so unexpected that I didn't know what to say. I had never seen her before.

'Sofia Grigorievna,' I said, struggling to breathe. 'I'm looking for Sofia Grigorievna Azarova.'

The woman's eyes narrowed. 'This is my apartment now!' she said. 'The government gave it to me. It's legally mine!'

She slammed the door in my face. I stood there in shock, my heart thumping in my chest. Where was Mama? Had she been arrested despite my false confession?

My head became light and I sat down on the first step of the staircase, panting for breath. Doctor Polyakova had told me that my heart had been damaged when the brigadier jumped on my chest. I would have to be forever careful of it.

A door on the floor below opened and an elderly woman came out and peered up the stairs at me. I stood up, afraid that she was about to scream at me too. Instead she gestured for me to come down to her apartment.

'You're looking for Sofia?' she whispered. 'You are ...?'

'A friend,' I said.

She seemed to be expecting a different answer but she welcomed me inside her apartment anyway. 'It's very hot today. Let me give you some juice,' she said, helping me to a chair. 'My name is Arina. I became friends with Sofia when I moved here three years ago.'

'Where is she?' I asked.

Arina hesitated, her eyes full of sympathy. She stared at my face again as if she were trying to see something there. 'Sofia is dead. She passed away six months ago.'

For a few seconds I couldn't move. My vision darkened as if I had fallen down a deep hole. I tried to stand but didn't have the strength. Instead, I dropped my head into my hands.

Arina touched my shoulder. 'I'm sorry to be the one to tell you,' she said. 'You've come from the camps, haven't you?'

I nodded. She went to her kitchen and poured me a glass of orange juice. Orange juice! I hadn't seen the stuff for years. She placed it next to me on a side table and sat down in a chair opposite.

'My son was sent to the camps in 1937,' she said. 'He died there. Vorkuta. Where were you?'

I couldn't answer her; I'd gone numb from head to foot. Mama was dead! I wanted to cry, to release the grief that welled inside me, but I couldn't. It sat in my stomach like a rock.

'Sofia's daughter was a famous pilot in the war,' Arina continued, studying me carefully, 'but she disappeared in enemy territory. Sofia's husband was executed during the purges and her son died in an accident. All she had left in the world was her little dog. She doted on that dog, but when Dasha passed away Sofia no longer had any reason to go on living. Her health went from bad to worse after that.'

I drank the juice but I couldn't taste anything.

'Do you have somewhere to stay?' Arina asked me.

The camp commandant had given me the address of a communal apartment, but I'd planned to stay with Mama. I shook my head.

'Well, stay here,' she said. 'Until you get on your feet.'

Our eyes met. 'I signed a document agreeing never to talk about my experiences,' I said. 'I could be re-arrested if I do ... along with anyone I've confided in.'

Arina nodded. 'I understand.'

The truth stood unspoken between us. Arina had guessed that I was Sofia's daughter. She also realised that it was a secret that must be kept at all costs.

That night, after a warm bath, I lay on Arina's couch and stared at the ceiling. Moscow was a strange city to me now. With Mama gone it had lost its charm. Yet I knew I must keep my promise to Valentin and find him. He was all I had left now.

After a week with Arina, my strength began to return, although I was still startled by unfamiliar noises: footsteps in the hall outside; the radio; the hum of Arina's stove exhaust when she cooked. I spent many hours staring at my face in the mirror, trying to find in my reflection the adventurous young woman I had once been. Age and the camps had changed me sufficiently so that I didn't fear being easily recognised, even though my youthful picture had appeared in the popular newspapers. When Valentin and I were in the regiment, we'd said that if we became separated and weren't able to contact each other through Mama's address, we would go each Sunday afternoon to Sokolniki Park and search for each other there. But I couldn't face Valentin looking so haggard and worn. I had to improve my appearance first.

'What will you do for work?' Arina asked me one day. 'It's difficult for you people to find anything. Even those who see through the propaganda are afraid that if they employ ex-prisoners and things change again, they might be arrested themselves.'

I thought about it for a few moments. 'I used to work in a factory. We built airplanes.'

'Let me speak to my son-in-law,' Arina said. 'He works at the oil refinery. He might be able to help you.'

Arina's son-in-law found me a job as a laboratory assistant at his refinery, and I moved into a communal apartment. My room had cracks in the walls that had been patched with newspaper and it reeked of mildew and stale cooking oil. I didn't care; it was still better than the camp. With the salary I earned I bought food and clothes.

Every Sunday afternoon I caught the metro to Sokolniki Park. I never allowed for the possibility that Valentin might have been killed in the war. The park was over six hundred hectares in size and included woodlands, dancing pavilions, lakes, cafés and a swimming pool. In our ardour, we hadn't thought to designate an exact meeting point.

The previous year the park had hosted an American exhibition and some of the posters remained. I studied the American fashion models and dyed my hair butterscotch-blonde again. I wore black eyeliner and pale pink lipstick and arranged my hair into a half-upswept ponytail with curls spiralling around my ears. The style and colour were flattering and drew attention away from the grooves around my mouth and my jawline, which had thickened with age. Cosmetics became war paint for me again; a sign that Kolyma hadn't destroyed me.

'Ah, here comes Moscow Oil Refinery's beauty,' the

foreman said one day when I arrived for work. His words reminded me of when Roman used to say the same thing at the aircraft factory before the war. Of course, I wasn't a beauty any more. There were younger girls at the refinery who were prettier and fresher looking than me, but the compliment put a spring in my step.

One summer afternoon, I was walking around Sokolniki Park when the new shoes I wore began to pinch. I sat down on a bench and glanced at the issue of *Pravda* someone had left there. I hadn't read a newspaper or listened to the radio since returning to Moscow. It was best to remain ignorant of politics. But the cover picture caught my eye. It was of two little dogs in jackets with collars around their necks. *Belka and Strelka return safely!* the caption read. I scanned the article and was amazed to discover that the Soviet government had sent dogs into space, along with a rabbit, mice, rats, flies and some plants and fungi.

'They don't tell you about all the dogs that have died, do they? Poor Dezik and Lisa, Bars and Lisichka, or little Laika, who they knew wouldn't survive but they sent anyway.'

I looked up to see a man in a well-cut suit speaking to me. His Russian was good but his accent was strange. Perhaps he was American. He was walking two boxer dogs whose coats had been brushed to a high shine.

How did the man know about the dogs that had died? The Soviet Union wasn't one for publicising its failures. I'd had no idea that the government was exploring space, and was as appalled as the man that innocent animals were being exploited like that. But I couldn't afford to speak to a foreigner. I remembered the ballerina at Kolyma who was arrested for accepting flowers from an American admirer. I knew what the consequences would be if an NKVD agent saw me conversing with him, especially if we were heard to say anything critical of the government.

'Excuse me,' I said and hurried away.

Even when summer came to an end, I continued to make my Sunday-afternoon trips to Sokolniki Park. The magnificent masses of gold and red foliage that adorned the grand maple and elm trees were beautiful. I walked the paths around the lakes, fallen leaves rustling at my feet. I will never give up hope, I told myself. Then, one afternoon when I was walking along an avenue of saffron-leafed birch trees, I saw Valentin sitting on a bench and gazing into the distance. He was older but no less handsome.

Part of me wanted to run to him straight away and fall at his feet: 'Darling, I've been waiting for you for so long!' But I stood still for a moment to take him in. He was wearing the parade uniform of an air-force general and medals crowded his chest. Yes, of course Valentin would have made something of himself. We hadn't seen each other for seventeen years and he had lived a life I knew nothing about. But I had found him, and he was waiting for me, here in Sokolniki Park, just as we'd promised each other.

Tears of joy ran down my face and I started towards him. He rose, still looking into the distance, and lifted his arm to wave to someone. I stopped and turned to see a dark-haired woman in a tailored dress and a boy in his teens walking towards him. When they met, Valentin embraced the woman and they kissed each other on the lips. Pins and needles pricked my flesh. No! It was impossible!

Valentin and the woman linked arms. All three were well dressed; it looked as if they were about to attend an official event together. The boy peered up at the sky and I saw how closely he resembled the woman. My throat tightened and my head ached as the truth hit me: the woman was Valentin's wife and the youth was their son. I was an invisible ghost staring at the life that should have been mine. I had lived on my youthful memories of Valentin, but he had moved on. He hadn't been waiting for me at all.

I watched the happy threesome walk off while I trembled like a dying bird. Valentin was lost to me forever.

I lay on my mattress and sobbed. What was left for me now? Nothing! The dream of being reunited with Valentin had sustained me, but all I saw before me now was emptiness. Everyone and everything I loved had been taken from me. I didn't even have my own name any more.

I caught sight of the copy of *Anna Karenina* that Nikita had given me. Poor tragic Nikita. Was he still alive? I thought of Anna when she realised that Vronsky no longer loved her and only misery lay before her. She had thrown herself under a train. I sat up and understood what I needed to do. It was the only choice left to me. It was what should have happened all those years ago when I shot Svetlana.

It was drizzling as I headed towards the metro station. Moscow was only pretty in the sunshine and the snow; the overcast sky robbed it of all its allure. As I made my way along the street I felt as if I were pushing through a thick fog. I pictured how the final moments of my life would play out: I would descend the escalator, step onto the underground platform and then ... into oblivion.

I was about to enter the station when I heard strange cries. I stopped to listen. Was it a child?

The noise stopped. I rubbed my temples and stepped onto the staircase when the sound came again. I looked around for its source. Curled up in the doorway of a disused shop was a female dog with puppies. I moved closer. The mother was dead, with blood around her nostrils and mouth. Perhaps she had eaten something poisonous, or some cruel person had beaten her to death. Three of the puppies were dead too, but when I lifted the mother's body I saw where the cries were coming from. Two black-and-white puppies looked at me with sorrowful eyes. They reminded me of Ponchik, the stray dog my father had rescued from the metro when I was a child.

I lifted one of the puppies, a girl. She was so cold! I picked up her sister and her paws were cold too. If I left the dogs here they would be dead by the evening. I leaned against the wall, thinking about what I had planned to do. But these two creatures needed my help; I was no good to them dead. I remembered the space dogs the foreign man had told me about. The Soviet government had used them and betrayed them, just as it had me. I couldn't help those dogs, but I could save these ones.

I tucked them into my jacket and headed back to my room. I no longer had a glorious and happy life ahead of me, but I did have a reason to go on living. The puppies that I had decided to rescue had in turn saved me.

THIRTY

Moscow, 2000

Lily sat on the train in a daze, thinking over all that Natasha had revealed the night before. Something was unravelling inside her; she thought about the helplessness she'd felt when Adam was diagnosed with cancer. When he died, Lily had been alone with her loss. Her friends couldn't fully understand what she was suffering: none of them had lost a fiancé, or even a close friend. She hadn't met anyone her own age who had experienced that kind of misery; not until Kate's death. The tragedy Natasha had suffered had been shared by millions of people. She had survived but many others hadn't. And the lives of those like her who returned from the camps were never the same. Lily couldn't stand it. As soon as she arrived at the office she called Oksana.

'The State funeral was so wrong!' she whispered into the receiver. 'Natalya Azarova didn't die in the war. She was screwed over by the government! The Russian people should know that!'

'It's too late for justice, Lily,' Oksana told her calmly. 'What Natasha needs now is peace. The last thing we'd want for her is the frenzy of attention that opening a can of worms like that would cause.'

Oksana was right, Lily knew, but there was something else that bothered her. From what she'd seen of Valentin Orlov during the broadcast of the funeral, he didn't look like a man who had forgotten the woman he'd loved. The newspaper article had said that he'd been searching for her crash site for nearly sixty years. Lily remembered what Luka had told her about relic hunting and how people gained a sense of closure from knowing what had happened to their loved ones. Didn't Valentin Orlov deserve to know what had become of the woman he'd loved?

Later in the afternoon, an email popped up in Lily's mailbox from Luka.

> *Hi Lily,*
> *Would you like to join me for a meditation class after*
> *work? The Philosophical Society is only five minutes*
> *from your office and we can meet beforehand in the café.*
> *Let me know.*
> *Best,*
> *Luka*

Lily leaned back in her chair and ran her hands through her hair. She felt uncomfortable about going out with Luka now that she knew he wasn't gay. If she'd never had Adam in her life, she would enjoy being with him: meditation, art-house films, relic hunting and salsa dancing — Luka opened up a world of interesting things to do. But it didn't matter how much time passed, the pain of Adam's death remained raw, and nothing and no one could cure it. Still, Luka was a good person and he deserved to be told the truth.

Lily replied that she couldn't do the class because she had to visit Oksana's family friend in hospital, but she'd meet him beforehand for a coffee.

Luka was sitting in the café of the Philosophical Society when Lily arrived. He stood up and pulled out a chair for her.

'I don't drink coffee before meditating,' he told her. 'I can recommend the Siberian mushroom tea they serve here and the salad sandwiches.'

Lily nodded and looked around the room with its block-print tablecloths, unfinished wooden floor and a table displaying pamphlets for meditation and yoga classes. The atmosphere reminded her of the alternative therapy centres she'd gone to with Adam.

'What's wrong?' Luka asked her.

She shook her head, embarrassed.

'It's all over your face,' he said. 'You're upset.'

'Sorry,' Lily replied. 'I'm not the best person to see before a meditation class.' She had rehearsed what she was going to say on the way to the café but she found herself stammering. 'I-I'm not ready to see anyone ...'

Luka looked startled. Perhaps Oksana had misread the situation and he wasn't interested at all. Now on top of everything Lily felt like an idiot.

The waitress arrived with the teapot and cups. She poured the tea and left them.

Luka pushed one of the cups towards Lily.

'Breathe,' he said. 'Allow yourself to breathe. I haven't been pressuring you for anything. I simply like your company.'

'I know,' Lily said, trying to smile. 'Don't think I don't appreciate your company.'

The waitress brought the sandwiches. Despite the awkwardness of the situation, Lily had worked up an appetite. The filling of diced tomato, onion, red and green peppers, potato, peas and mayonnaise reminded her of her school days.

'My mother used to make me sandwiches like this to take to school,' she said. 'The Australian kids would eat this brown paste called Vegemite. I used to feel odd then, but now I realise what the Aussie kids were missing out on.'

Luka's gentle smile pierced her heart. 'I respect you being honest with me,' he said. 'Most people run off without a word.'

Lily fought the tears that were welling in her eyes. 'That's what your ex-wife did, isn't it?' she said with sympathy. 'She was a fool to throw away someone like you!'

'I'm over her,' Luka said. 'Oksana thinks I'm not because I haven't dated anyone seriously since my divorce. But, truth be told, I've been busy taking advanced courses and helping my uncle in his practice.'

He picked up a sandwich and cocked his eyebrow at Lily. 'This doesn't have anything to do with me being gay, does it?'

'Oh God!' said Lily, putting down her sandwich. 'Did Oksana tell you about that?'

'You didn't think she'd be able to keep something like that to herself, did you?' he asked, a grin twitching at the corner of his mouth. 'I saw her today when she brought me a cat with an ear infection.'

He laughed out loud and to her surprise Lily found herself laughing too.

'I'm really sorry,' she said. 'You're taking it much better than an Australian guy would. It's just that you dress well and you've got a lot of style.'

'How can that not be a compliment?' asked Luka, biting into his sandwich and chewing thoughtfully for a while. 'It must have been strange growing up in Australia and having Russian parents,' he said.

He seemed genuinely interested and Lily found herself telling him about life in Narrabeen.

'It's a beach culture,' she said, 'but I wasn't really the beach kind. My parents sent me to ballet classes and piano lessons and I was studious. Everyone was surprised when I fell in love with a boy who surfed.'

Luka ordered them more tea and Lily told him about Adam. How they'd met when her father had trained Adam to be a volunteer lifesaver and how he used to make her laugh; she even told him about how he'd come to her twenty-first birthday party dressed as Humphrey B. Bear, which had been her favourite childhood television show.

'He must have been a special guy,' Luka said. 'And Australia sounds wonderful. I'd like to go there some day and see the possums, koalas and kangaroos.'

Lily glanced at the clock on the wall and saw it was time for Luka's meditation class. But she had something that she wanted to ask him. She took a sip of tea, as if to steel herself.

'When you were on the dig ... did you get the impression that Valentin Orlov cared about Natalya Azarova, or do you think he was simply performing his duty to a pilot who had served under him?'

Luka considered her question for a moment before responding. 'Well, according to Yefim there was a rumour of a love affair between Orlov and Natalya Azarova during the war, although they were discreet. Orlov married after the war but is a widower now. As to what he feels all these years later ...' He paused and then grinned. 'Well, he never stopped looking for her so I like to think he is still in love with her, but then I'm a romantic.'

Luka paid the bill and they stood up to go their separate ways. Despite the tension she'd felt earlier, she had enjoyed their time together.

'Listen,' he said, 'I'm not going to call you any more although you're welcome to call me any time you want to. No bad feelings. But there is something I want you to know, Lily: your life isn't over. I don't think you came to Moscow to run away from Sydney; I think you came here to find something. Your spirit knows there's an adventure out there for you.'

On her way home on the train, Lily thought about Luka's words. She felt a kernel of hope stirring inside her: maybe there was something more for her out there in the future only she couldn't see what it was yet.

THIRTY-ONE

Moscow, 2000

Several weeks after the State funeral, when Lily and Oksana were kissing Natasha goodbye at the end of a visit, the old woman caught hold of Lily's hand.

'There is something I would like to do,' she said, looking into Lily's eyes. 'I want to go to the grave ... to see where my dearest friend is buried.'

'We can do that,' said Oksana. 'I'll speak to Polina. Let's make it first thing Sunday morning when the cemetery won't be crowded.'

The matron gave her permission and early on the following Sunday morning Oksana drove Lily and Natasha to Novodevichy Cemetery.

'Why don't I go and find the grave first?' Lily suggested, casting a glance at Natasha's drawn face. 'That will save walking around unnecessarily.'

'Good idea,' agreed Oksana.

Lily had been to the cemetery once before, when she'd first arrived in Moscow, but it had been snowing then and the trees had been bare. This time, when she entered the gate and asked the attendant to mark the location of Natalya Azarova's grave on the cemetery map, the maples and birches were still in full leaf and were only just beginning to turn gold at their tips.

Lily had been enchanted by the romantic cemeteries of Père Lachaise and Montmartre in Paris when she and Adam had been exchange students there, and she'd found the monuments in Novodevichy harsh compared to the cherubs and doves in the French cemeteries. During the Stalin era the graves of noblemen had been destroyed, and in their place had risen tombstone blocks showing lifelike sculptures of the deceased. Apart from the occasional ballerina or actress, it had seemed to Lily on that first visit that the statues were mostly masculine: a doctor in scrubs holding a newborn baby; a tank on top of the grave of a major general. Now, softened by the foliage, the blank-eyed stares of the sculptures appeared less severe, and sparrows flitted across Lily's path as she made her way to the section where Svetlana was buried.

She saw a bride and groom, and assumed they were paying their respects to an ancestor on their significant day; and she noticed an artist with an easel, painting a view of a mossy path. Other than that, the cemetery was quiet. Lily turned a corner, passed a cluster of birch trees, and found herself before the grave of Natalya Azarova. The life-size sculpture was of Natasha as a young woman looking towards the sky, shielding her face with her hand. She was wearing a flowing robe, and the only homage to her military career was the medals pinned to her chest and the pilot's cap she clutched in her other hand. Lily thought it was the most beautiful sculpture she'd ever seen.

The grave was covered by bouquets of hyacinths, roses, lilies and carnations. Lily teared up at the sight of them. Whether the government had any record or not of the fate of Natalya

Azarova, she had been immortalised. People from around the world would see this grave and know about her daring and heroic life.

'It's beautiful,' Lily told Natasha and Oksana when she returned to the car. 'Come and see.'

Oksana had brought a wheelchair, but when she offered it to Natasha, the old woman pretended she hadn't heard her. Instead she slipped her hands through the two younger women's arms and let them lead her into the cemetery. Despite their slow pace, Lily noted Natasha's shoulders set straight and that she held her chin high.

'I am glad Svetlana is buried here,' she said. 'She deserves to be honoured. She was the most courageous of us all.'

They walked past the artist Lily had seen earlier, and approached the corner with the birch trees. When the grave came into view, Lily saw there was a man standing next to it, gazing at the sculpture as longingly as a lover regards a real woman. Lily recognised him immediately: it was Valentin Orlov.

She turned to Natasha. From the look on her face, Natasha had recognised him too. Her body trembled and she loosened her grip on Lily's arm and brought her hand to her lips as if to stifle a cry.

'He never forgot me,' she said in a quiet voice. 'Look. He has never forgotten me!'

Lily glanced at Oksana, who, for the first time, seemed uncertain about what to do.

'Do you want to speak to him?' she asked Natasha.

Lily swallowed the lump in her throat. Were Natasha and Valentin going to find each other again?

Natasha hesitated, then took a step forward. A legion of emotions seemed to sweep across her face. She stopped and clenched her fists.

'No,' she said, so softly Lily had to lean towards her to hear. 'I can't do that to him.' Her eyes welled with tears. 'Look at him! He thinks he has buried me and reclaimed my honour. What would it do to him if he knew that I didn't die in the war? That for all these lost years we have been living in the same city?'

Lily could see the struggle that was taking place in Natasha, between the young woman she once was and the wiser woman she had become.

'Let him remember me as I was then,' she continued. 'Let him have the pleasure of knowing that a beautiful young woman loved him with a pure heart in the midst of a terrible war. May those two youthful beings remain forever entwined, not destroyed by the broken people we have become.'

Natasha gazed at Valentin and Lily longed for him to turn around and see the three women watching him, one of whom had been the love of his life. But he continued to stare at the statue.

'I love you, my dear Valentin,' Natasha whispered. 'We will meet again in heaven.' Then she turned to Lily. 'Please take me back.'

The determined set of the old woman's jaw made her wishes clear. With a heavy heart Lily walked with Natasha and Oksana back towards the cemetery gate. Natasha kept her eyes lowered to the path as if every step that took her away from her lover was tormenting her. When they reached the car, she slumped against it for support while Oksana searched her pockets for her car keys. Lily gave the old woman a hug, knowing there was nothing she could say.

'My keys!' said Oksana, fumbling around in her other pocket. 'I must have dropped them somewhere inside the cemetery.'

Lily stared at her friend. Was this a ploy to get Valentin and Natasha to meet? No, Oksana's face was flushed and she was unusually flustered. She really had lost her keys.

'Wait here with Natasha,' Lily said to her. 'I'll go back and find them.'

It's fate, Lily told herself as she ran back into the cemetery. It's Valentin and Natasha's destiny to be reunited. I'll find the keys and I'll find him. Her eyes scanned the ground for the car keys but her mind was racing far ahead. I'll tell him that Natasha is waiting for him outside the cemetery gates. Lily knew that true love was a force that couldn't be destroyed. If she could have one more day with Adam, even if she knew she would lose him again, she'd take it. She would give everything she had to kiss Adam's soft lips one more time.

But when she arrived at Natalya Azarova's grave, Valentin was gone. She felt tears burn her eyes and bent over to catch her breath. She went back to the corner to look past the birches and nudged the slushy leaves with her shoe, searching for the keys. She saw something shiny and bent to pick it up, but it was only a bottle top.

'Are these what you are looking for?'

Lily straightened and found herself facing Valentin, Oksana's keys in his hand. Her heart thumped in her chest as she stared at him. His voice and appearance exuded formality and yet she felt a sense of intimacy towards him. He returned her gaze with a curious one of his own. It was as if he too recognised her from somewhere, but of course that was impossible. Perhaps it was the weight of power that hung between them. Lily could change the course of his life with just a few words.

She could feel the truth on her tongue, longing to be spoken. But what she'd been so sure about a few seconds ago now seemed more doubtful. Would her revelation change Valentin's life for better or for worse? She didn't know. She could make a decision like that for herself and accept the consequences, but was it right to foist her will on others? She remembered the bittersweet expression on Natasha's face and her words: 'I love you, my dear Valentin. We will meet again in heaven.' She knew then that Natasha had chosen the best course, or at least the best that could have been chosen after all the cruel turns of fate. She had said her goodbyes, and so had Valentin at what he believed was Natasha's funeral. The love Natasha and Valentin once shared was gone. It couldn't be brought back to life, just as Adam couldn't be brought back to life. Lily wouldn't open old wounds.

'Thank you,' she said, taking the keys from him.

Their eyes locked for a few seconds more, then Lily turned and walked with unsteady legs towards the cemetery exit, tears pouring down her face.

A few nights later, Lily was at home, watching Tuz, who was now venturing out from the safety of his cage and exploring the apartment. She hadn't been able to stop thinking about Natasha and Valentin. They'd had the love of a lifetime and now it was over. Like Adam and me, she thought.

Sometimes, when she opened her email in the morning or pressed the button on her answering machine, she hoped that Luka might have contacted her after all. But he was true to his word. She realised it was for the best. 'I'm done,' she said to herself. 'The possibility of love is over for me too.'

The telephone rang, startling her and sending Tuz darting back into his cage. She picked up the receiver. Her mother's voice came on the line.

'Hello, darling!'

'Mum! Is everything all right?' Lily asked. She glanced at the clock. It was the wee hours of the morning in Sydney.

Her mother only called when she had something important to share, otherwise she wrote letters. Telephoning Russia from

Australia was expensive, but Lily suspected the real reason her mother preferred to write was that she was afraid the phone lines were still being tapped.

'Yes, darling. I called to see how you are. We went out dancing at the club with Vitaly and Irina and I thought I'd call you before I went to bed.'

Lily was glad that her parents were still active, but she grimaced at the realisation that they had a better social life than she did.

'Listen,' her mother said. 'Shirley came to see me today.'

The mention of Adam's mother made Lily even sadder than she already was. 'Yes?'

'She wanted to know your address and if it was all right to write to you?'

Lily's mother paused, waiting for her to respond. Of course it was all right for Shirley to write to her, but why did she want to do so now, Lily wondered. Shirley hadn't wanted to see her after Adam's funeral.

When Lily didn't say anything, her mother continued. 'She told me that she can't forgive herself for what she said to you after Adam died. She knows how much it hurt you.'

Lily's eyes filled with tears as she recalled Shirley's words to her: 'You'll get on with your life, and in a year or two you'll meet somebody else. But for our family, the grief will last forever.' Those words had wounded her savagely. If Lily did anything that made her happy, she remembered them and felt guilty.

'Lily?'

'Yes, Mum, I'm listening.' Tears were flowing down Lily's cheeks. How had her mother known to call at this moment, when she needed her comfort most?

'Lily …' her mother paused. 'What you and Adam had was special. You weren't only an engaged couple; you were childhood friends and soulmates. You've suffered a terrible blow ... but I want you to know that you can be happy without Adam, and one day you will be.'

Lily tossed and turned in her bed that night. Her mother's words had unsettled her: ... *you can be happy without Adam, and one day you will be.* She couldn't see how that could be true. She didn't *want* to stop feeling the pain, because that would be like forgetting Adam, and she could never do that.

After the visit to the cemetery, Natasha never spoke about her past again. It was as if in retelling it she had let it go. She seemed to live in the present: relishing her meals; admiring the sunrise and sunset from the hospital window; enjoying seeing Laika, Oksana and Lily when they came to visit.

Because of her animal responsibilities, Oksana couldn't always stay long during the visits. When Natasha and Lily were alone, Lily would read to the old woman. She was no longer interested in Tolstoy; she wanted Lily to read Turgenev and Pushkin. One day after Lily had finished *Eugene Onegin*, Natasha reached out and touched her arm.

'I used to wonder what it would be like to have a daughter and grandchildren,' she said with a smile. 'And now I know. Oksana is like my daughter and you are my golden grandchild.'

While Natasha was anything but a typical *babushka*, Lily too felt that she had found herself a grandmother again.

'I love you,' she told Natasha when she kissed her goodnight.

A beautiful expression came to Natasha's eyes. It was as if the years faded away and a young woman looked back at her.

'I love you too,' she replied, squeezing Lily's hand.

Lily now had eleven cats as well as Laika living in her apartment. Pushkin was too old to be adopted out, and while Mamochka no longer snarled and hissed unprovoked and allowed Lily to pick her up, she still ran away from strangers, so it would be some time before that cat could be found a home. The other occupants were Tuz and some juveniles. Now that Scott had volunteered to organise finding homes for the rescued cats, things had stepped up and Lily had had to speed the socialisation process of the cats. She left the television on when she went to work so they'd get used to human voices, and she taught them to enjoy being cuddled by starting with embraces on the floor and gradually progressing to cradling them to her chest. 'Lily's Finishing School for Cats' she renamed her apartment.

She got up an hour earlier in the mornings to feed the animals, pet them and clean the litter boxes before going to work. In the evenings, she'd take Laika for a walk before visiting Natasha, and afterwards she'd come home and play with the cats. Their transformation from vicious and frightened to affectionate and friendly made Lily wonder if miracles might truly be possible.

One evening when she returned from the hospital, she checked her mailbox and found a letter with her mother's handwriting on the envelope. She wondered if it contained the letter Shirley had intended to send. She had forgiven Adam's mother — grief confused people and made them say things they didn't mean — but she was still fragile and didn't want to be wounded again by an insensitive remark.

Lily sat down on the sofa with Pushkin on her lap and Laika near her feet, and steeled herself. She opened the envelope but the only correspondence it contained was from her mother.

My darling Lily,
Do you remember the key with the Parisian bow that I
keep in my jewellery box, the one you found when you
were a little girl? I told you that it belonged to my house

*in Harbin, but that wasn't true. When I was very young,
I was married to a man named Dmitri. The key came
from our apartment in Shanghai. He was the manager of
the most glamorous nightclub in the city, the Moscow-
Shanghai, and I loved him with all my heart. He died
trying to save somebody, and for many years I believed
that I would never love anyone again. I refused your
father's first proposal for that reason. But marrying Ivan
was the best decision I ever made. I have a wonderful life
with a man I love deeply and a daughter I am so proud
of. What I want you to know is that you don't leave your
first love behind when you meet someone else. You carry
him with you always — in your heart. But it is possible
to live in both worlds — with your past love and your
new one — and still be true to both.*

Lily read the letter again, unable to believe what it said. It had
been enough of a shock to learn before she came to Russia that
her father had been married before and that his wife and two
young daughters had been brutally murdered. Were there any
more family secrets?

She looked at the letter a third time and on this reading paid
attention to the words: ... *you don't leave your first love behind
when you meet someone else. You carry him with you always —
in your heart. But it is possible to live in both worlds — with
your past love and your new one — and still be true to both.*

She sat still for a long time, wondering if that could be true.
Then she thought about Luka at the police station, when he'd
rescued her and Oksana. She realised that she'd always known
he wasn't gay, she'd just tried to convince herself he was. She'd
liked him the moment she'd met him, only she couldn't admit
that to herself without feeling guilty about Adam.

*

Two nights later, Lily and Oksana were back at the Zamoskvorechye building site trying to catch the last of the cats. Scott came along too these days, bringing camp chairs and thermos flasks of hot tea for everybody. Tonight was crucial: they'd learned that work on the building site would commence in December so they had to have all the cats out by then. But after several hours of sitting in the cold, they hadn't seen any of the colony.

'Have you ever used affirmations?' Scott asked Oksana.

She raised her eyebrows. 'No. Is that a type of cat treat?'

Lily shot Oksana a glance but she didn't see it.

'It's a way of focusing your thoughts to get the outcome you want,' Scott said, edging his chair closer to Oksana. 'Perhaps our fear that we're not going to trap these cats in time is keeping them away.'

Oksana frowned then nodded. 'Yes, that could be so. Cats, especially stray ones, are sensitive to the slightest change in their environment. They pick up on everything, including our thoughts, I suspect.'

'Exactly!' said Scott. 'Perhaps the three of us could think an affirmation together: *Tonight we catch all of the cats easily and effortlessly.*'

'Excellent suggestion,' said Oksana. 'Let's do that.'

Lily couldn't believe what she was hearing, but if Oksana was willing to go along with Scott's idea she didn't want to be the one who resisted. So the three of them focused their thoughts on the affirmation.

'What was that?' asked Lily.

'A trap went off,' said Oksana. They peered through the darkness. 'Yes, there's a cat in it! Lily — quick, go cover it!'

Lily ran towards the trap with a blanket. As she reached it another trap closed. Scott rushed towards that one and covered it. They put the cats in Oksana's jeep and set more traps.

'What good fortune!' said Oksana. 'Are you willing to wait for the others?'

Lily and Scott nodded.

They'd never managed to trap more than three cats in a night, but this time they caught all of the remaining cats before midnight. They loaded up Oksana's jeep with the covered traps. As there was no room left in Oksana's car, Scott gave Lily a lift back to her apartment. When they pulled up outside, he stepped out of the car to open the door for her.

'I love cats,' he said. 'I've made some inquiries and apparently there's no problem taking a cat back to the States as long as it's certified and checked. Do you think Tuz might be a good cat for me?'

'Tuz is still a bit nervous,' Lily explained. 'I'm not sure how he'd be around your kids. I've got some cats in my apartment that are very settled and affectionate. Would you like to see them sometime?'

Scott glanced up at the building and she realised that he was keen to see them now. She invited him in, wondering what he'd think about the apartment's funky décor.

Lily opened the door and turned on the light, catching Mamochka making her way from the litter box in the bathroom. She froze and stared at them like a deer caught in a car's headlights.

'What a beautiful cat!' Scott said.

Lily was about to warn him not to touch Mamochka, but Scott had scooped the cat into his arms before she could speak. Lily's adrenalin surged. She was sure their next stop would be the hospital emergency room after Mamochka had bitten off

Scott's thumb. But to her surprise Mamochka returned the adoring expression that Scott was bestowing on her. It was love at first sight.

'Huh!' Lily said, amazed. 'I think Mamochka has chosen her new home!'

'Can I take her now?' Scott asked, playing with Mamochka's paw.

Lily smiled. 'It's best that I bring her to you. That way she won't feel I've abandoned her.'

'When?'

He was like a child waiting for Santa Claus, Lily thought. 'Sunday,' she said. 'I'll bring her over to your place.'

After Scott left, Mamochka kept her eyes on the door as if hoping that he might reappear. Lily bent down and patted her. 'What a lucky cat you are, Mamochka. You're getting a second chance at life. You've found a good man who will adore you forever.'

As Lily changed for bed, she thought again about the letter her mother had written. Her parents had suffered tragedies but had found love again. Maybe second chances do come, she thought as she drifted off to sleep.

In the early hours of the morning, Lily received the call she'd been dreading. As the weather turned colder, Natasha had grown weaker, and there were more days when she couldn't get out of bed. Doctor Pesenko told Lily and Oksana that while good nutrition and care had improved Natasha's quality of life over the past few months, the X-rays showed her heart had worsened.

'It's time,' the night matron from the hospital told Lily now. 'You'd better come. The priest has already seen her.'

Lily knocked on Oksana's door, then remembered that after bringing home the cats from the building site, her friend had gone out again to feed other colonies in the area. Lily slipped a note under her door and then caught a taxi to the hospital, taking Laika with her.

'I'm afraid she's reached the end now,' the night matron told Lily. 'But in many ways that's a blessing. She was cheerful after your visit last night then began to fade after the shift change.'

Lily found Natasha dozing. Every so often her eyes would flicker open and then close again. Laika jumped up on the bed and lay her head on Natasha's shoulder. At first Natasha recognised them: she gave Lily a calm smile and stroked Laika's head. But gradually her lucidity diminished. It was as if her spirit was transcending her body and preparing to take flight. Lily had seen it before: she had stayed with Adam and her grandmother until their passing. There was no need for words at this stage; Natasha knew she and Laika were there.

Lily held Natasha's hand in her own and stayed beside her until the sun peeped through the blinds and Polina appeared at her side. The matron checked Natasha's vitals and squeezed Lily's shoulder. 'It won't be long now. Her pulse and breathing are slowing. Is there anything you would like me to do?'

'She's not in pain, is she?'

'No,' Polina assured her. 'We've made sure of that. She's not struggling; she's simply fading.'

'If you could call Oksana, I'd appreciate that,' Lily said. 'She was out last night and I couldn't tell her. I'm not sure if she saw my note.'

'She called just now,' Polina said, squeezing Lily's shoulder again. 'She's on her way.'

Polina left and Lily continued her vigil. She thought about the day she'd first seen Natasha in Pushkin Square, and about the bombing. Then she remembered the moment in Novodevichy Cemetery when Natasha had refused to speak to Valentin.

She could see clearly the wisdom in Natasha's decision not to disturb him. Love lasted beyond the physical life; Natasha would always be with Valentin.

Suddenly the old woman's chest rose high and sank quickly again. There was a sense of quiet in the room, even though there was a television playing down the hall and the sounds of breakfast being prepared in the kitchen. Lily leaned forward and realised that Natasha was no longer breathing.

Laika lifted her eyes to look at Lily but didn't move from her position.

'Your mistress has gone,' Lily whispered to her, 'but her love for you will always remain.'

She leaned over and put her arms around both Natasha and Laika. She kissed Natasha's forehead and saw her as a young pilot again, taxiing down the runway before soaring into the sky.

THIRTY-TWO

Moscow, 2000

Natasha's funeral was held in a small church not far from the hospital. Polina had put Oksana and Lily in contact with a Russian Orthodox priest who was willing to officiate over a cremation — because Natasha had left them with a specific request about what she wanted done with her ashes.

It was a sunny but icy-cold day and the mourners who gathered around the church door were wrapped in coats, scarves and gloves. Oksana and Lily had brought Laika, and Doctor Pesenko, Polina and two other nurses who had cared for Natasha were there too. Lily was about to go into the church when she saw Luka arrive in the Yelchin Veterinary Hospital's van. The sight of him lifted her spirits but she wondered why he had brought the van instead of his car. Then he opened the doors and Lily saw that he had six elderly ladies with him all carrying bunches of red carnations. She recognised Alina from Natasha's apartment building and assumed that the other women were also residents.

Seeing Alina reminded Lily that Natasha was being farewelled as Zinaida Rusakova. When she had explained this to Polina she'd been relieved that the matron didn't even raise an eyebrow. In a country of revolutions, purges and wars that had left millions orphaned, widowed, separated from their families or suffering trauma, there could be any number of reasons for going by one name while being cremated under another.

Lily went with Oksana to help the old women into the church. 'Thank you,' she said to Luka. 'I didn't know Oksana had organised for you to bring the ladies.'

Luka smiled. 'You should know that when there is a task to be done there's no one better than Oksana to find the right person to do it.'

Despite the heaviness in her heart, Lily managed to smile back.

When everyone was seated inside the church, the priest began the ceremony by singing prayers and waving a censer. Lily's eyes drifted to Natasha in her coffin. She knew that what she was seeing was only a shell; the spark that animated human life was gone. And what a spark Natasha had possessed! She'd been courageous and strong-willed until the end.

Lily remembered what it had been like to touch Adam's body after his heart had stopped beating. The nurses had allowed her and Shirley to sit with him until the time finally came to take him away. When she'd seen his coffin at the funeral she couldn't grasp that the man who had been so full of life was now silent and shut away in a box. That was how she felt about Natasha now, and the idea of it made her weep. Oksana put her arm around her and Luka sent her a sympathetic glance.

The mourners formed a guard of honour as Natasha's coffin, covered in red carnations, was driven away to the crematorium. The old women wept but Lily cried the hardest. The ceremony had been different from the lavish State funeral with all its pomp, but Lily knew that Natasha would have preferred this one. She and Oksana had arranged everything as if Natasha had truly been their relative; and had done everything with love, including washing Natasha's body and dressing her in white. Medals and glory hadn't meant much to Natasha; love had meant everything.

Doctor Pesenko hosted the wake at his apartment in the Arbat. As Oksana drove through the streets of the quarter, Lily stared at the buildings and stores and imagined Natasha as a young woman, looking in the windows and fixing her hair.

Doctor Pesenko's mother had made *blintzes*, crepe-like pancakes filled with sweet cheese that were traditional at funerals, and everyone gathered in the living room to eat them. Although Lily was sad, she enjoyed listening to Alina and the women talking about 'Zina' and her dogs.

'Mushka was my favourite,' said one of the women. 'She bit my husband on the backside once. She knew he was a good-for-nothing drunkard!'

The story brought laughter from the other women.

Lily went to the kitchen to help Doctor Pesenko's mother with the tea and found Oksana and Luka talking there.

'Oksana's been telling me about all the cats you have in your apartment now,' Luka said, with a twinkle in his eye that warmed Lily's heart.

'Not for long,' Lily replied. 'Laika and Pushkin will stay with me, but Scott and his wife have found homes for all the others.'

'We should have enlisted them earlier,' said Oksana. 'That couple are a godsend!'

Lily took the teacups out on a tray to the women. When she returned to the kitchen, Luka was preparing to leave. He kissed her and Oksana on the cheeks.

'I've got a hip replacement to perform on a Rottweiler this afternoon,' he said. 'The dog's in a lot of pain and I couldn't postpone it.'

As he walked to the door, Oksana grabbed his arm. 'Now that Scott has found homes for the cats Lily's been looking after, I want to re-do her apartment. It's time to strip that old wallpaper and paint everything white. Lily can add her own dashes of colour with cushions and lamps.'

Lily lifted her eyebrows. It sounded wonderful but Oksana hadn't mentioned these plans to her.

'Lily and I can do all the painting,' Oksana continued. 'But there are these terrible tiles in the kitchen that will be difficult to chip off. Your uncle told me that you did the remodelling of your apartment yourself? Perhaps you can come over to show us what to do?'

Lily felt herself blush. Luka had been right: Oksana was good at finding the right person for the task. But she knew that this enlistment had another purpose. That's why her heart skipped a beat when Luka replied, 'I'd love to. Just call me and let me know when you need my help.'

'That wasn't half obvious,' Lily said to Oksana after they'd shut the apartment door.

'Well, it's up to you now,' Oksana replied with a grin. 'You can't expect me to do all the work.'

The Sunday after the funeral, Lily experienced a beautiful dream. She found herself sitting at a long table outside a dacha. The house faced a lake and was surrounded by a vegetable garden brimming with cucumbers, onions and beets, and bordered by beds of pink and red asters, tulips and chrysanthemums. At the table sat everyone Lily had ever loved, those who were living and those who had died. Her grandmother glowed with good health and strength. Lily's parents flanked her, looking blissfully relaxed. Adam was there too, strong and tanned as he'd always been before he got sick. Lily looked up to find a young Natasha sitting opposite her and pouting her perfectly made-up red lips. Even Lily's old cat Honey was there, rubbing everyone's legs under the table. Vitaly and Irina appeared along with Betty and her siblings, and Oksana and Luka came out of the house carrying platters of sliced watermelon and peaches. Out of the woods emerged people Lily had never met but somehow recognised: a handsome man with ginger hair, and two little girls with white bows on their heads.

She was filled with joy, which didn't leave her even when she awoke and stared at the ceiling. She didn't know how it was possible, but she understood that every person she'd loved and who had died was still with her, living alongside her.

Later that day, she walked to the metro station, intending to visit some of the stations she hadn't seen before. She still felt exhausted with grief over Natasha, but inside her a sensation of buoyancy stirred, something she could not remember experiencing before. Even before Adam had got sick, she'd never felt so weightless. It was as if she'd stepped away from the tragic family history that had haunted her and into a plane of light.

She'd just taken a seat on the train when a caramel-coloured dog entered the carriage and jumped up onto the seat opposite her. He lay his head on his paws and fell asleep. The commuters stepped around him to avoid waking him up.

The woman sitting next to Lily looked around with a concerned expression on her face. 'That dog must have got separated from his owner,' she said. She had an Australian accent and obviously hoped someone in the carriage understood English. 'We'd better call the guard or they'll never find him again. He could end up anywhere.'

'He's a metro dog,' Lily told her.

'A what?' asked the woman, looking surprised to find a fellow Australian sitting next to her.

'A stray,' Lily explained. 'You often see them on the trains, and some people swear they know exactly where they're going. Sometimes a guard shoos them away, or a cruel person kicks them or gives them a poisoned sandwich. But most of the time people either feed them or let them be.'

The woman looked flabbergasted and Lily giggled. The woman was so Australian — used to order, public safety and rules. In Russia, those things contradicted each other. Lily wondered whether she was more Russian than Australian now. She looked at the dog again. A woman in a leopard-print coat took a sausage from her shopping bag. She snapped it into pieces with her manicured fingers and fed it to the dog.

Russia was all contrasts, Lily thought: breathtaking beauty alongside hideousness; it was brutal yet compassionate; shabby yet grand. It was a country of traumas that ran so deep they were passed from one generation to another. Even Lily, born in Australia, hadn't been left untouched by the gaps in her family tree. But perhaps Russia had shown her how to stand up again after receiving a blow; and that no amount of evil could obliterate hope.

Lily remembered what Oksana had said when she and Lily had taken Natasha to see Doctor Pesenko. She'd told Lily that she believed the dying animals that came to her were angels in disguise, because in caring for them she found they left her with a gift.

Is this Natasha's gift to me, Lily wondered. This sense of renewal?

Lily saw Luka walking towards her along Tverskoy Boulevard and rose from the wrought-iron bench she'd been sitting on. 'I'm glad you could come,' she told him. 'I want to show you the house where my grandfather lived.'

She pointed to the yellow-and-white mansion opposite and invited Luka to sit down next to her.

'It's magnificent!' he said. 'And they've restored it beautifully.'

'The exterior only. Unfortunately the interior's now ultra-modern.'

'Still,' said Luka, 'at least the whole thing hasn't been torn down like in other parts of the city.'

'I thought you'd like to see it,' Lily said, loosening her scarf. Despite the snow that had started to fall she was feeling very warm. 'I know you like history.'

'I love this whole area,' he said. 'When Napoleon invaded, the French soldiers pitched their tents here and hanged any Russian resisters from the lampposts. They cut down the trees for firewood. But when the French retreated, the Muscovites restored their beloved boulevard to its former glory.'

Lily looked at the house again. 'I'd like my parents to come and visit me here — I want my mother to see it for herself. But she's too afraid.'

'Really?' Luka looked at her with interest.

Lily explained about the trip her parents had made in 1969 to smuggle her grandmother out of Russia.

'What a story!' he exclaimed. 'But your mother's fear is common among Russian émigrés, especially after what went on here during the Stalin years.'

Lily thought of Natasha and flinched.

Luka nudged her. 'I can think of a way to get your parents to come here for sure.'

'Is that so?' Lily asked, curious to hear what Luka was about to suggest.

He put his arm around the back of the bench behind her. 'Well, say for instance you were to meet this Russian guy who really liked you and who you liked. If your parents are anything like mine, I'm sure they'd want to meet him right away.'

Lily shifted in her seat. 'I thought we might go slow,' she said. 'This is a big step for me.'

'I know it is,' said Luka, looking at his lap. Then he turned to her again, a bright smile on his face. 'But it isn't for me. I figure if you know someone is right for you, you know.'

'Is that how you feel?' Lily asked him.

He nodded and gazed at her intently.

I'm not fighting this any longer, Lily told herself. When Luka kissed her she didn't pull away. His lips were as beautiful to kiss as she'd imagined they would be.

'Well,' she said afterwards, 'now that my parents are coming to Moscow, you'd better help me fix up my apartment.'

Luka looked into her eyes. 'I intend to. There's nothing that us gay guys can't do!'

Lily punched his arm. 'You're never going to let me forget that, are you?'

He shook his head and grinned. 'No, it's the story I intend to tell our grandchildren about how we met.'

Lily laughed. Luka took her hand and together they walked towards the metro. She stopped for one last glance at her grandfather's house, and thought about Adam and about her mother's words: ... *you don't leave your first love behind when you meet someone else. You carry him with you always — in your heart. But it is possible to live in both worlds — with your past love and your new one — and still be true to both.*

She turned to Luka and smiled. It's going to be okay, she told herself, with a conviction that penetrated every bone and muscle in her body. Everything's going to be great. I've got an adventure ahead of me and I intend to live it.

THIRTY-THREE

Moscow, 2000

The afternoon was turning dark and icy when Lily arrived at Novodevichy Cemetery. Oksana was waiting for her by the gate, clutching an oversized handbag. At that hour the cemetery was too cold and spooky for the tourists, which was how the women had planned it. They wanted as few people around as possible.

'I've had a look at the grave,' Oksana told Lily. 'There's a gap under the base of the statue that opens into the tomb itself. We can slip the box in there. It's a much better plan than our one of scattering the ashes around the grave. I'm sure Natasha would approve.'

When they reached Natalya Azarova's grave, Lily was touched to see that the number of bouquets of brightly coloured flowers that covered it hadn't diminished with the cold weather.

Oksana opened her bag and took out the wooden box that contained Natasha's ashes. She and Lily held the box together and recited the Lord's Prayer. Then they each kissed the box reverently, and Oksana showed Lily the gap she'd found earlier.

'I declare that Senior Lieutenant Azarova is no longer missing,' Lily announced, and she and Oksana pushed the box through the gap. It landed inside the tomb with a thud.

'There,' said Oksana, 'Svetlana and Natasha are together again. And when people come to visit this grave, they will be honouring both of them.'

They spent some moments at the grave in contemplation, then the two women linked arms and walked back to Oksana's car. They were pleased — and somewhat amazed — that they'd accomplished their sacred task without being seen, or stopped by the cemetery officials.

'Natasha must have been watching out for us,' Oksana said.

Valentin Orlov had visited Novodevichy Cemetery every day since the funeral. He liked to come early in the morning or last thing in the afternoon to avoid the tourists, students and other visitors. It was bitterly cold that afternoon as he stepped out of the taxi and noticed the two women who passed him, deep in conversation. He recognised the younger of the two as the woman who had lost her keys near Natasha's grave. He wondered what her interest in his beloved was. He was tempted to follow her and ask her, but the cemetery gates would close soon.

He placed the single rose he always brought with him among the bouquets left by admirers. He had hoped that once Natasha's body and plane were recovered, and she'd been recognised officially as a heroine of the Great Patriotic War, he would gain a sense of finality. But the feeling never came. Time was supposed to heal all wounds, but his was still a black hole inside him. The skeleton he and Ilya had discovered in Orël Oblast was buried here, but Natasha's essence wasn't. I found her and yet I didn't find her, he thought.

But the sculpture on the grave captured Natasha's femininity and strength, and it was something tangible that he could touch, like the photograph he kept at home of himself and Natasha standing by his Yak. That was why he came to the cemetery every day: to have some contact with her. He expected his life would continue in this same melancholic manner until he was too old and weak to come any more. But then something happened that changed everything.

He was standing by the grave, looking at the flowers, when he saw a flash of light. Now, the bouquets shimmered with vivid colours. A warm sensation surrounded him and he felt a gentle pressure at his side. It was her, Natasha! He knew it!

He couldn't see her but he could hear her. She was saying something, but not using words that were part of any human language. Then she laughed and Orlov found himself laughing too, and his whole being seemed to rise above the earth and expand with joy.

He remembered when she had first joined the regiment in Stalingrad. It had been exactly like this: she had come into his life and unshackled him. *Did you ever consider the possibility that I might surprise you?* she'd asked him; and she had. After all these years of separation, she had returned to him.

Orlov touched his side. 'Natasha?'

This time she spoke clearly and straight into his heart: 'I love you, my dear Valentin. We will meet again in heaven.'

'I love you too,' he said out loud. 'I never stopped waiting.'

'I know.'

Then she was gone.

Orlov sat on a bench near the grave, trying to digest what had happened. The weight that had pressed on his chest for so long had lifted. The ever-present regret had fallen away. The world seemed to be adjusting itself into a new pattern and he was filled with a sense of optimism. If he didn't feel so peaceful, he might have wondered if he'd lost his mind.

I'm eighty-three, he told himself. Maybe I have one year left. Maybe I have ten. Why waste them?

His mind drifted to Leonid and Irina and their children, Nina and Anton. Fine people, all of them. They had said that they wanted to know him better. Well, maybe that could happen, he thought. After all, I've lived an interesting life.

He stood and touched the gravestone one more time. He knew that he wouldn't come to the cemetery again. Natasha wasn't here. She was in his heart, where she always had been, and where she would always remain.

'I love you, Natasha,' he said. 'We will meet again in heaven.' Then he turned and walked towards the cemetery gate.

Wait for Me

To Valentina Serova

Wait for me, and I'll come back.
Wait with all you've got.
Wait, when dreary yellow rains
Tell you, you should not.
Wait when snow is falling fast,
Wait when summer's hot,
Wait when yesterdays are past,
Others are forgot.
Wait, when from that far-off place,
Letters don't arrive.
Wait, when those with whom you wait
Doubt if I'm alive.

Wait for me, and I'll come back.
Wait in patience yet
When they tell you off by heart
That you should forget.
Even when my dearest ones
Say that I am lost,
Even when my friends give up,
Sit and count the cost,
Drink a glass of bitter wine
To the fallen friend —
Wait. And do not drink with them.
Wait until the end.

Wait for me and I'll come back,
Dodging every fate.
'What a bit of luck,' they'll say,
Those that would not wait.
They will never understand
How amidst the strife,
By your waiting for me, dear,
You had saved my life.
Only you and I will know
How you got me through.
Simply — you knew how to wait —
No one else but you.

Konstantin Simonov, 1941

AUTHOR'S NOTE

Sapphire Skies is a fictional story set against a historical background. While I was inspired by the glamorous Soviet female fighter ace Lydia Litvyak, who disappeared in combat and was denied the distinction of Hero of the Soviet Union until her body was discovered in the late 1970s, Natalya Azarova is a fictional character. I found Litvyak a fascinating woman, but I wanted to create a character of my own in order to show what life was like under Stalin, and to invent a fictional mystery with my imagination.

Marina Raskova was a famous female aviator who formed women's air regiments during the Great Patriotic War, the most well known of which is the 46th Guards Night Bomber Aviation Regiment. The members of this highly successful regiment were nicknamed 'Night Witches' by the German army because of their tactic of cutting their engines and gliding quietly in for an attack at night. There are many resources, including documentaries and books, about Raskova's regiments, and if *Sapphire Skies* has sparked your interest, then I encourage you to learn more about these amazing and courageous heroines.

Moscow Animals is an organisation that saves dogs and cats from the street and has the space dog Laika on their emblem. You can find out more about them here: www.moscowanimals.org. The rescue and socialisation techniques for stray cats described in this book are based on my experience as a volunteer with the World League for Protection of Animals, Australia. I am very proud to now be the patron of this wonderful organisation: www.wlpa.org. Valentino and Versace are two cats I rescued this way and are now part of the bevy of beautiful felines that keep me company when I write.

A note about transliteration of Russian words and names

The system used to transliterate Cyrillic words in this book is mainly the British Standard System. However, where there is a common English spelling, that spelling has been used in preference to strictly observing the system; for example, using Alexander instead of Aleksandr. Similarly if there is a simpler way of transliterating a name than the system provides, that has usually been preferred; for example, Anatoly instead of Anatoliy. (Occasionally I have used the version of the name that sounded most exotic to suit my purpose.) This latitude would not be acceptable in an academic text, but my aim here is to make Russian words and names as easy on the eye and tongue as possible for English-speaking readers, while still giving something of the essence of the Russian language and the culture in which the story is set.

A thank you to readers

Sapphire Skies is my sixth book, and as I've progressed in my writing career I've been very pleased to have collected along the way a loyal following of readers. I want you to know that I think of you all when I am writing and always give each book the very best of myself with you in mind.

Please feel free to join the friendly community of readers on my Facebook page: facebook.com/BelindaAlexandraAuthor.

I am also happy to receive mail, but please be sure to write your name and address clearly on your letter so that I can reply to you. It breaks my heart when someone has taken the trouble to write to me but I can't reply to them because there isn't a legible address.

I can be reached:
    C/- HarperCollins Publishers Australia
    PO Box A565
    Sydney South, NSW, 2000
    Australia
Bless you all!
Belinda Alexandra xx

ACKNOWLEDGEMENTS

I would like to thank the wonderful people who helped me with *Sapphire Skies*. In particular, I would like to express my sincere gratitude to my legendary literary agent, Selwa Anthony, for her enthusiastic support and her sage advice. I'm also thankful for the brilliant team at HarperCollins Publishers Australia. In particular: Anna Valdinger; Shona Martyn; James Kellow; Sarah Barrett; Simon Milne; Michael White; Jessica Bramwell; Mary Rennie; Karen-Maree Griffiths; and Kelly Fagan.

Sapphire Skies has an intricate and detailed plot line and I was fortunate to have the talented Nicola O'Shea as my editor to work with me on it. I'd also like to thank Drew Keys and Pam Dunne for proofreading.

I'm grateful to the experts and scholars who shared their knowledge with me: Paul Wesley of the Australian Federal Police; Paul Marelic of the Royal Australian Air Force; Irina McCarthy for advice about the Russian language and Russian cultural issues; Professor Konrad Kwiet for answering my questions about Auschwitz. Pauline O'Kane and the staff at Ku-ring-gai Library deserve a special mention for all the assistance they gave me with sourcing research materials.

Finally, I would like to thank my beautiful friends and family for their constant support and encouragement. I would especially like to thank my husband, Mauro, my father, Stan, and my brother, Paul; and at the risk of sounding a little nutty, I'd also like to thank my cats — Gardenia, Lilac, Gucci, Valentino and Versace — for their excellent and amusing company while writing this novel.

Thank you all from my heart.

Belinda Alexandra

White Gardenia

In a district of the city of Harbin, a haven for White Russian families since Russia's Communist revolution, Alina Kozlova must make a heartbreaking decision if her only child, Anya, is to survive the final days of World War II.

White Gardenia sweeps across cultures and continents, from the glamorous nightclubs of Shanghai to the harshness of Cold War Soviet Russia in the 1960s, from a desolate island in the Pacific Ocean to a new life in post-war Australia. Both mother and daughter must make sacrifices, but is the price too high? Most importantly of all, will they ever find each other again?

Rich in incident and historical detail, this is a compelling and beautifully written tale about yearning and forgiveness.

ISBN: 978-1-47113-874-4
eBook ISBN: 978-1-47113-875-1

Belinda Alexandra

Wild Lavender

At fourteen, Simone Fleurier is wrenched from her
home on a Provençal lavender farm and sent to work
in Marseille. Her life there is hard and impoverished,
but Simone discovers the music hall and a dream: to
one day be a famous dancer and singer. But when war
threatens, Simone makes a decision that will lead to great
danger – yet ultimately prove that love, just like wild
lavender, can grow in the least likely of places . . .

Belinda Alexandra has created a tale of passion and courage
that moves from the backstreets of Marseille to the grand
music theatres of Paris, from the countryside of Provence
to decadent pre-war Berlin and jazz-age New York.

ISBN: 978-1-47113-876-8
eBook ISBN: 978-1-47113-877-5

Belinda Alexandra

Silver Wattle

A dazzling novel about two exceptional sisters,
set in the Australian film world of the 1920s.

In fear for their lives after the sudden death of their
mother, Adéla and Klàra must flee Prague to find refuge
with their uncle in Australia. There, Adéla becomes a film
director at a time when the local industry is starting to
feel the competition from Hollywood. But while success
is imminent, the issues of family and an impossible love
are never far away. And ultimately dreams of the silver
screen must compete with the bonds of a lifetime . . .

Silver Wattle confirms Belinda Alexandra as one of our
foremost storytellers. Weaving fact into inspiring fiction
with great flair and imagination, this is a novel as full of
hope, glamour and heartbreak as the film industry itself.

eBook ISBN: 978-1-47113-947-5

Belinda Alexandra

Golden Earrings

Let me tell you a story . . . The granddaughter of
Spanish refugees, who fled Barcelona after the Civil
War, Paloma Batton is an attentive student of the Paris
Opera Ballet, that is, until she is visited by a ghost . . .

Leaving her a mysterious gift – a pair of golden earrings
– the ghost disappears, setting Paloma off on a quest.

Paloma's exploration of her Spanish heritage leads
to a connection between the visitor and 'la Rusa',
a woman who died in Paris in 1952, known for her
rapid rise from poverty to flamenco star. Although
her death was ruled a suicide, Paloma soon discovers
that many people had reasons for wanting la Rusa
dead . . . including Paloma's own grandmother.

Golden Earrings is a story of passion and betrayal,
and the extremes two women will go to for love.

ISBN: 978-0-85720-888-0
eBook ISBN: 978-0-85720-889-7

Belinda Alexandra

Tuscan Rose

A mysterious stranger known as 'The Wolf' leaves an infant
with the sisters of Santo Spirito. A tiny silver key hidden
in her wrappings is the one clue to the child's identity . . .

When Rosa turns fifteen, she must leave the nuns who have
raised her and become governess to the daughter of an
aristocrat and his strange, frightening wife. Their house is
elegant but cursed, and Rosa – blessed with gifts beyond
her considerable musical talents – is torn between her
desire to know the truth and her fear of its repercussions.

Meanwhile, the hand of Fascism curls around
beautiful Italy, threatening her citizens. In the face
of unimaginable hardship, will Rosa's intelligence,
intuition and her extraordinary capacity for
love be enough to ensure her survival?

ISBN: 978-0-85720-878-1
eBook ISBN: 978-0-85720-879-8